About the Authors

GU01007094

Author of more tha[...]
Arkansan **Gina** [...]
romance novels by [...]
sharing her own st[...]
celebrating familie[...]
by her husband of [...]
and their son, their librarian son-in-law who fit perfectly
into this fiction-loving family, and an adorable grandson
who already loves books.

Raye Morgan has been a nursery-school teacher, a
travel agent, a clerk and a business editor, but her best
job ever has been writing romances – and fostering
romance in her own family at the same time. Current
score: two boys married, two more to go. Raye has
published more than seventy romances, and claims to
have many more waiting in the wings. She lives on the
Central California Coast with her husband.

Abigail Gordon loves to write about the fascinating
combination of medicine and romance from her home
in a Cheshire village. She is active in local affairs, and
is even called upon to write the script for the annual
village pantomime! Her eldest son is a hospital
manager, and helps with all her medical research. As
part of a close-knit family, she treasures having two of
her sons living close by and the third one not too far
away. This also gives her the added pleasure of being
able to watch her delightful grandchildren growing up.

Seasons in Love

COLLECTION

One Spring Baby

GINA WILKINS

RAYE MORGAN

ABIGAIL GORDON

MILLS & BOON

First Published in Great Britain 2020
By Mills & Boon, an imprint of HarperCollins*Publishers*
1 London Bridge Street, London, SE1 9GF

ONE SPRING BABY © 2020 Harlequin Books S.A.

The Bachelor's Little Bonus © 2016 Gina Wilkins
Keeping Her Baby's Secret © 2009 Helen Conrad
A Baby for the Village Doctor © 2009 Abigail Gordon

ISBN: 978-0-263-28105-7

MIX
Paper from
responsible sources
FSC® C007454

This book is produced from independently certified FSC™ paper to ensure responsible forest management.

For more information visit: www.harpercollins.co.uk/green

Printed and bound in Spain
by CPI, Barcelona

THE BACHELOR'S LITTLE BONUS

GINA WILKINS

For my family – immediate, extended and family of the heart. You have all enriched my life beyond measure!

Chapter One

Returning home from a mundane business trip, Cole McKellar stepped out of a dreary February evening and into a scene from one of his increasingly recurrent fantasies: A pretty blonde asleep on his oversized brown leather sofa.

The sight aroused and disturbed him—the same reaction he usually had to those unbidden daydreams. He squeezed his eyes shut, but when he opened them the blonde in question was still there. What was wrong with him? He shouldn't be having these feelings about Stevie, especially when she viewed him merely as a neighbor and a friend. And yet…

Illuminated by the lamp on the table nearest her head, she lay on her left side, her hand beneath her cheek, her jeans-covered legs drawn up in front of her. Her shoes were on the floor, leaving her feet exposed in bright red socks that matched her sweater. Golden curls tumbled around her sleep-flushed face, and her soft, full lips were slightly parted. Long lashes lay against her fair cheeks, hiding eyes he knew to be a vivid blue. Notably colorful and feminine in contrast to his muted bachelor decor, she looked young and vulnerable lying there, though he knew Stevie McLane to be a capable and accomplished thirty-one year old, only two years his junior.

Dusty, his little gray tabby, snuggled into the crook of Stevie's arm. In response to Cole's arrival, the cat lifted her head and gave him a look as though warning him not to disturb their sleeping guest. He frowned and studied Stevie more closely. Was there a trace of tears on her face? Had she been crying?

Gripping his overnight bag tightly in one hand, his computer case in the other, he shifted his weight uncomfortably, unsure what to do. Should he wake her? Should he let her sleep? He couldn't just stand here watching her. It was sort of…creepy.

Dusty stood and stretched. Roused by the movement, Stevie blinked her eyes open. Finding Cole standing there, she gasped.

The last thing he'd wanted to do was frighten her. "I'm sorry, Stevie, I—"

"Cole! I didn't—"

Both stopped talking to let the other speak, then hurried again to fill the awkward silence.

"I didn't mean to—"

"I thought you—"

Cole held up a hand with a rueful smile when their words overlapped again. "I'll start. I'm sorry I startled you. I didn't know you were here. Now your turn."

On her feet now, his next-door neighbor pushed back her tumbled hair with both hands and smiled up at him.

Though just over average height himself, he still felt as though he towered over Stevie, who topped out at about five-two in her red-stockinged feet. "I thought you weren't going to be home until tomorrow," she said.

"I rescheduled my flight because of the weather. I didn't want to get stuck in Dallas for an extra day or two, especially since I have to be in Chicago a few days next week."

"And now you must be tired." She shook her head. "I'm sorry, you weren't expecting to find uninvited company in your house."

She had no idea just what a welcome surprise that had been, nor would he fully enlighten her. When it came to Stevie, he'd gotten pretty good at concealing his feelings during the past year. "Usually when I come home, the house is empty except for Dusty, and she likes to play it cool with her royal greetings. It's a pleasant change to be welcomed with a smile."

He'd answered lightly while studying her suspiciously puffy eyelids. Would it be intrusive to mention his impression that she'd been crying? He settled for what he hoped was a vaguely concerned tone. "Is everything okay?"

She wiped nonchalantly at her cheeks, as if smoothing away the effects of sleep rather than any hint of tears. "Oh, sure. It was just too quiet at my house tonight, so Dusty and I were keeping each other company. I guess I fell asleep."

His cat had climbed on the arm of the couch and now demanded a greeting from him. Cole reached down to rub the tabby's soft, pointed ears. "Did you give Stevie your sad-eyes act to keep her from leaving after she fed you? I bet you added a few of those pitiful meows you've perfected."

Stevie wrinkled her nose with a little laugh. "I'm pretty sure she even threw in a couple of forlorn sniffles."

He ran a hand absently down Dusty's back, stopping to scratch at the base of the tail, a spot that always made his pet arch blissfully. "She's shameless."

"Yes, she is," Stevie agreed, giving the tabby a fond smile.

Cole claimed occasionally that he'd bought the cat with the house. He'd lived here only a couple weeks when a pathetic kitten had appeared on his doorstep out of a winter rainstorm, wet and hungry and miserable. Hearing the meows, he'd opened the door to investigate and the little stray had darted past him into the living room. Other than visits to the vet, she hadn't been outside since.

He'd planned initially to find a good home for the stray, but somehow she'd ended up staying. He and Dusty, who was named for her habit of emerging from under furniture with dust bunnies on her nose, got along like a couple of contented hermits. Still, it was always a treat for them when Stevie dropped by. Sometimes he thought they were both a little too eager for her visits.

Weren't cats and computer analysts supposed to be contentedly independent and naturally aloof? He'd wondered more than once what sort of special magic Stevie wielded to enchant them so thoroughly, though he hoped he was a bit more discreet about his fascination with her than his pet. He treasured his unconventional friendship with Stevie too much to risk it with the awkwardness of an unrequited infatuation.

A data analyst for a national medical group, Cole worked primarily from home. He made a few business trips a year for planning and progress meetings, but mostly he communicated with the outside world via computer and smartphone.

His late wife had teasingly accused him of taking introversion to the extreme. But it wasn't that he disliked people. He was just more comfortable with computers, especially since Natasha's difficult illness.

It was suddenly very quiet in the room. Pushing thoughts of the painful past from his mind, he cleared his throat and glanced toward the window. "Sounds like the sleet has stopped. Maybe it's finally changing over to snow. I'd rather have snow than ice."

Stevie nodded with a bit too much enthusiasm for the banal comments. "No kidding. At least this weather hit on a Friday so most people don't have to get out for work or school tomorrow. Not that local schools would be open, anyway. You know they close at the first sign of a snowflake. But still, I hope we get enough snow for the kids to build snowmen and have snowball fights. That's not something they get to do very often around here, so they'll want to make the most of it. I remember how disappointed I always was when we got all psyched up for snow and had to settle for just a dusting. Still, I hope it's gone by Monday. I have a couple of meetings I'd really hate to have to put off."

He chuckled, accustomed to her characteristic, stream-of-consciousness prattling. "Let's hope there's enough snow for the kids to enjoy over the weekend but that it melts quickly enough not to cause too many issues for the coming week."

"That would work." She smiled, but he had the distinct feeling something was wrong. For one thing, she was twisting a curl tightly around her fingertip, a nervous habit he'd noticed several times during the past few months.

Stevie was one of the most naturally effervescent women he'd ever known, outgoing and optimistic and a little quirky. She'd grown up in the comfortable bungalow on the corner lot next door in Little Rock, Arkansas. She'd been the first to welcome him to the street when he'd bought this house in the midtown neighborhood that was currently undergoing a revival after a decade-long slump. He'd made a tidy profit on the condo he'd sold last year, and he thought he'd do the same with this place if his needs changed again. Even better than that, he'd gained Stevie as a neighbor.

He wondered if it was only the bad weather that had left her free on a Friday night to keep his cat company and doze on his couch. As far as he knew, she hadn't dated anyone since a breakup some three months ago. When they'd first met, he'd had designs on her, and maybe he'd even had a few fantasies about her since, but he'd never acted on any of them. She'd been involved with the hipster musician, which had made her off-limits. Not that he had a chance with her anyway.

Inherently candid, Stevie had once confessed to him during a rambling conversation that she had a lamentable weakness for footloose artists and musicians, a penchant that had left her soft heart bruised more than once. He'd gotten the message, whether intentional or not on her part. Reclusive computer geeks were not her type romantically, though she seemed pleased to have one among her many pals.

Since she'd split with Joe, she'd been slightly more subdued than usual, but tonight she seemed even more dispirited. Had she been crying because she was lonely? Or—he swallowed hard, very much disliking the other possibility—because she missed the guy who'd caused her so much grief before he'd left town to start a new single life in Texas?

He tried to think of something more to say, but small talk wasn't his forte. Stevie usually carried their conversations, chattering away while he enjoyed listening and responding when prompted. Yet she never seemed bored by him, another trait that made her so special. Stevie would never yawn and check her watch during dinner with him.

He winced as he remembered the recent blind date he'd been stupid enough to consent to after being nagged by a friend's wife. He'd been just as disinterested during the evening, but he'd at least had the courtesy to not be so obvious about it. When he wanted to spend time with a woman, he had a few numbers he could call, a couple of women friends who wanted nothing more from him than a few hours of mutual pleasure. He didn't make those calls often—and even less so during the past couple of months, for some reason.

He didn't know why his mind had drifted in that direction at the moment, though the thought of dinner gave him inspiration. "Have you eaten?" he asked Stevie. "I've been on a plane all afternoon and I'm hungry."

She hesitated, then smiled a bit more naturally. "No, actually, I haven't had dinner. I might have even skipped lunch. I don't remember."

The admission made him even more convinced that something was troubling her, but he figured she'd tell him when and if she was ready. Maybe over a hot meal.

"I froze portions of that big pot of soup you made for me last week. It'll take just a few minutes to thaw and heat a couple bowlfuls."

She smoothed her tousled hair with one hand and

nodded. "Sounds good. Just let me wash up and I'll help you."

"I'll meet you in the kitchen."

Hastily stashing his bags to unpack later, he busied himself preparing the impromptu meal. Had he found the empty house he'd expected when he'd returned, he'd have nuked the soup and eaten in front of the TV with a beer straight from the can. But since he had company, he made more effort, setting the table with placemats and flatware, making sure the bowls weren't scratched or chipped.

For the most part, he'd learned to be content with his quiet life, so why was he so pleased by the prospect of sharing a simple bowl of soup with Stevie on a bleak, winter evening?

After splashing water on her face in Cole's guest bathroom, Stevie pressed a hand to her still-flat stomach, drew a deep breath and assured herself she looked reasonably presentable considering she'd just been startled out of a sound sleep. She seemed to be sleepy a lot these days. She hadn't even heard Cole enter the house.

The thought of him standing there watching her sleep made her pulse flutter. She supposed it was embarrassment at being caught off guard in his living room. He didn't seem to mind that she'd made herself at home while he was away, but then, she wouldn't have expected anything different from laid-back Cole.

In the year she'd known him, she'd never seen him rattled. She'd rarely observed any display of strong emotions from him, actually. He was the steadiest, most sensible person she knew, a calming presence in her sometimes hectic life. Maybe that was why she'd instinctively taken refuge in his living room when she'd been sad and stressed, though her cat-sitting duties had made a convenient excuse.

She scrutinized her reflection in the mirror. Had Cole seen the tear stains on her cheeks? She thought maybe he had and felt the heat of embarrassment. Though she wasn't usually shy about expressing her emotions— even tended to overshare at times—Stephanie "Stevie" McLane liked to think of herself as resilient, feisty and courageous. Not the type to hide in a friend's house and sniffle into his cat's soft fur. Still, Cole had merely searched her face with his dark, perceptive eyes, calmly asked if everything was okay, then offered her a hot meal. Somehow he'd seemed to know it was exactly what she'd needed, and not just because she was hungry.

He glanced up with a smile when she joined him in the kitchen. His thick, wavy dark hair was a bit messy, but then it always was. A hint of evening stubble shadowed his firm jaw. His eyes were the color of rich, dark chocolate. She'd always thought those beautiful eyes gleamed with both kindness and intelligence. Broad-shouldered and solidly built, he was not what she would call classically handsome, nor did he have that somewhat ethereal artist quality she'd always been drawn to in the past. He didn't talk a lot, and he wasn't prone to sharing his feelings. Still, there was something about Cole that automatically evoked trust and confidence.

She'd liked him from the day he'd moved into this house. There'd been a definite tug of feminine interest, but within her first hour of chatting with him— okay, interrogating him, as he'd humorously referred to that initial conversation—she'd found out he was a computer whiz, a widower and a country music fan who usually listened to news radio in his car. He was practically her total opposite, a stalwart Taurus to her capricious Gemini.

She'd tried to convince herself since then that her latent fascination with him was due more to those intriguing differences than to an underlying attraction she couldn't entirely deny. Despite being involved in an on-again, off-again relationship with a commitment-phobic musician for most of the time she'd known Cole, she'd have to have been brainless not to notice what a great guy he was. So different from her other male acquaintances, he was an enigma to her in many ways, but still they'd become friends. Maybe they could have become more than friends, had circumstances developed differently. She always enjoyed hanging out with him, and she missed him when he was away.

She had missed his steady, solid presence even more than usual during the past few days.

With old-fashioned courtesy, he held her chair for her as she took her seat at the table. "I don't have much to offer by way of a beverage," he said apologetically. "I can make coffee or there's beer or I can open a bottle of wine…"

"This is fine, thank you," she said, motioning toward the water glass he'd already filled and set beside her steaming bowl.

To quickly distract herself from her problems, she picked up her spoon and asked, "How was your trip?"

Seated now across the table from her, he grimaced. "Let's just say it's a miracle I'm not spending tonight in jail rather than having a nice bowl of soup with you."

She smiled. "Annoying associates?"

"To quote my late country grandpa, a couple of them were as dumb as a bag of rocks."

That made her laugh. She always loved it when Cole

quoted his "country grandpa," who had apparently been a treasury of old adages. "Knowing you, I'm sure you were completely polite and patient with them."

"I don't know how patient I was, but I tried not to tell them what I really thought. They didn't even try to pay attention half the time, then complained because they missed a few important points. It gets frustrating. Which is one of the main reasons I prefer telecommuting to pointless meetings and endless deliberations."

As a busy kitchen designer, Stevie knew all about frustrating collaborations. "Totally understand. There are plenty of times I want to dump a pitcher of ice water over a superpicky client or a lazy subcontractor."

He chuckled. "I'm sure you're able to sweet-talk all of them into seeing things your way. That's a talent I don't have."

She had to concede that no one would describe Cole as a "sweet talker." Or a talker at all, for that matter. Still, when he did speak, he always had something interesting and thoughtful to contribute. She'd consulted him several times about perplexing business issues, and had valued his measured, practical advice.

Biting her lip, she wondered what he would say if she confided her current, very personal predicament. She clenched her fingers in her lap.

Cole cleared his throat. She glanced up to find him studying her face with those too-knowing eyes. "Your food is getting cold," he said quietly.

Had he sensed somehow that she'd hovered on the verge of another meltdown? Either way, his reminder had been just what she'd needed to bring her back from the edge. Gripping her spoon so tightly her knuckles whitened, she concentrated on the soup and the cheese and crackers he'd served with it. In an attempt to keep him—and maybe herself—diverted, she talked as she ate, babbling away about anything that randomly occurred to her.

Seeming to have little trouble following her rapid changes of topic, Cole finished his meal then pulled a bag of cookies from the pantry for dessert. She declined the offer, finishing her rapidly cooling soup between sentences while he munched a couple of Oreos.

When he finished, he carried his dishes to the sink, sidestepping the cat munching kibble from a bowl on the floor. Stevie helped him clear the table, smiling up at him as they reached at the same time to close the dishwasher door.

"Thank you, Cole."

"For the soup? Wasn't any trouble, I just warmed it up. You actually made it."

She gave him a fondly chiding look. "Not for the soup, though I guess I needed that. Mostly, thanks for the company and conversation. I needed that even more tonight."

Wiping his hands, he turned to face her with a slight smile on his firm lips. "I didn't say much."

"I didn't give you much chance."

"Well, no, but I'm used to that."

She giggled, pleased to feel like laughing now, even at her own expense. She reached up to pat his cheek. "Are you calling me a chatterbox?"

"Just stating facts." His rare, full grin lit his eyes and carved long dimples around his mouth. Tousled and scruffy after his long day, he looked…well, adorable. His evening beard tickled her palm, and the warmth of his skin tempted her to nestle closer to his solid strength to alleviate her own nervous chill.

A bit unnerved by the impulse, she dropped her hand

quickly and laced her fingers together. This was not the time to be distracted by the physical attraction that had always underscored her friendship with Cole, an attraction she'd always assured herself she had very good reasons to keep private.

"You've been traveling all day," she said, rallying her inner defenses and taking a step back. "I'm sure you're tired. I should go and let you relax."

"There's no rush. We could stream a movie or something. I think I have some popcorn."

Her smile felt a little tremulous. He was being so sweetly concerned about her, even though he hadn't a clue what was troubling her. He'd probably looked forward to crashing on his couch or bed when he'd returned from his business trip. Instead, he'd found himself preparing dinner for a surprise guest and offering to entertain her even longer in case she was still reluctant to return to her own empty house. Was it any wonder she considered him one of her dearest friends?

"Thanks, Cole, but I think I'll just turn in early."

He frowned. "What if your power goes out tonight? With the layer of ice underneath this snow, it's a definite possibility."

"I have plenty of blankets to snuggle under, a couple of good flashlights, and a gas stovetop for heating water for tea."

"Your phone is charged?"

"Almost completely. And I'll plug it in as soon as I get home."

He nodded, though he didn't look entirely reassured.

She slid her hands down her sides in a nervous gesture. "So…"

Just as Cole wasn't much of a "talker," he wasn't much of a "toucher," either. Casual hugs and pats didn't come naturally to him, the way they did for her. He never seemed to mind being on the receiving end, though he'd once teased her about patting his cat goodnight, then doing the same to him as she'd prepared to leave.

So, it surprised her a little when he rested a hand on her shoulder as he gazed somberly into her eyes. "You know, Stevie, I'm not much of a conversationalist, but you've told me more than once that I'm a very good listener. And I'm your friend. If there's anything at all I can do for you, I hope you'd feel comfortable telling me."

Though she tried to hold on to her composure, all it took was a slight squeeze of his fingers to make her eyes fill with tears. To her consternation, sobs burst from her chest as an overtaxed emotional dam finally gave way, and there seemed to be nothing she could do to stop them.

After only a heartbeat's hesitation, Cole stepped forward and gathered her into his arms. He patted her back somewhat awkwardly, a bewildered male response that only made her cry harder.

"Stevie, tell me. What's wrong?"

"I'm—" She choked, then blurted out, "I'm pregnant."

Cole's hand froze in midpat. Of all the answers he had imagined, that was the lowest on his list.

Her voice muffled by his shoulder, she spoke in a flood of jumbled words interspersed with gulping sobs. "I'm sorry. It's just that I haven't told anyone, not even my best friends. This has been building up for weeks, ever since I first suspected I was pregnant, but I didn't want to even think about it. I tried to believe it was just stress or miscalculation, but it's real, and now I'm almost three months along. Joe moved to Austin and I'm pretty sure he has another girlfriend there already. He said he doesn't want a kid and he'd be a terrible father, anyway. I'm not even brokenhearted about the breakup because it wasn't working out and neither of us was really happy. Still, my brother and I grew up without our fathers and I always said I'd never do that to a child and I can't believe I was so stupid at my age. I'll do my best to give my baby a happy childhood. I mean, I turned out okay, right? But the weather was terrible tonight and I was home all alone and I just wanted company, even if it was only your cat," she finished in a soft wail.

He followed the tangled monologue, but just barely. It was a lot of information to digest in a very short amount of time. Fortunately, interpreting massive amounts of data was what he did every day. Stevie was three months pregnant. Joe was out of the picture. Stevie planned to raise the child alone. And she was obviously scared spitless.

Because a calm tone usually trumped overwrought emotion, he asked, "Have you seen a doctor?"

She nodded into his shoulder. "Twice."

"Are you okay? Healthy?"

Her sniffles slowed and she bobbed her head again. "Both of us are."

Both. He swallowed at the reminder that he wasn't holding just Stevie. He couldn't think of anything reassuring to say, so he fell back on practicality. Reaching around her, he snagged a paper towel from the counter and offered it to her. "I don't have a clean handkerchief on me, but maybe you could make use of this?"

His prosaic offer seemed to jolt her out of her meltdown. She made what appeared to be a heroic attempt to get her emotions under control. When she raised her head slowly to look at him, her wet, vivid blue eyes looked huge against her pale skin. She clutched his shirt in both fists as though anchoring herself in a whirlwind. Drawing a deep, unsteady breath, she relaxed her grip, carefully smoothed his crumpled shirt and stepped out of his arms. He hovered close. She still looked fragile enough to collapse at his feet.

"I, um—" It seemed to annoy her that her words were interrupted by a little catch of her breath. She cleared her throat and said, "I'm sorry I fell apart on you. The words just started flooding out and I couldn't stop them."

"You needed to unload," he said simply.

"I guess you're right," she said after a few moments. "Like I said, I haven't told anyone except Joe and my doctor. I just… I didn't know what to say."

"Keeping it to yourself for so long had to have been hard for you." It must have been especially difficult for naturally forthcoming Stevie.

Wiping her cheeks with the paper towel, she nodded. "Especially with Jenny and Tess. They're my best friends and we tell each other everything. Or we always have until now. But Tess is busy planning her wedding and Jenny and Gavin have been trying to get pregnant ever since they got married. How can I tell her that I accidentally got knocked up by a guy she never really liked all that much, anyway?"

He filled a glass with water and handed it to her without comment. She accepted it with a nod of thanks and took a few sips. He was relieved to note that the color was returning to her face, that her hand was steadier when she set the glass on the counter.

She drew a deep, unsteady breath before speaking

again. "It was after Christmas when I first suspected I was pregnant, but another couple of weeks before I let myself believe it."

"Had to have been a shock to you." It had certainly stunned him.

"To say the least. I felt obligated to call Joe, but he made it clear he won't be involved, so I'm on my own, which is fine with me since I'm not interested in seeing him again. I mean, yeah, it was irresponsible of me, but I'm thirty-one, you know? I'll be thirty-two in May. I've always thought I'd have a baby someday, and this could be my best chance. I've completely sworn off stupid fairy-tale fantasies for the future. It's taken me way too long and too many heartaches to figure out that I have not a shred of good judgment when it comes to romance. I've always been drawn to the guys who are the least likely to settle down, and I've always ended up on the losing end. No more. I'll figure out a way to raise this child on my own. Sure, it'll be tough making my schedule work out for the next few months and budgeting my savings to tide us over during the time I'll have to take off for maternity leave. I mean, my business is still pretty new and this is like the worst time to try to juggle contracts and finances and time off, but somehow I'll—"

"More water?" He motioned toward the glass as her nervous babbling threatened to lead to tears again. It was obvious she was on to him.

Drawing in another long breath, she smiled a bit wryly as she shook her head. Dusty wound around her ankles and she reached down to give the cat an absent stroke before straightening to speak more calmly again. "So, here I am. Single and pregnant, just like my mother was twice in two years with my brother and then me.

I haven't been sick a day and my doctor says I'm very healthy and so is the baby. I guess hormones just got the best of me tonight. I'll be fine, really."

"I have no doubt of it," he said. "You'll be a good mother."

She moistened her lips. "You really think so?"

"Absolutely." She should know by now that he didn't say things he didn't mean.

Her smile was sweetly tremulous. "Thank you, Cole. For the dinner, for letting me cry all over you, for being such a good friend. And now I really am going to leave so you can rest."

A good friend. He could be that for her.

He wasn't entirely sure she should be alone in her agitated mood, but he figured she would decline if he tried again to detain her. So he merely nodded and said, "I'll walk you home."

Tossing the crumpled paper towel into the trash, she glanced over her shoulder with a lifted eyebrow. "Since when do you need to walk me next door?"

"Since there's ice all over the walkway and you're pregnant," he replied bluntly. "I want to make sure you don't fall."

"It's not necessary, but I can see you're going to insist." Her smile looked a bit more natural now, though still not the high-wattage grin he associated with her.

With a faint smile in return, he nodded. "You're right. I am."

Minutes later, bundled into their coats, they walked out into what amounted to an Arkansas blizzard. Snow fell so hard he could hardly see Stevie's white house on the big corner lot next door. The ground was already covered and no cars drove down the street, most of the

locals having taken the advice of forecasters and bur-
rowed safely into their homes for the night.

It wouldn't stay this peaceful, of course. He'd bet
the generally well-behaved but exuberant Bristol kids
across the street would be out playing in the snow as
soon as their mom gave them permission. Snow days
were always a rare treat around here, even though they
proved a headache for road crews and first responders.

He kept his gaze trained on Stevie as they stepped
off his porch. Her disposition changed the moment they
moved out into the winter storm. She couldn't seem to
resist turning her face up to let the snow fall against her
cheeks. The security lamps above them provided just
enough light for Cole to see the white flakes glittering
on her skin and in her golden curls. With her signature
musical laugh, she held out her arms and turned in a
little circle, her shoes crunching on the thin layer of
ice beneath the accumulating snow. Bemused by her
mercurial mood shifts, and well aware they had more
to do with her unique personality than to fluctuating
hormones, he chuckled and caught her arm to make
sure she didn't fall.

"Isn't it beautiful?" she asked with a sigh, wrapping
her hands around his arm and smiling companionably
up at him.

"Very."

Her lashes fluttered, though he wasn't sure whether
that was due to the snow or his husky tone. He cleared
his throat. He must be more tired than he'd realized, or
more shaken than he'd have expected by Stevie's bomb-
shell. Whatever the reason, he found himself wanting
to prolong this cozy walk in the snowy night with Stevie tucked close to his side, breath clouds mingling and
drifting in the air in front of them. For the second time

in just over an hour, he felt almost as if he'd stepped into one of his private fantasies. He was glad mind reading wasn't among Stevie McLane's many talents. He wasn't sure how she'd react to knowing that just watching her catching a snowflake on her tongue sent his imagination down a path much more hazardous than the one on which they walked.

Burying those uncomfortable thoughts deep inside his mind, he made an effort to keep his expression blandly friendly until they were on her small porch. She unlocked the front door she'd painted bright blue to match the shutters. One hand on the knob, she smiled up at him. "Okay, I'm safely home. You can relax."

He searched her face in the soft glow of her porch light. "You're sure you're okay? If you need anything else this evening, even if just to talk more, I'm available."

In a gesture that was both impulsive and entirely characteristic, she wrapped her arms around his waist for a hug. "Thank you," she said. "You're a very nice man, Cole McKellar."

A very nice man. As flattering as her comments were, they were hardly the words she'd have whispered in one of those steamy daydreams. Giving himself a mental slap, he returned his friend's hug with a brief squeeze before stepping back. "Good night, Stevie. Call if you need me."

She opened her door. "Good night, Cole."

He stepped down from the little porch into the falling snow, which was already hiding the footprints they'd left on the way. He'd taken only a step when something made him turn back around. "Stevie?"

She paused in the act of closing the door. "Yes?"

"You aren't alone."

With that blurted promise, he turned and headed home, his head down, his fists shoved into the pockets of his coat. He'd taken quite a few steps by the time he heard Stevie close her door.

Chapter Two

Stevie woke late Saturday morning feeling more positive than she had since she first suspected she was pregnant. She wandered to her bedroom window to look over an expanse of glittering snow toward Cole's house. Simply sharing her predicament with him last night had seemed to take a load off her shoulders.

You aren't alone. She could still hear the echo of his deep voice. The words had lulled her to sleep last night, and were still drifting through her mind when she'd awakened. She couldn't begin to express how much it had meant to her to hear them.

Cole was such a great guy. Quiet, but with his own sly sense of humor. Fascinatingly intelligent, in a math-ish sort of way. And completely nonjudgmental, a particularly appealing trait at the moment.

A habitual matchmaker for her friends, she'd occasionally tried to think of someone who'd be a good match for this supernice man, but for some reason she could never come up with anyone who seemed just right for him. A secret part of her had acknowledged on occasion that she'd selfishly wanted to keep him to herself. She had pushed that unsettling voice aside, reminding herself that she'd been in no position to make a play for Cole even if he'd encouraged her.

She wasn't even sure he'd dated seriously in the year she'd known him, though he went out sometimes in the evenings, casually alluding to gatherings with friends. He didn't talk about his late wife much, but on those rare occasions his face warmed and softened. She could tell he had truly loved her. Natasha had been gone for several years, but maybe he still mourned her too deeply to be interested in a new relationship. It was hard to be sure with Cole. He tended to keep his deepest emotions to himself.

It made her sad to think of him still grieving, unwilling or unable to fall in love again. Only because he was her friend and she wanted all her friends to be happy, she assured herself. Still, he seemed content with his home, a job he enjoyed and the friends she hadn't met, so maybe that was enough for him.

She dressed in jeans and a multicolored sweater with colorfully striped knee socks, figuring she'd be out in the cold at some point. As had been her habit the past couple weeks, she turned sideways in front of the mirror to check her figure. Her jeans were getting a little snug in the waist and her bras were a bit tight on her already-generous bustline, but she doubted even her closest friends would be able to guess her condition by looking at her.

She must tell Tess and Jenny soon. She felt incredibly guilty that she hadn't already, even more than not having told her mother and brother. Her two closest friends would forgive her, would even understand why she'd kept her secret for so long, but she wouldn't blame them if they were a bit hurt, at least at first. Especially Jenny, who'd been her best friend since their school days. They'd met Tess almost two years ago and they'd been a tight trio ever since, though they couldn't spend quite as much time together now that Jenny was married and Tess was busily planning a June wedding.

Being human, after all, and the most unabashedly romantic of the small group, Stevie couldn't help feeling a little envious that both Jenny and Tess had found the loves of their lives while her own romances always fizzled. Perhaps she'd been destined all along to follow in her mother's self-reliant footsteps. Was it in her genes to habitually fall for the men who were least likely to settle down to marriage and families?

Shaking her head in exasperation, she turned away from the window.

After eating breakfast, she went into a spare bedroom she used as a home office. Sitting at her desk, she thought of Cole. Like him, she worked from home a lot, but she also leased a small office in a midtown strip center, though most of her work hours were spent in on-site meetings with clients. She was glad she had a third bedroom so she wouldn't lose her office when the baby came.

She'd been at it only an hour when she was interrupted by the chime of the doorbell. Glancing at the clock, she saw that it was just after eleven. She wasn't expecting anyone. Thinking Cole had come over to check on her, she opened the door with an eager smile that wavered only a little when she saw the caller.

"Hi, guys, what's up?" she asked the three pink-cheeked, heavily bundled kids grinning up at her. The Bristol siblings were cute little peas from the same pod, all red-haired, green-eyed and snub-nosed. The boys, Leo and Asher, were nine and seven. Charlotte was five. Baby sister Everly—the "surprise baby," according to their mother, Lori—was presumably at home with their mom. A rather chaotic pathway of little footprints in the snow led from their house across the cul-de-sac to Stevie's small porch.

"Can you come out and help us build a snowman, Miss Stevie?" Charlotte asked with wide, hopeful eyes. "Mommy's taking care of Everly and Daddy's at work."

She wasn't surprised by the request. Since the baby's birth six months ago, she'd played with them several times to give their somewhat harried mother a few minutes to rest on days when her firefighter husband was on twenty-four-hour shifts. They'd thrown basketballs at the hoop mounted above their garage door, played tag and catch, even sat at the picnic table in their backyard with board games. Lori had been almost tearfully grateful for the breaks, but Stevie never minded. She liked kids, particularly these funny and well-behaved siblings.

"Give me five minutes to bundle up and I'll join you in your yard."

The children cheered happily.

"Leo, hold Charlotte's hand on the way back across the street," she instructed. "And look both ways before you cross."

Leo made an exaggerated show of taking his little sister's hand to lead her across the empty street to their own yard. Smiling, Stevie closed her door and turned toward the bedroom.

Half an hour later, she was breathless and covered

with snow from the bright blue knit cap on her head to the waterproof pink boots into which she'd tucked her jeans. Her hooded jacket was yellow, her gloves the same blue as her hat. Charlotte told her she looked like she was wearing a rainbow. Laughing, Stevie showed her how to make a snow angel, adding to her frosty coating.

With the thin layer of sleet beneath, the snow crunched when they played in it. Gray clouds hung low above them, but happy laughter reigned in the Bristol's front yard. From inside the warm house, Lori and baby Everly appeared occasionally in a window to watch, and Stevie waved to them. Next year that little angel, too, would be out playing in the snow. And she would have a baby of her own to watch, she realized with a hard thump of her heart. To soothe the fresh attack of nerves, she focused on the Bristol kids.

The boys had nearly cleared the front lawn of packable snow in the quest to make their snowman "supersized." It was so big that Stevie was elected to lift the giant head onto the body. She drew a deep breath and prepared to give it her best shot. Two strong, black-gloved hands came from behind her to offer assistance. She looked over her shoulder and smiled when she saw Cole standing there. He wore a black watchman cap over his thick dark hair, a black jacket and black boots—a more somber, coordinated ensemble than her own.

His chocolate eyes gleamed with amusement as he grinned down at her. "Need a hand?"

"Or two," she agreed. "These kids like their snowmen on the larger side."

"We're building a snow giant!" Asher exclaimed eagerly, carrying a large stick he'd found in the backyard. "This can be one of his arms. Leo's looking for another."

With Cole's help, they made short work of completing their snow friend, accessorizing with a battered ball cap and frayed scarf donated by Lori. They created facial features with decorative river rocks filched from the flower beds. It had started to snow again, to the children's delight. Another half inch was predicted on top of the six inches that had collected during the night. Stevie figured the snowman would survive a day or two before the warmer temperatures forecast for later in the week melted him away.

After being summoned for lunch by their mother, the siblings politely thanked Stevie and Cole for their assistance in building "the best snowman ever!" They tramped reluctantly inside their house when their mother called out again. Stevie grimaced sympathetically as she imagined the wet mess of clothing and puddles Lori would deal with, but maybe the busy mom would consider it a fair trade-off for the hour of volunteer babysitting. From the open doorway, with Everly on her hip, she called out an offer of hot chocolate, but they declined cordially.

"Though, actually, hot chocolate sounds like a good idea," Stevie confided to Cole as they tramped across the street. She wiped snowflakes from her eyelashes with the back of one damp glove. "I'm freezing."

"Your jeans are wet from rolling around in the snow with Charlotte. You should get into dry clothes."

She noted he'd stayed much drier, maybe because he'd been a little less enthusiastic about getting down in the snow, she admitted with a grin.

"Come in, if you have time," she said, motioning toward her house. "I make a mean mug of cocoa."

"That sounds really—"

His right foot slipped on a slick spot on her driveway. Flailing comically, he went down flat on his back in the snow. Stevie almost burst into laughter at the funny expression he made as he lay there, but she managed to contain her amusement to a grin.

"Are you hurt?" she asked, though she could tell at a glance that he'd damaged only his pride.

Very deliberately, he spread his arms and legs into Vs, then climbed to his feet, surveying the resulting snow angel with a nod of satisfaction. "I meant to do that."

Delighted by his quick wit, she laughed and tucked a hand companionably beneath his arm. "Let's go get warm."

"Sounds good to me," he said, covering her hand with his own. And though they both wore gloves, she could still feel the warmth of his touch spreading through her.

Having shed their wet boots on the porch, Cole insisted that Stevie change into dry clothes before she played hostess. She left him to wash up in the guest bath while she ducked into her bedroom to change into a loose sweater and leggings. Fluffing her curls with her hands, she gave herself a quick once-over in the full-length, silver-framed, art deco mirror that coordinated with her sage, silver and cream French deco bedroom furnishings. Her cheeks and nose were still pink from the cold but she resisted an impulse to touch up her minimal makeup for her guest's benefit. After all, it was just Cole, right?

Her country French kitchen was her favorite room in the house. The walls were warm sage, the cabinets knotty pecan with leaded glass inserts, the counters brown-and-tan granite with antique bronze hardware. Cole joined her there, looking casually at ease in his sweater, jeans and wool socks. His dark hair was disheveled from the hat he'd removed, and her fingers itched with a sudden urge to play in those thick, unruly waves. She opened the refrigerator instead. "How about a sandwich before we drink our cocoa? Playing in the snow always gives me an appetite."

"Sounds good, if it's not too much trouble. What can I do to help?"

When they sat down to lunch, to her relief, he didn't bring up her pregnancy. He merely ate his grilled cheddar-and-tomato sandwiches and munched salt-and-vinegar chips while she babbled nervously about everything and anything—except her predicament.

After the dishes were cleared away, they moved to the living room with steaming cups of cocoa topped with marshmallows. She'd indulged her love of eclectic European and American deco design in here, too. Flames crackled among the gas logs in the fireplace framed in white-painted carved wood, spreading warmth through the room. With her feet curled comfortably beneath her, she sat on the dove-gray couch that faced the fireplace. Cole had settled in a tapestry armchair near her end of the couch. She couldn't help admiring the way the firelight brought out the highlights in his hair.

"I've always liked this room," he commented, stretching his legs in front of him toward the fire. "It always impresses me that it can look so classy yet still be so comfortable. Not fussy and formal like some people's decorated places."

Pleased by the comments, she beamed. "That's exactly what I aim for in my decorating. Stylish, but welcoming. Home design is meant to be enjoyed. Lived in, not just admired or photographed."

He nodded in approval. "That's as it should be. I've always said it was a waste to have furniture you can't sit on or carpet you feel guilty walking on. Tasha—"

He stopped talking and took a sip of his cocoa.

She swirled her beverage gently in her mug to better distribute the melting marshmallows. "Natasha agreed with your design aesthetic?" she prodded gently. She was curious to hear more about the woman he'd married, but she didn't want to cause him pain talking about her.

He shrugged, his expression wry. "She wasn't really into decorating. As long as she had a comfortable chair for reading, she was happy."

"She liked to read?"

"Almost obsessively, especially as her health declined and there was little else she could do."

"Was she sick for a long time?"

"Yes," he replied quietly.

And Cole had taken care of her during that time. She had no doubt that Natasha had received the best of care from him. Unlike most of the men in her own past, Cole wasn't the type to walk away from his responsibilities and commitments, even when those challenges were daunting. Any woman who captured his heart would be very fortunate, indeed, she thought a bit wistfully.

"Do you have plans for the day?" he asked, and it couldn't be more obvious that he wanted to change the subject.

She obliged. "I was going to spend a few hours at my office, but I think I'll just work at home this afternoon instead, considering drivers around here go insane when there's snow on the roads."

"Good plan. So, are you, um, feeling better today?"

She managed not to grimace in response to the oblique reminder of last night's meltdown, but it still embarrassed her. "Much better, thank you. I had fun playing with the Bristol kids this morning."

"Nice kids. They're obviously crazy about you."

"I like them, too."

He finished his cocoa. A dab of marshmallow dotted his upper lip when he lowered the mug. She eyed it from beneath her lashes. She wasn't sure why she wasn't teasing him about it. Normally she would have, but something held her back just then. Maybe it was the crazy image that popped unexpectedly into her head—herself licking away that tempting smudge and then sampling the taste of chocolate on his firm lips.

She blinked rapidly, shocked at the direction her thoughts had taken. *Hormones.* That had to be the explanation. Sure, she'd always been aware of Cole as an attractive man, not to mention his other fine qualities, but she'd deliberately avoided thinking of him in that way. She'd made some really bad decisions when it came to romance, leading, if not to heartbreak, at least to frequent disappointment. Tragically widowed, Cole had shown so signs that he wanted more from her than friendship. And besides, she treasured their relationship too much to risk ruining it by trying to convince themselves they were a compatible match. Most especially not now, considering her awkward predicament.

He wiped off that distracting bit of marshmallow with a napkin, then stood to carry his mug to the kitchen. She followed with her own. He turned just as she approached the sink, and they very nearly collided. With a low laugh, he caught her shoulders. "Steady there."

Heat flared from his touch. For a moment, her mind went blank. She took a jerky step backward, then tried to cover her discomfiture with a laugh. "Were you afraid I was going to knock you over?"

He smiled. "Maybe. I've already landed at your feet once in the past twenty-four hours. And there's no snow in here to give me a credible reason for being on the ground."

She laughed and moved to rinse her mug in the sink. When she turned back around, she found Cole looking up at her high ceiling with a frown. "You have a bulb out," he said.

She followed his glance and saw the dark bulb in one of the recessed canisters that provided auxiliary lighting to the pendant lamps over the island. "I thought something looked different in that corner."

"Do you have a spare bulb?"

"Yes. I'll change it later."

He was shaking his head before she'd completed the sentence. "You don't need to climb ladders in your condition. I'll take care of it."

She had to admit it was difficult for her, at five-two, to change the bulbs in her nine-foot kitchen ceiling. Grateful for his assistance, she fetched a bulb and a stepladder, then turned off the light switch. She leaned against a nearby counter while Cole climbed onto the stepladder and reached overhead. For a self-professed "computer nerd," the man did stay in good condition, she thought, watching muscles ripple as he stretched upward and his shirt exposed part of what looked to be a perfectly formed six pack.

"Well, damn."

She lifted an eyebrow in response to his growl. "What's wrong?"

"Bulb broke off in my hand and now the cap's stuck in the socket."

"Hang on, I'll grab a potato."

He stepped off the ladder to toss the broken bulb into the trash, watching while she sliced a fat potato neatly in half. "So you know that trick."

She smiled as she handed him one half of the potato. "I've broken a few bulbs in my time. My mom taught me this trick years ago. Our budget was usually tight, so she was the 'handyman' around here when we were growing up, at least until my brother and I were old enough to do our share of maintenance."

"She sounds very self-sufficient."

"I suppose she had to be. I've told you, of course, that Mom never married the fathers of either of her kids. She had issues with commitment, and she said neither of them were the home-and-hearth types, anyway. My father died when I was just a toddler, leaving nothing for my support. Mom didn't get much help from my brother's dad, either, but she supported us well enough on her own. She put a down payment on this house with a small inheritance from her parents when Tom and I were very young, and then paid it off over the next ten years with her salary. She was a shrewd budgeter. She gave us a good home here—even though working nine to five in a state job smothered her gypsy soul, as she informed us too many times to count."

Back up on the ladder, Cole glanced down at her when she stopped for a breath. "She sounds like a unique woman."

She smiled. "She is that."

Practically the day Stevie had graduated from college, her accomplished but unconventional mother had announced she was retiring from her job with the state and moving to Hawaii. Upon her retirement, she'd sold Stevie this house for a bargain price and had gone off to find herself on a warm beach.

She turned to pull a bottle of water from the fridge, speaking almost to herself as she twisted off the cap. "I only hope I can handle the challenges of single motherhood as well as Mom did."

"You'll be great." He pushed the potato into the broken bulb and twisted. The resulting metallic squeal made them both grimace, but the trick worked. Stevie held up a wastebasket for the potato and broken parts, then handed him the new bulb.

"Thanks," he said, reaching up again before asking in a conversational tone, "Do you remember your father at all?"

"No. Like I said, I was just a toddler when he was killed in a car wreck, and he'd never even seen me."

"And your brother's father?"

"Tom's dad is still living, as far as we know, but they've never had a relationship. It was just the three of us here."

She gave a little sigh. "I have to admit I was always envious of my friends who had fathers in their lives. Jenny grew up without a dad, too, so she and I bonded in childhood over that, but we were both a little jealous of the girls who had dads to take them to father-daughter dances or even to give their boyfriends the third degree," she added with a rueful laugh. "I know Tom would have liked having a father to play catch with him and take him fishing and other male bonding stuff. Mom threw a mean curve ball and taught us to ride our bikes and drive and do basic home and car maintenance, everything we needed, really…but I've always thought if I ever had a kid, I'd give him or her the one thing missing from my own otherwise happy childhood. A dad."

Dusting off his hands, Cole climbed down and folded the stepladder. "Not everyone is lucky enough to have a close relationship with their father," he muttered as he carried the ladder toward the laundry room.

She watched him thoughtfully. Though he hadn't said much about his family issues, she knew Cole wasn't close to his father. He'd told her his parents were divorced, and both remarried. His mother had moved to another state several years ago, and he'd spent most of his childhood with his paternal grandparents—the "country grandpa" he quoted often—but he hadn't given details of his estrangement from his dad.

Maybe it was just as well she was doing this on her own, she thought with a sigh. Her child's biological father had no interest at all in fatherhood. Had she been with someone different, someone more steady and reliable and responsible—someone like Cole, she thought with a hard swallow—well, that could have had a very different outcome.

Rejoining her, Cole glanced around the kitchen. "Is there anything else I can do for you before I go? Any more repairs you need seen to? It's the least I can do in return for all the cat sitting you're doing this week."

She smiled. "No, that's it, thanks."

"You have food and supplies so you don't have to go out this afternoon? The roads are still a mess."

She patted his arm. "I'm good, Cole, thank you."

He caught her hand in his, gave the fingers a little squeeze, then released her quickly and took a step back. "I'd better go, then. I have a conference call later this afternoon and I need to get ready for it."

"You have a conference call on a Saturday afternoon?" she asked as she followed him into the living room.

He reached for his coat and hat. "Yeah. A lot going on with work this week. I'll probably be tied up for a couple hours, but if you need anything don't hesitate to let me know, okay?"

"I'll be fine. Be careful walking home. I think we have enough snow angels out there."

He made a face that drew a laugh from her. "I'll watch my step."

His faint smile fading, he paused with his hand on the doorknob, looking as though there was something on his mind. Her fingers laced tightly in front of her. She waited, but he remained silent.

His gaze lifted, locking with hers. Lost in his bottomless dark eyes, she stared back at him. It felt as though something important hovered between them, but she couldn't quite figure out what it was. Something he wanted to say? To do? Something he was waiting for her to say or do?

"Call if you need me," he said and opened the door. He was gone before she could even respond.

Biting her lip, she locked the door behind him, then crossed the room and sank onto the couch. Something had changed between her and Cole since she'd shared her news with him, she thought wistfully. She couldn't define it, exactly. Cole certainly wasn't showing disapproval. Just the opposite, in fact; he'd been supportive and considerate. He'd sounded sincere when he said he had faith in her. As the first of her friends she'd told, he'd reacted exactly the way she hoped they all would.

And yet, something was different. She could only describe it as an awareness she hadn't acknowledged before. Whether it was only on her part, she couldn't say, but what else could it be? Maybe it was all in her head. Maybe those wonky hormones and jumbled emotions were making her imagine things that weren't real. Whatever the reason, she had to get a grip. She'd made quite a few foolish mistakes in the past few months, but she would never do anything that would put her treasured friendship with Cole at risk.

Her phone rang some three hours after Cole left. Looking away from the kitchen design on her computer monitor, she glanced at the ID screen on her phone. She smiled when she saw Cole's name. Was he checking on her again already? Very sweet, but she'd have to convince him she was fine so he would stop worrying about her. It hadn't helped, of course, that she'd blubbered all over him last night, she thought with a wince.

With that embarrassing memory in mind, she answered cheerily. "Hi, Cole. What's up?"

"Just letting you know I'm going to have to catch a plane to Chicago first thing in the morning."

She frowned. "I thought you weren't leaving until later in the week."

"So did I. But the conference call I mentioned was a nightmare. I have to go sort out some stuff. And try not to knock heads together while I'm there," he finished grimly.

She giggled, but a bit wistfully. He'd only just gotten back from the last trip. She wished he didn't have to go again so soon. She was sure he felt the same way, though probably not for the same reasons. "I'll take good care of Dusty."

"You always do. I'm pretty sure you're her favorite person. Which I understand completely," he added, and she could hear the smile in his voice now.

"Why, thank you, kind sir."

His low chuckle rumbled pleasantly in her ear. "The roads should be much better tomorrow, but don't take any chances, okay? Be careful."

"I will. You do the same."

She set her phone aside with a little sigh after they disconnected. She would miss him again. But maybe it would be good to have a little distance from him for a few days. She was quite sure everything would be back to normal—as much as possible considering the circumstances, anyway—once he returned.

It had been a long, frustrating day, but that wasn't what kept Cole awake Tuesday night. Ultimately, the business problems had been settled to everyone's satisfaction, and he would be able to return to Little Rock Thursday and get back to work in his much-preferred home office. So, it wasn't the job that had him tossing and turning in the hotel bed, or that made him finally give up and move to the window to stare blankly out at the midnight Chicago skyline. His thoughts were several hundred miles away. With Stevie McLane, to be precise.

Even when he'd been immersed in discussions about figures and trends and mathematical models, he'd been aware of thoughts of her hovering at the back of his mind, ready to push to the forefront as soon as he was alone. It was rare that he allowed himself to be distracted from work, but he hadn't been able to stop thinking about Stevie since she'd confided her pregnancy to him Friday night. He'd acknowledged privately that Stevie had been in his thoughts increasingly often during the past months, but even more so this week.

Something she'd said Saturday kept replaying in his

mind. *I've always thought if I ever had a kid, I'd give him or her the one thing missing from my own otherwise happy childhood. A dad.*

A brainstorm had occurred to him in the middle of that night, and he'd been pondering it ever since, giving it his usual thorough contemplation of all potential consequences. He still had nagging doubts about whether he was qualified to even make the offer, considering the poor example his own father had set, but he'd decided he should at least discuss the idea with Stevie.

He wasn't sure which possible outcome unnerved him most. That she would turn him down…or that she would accept.

He turned away from the window and padded back over to the tousled bed. He always kept a few interesting nonfiction books on his tablet. Maybe if he read awhile, he'd lull himself to sleep. Reaching out to turn on the bedside lamp, he muttered a curse when he knocked his wallet off the nightstand. He reached down to scoop it up and it fell open in his hands. He started to close it when something made him pause. Very slowly, he reached into the back of the wallet and drew out a small photograph with worn edges.

He'd once commented to Natasha that she had the face of a Renaissance Madonna. She'd laughed and told him not to be silly, but that hadn't changed the fact that she could have posed for one of those famous paintings. Framed by straight, dark hair, her oval face had been delicate, her skin a flawless olive. Her dark hazel eyes had been striking in their intensity and clarity, making him feel at times as though she could see right into him. Despite that serene exterior, she'd had a warrior spirit, refusing to accept the health issues that had eventually led to her death. She'd made plans for a long marriage, for a career, for a family. She'd clung to those dreams until the very end of her life.

He ran his fingertips slowly across the face in the photo. Natasha had been gone five years, leaving him a widower before he'd turned thirty. She wouldn't have wanted him to spend the rest of his life alone. But still, he felt a niggle of remorse whenever he envisioned himself having all the things she had wanted so badly and would never have.

She would understand, he told himself, sliding the photo back into place. She'd have liked Stevie, though they had little in common other than kind hearts and innate optimism. Natasha would certainly understand his compulsion to offer assistance to a valued friend, someone in a difficult situation. She had once described him as a compulsive caregiver.

His growing attraction to Stevie during the past year had made him both uncomfortable and vaguely guilty, despite his assurances of what Tasha would have wanted for him. He'd thought it a futile fantasy, a sometimes-lonely bachelor's natural infatuation for a desirable and fascinating woman. But now Stevie's circumstances had taken a daunting turn. And he'd promised her she wouldn't be alone.

Maybe he could give Stevie what he had failed to provide for Natasha no matter how hard he'd tried, he thought bleakly, tossing the wallet aside. Moving to stare out the window again, he wished he could erase the nagging apprehension that he didn't have enough to offer.

After several business meetings Monday and another appointment with her obstetrician Tuesday, Stevie spent Wednesday evening relaxing with her friends

Jenny Locke and Tess Miller for an ever-more-rare girls' night out. In addition to their changing personal lives, all of them stayed busy with their successful careers. Jenny owned two fashion and accessories boutiques and planned to open another within the next year. Tess was the office manager for her fiancé's thriving commercial construction company. Stevie's kitchen design business was growing increasingly in demand due to recommendations from her satisfied customers. It was getting harder all the time to find a night when all three were free, but they made an effort to nurture the friendship that meant so much to all of them.

They enjoyed gathering occasionally at Jenny's boutique, Complements, after business hours. With no other customers in the store, Stevie and Tess could try on new outfits, play with the latest bags and jewelry and supplement their wardrobes with the "friends and family discount" Jenny always extended to them. Tonight they huddled around a counter spread with magazines, photographs and fabric samples Tess had brought with her. Two computer tablets lay amongst the clutter, different bridal websites displayed on the screens.

"So, we all agree?" Tess asked. "We like these colors? Poppy red and pale yellow? And what about the bridesmaids' dresses? Is there any particular style you both prefer?"

Stevie bit her lip as she did a quick mental calculation. Tess's wedding was scheduled for mid-June. Stevie would be seven months pregnant and sporting a big belly by then. It was time to come clean with her friends. She didn't know why it was so much harder to confide in them than it had been with Cole. She was sure Jenny and Tess were going to be supportive, though she wouldn't be surprised if tears were shed, and not all of them hers. She drew a deep breath.

"Hello?" Tess studied both Stevie and Jenny with a quizzical expression. "Neither of you is answering me. Which style do you like for the bridesmaids' dresses?"

Jenny spoke before Stevie had a chance to share her news. "Um, Tess? If it's okay with you, I think we should choose a loose, nonfitted style."

Something in Jenny's tone made both Stevie and Tess look at her curiously. Her expression made Stevie's breath catch, and she heard Tess give a little squeak.

"Jen?" Tess's voice was breathless with anticipation.

A shaky smile spread across Jenny's beautiful face. "I'm pregnant."

The words Stevie had been prepared to say lodged in her throat.

Jenny looked at Tess when she added, "I'm only four weeks along, so I'm a little nervous about even mentioning it yet. But with the wedding preparations moving along, and the need to order dresses soon, I thought you should know now."

Tess squealed and reached out to her friend. Though usually the most exuberantly demonstrative of the trio, Stevie paused a beat before throwing herself into the group hug. She hoped her hesitation, if noticed, would be attributed to happy surprise.

Jenny was already answering a barrage of questions from Tess. Yes, she felt fine other than some morning nausea; yes, Gavin was super excited; yes, they'd told their families and everyone was thrilled.

Swiping at her damp cheeks, Tess beamed and started gathering the wedding materials. "All of this can wait. Let's go to the restaurant next door and we can talk about your news over dinner. I want to hear how your mom and grandmother reacted. I know Gavin's big family must have gone crazy. Do you know when you'll start decorating the nursery? I bet Stevie can help you with that, can't you, Stevie?"

"Well, I'm more comfortable with kitchens, but I'm sure I can come up with a few suggestions for decorating a nursery." Stevie smiled brightly as she set her own momentous news aside for now. Jenny glowed with happiness about her pregnancy, and Tess was still eager to discuss the simple, but certain-to-be-beautiful wedding she was trying to put together quickly. This seemed entirely the wrong time to mention that she was already three months pregnant herself.

She hid her inner turmoil for the remainder of the evening behind mile-a-minute chatter and animated laughter, giving her friends little opportunity to ask anything personal of her. They had an absolutely delightful evening, yet Stevie had trouble fully enjoying it.

"I just couldn't tell them," she said to Cole the next afternoon, restlessly pacing her living room. "Jenny was so happy to make her announcement—and very nervous that it's still early so something could yet go wrong. And Tess is focusing on her wedding arrangements. She's seeing everything through orange blossom-colored lenses right now. If I'd told them my situation, they'd have started worrying about me and obsessing about my situation rather than their own excitement and I didn't want our special evening to veer off into that direction last night, so I—"

"Breathe, Stevie." Watching her from an armchair, Cole broke in to interrupt the rush of words she'd been holding in for hours. His deep voice was a soothing balm to her frayed nerves. "You'll hyperventilate."

He'd arrived only a few minutes earlier to let her

know he was back in town and thank her, as he always did, for taking care of Dusty while he was gone. Stevie had barely waited until he was seated before she'd started pacing and venting to the only person who truly understood what she'd been going through recently.

She inhaled deeply. Staying busy with work, she'd held herself together pretty well since she'd parted from her friends last night with warm hugs and too-bright smiles, but just seeing Cole on her doorstep had brought her emotions dangerously close to the surface again. She paused in front of him, pushed her hair from her face with both hands and managed a smile of sorts.

"Sorry. I don't mean to keep unloading all my problems on you. It's your fault for being such a good listener," she added, trying to lighten the mood with teasing.

"I don't mind," he assured her, and made her believe him. "Actually, I've given your situation a great deal of thought, and I have some suggestions for you, if you're interested in hearing them."

He looked so solemn that she had to smile despite her agitation. "You've given this careful consideration, have you?"

His lips twitched. "I've analyzed the data you presented to me and I would like to suggest some viable alternatives for your consideration."

She chuckled in response to his self-mocking expression, then grew serious again. "That's very sweet of you, but I'm sure I'll work out a plan of some sort."

His faint smile vanished. "You're stressed, and that's not good for either you or the baby. I understand why you were reluctant to talk to your girlfriends last night, under the circumstances, and apparently you aren't quite ready to turn to your family. But I'm your friend, too, and I'm here for you. This is what I do, you know. I look at all the angles of a problem and identify solutions."

She twisted a shoulder-length curl around her finger in her habitual nervous gesture. "I know you're a genius at your work. But I'm not sure my current situation is in your wheelhouse."

"Not exactly, but I'd like to try to help. I made a few notes." He reached into his shirt pocket, drawing out his ever-present, tablet-sized smartphone. He pushed a button, then studied the words on the screen intently.

Seriously? He'd made notes? Was this the cutest thing ever?

"You said you didn't want to raise your child without a father. Is there any chance the biological father will change his mind about being involved?"

"None," she said with absolute certainty, amusement evaporating. "He made that very clear."

Cole nodded, then moved on to his next point. "You said you worried about keeping your business afloat, both financially and logistically, while juggling maternity leave and infant care."

"That will be a challenge," she admitted, twisting the curl more tightly. "I've already started saving as much as I can stash away and I'm trying to keep my calendar organized around my due date."

"You're going to need help," he said bluntly. "I believe there's an obvious solution. The ideal option is for you to marry someone who likes and wants kids. Someone who can help you with the myriad daily responsibilities of raising a child and running a successful business."

Taken aback, she shook her head in bemusement. This was the strategy Cole thought was obvious? That she should simply find someone to marry before her baby's arrival?

"Cole, that's—"

He seemed intent on quickly spelling out his reasoning. "You said you're done with unstable romances. I'm of the opinion, myself, that marriages built on practical foundations are more sustainable than those based on fantasy and infatuation. My parents, for example, married in a youthful whirlwind romance that ended in a bitter and acrimonious divorce. Both wed for the second time for far more sensible purposes and those marriages have been much more successful."

"You're suggesting I should marry a friend to help me raise my child?"

Cole nodded, looking for all the world as if his improbable conclusion made perfect sense. He set aside the phone. "It's the ideal solution."

She gave him a quizzical smile. "So, are *you* offering to marry me, Cole?"

His look of surprise almost made her laugh again. He must not have realized how his suggestion could be interpreted, she mused in fond indulgence.

"I thought you understood," he said, his expression very earnest now. "That's exactly what I'm doing."

Chapter Three

Stevie's soft laughter ended with a choke. She coughed a couple of times, waving Cole off when he stood and stepped forward as if to pound her back. Once she'd recovered her breath, she told herself she must have misheard him. "You, um—what?"

"I'm asking you to marry me," he repeated. Slowly this time, as if to make sure she comprehended.

Though her first reaction was shock, as his words sank in she found herself almost unbearably touched. A lump formed in her throat when she looked at him standing there all rumpled and noble and earnest. And sexy as all get-out, but she pushed that particular observation to the back of her mind to concentrate on the conversation.

She rested a hand lightly on his arm and spoke in a voice that wasn't entirely steady. "That's very sweet of you, Cole, but you understand pregnant women don't have to get married these days, right?"

He covered her hand with his own. "Yes, I know. But you have to admit it would be much easier if you have someone to share the responsibilities. I like kids. Always thought I'd have at least one of my own some-day, but I'd sort of given up on that expectation. I wasn't sure I'd ever marry again. I liked being married, but I get frazzled just thinking about the pressures and so-cial expectations of courtship. Yet I can picture myself raising this child with you."

She drew her hand slowly from beneath his to latch on to a lock of her hair, twisting it so tightly her finger-tip went numb. Was this real? Cole wasn't one to play practical jokes. And even if he were, this would hardly be funny. "I'm not sure what to say."

Still standing close, he studied her gravely, as if try-ing to read her mind. She wished him luck with that. The way her head was spinning, even she couldn't make sense of her thoughts.

"I can tell you're surprised, and I understand. But think about it, Stevie. It makes perfect sense. We could have a good life together. With my telecommuting job, I could watch the baby while you're working. Your career is flexible enough that we could coordinate our sched-ules around my business trips. I make a good living, so between the two of us, the child would be well cared for. I'm good with kids—and you have to admit I build a really great snowman," he added with a disarmingly self-deprecating smile.

"Wow." She swallowed, then said again, "Wow! You're actually serious."

He nodded. "It's a good plan, right? Win-win. For me, for you—and for this baby."

Oh, that was hardly a fair argument, she thought with a hard swallow. She'd told him she wished she could give her child a devoted dad. And she could hardly imagine a more upstanding candidate for the position.

She became aware that the hand not tangled in her hair had gone subconsciously to her stomach. She was still having trouble believing this was an actual proposal of marriage, but still she had to ask, "You'd really have no objection to raising another man's child as your own?"

Cole looked genuinely startled by the question. As straightforward as ever, he replied, "I've never had a particular desire to see my own face in miniature. My childhood best friend was adopted, something he discussed openly. He was closer to his adoptive family than I was to my biological one."

Though she didn't know the details of his estrangement from his father, she couldn't imagine why anyone wouldn't be grateful to have a son like Cole.

"Kids don't need a certified pedigree to make them happy," he added, just a hint of uncharacteristic wistfulness in his voice now. "They need love. Encouragement. Unwavering support. I can offer all those things to this child we can welcome together. Let's face it, neither of us expected this development, but we're both in the right place at the right time to accept the challenge."

Something deep inside her tightened in response to his words. "You've really given this a lot of consideration, haven't you?"

He nodded. "I've been thinking about it for days. I had to consider all the ramifications before I came to you. I'd never make a commitment I wasn't prepared to honor completely and permanently. I'm absolutely sure about this."

It wasn't often that naturally talkative Stevie found herself without words, but Cole had managed to strike her speechless. She almost wondered if she were dreaming this entire conversation, drifting into foolish daydreams about what might have been...

Cole reached out to gently untangle her hand from her hair, then cradled both her hands in his. She wasn't sure if he'd practiced this proposal, but he spoke without hesitation, visibly sincere. "Marry me, Stevie. You said I'm one of your best friends. I feel the same about you. We mesh well together, have from the start. We can make this work. We can give this child the type of home and family you and I both wanted growing up. I'm not making a sacrifice or being unselfish in this offer. I want very much to be a dad to this kid. I think I'd make a good one."

She'd spent her whole life acting on impulse, following her heart, her hunches, her instincts. Every one of those usual prompts urged her now to accept Cole's offer on the spot. Still, she owed it to him, to herself, to her child to take time to consider before she leaped this time.

"Think about it," he urged, reading the emotions chasing themselves across her face. "I don't want to rush you into anything that doesn't feel right to you, and nothing has to change between us if you choose to decline my proposal. We can still be friends. I just want you to know that I'm here for you and the baby, and that I hope—"

"Yes."

So much for caution.

He went still, his head cocked to one side as he eyed her closely. "Yes?"

She felt her fingers tremble in his big strong hands. His grip tightened just enough to show her that he felt it, too. She freed her hands and stepped back to give herself a little distance, drawing herself up to her full height, such as it was. Her voice was satisfactorily steady when she demanded, "Do you promise you'll always be a caring, committed father to this child, no matter what happens?"

"You have my word," he answered without a hint of hesitation. "You both do."

If there was one thing she'd learned about Cole Mc-Kellar during the past year, it was that he was the most honest man she'd ever met. Bluntly so, at times, but that was only part of his unique charm.

"Then the answer is yes."

It wasn't the hearts-and-flowers-and-violins marriage proposal she'd vaguely imagined for herself in youthful, Hollywood-tinted fantasies, but look where those silly daydreams had led her, how many times they'd let her down. She was going to be a mother now, and it was time to put unrealistic expectations behind her.

If she made a list of all the attributes she'd want for her child's father, Cole would match nearly every item on the page. Maybe he wasn't the type to write love songs for her or shower her with grand, romantic gestures, but the men who had done those things in the past hadn't stayed around to deal with the everyday realities of life. He wasn't claiming a grand passion for her— perhaps his late wife would always hold that position in his heart—but she knew he was quite fond of her, and she didn't doubt that he respected her intelligence and admired her success in her business. That meant a great deal to her.

Other men had claimed to love her, but hadn't stayed around to make a life with her. Cole would be there, stable, dependable, practical. She needed to work on being more like him—starting now.

"Yes," she repeated, more firmly this time.

A smile spread across his face and she had to admit he looked pleased. If he had any doubts about this plan, it wasn't visible in his expression. As for herself, she was still nervous—oh, hell, she was scared to her toenails—but she'd made her decision. She gave her tummy a little pat, sending a silent message in that direction. *You're welcome, kid.*

"Great," he said with obvious satisfaction. "We'll make this work, Stevie, I promise."

"I believe you." She would certainly do her part, she vowed.

Her legs seemed to have weakened, so she moved to sit on the couch. Cole sat beside her, drawing his phone from his pocket. She frowned a little. Was he already calling someone with the news? Was he really this excited about—

But he'd merely opened his calendar. "So when do you want to do this? The baby is due in—six months, right?"

She nodded, trying to focus on practical details. "Yes."

"So that doesn't give us a lot of time to take care of things. We'll have to decide where to live, set up a nursery, work out our schedules, that sort of thing. You, um—do you want a big wedding? Because if you do—"

"No," she assured him quickly. "I'd prefer something small and simple."

She could see relief cross his face, though knowing Cole, she suspected he'd have agreed to a huge affair if she'd said she wanted one.

"I don't need my parents there," he said. "Considering they don't even like being in the same state at the same time, they'd hardly want to attend the same wedding. They'll probably be relieved they don't have to make the effort. I'm pretty sure my mom will be pleased at the prospect of having a grandchild. I think she'd pretty much given up on the idea."

She twisted her fingers in her lap. Would his mother really welcome this child, even though her son wasn't the biological father? "Are you, um, going to tell your parents that I was already pregnant when you and I decided to get married?"

Cole shrugged. "As far as I'm concerned, it's unnecessary. I won't lie, but there's no need to tell everyone our business. You can make the decision with your mother and brother. We'll tell the child when he or she is old enough to understand, of course, and I guess your closest friends will know the truth, but I'd be fine with letting the rest make their own assumptions."

"That works for me, too," she murmured.

He nodded, putting that item behind them before returning to the previous one. "What about you? Do you want to wait until your mother and brother can get here to have the ceremony?"

She barely had to think about it before shaking her head. "Mom isn't really interested in ceremonies—and she's never been a big fan of marriage," she added with a wry laugh. "She'll be satisfied with hearing the details afterward and then flying in for a visit after the baby arrives. Same goes for my brother."

"And what about your friends?"

"Jenny and Tess are going to be…surprised." Which was the understatement of the year, of course.

Cole studied her expression. "How do you think they'll feel about our plans?"

"I don't know," she admitted.

She was sure her friends would be concerned she was acting on impulse and would urge her to take more time to think about all of this, despite the pregnancy deadline. Bonded with their soul mates, they would obviously want the same for her. Jenny had turned down a socially advantageous proposal from a wealthy and connected attorney to wed the cop she'd loved since their college years. Tess's engagement to her employer might have started out as an arrangement meant to assuage their matchmaking relatives during the holidays, but it hadn't taken them long to realize they'd been deeply in love for some time.

Both Jenny and Tess would certainly remind Stevie that she had always been the one to defend the fairy tale version of romance, to insist marriage should be based on passion, not practicality. But their circumstances were very different from her own, she reminded herself. They'd had only their own best interests to consider during their courtships. Jenny understood the pain of growing up without a father, her own having died before she was even born, but would she approve of Stevie's decision to provide for her baby's needs over her own silly fantasies?

"I don't know," she repeated.

"Would you change your mind if they do disapprove?"

She shook her head firmly. "Of course not. It's just that I'm not quite sure how to explain it to them. As I've said, I haven't even told them yet that I'm pregnant. I just don't want them to worry about me."

As much as she hated to admit it, things were changing between her and her friends with marriages and babies coming into the picture. It was inevitable, she supposed. They would always be close, but the time they could spend together would be even more limited with these new responsibilities.

"Here's an idea." Cole drummed the fingers of one hand lightly against his thigh. She could tell by his expression that he'd turned his full attention to solving her latest dilemma. "Instead of telling them ahead of time and dealing with their questions and opinions, why don't you just present it to them as a fait accompli? We could elope, then tell them we're married and we're committed to raising this child together. There would be little they could say at that point except to congratulate you and wish you well."

She blinked. "Not tell them beforehand? But Jen and I have always told each other everything. Tess, too, since we met her."

"You haven't told them you're pregnant."

She winced in response to that very reasonable rebuttal. "No."

"What's your schedule tomorrow?" he asked after a moment.

The seemingly abrupt change of subject made her blink again before answering, "I have a meeting in the morning, but it should only take a couple of hours."

"Can you be done by noon? I have a few things to deal with, but I can be finished by lunchtime. There's no waiting period to be married in this state, so we could leave at around one o'clock tomorrow afternoon, pick up a marriage license and stop at one of those little wedding chapels in the Ozarks. Afterward, we'll drive into Missouri and spend a couple nights at a nice inn in Branson, and be back at work Monday morning. I wish I could take you somewhere special for a real honeymoon, but my schedule is pretty tight at the moment and I'm sure yours is, too, getting ready for your maternity leave and all."

"Tomorrow," she repeated somewhat blankly, feeling swept along by a current that had surged out of control. She'd already agreed to marry him, so why did setting a time cause a flicker of panic inside her? "You're talking about getting married tomorrow?"

"Well, we could wait a little longer if you need more time."

"I—" She chewed her lower lip as she considered. Though she felt a bit cowardly to admit it, she could see the appeal of telling her friends after the fact rather than facing a barrage of questions and doubts and advice. Cole was right—this way it would be too late for them to try to talk her out of marrying him. Too late to talk herself out of it. "Tomorrow works for me."

He gave her knee a little squeeze, his fingers lingering long enough to make her vividly aware of his touch. "I'll make the arrangements with the chapel and a hotel. February is hardly peak tourist season, so we shouldn't have trouble getting reservations. Some of the Branson theaters are probably closed for the season, but I'm sure a few are still open. It'll be fun, right?"

"Fun." Stevie laughed in bemusement and pressed her cold hands to her warm cheeks. "How is it that you can make even the craziest plan sound absolutely rational?"

Cole had the grace to smile crookedly as he rose from the couch. "My special talent?"

"Apparently."

"Well?"

Rising as he did, she drew a slightly shaky breath and pressed a hand to her stomach. "Okay. I have a consultation at nine in the morning, but I can be ready to leave by one o'clock."

As matter-of-fact as Cole was being about all this, she wouldn't have been entirely surprised if he'd sealed the deal by offering his hand to shake. Instead, he reached into his pocket. For the first time since he'd blindsided her with this plan he'd obviously considered so carefully, she saw a hint of uncertainty in his expression. "I picked up something for you while I was in Chicago. I hope you like it."

"I'm sure I'll—" Her voice faded when she saw the little velvet box resting on his palm. "Oh."

"I wanted to be prepared in case you said yes." He opened the hinged lid to reveal the contents.

Her breath caught when the overhead light glittered off a diamond set on a white gold band. It was exactly the type of ring she'd have expected Cole to choose, simple and classic. Even the choice of square-cut over the slightly more traditional round stone was typical of him—though the gesture itself was certainly unexpected.

"It's beautiful, Cole." Her voice sounded husky to her own ears.

He caught her hand and slid the ring on her finger. She told herself it was a good omen that it fit surprisingly well. Her hands were small, but the ring wasn't overpowering. In fact, she'd have said it was exactly right for her.

He was watching her face. "If you'd prefer another style, we can swap it for—"

She curled her fingers protectively around the ring. "This one is perfect."

"I'm glad you like it. So, I'll go now and start making arrangements. This time tomorrow, we'll be in Branson."

And married, she added silently, swallowing hard.

She could tell his mind was already engaged with lists of tasks he wanted to complete before tomorrow. She knew how he got when he was focused on a deadline. He was probably itching to tap away at his trustworthy little tablet. "All right. See you tomorrow."

She walked him to the door, feeling as if she were moving in an odd sort of slow motion. She'd begun the day as an anxious, single mother-to-be. Only a few hours later, she found herself engaged to be married to a man who was busily planning their future while she still reeled from his proposal.

He let himself out, closing the door behind him. With a little sigh, Stevie started to turn away. She paused with a start when the door swept open again. Cole stepped back inside, his expression rueful.

"That was a lousy way to conclude our conversation, wasn't it?" he asked. "I think I can do much better."

Before she quite realized his intention, he gathered her into his arms and pressed his lips to hers.

As first kisses went, especially with such little fanfare, this one was impressive. Solid and sturdy, Cole enveloped her, engulfed her. Every feminine nerve ending inside her responded to that potent masculinity with a rush of sensation unlike anything she'd experienced before.

She was kissing Cole! Or he was kissing her. And if ever she had contemplated what it might be like to do so—and she'd imagined it on more than a few occasions, just for curiosity—the reality was more explosive than she could ever have predicted. How could she possibly have suspected that the quiet numbers cruncher next door kissed like a dashing pirate?

His lips were firm, warm, skilled. The hint of his late-day beard was pleasantly rough against her softer skin. He tasted of sexy, spicy, virile male; a potent combination that made her suddenly, unexpectedly hungry for more. She couldn't quite hold back the tiny murmur of protest when he drew his mouth a couple inches from hers, breaking the contact.

Cole looked almost as dazed as she felt when their gazes locked. And then he swooped in for another taste, and she discovered to her amazement that the first kiss hadn't been a fluke. She couldn't have said how long it lasted, or which of them moved closer to deepen the kiss, to press their bodies together. She couldn't help noticing that Cole was tautly aroused as he thrust his tongue between her parted lips for a more thorough exploration.

How long had this embrace been building? Hours? Days? Months? Was it possible she wasn't the only one who'd wondered what it would be like, who'd secretly wished to find out?

She didn't realize she was gripping his shirt in both white-knuckled fists until he finally, firmly set her back a step, carefully untangling her fingers from the now-wrinkled fabric. Wow. Did she say that aloud or was the word just echoing in her otherwise blank mind?

His face a bit flushed, Cole shifted his weight uncomfortably, then cleared his throat before saying, "Well. That was…reassuring."

She blinked, not entirely sure how to respond to that comment. It wasn't the adjective she'd have chosen to describe the embrace. Amazing, maybe. Spectacular. Toe-curlingly stimulating, even. But…reassuring?

After only a moment, Cole chuckled huskily, gave her shoulder a little squeeze, then opened the door. "I'll call you later. If you need anything in the meantime, you know where to find me."

The door closed behind him again and this time it stayed shut. Stevie stood without moving for what seemed like a very long time. In a daze, she pushed her hair from her overwarm face.

As she turned slowly back into her living room, she felt as if she should pinch herself to make sure she was really awake. Either this was one truly bizarre dream, or she'd just agreed to marry her next-door neighbor. Tomorrow!

Stevie could usually pack for a week in a carry-on bag, and rarely spent more than a few minutes deciding what to take. Yet it took her more than an hour to choose and pack the next day. And all for a two-night trip, she thought with a shake of her head as she stood in the middle of her bedroom, dithering over shoe choices.

It wasn't as if she needed anything different from her usual informal, somewhat bohemian wardrobe, not in Branson. With its live theaters, shopping malls, themed restaurants, golf courses and arcades, the town nestled in the Ozarks on the banks of sprawling Lake Taneycomo was a cheerfully cheesy tourist magnet.

There hadn't been a lot of extra money for vacations and travel when she'd been a child, but two or three times each year she and her mother and brother had made the just-over-three-hour road trip to Branson for a relatively inexpensive family weekend. She still had warm memories from those trips, which she'd mentioned to Cole during a couple of their rambling, lengthy chats. Did he remember? Probably. Cole didn't forget much.

She zipped her suitcase, then frowned at it, wondering if she'd packed enough. No. She wasn't going to second-guess this. It was only a weekend trip.

It was also her honeymoon, she thought, chewing on her lower lip as she gazed down at her ring. This wasn't at all what she'd imagined when she'd ever fantasized about a honeymoon.

Was she dressed appropriately for an elopement? Had the weather been warmer, she'd have worn something sleeveless and lacy, perhaps. There was no snow on the ground now, but it was cold enough that she'd have shivered in lace. She'd chosen, instead, a dusky blue sweater dress with black leggings and tall boots. The dress had come from Jenny's shop, and Jenny had told her the color made her eyes look brighter and bluer. Sometimes she wore a wide belt with it, but she left off the belt this time, accessorizing with a chunky ebony-bead necklace, instead.

Posing in front of the mirror, she looked hard at her midsection. She still doubted anyone could tell her condition just by looking at her. Had she not seen the positive pregnancy test and heard the doctor's confirmation, she would hardly believe it herself. It still didn't seem quite real. Nor did the fact that she was going to be a married woman in a few hours.

She opened the silver jewelry box on her dresser to take out the hoop earrings she planned to wear today. As she removed them, a narrow slip of paper caught her attention. She'd saved it from a fortune cookie; she didn't even remember exactly when, but she'd had it for several years. Something about its message had spoken to her: *You will live an unexpected life.*

She laughed shortly. "You surely got that right, Confucius."

Cole was pleased that they were in the car and on the road exactly on the schedule they'd agreed upon. Though he and Stevie hadn't confided the reason they'd both be out of town for the next two nights, they'd arranged for Lori to check on Dusty tomorrow, so the long weekend was all cleared for their brief honeymoon. Even the weather was cooperating. It was cold, but the roads were dry and the sky a cloudless pale blue. He took that as a good sign.

He was very much aware of how close they sat in the front seats of his SUV. He could reach easily enough across the narrow console to take her hand or rest his on her knee. Because that thought was all too tempting, he tightened his fingers on the steering wheel and tried not to think about the kisses that had left him tossing and turning in his bed most of the night.

He didn't have to worry about awkward silences during the drive. Though he'd seen the self-consciousness in her eyes when she'd answered the door, Stevie wasn't the type to be quiet when she was flustered. Just the opposite, actually; she tended to babble. Cole wasn't sure she took a breath during the first hour of their drive. She chattered about so many random topics he couldn't even keep up, her hands fluttering around her like restless little birds.

Though he didn't say much in return—couldn't have slipped in more than a word or two if he'd wanted to— he didn't mind her frenetic monologue. Nor did he try to calm her. She had every reason to be jittery. He was a little nervous, himself—not because he had doubts about the plans they'd made, but because he hoped he was up to the massive responsibilities he was taking on. He had to admit he'd assigned himself a daunting task. Torn between bittersweet memories of the past, concerns for the future and frustrated physical desire, he hadn't gotten much sleep last night.

"Oh, my gosh." Stevie covered her cheeks with her hands, laughing ruefully. "I'm talking a thousand miles a minute, aren't I? I haven't given you a chance to speak at all. Sorry."

"No need to apologize. I enjoy listening to you. It makes the drive go by faster."

"Yes, well, I've run out of small talk."

"Maybe we should discuss some of the decisions we have ahead of us. I made a list last night…"

She chuckled softly. "Of course you did. Should I pull out your trusty notebook?"

He didn't mind her teasing any more than her chattering. It was all just part of what made up Stevie, and he couldn't imagine why anyone would want to change her.

"There's no need," he said with his own attempt at levity. "I memorized the list."

It pleased him that she laughed before asking, "Okay, what's the first item on the agenda?"

He started with an easy question. "How are you feeling? Still no morning sickness?"

"Not a day. Unlike poor Jenny. She said she starting getting sick almost immediately. She didn't tell us about the pregnancy until Wednesday because she said she was afraid she'd jinx it, but she's been dealing with morning sickness for a couple of weeks."

"You're lucky, then."

"I suppose." As if hearing how the words might have sounded, she shook her head quickly. "It's not that I want to be sick, of course. I just don't really feel pregnant, you know? I've seen the tests and I saw an ultrasound and heard the heartbeat at this week's doctor's appointment, but sometimes it still just doesn't feel real."

"I can imagine. Well, not really, because it's not something I'll ever experience, obviously, but it must be an odd sensation. You said you saw an ultrasound?"

"Yes. I have the printout at home. It's pretty cool. Still just a little peanut a couple inches long, which I guess is why I'm not really showing yet, but you can see the little arms and legs and some facial features."

Another ripple of nerves coursed through him at the thought of actually seeing the baby he planned to raise as his own. "Can you tell yet if it's a boy or a girl?" Not that it mattered to him.

"No, not yet. I'll have another ultrasound after twenty weeks and we should be able to tell then."

"Will you want to know then or would you rather be surprised at delivery?"

She laughed wryly. "I wouldn't be patient enough to wait that long. It'll be hard enough waiting until the ultrasound to find out."

Exactly as he'd have expected from her. And, being the type who always liked to be prepared, he felt the same way. "Have you bought any baby supplies yet?"

"Nothing yet. Except…"

"Except?"

"I bought a night-light shaped like a turtle. It's made to sit on a table beside the crib. The shell glows and there's a battery backup that keeps it illuminated even if the power goes out. I was afraid of the dark when I was little, and I thought maybe the baby will be, too."

Curious, he slanted her a sideways glance. "Are you still afraid of the dark?"

"Sometimes," she admitted. "I still sleep with a flashlight close at hand."

That surprised him. He hadn't thought Stevie was afraid of anything. "Is there a particular reason you're afraid of the dark?"

She hesitated a minute, then sighed. "I've always had that tendency, but it got worse when I was nine and Tom was ten and a half. I had a night-light in my room, but I still got scared when I heard funny noises. I didn't say much about it because Tom made fun of me, and you know how siblings can be."

"I was an only child, but I saw enough of my friends' siblings to get the picture."

"Anyway, Mom had taken a part-time second job working at a hotel desk in the evenings, earning extra money for Tom to get braces. Mrs. Clausen from next door came over to stay with us on those evenings. One night there was a thunderstorm and the power went out. I woke up in a totally dark room and got scared. I called and called, but no one answered and I was certain I was alone in the house—well, except for maybe the monsters under the bed or in the closet," she added ruefully.

"Where was Mrs. Clausen?" he asked, caught up in the story.

Stevie gave a low laugh that held little humor. "Stuck in the front bathroom. She got flustered in the dark and couldn't find the door lock. It was probably no more than minutes before she managed to get to me, but it seemed like hours. I was sobbing hysterically by the time she made her way to me."

"And your brother?"

"Slept through the whole storm."

"I'm sure you were frightened. That must have been traumatic for you."

Her hands fluttered again. "I grew up. Got over it to an extent. I still keep a flashlight on the nightstand, but I'm pretty confident now that there are no monsters under the bed or in the closet."

"Thank you for sharing that with me. I know it must be a painful memory but it means a lot that you trust me with it."

She reached over to pat his thigh, her soft laugh more natural this time. "It was just an anecdote, Cole, not a confession to my priest."

Reaction to that familiar touch surged through him, but he pushed it away. She had a way of gently poking at him when he got too formal and serious. He covered her hand with his and squeezed before gripping the steering wheel again, silently acknowledging he'd gotten the message. Still, he'd meant every word. If he and Stevie were going to make this work, they had to be honest and open with each other.

Stevie drew her hand away and laced her fingers in her lap. Her voice sounded a bit higher-pitched when she said, "Anyway, Mom stopped working nights after that incident. She bought Tom's braces on a payment plan. Fortunately my teeth were straight."

He laughed, then asked, "How do you think your mom will feel about becoming a grandmother?"

"She most definitely won't be a traditional grandma. She'll wonder why we're bothering with what she calls 'the obsolete and unnecessary institution of marriage.' I'm sure she'll come see the baby as soon as she can make arrangements. We gathered in Tennessee at my brother's house for Christmas, but I didn't know about the pregnancy then—or hadn't accepted the possibility yet."

"I'll bring her here for your due date, if she'd like to be here. You should have your mother with you."

"That's sweet of you, but I'll buy her ticket. I do okay financially, you know. Well enough to live comfortably, if not extravagantly. As I told you, I'm budgeting for my leave time, so…"

Her voice drifted off with another vague gesture of her hands. A very self-sufficient woman, his wife-to-be. That was only one of the many things he admired about her, though he still hoped she'd let him help her out.

He slanted a sideways glance at her. She looked very pretty today. That blue dress was especially flattering with her blond hair and big blue eyes. The soft knit fabric hugged her curves—and for such a petite woman, she had very nice curves. He cleared his throat, shifted in his seat, and tightened his grip on the steering wheel.

"I want to buy the kid a stuffed tiger," he said to distract himself. "Maybe we'll find one this weekend."

"A tiger?" Stevie twisted in her seat to look at him.

He nodded. "You had a night-light, I had Stripy. My uncle Bob—my dad's younger brother—gave him to me when I was four, maybe five. My parents were fighting then, splitting up and getting back together, shuttling me between them and my paternal grandparents. I never knew where I'd be spending the next night or whether my parents would be too quiet or yelling at each other. I started having nightmares, waking up screaming nearly every night. Uncle Bob bought me the tiger to chase away the monsters at night. He was a big *Calvin and Hobbes* fan. He'd read the comic strips to me from the newspaper."

"The tiger stopped your nightmares?"

He shrugged. "Didn't stop them. But when I woke up, Stripy was always there, and it made me feel better. The nightmares stopped after my parents split up for good and we all settled into new, more peaceful routines. I spent most of my childhood on my grandparents' cattle farm in El Paso, Arkansas, while Mom went back to college. Dad poured his energy into building his car repair business. With the exception of a couple of rocky years, I had a pretty good childhood. But I still have fond memories of Stripy. I think our kid should have one, though I can promise you we'll never put him—or her—through what my folks did to me. They got married too young, had a baby before they knew what they wanted for themselves. You and I are old enough and realistic enough to avoid all that foolishness."

"Absolutely," she said with almost grim determination. "We'll give him—or her—a stable, safe and secure childhood so he—or she—never has to depend on a night-light or a stuffed toy to chase away the monsters under the bed."

He frowned for a moment at the road ahead, processing her words as he drove in silence. He knew, of course, that she'd accepted his unexpected proposal for the benefit of her baby, just as the child's best interests had been a strong consideration for him when he'd offered. But he hoped she didn't see their marriage as a sacrifice on her part. "I want you to be happy, too, Stevie. We'll have a good life together. I'll always be there for you when you need support or encouragement."

She patted his thigh again, a vaguely unsatisfying gesture this time as it seemed entirely too indulgent. "And when you come back from those dull business trips, Dusty and Li'l Peanut and I will be there to welcome you with hugs and a home-cooked meal."

"Sounds great," he said, and meant it. It sounded ideal. He should stop trying to second-guess her thoughts and feelings—he wasn't good at it, anyway—and just accept his good fortune.

He pushed thoughts of the past away and focused instead on the future. After all, this was the beginning of their life together. He would be spending the weekend with this fascinating, desirable woman...and he planned to make this honeymoon a memory Stevie would always cherish.

Chapter Four

Cole really was an organizational genius, Stevie concluded an hour later. He'd taken care of logistical details for their elopement that hadn't even yet occurred to her, including the marriage license they dealt with immediately upon their arrival at their wedding destination.

She saw him caught off guard only once during those preparations.

"Stephanie?" he asked in surprise when they'd filled out their license application. "Your full name is Stephanie Joan McLane?"

She wrinkled her nose as she nodded. "Mom named me after Stevie Nicks—whose birth name was Stephanie—and Joan Jett, her two favorite women singers. My brother is Thomas Neil, after Tom Petty and Neil Young. He's always said it was a good thing Mom wasn't a country music fan or we might have ended up answering to Dolly and Porter."

That had made Cole laugh. He had such a rich, deep laugh. She hoped to hear it often during their upcoming years together, she thought wistfully.

The little wedding chapel he'd reserved was close to the state border, only some forty miles from their honeymoon destination of Branson, Missouri. Located in an old, white-frame church with battered but gleaming wood floors and rows of antique oak pews, it was generously, almost overly, decorated with white silk flowers and big red hearts. Romantic instrumental music played from speakers. A portly, sixtysomething officiate with a beatific smile and twinkling eyes welcomed them warmly, introducing himself as Pastor Dave and his equally plump and smiling wife, Luanne.

"You were very lucky we had this slot available today. Valentine's Day is our most popular day for elopements, you know," he confided, pumping Cole's hand and winking at Stevie. "Got five more weddings scheduled before the day's done."

Valentine's Day. Stevie just barely stopped herself from slapping her hands to her cheeks with a gasp. How flustered had she been today that she'd written the date probably half a dozen times without considering the significance? She'd been vaguely aware that the holiday was upon them, of course, but she hadn't watched much TV or spent much time on social media during the past few busy, emotionally stressful weeks. How on earth *had* Cole managed to make wedding and honeymoon reservations in less than twenty-four hours for this particular weekend? He'd assured her they would be staying at a very nice hotel and even had tickets to a couple of popular shows.

Watching him slip a couple of bills to their beaming host, she suspected he'd quietly greased a few palms.

And he'd done this all for her. She bit her lower lip, then released it immediately to keep from chewing off her freshly applied gloss. She wanted to look nice in the Elite Matrimonial Photo Package Luanne would take with her digital camera.

"Shall we begin?" Pastor Dave waved a hand toward the altar at the front of the little chapel, looking surreptitiously at the antique clock on the wall behind him as he turned. "You requested the nondenominational religious ceremony, is that correct, Mr. McKellar?"

"Yes," Cole agreed, glancing at Stevie as if for confirmation.

She managed a smile and a nod, resisting an impulse to nervously twist her hair. *No second thoughts*, she ordered herself. *For once in your life, you're doing the sensible thing.*

"Here you go, Miss McLane." Luanne pressed three long-stemmed red roses tied together with a white satin ribbon in Stevie's hand, then stepped back to raise her camera. "Give us a big smile, hon."

The roses were pretty, part of the Special Deluxe Elopement Package. Holding them gently in her left hand, Stevie set her small handbag on a front pew, rummaged in it for a moment, then turned toward her groom. "I'm ready."

"When I heard your fine Scottish surnames, I chose a special wedding song just for the two of you," Pastor Dave confided as he moved to the small lectern at the front of the room. He pressed a couple of buttons and after a brief pause, a bagpipe version of *Ode to Joy* poured from the overhead speakers. Stevie slanted a glance at Cole to find him smiling down at her in a way that almost elicited a completely inappropriate giggle. She heard the click-click of Luanne's camera as Pastor

Dave began his simple ceremony, barely referring to the little book in his hands as he recited words he must have intoned countless times before.

Somehow she managed to pay attention, and to respond appropriately at the correct times. She smiled faintly when the officiate read her almost-husband's full name. Cole Douglas McKellar. A fine Scottish name, indeed.

She moistened her lips as Cole's gaze locked with hers. A ripple of awareness coursed through her at the thought that this attractive, caring and complex man would now be bound to her. They would share a home, a future. A bed. As hectic as the past twenty-four hours had been, she'd hardly had time to even think about that part of their marriage. She realized suddenly that she was looking forward to the journey they'd embarked on together that morning.

What was Cole thinking? Feeling? He looked as at ease as ever. But on closer inspection, was there just a hint of tension in his dark eyes? She had no doubt he was taking these vows very seriously, but was he wondering whether he'd acted on an uncharacteristic and perhaps imprudent impulse? Was he having second thoughts?

Pastor Dave peered at them over the top of his reading glasses. "Do y'all have rings?"

"I do." Cole drew a white gold band from the pocket of the charcoal sport coat he wore with a pale blue shirt, lighter gray pants and a blue and gray patterned tie. Knowing how much he hated wearing ties, she was touched that he'd gone to the effort of dressing up for this occasion, even though they had no audience for their ceremony other than Pastor Dave and Luanne.

"I have one, too," she said, opening her left hand to

reveal the band she'd taken from her purse. Like hers, it was white gold, his with a brushed finish. She'd bought it that very morning. She'd stopped into a jewelry store in the same business center as her office and taken only a few minutes to select a ring that seemed to suit Cole's tastes, making a guess at his size. She saw surprise flit fleetingly across his face. Had he thought she'd forgotten to get a ring? Or had he never actually expected to wear a wedding band again?

And here she was, second-guessing his emotions again. She shook her head slightly and slipped the ring on his finger when prompted by Pastor Dave. It fit well enough, not snug but not so loose it would slip off. She saw Cole look down at his hand as if to admire the band there, and she hoped that was a sign that he liked it.

Luanne moved into position behind Pastor Dave with her camera raised as he pronounced them husband and wife. The camera snapped noisily when he added, "Y'all can seal this deal with a kiss now."

Stevie's giggle was smothered beneath Cole's willingly cooperative lips. And while the presence of their approving audience held the kiss in check, she was vividly reminded of the more heated kisses they'd exchanged in private yesterday.

Her heart tripped in her chest. She and Cole would be spending this night together as husband and wife. Judging by the fireworks that went off inside her whenever their lips met, this was going to be a very special honeymoon, indeed!

Cole had made a reservation at a nice hotel just off Branson's main thoroughfare. Stevie's palms felt damp as she followed him into the elevator for the ninth floor. Apparently she'd been so focused on the impromptu wedding that she hadn't looked much farther ahead. She certainly hadn't anticipated how nervous she would be at the prospect of officially beginning their honeymoon! Nervous—but excited, she realized with a flutter of anticipation.

Cole swiped the key card without looking around at her, then moved out of the way to allow her to precede him into the room. *Suite*, she corrected herself when she walked in and looked around. In addition to a king-sized bed and a small table with two chairs, there was a pretty little sitting area with what she assumed to be a sleeper sofa and an armchair. Her attention was drawn almost immediately back to that huge bed. She hoped Cole didn't hear her hard swallow.

Cole set down their bags before turning to her. Though she couldn't stop glancing toward the bed, he seemed to be making an effort to avoid looking at it. "Would you like to change before dinner, or are you good in what you're wearing?" he asked.

"This is fine, thanks."

"You don't mind if I get rid of this tie, do you?" He was already tugging at the knot.

She smiled. "I'm surprised you kept it on this long. By all means, make yourself comfortable. It's not like ties are the typical dress code for Branson."

He shed both jacket and tie and pulled a navy V-neck sweater from his bag to tug over his pale blue shirt. "That's better," he said with a sigh of such relief that she had to laugh.

She reached up to smooth his hair, resisting an urge to play in it for a bit. She really did love his springy dark hair.

Aware again of that big bed behind her, she dropped her hand and took a step back. "So. Dinner?"

Was his smile just a bit strained when he nodded? "Dinner," he said, and motioned toward the door.

Carrying a plastic mug shaped like a cowboy boot, Stevie reentered the hotel room later that evening with a slightly weary sigh. It had been a long, momentous day after an early start, and she was tired, but not in a bad way. On a whim, she retrieved the three red roses she'd stuck into a glass of water earlier and transferred them to the souvenir boot mug. The blooms were already starting to wilt, but she set them prominently in the center of the table, stepping back to admire them while Cole hung up their coats.

He turned to study her makeshift centerpiece, then pushed a hand through his hair, speaking wryly. "So, your wedding night festivities consisted of sitting on benches in an arena, eating pork and chicken and corn on the cob with our hands, while entertainers did tricks on horseback for the dinner show."

She giggled. He was not exaggerating. "Maybe the place didn't offer silverware, but the food was delicious and the show was fun."

Cole looked as though he tried to smile in response, but he wasn't very successful at it. Taking a step toward her, he placed his hands on her shoulders and gazed down at her gravely. "I feel as though I should apologize."

She felt her eyebrows rise. "For...?"

"I doubt very much that this was the wedding experience of your dreams. A one-day engagement. Pastor Dave and Luanne. Two nights in a town that's basically one big amusement park. A wedding night barbecue dinner shared at a long table with a group of senior citizens who came from Wisconsin on a tour bus. Not exactly a tropical resort or a European villa."

"I happened to enjoy that dinner," she assured him, letting her hands rest on his chest. "And the sweet little old man sitting at my other side kept me laughing all through the meal and the show. It was a pleasure to share a bench with him."

"He was flirting with you."

"Yes, he was. He said he's ninety, but he still has an eye for the ladies. He asked me to run away with him after dessert. I told him I would have, but I'm a married woman now."

She felt Cole's fingers flex on her shoulders in response to those words, perhaps a subconscious reaction. Probably he was still adjusting to the reality of being a married man again after so many years of bachelorhood. That was certainly understandable.

"I'm glad you didn't run off with the old guy," he said, a slight smile now softening his troubled expression.

Aware of how closely they were standing, she moistened her lips. It would require only a slight shift of her weight and she could be in his arms, cradled against that warm, strong chest. She shifted her hands a bit, savoring the feel of firm muscles beneath his soft sweater. Her shiny new rings glinted on her left ring finger. "So am I."

His gaze lowered, and if she wasn't mistaken he focused intently on her mouth. What was he thinking? she wondered. Before she could ask, he blinked, and the moment was over. He glanced at the bed, and those brown eyes darkened. Frowning, he turned his head to look at the sofa bed in the sitting area. "It's been an

eventful day. I'm sure you're tired. You can take the big
bed. I can sleep on the sofa bed."

"Cole." She tightened her grip on his sweater as she
interrupted. It was apparent that he was trying so hard
to keep his tone casual and considerate, careful not to
cause her any discomfort or embarrassment on their
wedding night. Nerves danced frantically beneath her
skin, but she held his gaze steadily. "First, you need to
understand that you don't owe me apologies for today.
We had a lovely wedding. The dinner show made me
laugh, which I always appreciate. I expect to have a fun
weekend with you here in a place that holds many happy
childhood memories for me. It doesn't take a tropical
resort or a European villa to make me happy."

He cupped her cheek with one hand. "Maybe you
don't need them, but you deserve them. I'd like to take
you to both someday. In the meantime, if there's anything special you want to do while we're here this weekend, just let me know."

He was trying so hard to please her. Very sweet, but
unnecessary. She wasn't that high maintenance.

Her hands still clutching his soft sweater, she rose
slowly on tiptoes, trying to read his expression as she
brought her mouth close to his. Did he truly want to
spend their wedding night on the sofa bed? Perhaps
they'd entered a marriage of convenience based on
building a stable family for this child and for themselves—but he needed to know she considered it a real
marriage. She didn't think either of them would be satisfied for long being nothing more than friendly roommates. She knew she wouldn't.

Now that she'd allowed herself to acknowledge her
attraction to him, just standing this close to him made
her skin tingle, her pulse accelerate. And from the way

his eyes darkened as she moved closer to him, it was clear he had healthy desires of his own. Though he'd kept his private life to himself for the most part, and rarely confided details of where he went on his nights out with friends, she'd never thought of her quiet neighbor as monk-like.

"Thank you for taking care of everything this weekend for us, Cole," she murmured against his lips. "You've done a wonderful job."

She kissed him before he could respond.

Fueled by simmering emotions, by nerves and uncertainties, hopes and resolve, the kiss was spectacular. Stevie threw herself into it, pushing away thoughts and doubts in favor of feelings and sensations.

When she pressed her abdomen to the gratifyingly hard ridge in his pants, he froze, then broke off the kiss as if he'd abruptly come to his senses. "I, uh…"

He cleared his throat, hard, his hands on her shoulders. To keep her close? Or to hold her away? He looked as though even he wasn't quite sure of his intentions.

"Look, Stevie, I know I rushed us into all of this. I mean, I tend not to waste much time when I get a good idea, but now that we've taken care of the formalities, there's certainly no pressure for you to…we have the rest of our lives to…I mean, just so you know, when the time is right, I'm here for you, but—"

"Cole," she said again, reaching up to lay her fingers against his clever mouth. It was so rare to see him flustered and babbling. She couldn't help being both amused and charmed. "We're married. We made promises to each other in that chapel today in front of Pastor Dave and Luanne. I want to share a bed with my husband, if he's interested."

"I'm interested." Cole's voice was husky. "Been interested for longer than I've wanted to admit."

A part of her had known, she thought as she took his hand. Just because they hadn't acknowledged the attraction didn't mean it hadn't always been there.

She took his hand and moved a step backward toward the big bed. Looking up at him through her lashes, she smiled. "I'm very happy to hear that."

She was already tugging at the hem of his sweater. Judging from touch alone, those clothes hid a seriously fine body. Plus, there'd been that brief glimpse of a chiseled chest the day he'd changed the light bulb. Now she was eager to explore it more closely. His hands joined hers where she worked at the buttons of his shirt, and she left him to finish while she shed her boots.

They tossed their clothes aside quickly as impatience took over. But she had the presence of mind to glimpse at his body as he revealed it. She took in the strong planes of his back and chest and the rock-hard muscles of his thighs. He stopped at a pair of boxers, and she was denied the full view she anticipated. Before she could remove her underwear he stepped forward and took her in his arms, tumbling her onto the pillows, his mouth on hers as their limbs tangled. He was so warm. Solid. Being in his arms was like being wrapped in armor. She felt safe. Protected. It was a novel feeling for someone who'd spent her whole life taking care of herself and taking care of others. Quite a seductive sensation in itself—not to mention how very good he felt on top of her.

For a man who spent so much time working on computers, Cole McKellar kept himself in excellent physical condition. And he proved very quickly that he knew exactly what to do with that great body.

It was no surprise to her at all that he was a thorough and unselfish lover, two adjectives that seemed the perfect description of the man she'd come to know during the past year. Now that they were in the bed, he took his time, lingering and savoring as he explored, caressed, tantalized, then unhurriedly moved on. He was so gentle at first, so obviously intent not to cause her discomfort. She was the one who lost patience, growling beneath her breath and tugging at him until he got the message with a low, willing laugh.

He stripped her bra, his hands moving more eagerly, less carefully now over her breasts as he revealed them. Then he slowly, excruciatingly slowly, slipped off her panties, dragging his fingers down her legs as he pulled them off. When he returned to hover over her, she wasted no more time. To convince him she was neither fragile nor shy, she matched his kiss hungrily, letting her tongue tangle with his. She slipped one leg around him and in one smooth motion his body merged with hers. Her breath escaped in a gasp of pleasure, echoed by Cole's deep groan. He brought her other leg around him and went even deeper, and she welcomed him into her. Moving with him in an age-old rhythm, she built inexorably toward a powerful climax, one so intense that she could not think or speak or even moan. Just feel.

He followed her immediately, and from the contented groan he gave right before his release, she reasoned he felt the same.

"Happy Valentine's Day, Stevie," she heard him murmur some time later, after he'd recovered enough breath to speak. Not quite to the point of speech, herself, she merely smiled sleepily and nestled contentedly into his bare shoulder.

Cole lay awake for some time after Stevie slept. He hadn't yet turned off the small lamp in the sitting area, and there was just enough light in the room for him to see her sprawled bonelessly beside him in the big bed, clutching her pillow into a ball with both arms. Her blond curls tumbled riotously around her shoulders, partially hiding her face, though he could see that her lips were parted in what he thought looked like a soft little smile. She looked sated and utterly relaxed. Though he hadn't been presumptuous enough to predict the evening would end this way, it had come as no surprise to him to discover that, along with her many other attributes and eccentricities, Stevie was a passionate and sensual woman.

In those fantasies that had haunted his nights since he'd gotten to know Stevie, he'd always imagined that making love with her would be an adventure. Hard as it was to believe, the reality had been even more spectacular. Fact was, just looking at her sleeping now made him harden again, already impatient to see if it would be just as mind-blowing the next time. He'd never met anyone quite like Stevie. Being on the receiving end of her enthusiastic passion was decidedly flattering. A heady ego boost for an innately introverted computer nerd. He couldn't help but smile.

A guy could spend a lifetime getting to know and appreciate all the facets of Stevie. He lifted his left hand, and the band on his finger gleamed softly in the dim light. He wasn't at all sorry he'd signed up for this mission. He just hoped he could keep up with her and make sure she never regretted accepting his proposal.

He wasn't her usual artistic type. He was no poet. Couldn't play a musical instrument. Sang like a bullfrog. Couldn't draw a stick figure. He had no expectations of sweeping Stevie off her feet. But he liked the image he'd formed of their future together, the one she'd described for him earlier—coming home from his business trips to a house filled with warmth and light, to the welcome of a woman who rarely stopped chattering and whose laughter was infectious. To a child's hugs and what-did-you-bring-mes?

He would do his best to make Stevie happy with what he had to offer in return for the family he'd thought he'd never have. He'd be there for her, take care of her even when she didn't know she needed it. That was what he did.

As for what he would receive in return . . . He brushed a light kiss against her warm, damp cheek, certain he'd gotten the best of this bargain. In addition to the cozy family home he'd just envisioned, he had more nights in bed with Stevie to look forward to. Considering how spectacular their first time had been, he was eagerly anticipating the next. He had a feeling he had just begun to explore all the fascinating facets of this woman who was now his wife.

After a surprisingly sound night's sleep, Stevie woke slowly, stretching and yawning before she opened her eyes to find Cole watching her with a smile. A little gasp escaped her before her sleep-clouded mind cleared enough to remind her of why he was there.

He reached out to touch her arm. "That's twice in the past week I've startled you out of sleep. I feel as though I should apologize again."

Rubbing her eyes, she laughed ruefully. "It's not your fault. I just tend to wake up disoriented."

"I'll keep that in mind in the future," he murmured.

She blinked a few times at the reminder of a future that included him now. "Oh, my gosh!"

His left eyebrow rose. "What?"

Struggling to sit up, she pushed at her tangled hair with a rueful little laugh. "Like I said, I wake up disoriented. I just remembered we got married yesterday."

Rising onto his elbow, he looked at her with both brows lifted now. A grin tugged tentatively at the corners of his lips, though he looked as if he wasn't sure whether he should laugh. "I'm not surprised you're befuddled. It all happened pretty fast."

She smiled to show him she recognized the humor in her admission. "You could say that again. Thursday morning I woke up thinking I'd be a single mom and by Friday afternoon I was a married woman. I mean, I've acted on impulse more than a few times in my life, but—oh, my gosh."

He did chuckle then. "You think it's hard for *you* to believe? Even after I'd spent several days considering the idea, I didn't really expect to be married within twenty-four hours of proposing. It just sort of happened. I'm not calling it an impulse, though. More like a plan of action expedited for maximum benefit."

Laughing, she cupped his face in her hands and murmured against his lips, "I just love it when you talk all analyst-y."

"I'm not sure that's a—"

She kissed him before he could finish the sentence.

Showing that he was still open to spontaneity—or, as he would consider it, efficiently taking advantage of an impromptu opportunity—he flipped her onto her back and rolled on top of her. Her delighted laughter quickly changed to murmurs of pleasure as he proved once again that her math genius husband was as clever with his mouth and hands as he was with that brilliant mind.

They enjoyed a leisurely breakfast at a farmhouse-style diner, during which Stevie chattered about trips to Branson as a child with her mother and brother. Cole mentioned that he'd visited only a few times himself, the first trip as a very young boy with his parents during one of their attempts to act the part of happy family—an attempt she surmised hadn't been particularly successful, though he didn't elaborate.

Taking advantage of a chilly, but otherwise beautiful day, they wandered through attractions and shops after breakfast. They were strolling at a leisurely pace through an outlet shopping center when Cole drew her into a store that specialized in baby supplies. An odd feeling gripped her as she drifted down the aisles beside him, rather intimidated by all the merchandise surrounding them. There seemed to be so much of it, so many options, colors, sizes. Was all this stuff necessary for one little baby? She didn't even know what some of these things were. Insecurity rose up in her. Shouldn't she know?

"Stevie? Are you okay? You look a little pale."

She tried to force a reassuring smile for Cole, who gazed down at her in concern. "Just a little overwhelmed. I don't even know how to use most of this stuff."

He placed a hand on the small of her back. "You'll learn what you need to know."

She wished she felt as confident as he sounded. She gave a determined nod. "I'll learn."

"Have you decided which bedroom will be the nursery?"

"The one I've been using as a guest room, I suppose—the one that was mine growing up. It's close to the master, and I've been using the third bedroom as a home office. Um, my house is a little bigger than yours, so it makes sense for us to set up there, right?"

He nodded. "I can keep my office in my house for now, but we'll probably want to discuss combining our households into a larger place eventually. One that will accommodate two offices and a guest room."

She wasn't ready to discuss selling or buying houses just then. It was a given that they would live together in one house, of course. After all, they were married.

She changed the subject quickly when she spotted a white wicker bassinet with a sage-and-off-white chevron-stripe liner. "Oh, look, Cole. Isn't it pretty?"

"That's the same color green you've used in your house, isn't it?"

"Sage. It's my favorite." She was already stroking the little bed, picturing it in a sage-and-cream nursery suitable to either gender. She could find some vintage nursery prints to frame for the walls, and invest in a comfortable nursing chair in a soft nubby fabric with one of her late maternal grandmother's hand-knit throws draped over the back. The turtle night-light would sit on an antique nightstand beside the crib. Perfect. "And look, it's on sale!"

This little basket was definitely going home with her.

"I've got this." Cole was already signaling for assistance from a clerk. "Is there anything else you want here? What about that little bouncy seat thing over there? The pad is the same shade of green, right? One of my friends swore his daughter was only happy when she was sitting in her bouncy seat after nursing. There's room in the back of the SUV for both the bassinet and that, if you like it. Maybe a few other items, if you see anything else you want."

He was already reaching for his wallet. Stevie shook

her head, moving to stand between him and the bassinet. "No, I've got it. You've done enough already this weekend."

"Not that much," he assured her. "I've provided a honeymoon of sorts for my bride. Now I'd like to get a few things for the baby."

"No. *I* want to buy this."

He went still, frowning as he studied her firmly determined expression. "Why?"

"Because it's my—" Realizing what she'd almost said, she bit her tongue before she could complete the blurted sentence.

Cole's hand fell to his side and he took a step back. His voice turned cool. "All right. Get what you want and I'll help you load it into the car."

She'd hurt his feelings. Guilt flooded through her with the realization. That had been the last thing she'd wanted to do. She needed Cole to understand that though their marriage was based on his selfless offer to help her raise this child, she had no intention of taking advantage of his innate generosity. She'd been independent for more than a decade. She'd married him to be a partner to her, not for financial support. They hadn't had time yet to talk about money or the other day-to-day responsibilities of marriage, but she knew it wasn't going to be easy for her to adjust to his new role in her life. To learn to lean on someone else for a change.

Before she could figure out how to apologize for her thoughtlessness, a salesclerk approached with a bright, friendly smile. "Can I help you?"

Conceding that this was the wrong time and place for a momentous discussion, Stevie purchased the bassinet and bouncy seat, then helped Cole carry them to his SUV. She wondered if he'd be mad at her, but quickly found he'd masked any feelings behind an easy smile. He even teased her about having to leave his suitcase behind if they bought much more on this trip. Apparently he was determined to put their brief clash behind them, intent on keeping this day a pleasant one. She was glad; it was their honeymoon, after all. Practical discussions could wait until later.

Glancing at his watch, he asked if she wanted to eat dinner before the musical variety show they would be attending that evening.

"Oh, my gosh, yes!" She pressed a hand to her stomach. "I'm starving. I'd never make it through the show without food. For the past couple of weeks, it seems like I'm hungry all the time."

He chuckled and opened her door for her. "As the old saying goes, you're eating for two now. What would you like?"

"Anything that sounds good to you. I'm not picky."

"We'll even find a place with silverware this evening," he assured her, then closed the door.

Watching him round the front of the SUV to the driver's seat, she was relieved he'd put that momentary awkwardness behind them so easily. She supposed she shouldn't be surprised. Cole wasn't one to let emotions rule his actions, something that was difficult for her even when she wasn't flooded with early-pregnancy hormones.

This was all going to work out, she promised herself. It was only to be expected that there would be some compromises in the process. But now that they'd gotten this first minor clash out of the way, she just knew the rest of their honeymoon would be nothing but enjoyable.

Cole stood beside the bed a few hours later, feeling helpless as Stevie curled into a ball and moaned. He'd dimmed the lights for her comfort, but even in the shadows her skin still seemed to have a slightly green tint to it. "Is your stomach still upset?"

The only response to his tentative question was another heartfelt groan.

He moved to the sink where he dampened a washcloth with cold water, then carried it back to her. "Let me put this on your throat. My grandma used to do that for me when I was nauseated and it always seemed to help."

She shifted on the thick pillows and allowed him to press the cloth gently to her throat. "I'm sorry," she murmured, her eyes squeezed shut. "I didn't mean for the evening to end this way."

"Don't apologize. I'm just sorry you're ill. Are you sure we shouldn't have you checked by a doctor?"

She shook her head and managed a weak smile as she peered up at him through barely cracked eyelids. "No. It's just nausea. I guess I bragged too soon about not being sick a day so far. At least we made it to the end of the show."

But only just, he thought with a wry shake of his head. He'd noticed Stevie had seemed subdued at intermission. At first he'd wondered if it was because he'd somehow annoyed her at the baby supplies store earlier, though they'd gotten along fine during dinner. But she'd confided that she was feeling a little queasy, so he'd bought her a soda to sip while the energetic young singers and dancers had taken the stage for the second half. He'd only halfway paid attention to the stage, surreptitiously watching Stevie instead as she'd wilted visibly in her seat. He'd all but carried her to the car afterward, and she'd barely made it into the room before bolting into the bathroom and slamming the door behind her. When she'd reemerged, it was only to collapse on the bed, still fully clothed.

He slipped off her shoes and set them on the floor. "Would you like to put on your nightgown?"

Her eyes were closed again, but he thought there might be a bit more color in her face now. "I'll change in a minute," she murmured.

He moved to the dresser. She'd brought a couple of nightgowns—one made of black satin, the other a warmer purple knit splashed with cheery red flowers. As diverse as the two garments were, each somehow seemed perfectly suited to Stevie. Though his hand lingered for a moment on the black one, he pulled out the more comfortable-looking gown and carried it to the bed. "Here, let me help you," he said.

A few minutes later, she was snugly tucked into the bed, the washcloth redampened and draped again on her throat. "Can I get you anything else? Some more soda?"

She shifted on the piled pillows, moistening her lips. "Maybe a little."

Sitting beside her on the bed, he handed her the glass of citrusy soda he'd purchased from a vending machine down the hall. She took a couple of sips, then gave it back to him. "Thanks. I feel better now. Just tired."

"I'll sleep on the sofa bed."

She shook her head and patted the bed next to her. "I'm hardly contagious. You'll be much more comfortable here in this king-sized bed than on that fold-out."

He wasn't so sure about that, considering she'd be snoozing beside him, temptingly close but needing her rest. Still, as she'd said, it was a big bed. It had been a long time since he'd shared a bed with anyone, and he had to admit he liked the feel of a warm, soft body next to him even if only in sleep.

She was mostly out by the time he climbed in beside her, taking care not to jostle the mattress or otherwise disturb her. He'd hardly settled onto the pillows before she turned and snuggled into him, her hair tickling his chin, her small hand resting on his chest. He wore pajama bottoms and a T-shirt, but he could feel her warmth through the fabric. Too warm? He rested a hand lightly against her face, reassuring himself that she wasn't running a fever.

"I'm fine," she murmured drowsily, and he wasn't sure she was actually awake. "I just never want to smell popcorn again."

He stroked a wayward curl off her cheek. There was no need to reply. She wouldn't have heard him, anyway, as she'd already drifted off again.

On impulse, he pressed a light kiss on the top of her head, then tried to relax. It wasn't easy. Even discounting the distraction of having her in his arms, he was having trouble turning off his thoughts. He kept replaying the day, from the exhilarating wake-up sex to that terse exchange in the baby store. He still wasn't sure exactly why she'd taken such exception to his offer to buy the bassinet and seat. He wasn't very good at reading emotional cues, being the type who preferred issues plainly spelled out. But he thought maybe he'd unwittingly stepped on her pride.

He hadn't tried to imply that she wasn't capable of providing for her child. He hadn't been trying to take charge or insist on having his own way. He'd simply wanted to show her that he shared her excitement about the baby.

Her baby, he reminded himself with a wince. It had been clear enough what she'd started to say before she'd swallowed the words. For all her talk about sharing the child with him, about commitment mattering more to her than biology, for all the nervous enthusiasm she'd shown so far toward their marriage even to the point of eagerly consummating their wedding night, there was still a part of herself she was holding back from him. A self-protective door that she hadn't yet unlocked, perhaps because of her past disappointments. And she didn't yet trust him enough to open that door for him.

He had to admit it had hurt when she'd snapped at him. When he'd realized what she'd almost said. *Her* baby. Not theirs. The words had hit him like a blow, though he'd tried to hide his reaction to keep the peace.

Because he wasn't one to dwell on injured feelings, he relied instead on his usual method for dealing with uncomfortable emotions. Objective analysis. He needed to be patient. This was all so new for both of them. In the long run, he still believed he and Stevie would make a success of this marriage. That they and the child they'd raise together would have a good life. A contented life.

He'd have to proceed cautiously, prove to her that he was here for the long term. That he would not walk away from her when life got difficult. With time, he would convince her that she could trust him completely. And that she and her child—their child—could rely on him. Always.

Chapter Five

The pale winter sunlight just seeped around the edges of the window curtains when Stevie woke Sunday morning. She turned her head to find Cole still sleeping beside her. Had he lain awake awhile after she'd fallen asleep? She certainly hadn't intended to cut their second night short that way. She was just relieved she'd made it through to the end of the show.

She slid carefully from the bed and padded into the bathroom, silently closing the door behind her. Fortunately there was no nausea this morning, so she felt much more herself when she emerged a few minutes later. She tiptoed back into the room, but it turned out not to be necessary. Cole was awake, propped against the pillows with his hands behind his head, watching her as she stepped into the room.

Smoothing her palms down the front of her red-flowered purple gown, she smiled at him. "Hey."

"Hey. Feeling better?" His voice was a deep, sleep-roughened rumble in the quiet room. Her throat closed in response.

He'd been so sweet last night when she'd been ill, taking care of her without hesitation. He had a lot of experience as a caregiver, of course—but she wasn't accustomed to being the one on the receiving end. She felt a sudden need to assure him that she really was fully recovered.

"I feel great this morning," she said as she approached the bed.

"The color's back in your cheeks and your eyes are bright again." He nodded in satisfaction as he studied her face. "You looked wrung out last night."

"Here's a hint, Cole." She sat on the bed beside him and leaned over him, her hands on his chest. "Don't mention that your new bride looked sickly on her honeymoon."

He chuckled and ran his hands up her arms. "Sorry. If it makes any difference, I still had trouble keeping my hands to myself when I helped you into this nightgown."

"Yes, that's much better," she assured him, giving in to an impulse to run a hand through his thick tousled hair. "Did I mention I'm perfectly fine now?"

With a grin, he tugged her into his arms. "I'm happy to hear that. For several reasons."

Her laughter was smothered by his hungry kiss.

Holding a bag in one hand, Stevie looked around the hotel room as they prepared to depart later that morning, her gaze lingering for a moment on the big bed. She found herself suddenly reluctant to leave this private retreat. Reality waited outside this door—the tasks of informing all their friends and families of their marriage and dealing with the reaction, figuring out how to combine their households, learning to live together, coordinating schedules in preparation for the baby's arrival...

She took a deep breath and stopped listing the tasks before she became completely overwhelmed. *One step at a time, Stevie.*

Cole stepped up behind her and rested a hand on her shoulder. "Ready to go?"

"No."

His fingers tightened reassuringly for a moment. "It will be fine."

She smiled faintly up at him. "I know. But it's been nice here."

He leaned his head down to brush a kiss over her lips. "I'd like to stay longer, too," he admitted when he stepped back. "Unfortunately..."

"The honeymoon is over," she finished, turning toward the door.

Cole gave a little grimace. "Maybe I wouldn't have phrased it quite that way," he murmured as he opened the door to the hallway.

Giving him a look of wry apology, she preceded him out of the room.

"Is there anything else you want to do before we head out of town?" he asked after a leisurely breakfast.

"Yes."

"More shopping? Another show?"

She smiled. "Let's just say it will involve a wager."

She noted that he looked both intrigued and a little wary in response, which made her laugh.

An hour later, she faced him with her shoulders squared, chin held confidently high. "Well? Still feeling good about that bet?"

"Pretty sure that was an unfair challenge." Cole tilted

his head as he eyed her in suspicion. "How many times have you played this course?"

Smiling nostalgically, she glanced around the indoor miniature golf course. The large space was dimly illuminated. Two eighteen-hole courses were lit by low walkway lights with multicolored plastic shades. Tiny fairy lights were strung in greenery arranged to replicate a nighttime garden setting. Tinkly new age music played from hidden speakers, and water splashed in artificial streams and falls, creating a mystical ambiance that explained why the few other players on this Sunday morning spoke in quiet tones, their laughter politely muted.

Holding putters, Stevie and Cole faced each other across the tee of the eighteenth hole. Only one stroke separated their scores, the advantage hers.

"I can't remember how many times, exactly," she said in answer to his question. "But every time Mom brought us to Branson for vacations, Tom and I begged her to let us play in here and in the arcade down the hall. We always bet on the outcome—doing dishes for a week, putting away the laundry, various household chores. Mom wouldn't let us bet money."

"You still haven't told me what we're wagering," he reminded her, his tone indulgent. "And by the way, I don't actually mind doing household chores."

"So, what are you offering if I win?"

He gave it a moment's thought, taking advantage of having no one behind them and waiting to play to stretch out the teasing conversation. "If you win, I'll wash and detail your car when we get home."

Having known her for a year, he was aware of how much she hated washing her car, and it was especially dirty after last week's snow and mud. "Ooh. Interesting."

He chuckled, tossing and catching his bright yellow golf ball in his right hand. "And what will you do for me if I win?"

She bit her lower lip for a moment in thought, then spread her hands, offering a vague pledge she was pretty sure she wouldn't have to make good. "If you win, I'll owe you a favor to be redeemed at your discretion. You name it."

His eyebrows rose. "Sounds intriguing. But you look awfully confident you won't have to pay up. You're pretty good at this next hole, huh?"

"Scared?"

He dark eyes gleamed with amusement. "Maybe."

He really was cute. More relaxed than she'd been in weeks, she grinned back at him. "Well?"

He swept a hand toward the course. "Take your shot."

Already picturing her car all shiny and clean, inside and out, she bent to place her hot pink golf ball on the rubber mat. As she did so, she glanced over her shoulder at Cole. Was he admiring the curve of her bottom? He looked away quickly and she thought his face might have flushed just a little, though it was hard to tell in the shadowy venue. Biting her lip against a smile, she stood and lined up her shot.

A short while later, she walked out of the golf course into a big indoor breezeway, still shaking her head in disbelief. Smiling from ear to ear, Cole wrapped an arm around her shoulders. "So now you owe me a big favor."

"I still can't believe you got a hole in one. And that I whiffed that last putt. Are you sure you weren't just taking it easy on me on the first seventeen holes?"

"I just got lucky with the hole in one, and you only missed your second putt by a half inch."

"So what's my penalty? Have you decided what you want for the bet you won?"

"Not yet. I'll let you know when I think of it."

She looked up at him through her lashes, enjoying his lazily teasing mood despite her pretend pouting. "Now I'm the one who's scared."

He laughed softly and gave her shoulders a little squeeze. "Don't worry, Stevie, I won't have you wash my car."

She made a show of wiping her brow in relief, drawing another laugh from him.

In addition to the mini golf courses and arcade, the building housed a restaurant, a couple of small theaters and several gift shops. Stevie paused to admire a display of scarves, momentarily tempted by their bright colors, sparkly threads and fluttering fringe. Making herself turn away without buying, she looked around for Cole, spotting him standing in front of a display of stuffed animals.

He held a stuffed tiger in his right hand when she joined him. The toy looked quite suitable for an infant, more funny than fierce, incongruously whimsical in Cole's strong hand.

She smiled. "You found a tiger."

He nodded, his expression a little odd. "It caught my eye."

Still he didn't move. She lifted her eyebrows in question. "Are you buying it?"

"Is that okay with you?"

She didn't know whether to sigh or wince in response to his hesitation. "Of course it's okay with me. I think it's adorable."

"Then I'll get it. A souvenir of our honeymoon for the kid."

She chewed her lower lip as she watched him pay for the toy. Had she overreacted about the bassinet yesterday? Or had she merely shown that her independence hadn't changed simply because she now wore Cole's ring on her left hand?

Transaction complete, Cole turned to her. "Ready to head home?"

Forcing a smile, she nodded. "I guess it's time."

They shared a long look before moving in unison toward the exit. Stevie wondered if Cole had been able to read the emotions in her eyes better than she'd been able to decipher his. Probably. She seemed to be an open book to him, while she saw only what he chose to reveal to her.

She figured she had years ahead of her to figure him out. It might just take that long.

They were halfway back to Little Rock when Cole cleared his throat to catch Stevie's attention. She'd been gazing out the side window at the winter-bleak scenery, but barely paying attention to the landmarks. She knew she'd been uncharacteristically quiet, her thoughts focused on the busy and complicated days ahead of them.

"Stevie?"

She glanced around at him when he spoke. "Yes?"

"We'll be passing my dad's place in another twenty minutes or so. Would you mind if we stop and say hello? Might as well get this introduction over with. We won't stay long."

She noted that he didn't look particularly enthusiastic about the prospect. "You want me to meet your father? Now?"

He shrugged. "Now's as good a time as any, since we'll be passing by, anyway."

"Should you call and make sure he's home?"

"He's home."

"Should you at least let him know we're coming?"

"No need. He and I don't stand on formalities."

She almost sighed at how little information he was offering, even though he was the one who'd made this suggestion. "Is there anything more I should know before I meet him?"

Cole shrugged. "I don't expect you to like him very much. Though I guess if anyone could charm Jim McKellar, it would be you."

It didn't reassure her that he sounded less than optimistic.

The house was a modest buff brick bi-level half a mile off the highway outside of Conway. A chain-link fence surrounded the closely cropped, but sparsely landscaped yard. Outside the fence was a large graveled lot filled almost to capacity with vehicles of many makes, models and vintages waiting to be serviced in one of the three metal garages, each with three service bays, lining the lot. Only one of the bay doors was open. A sign over a regular-sized door at one end of the nearest building read McKellar Auto Service and beneath that, in smaller letters, Office.

Stevie saw no activity around the business, which was no surprise at almost five p.m. on a Sunday. She expected Cole to park close to the house. Instead, he pulled into an empty parking space in front of the office.

"That door's up," he explained when he saw her looking at him in question. "That means he's working. He's out here seven days a week unless something unusual comes up. Precisely at five thirty he goes in the house to wash up for dinner, which he eats while he watches the six o'clock newscasts."

"A man of habit," she commented.

"Very much so."

"It looks as though he's quite successful with his business."

"Oh, yeah. He's damned good at what he does. There's not an engine he can't tear down and rebuild given the right equipment, and he's invested wisely in that."

"Does he ever take vacations? Time off?"

"Not unless someone forces him. There's nowhere Dad would rather be. What he can't understand is why I don't want to be under the hood of a car with him."

Hearing something in his voice, she tilted her head. "He wanted you to go into the business?"

"Yeah. He'd hoped to turn it over to me someday. I guess he took it personally that I never wanted it."

"That's why you and your dad aren't close? Because you didn't want his auto repair business?"

"There've been other issues, but no need to get into those now. Let's get this out of the way." With that grim statement, he opened his door.

Stevie jumped out of her own side without waiting for him to come around. She shivered as cold air surrounded her, seeping through her layered tops and pants. She reached back into the SUV and grabbed her coat, bundling it around her as she followed Cole toward the open bay door. He wore only his pullover and jeans, but he seemed oblivious to the cold even though his breath hung in puffy clouds in front of him as he called out, "Dad?"

In response to Cole's voice, a man emerged from beneath the raised hood of a battered sedan. Shop lights were trained on the car's engine, silhouetting the man in their bright beams, and Stevie had to blink to bring him into focus. Wearing an oil-smeared blue uniform shirt, faded jeans and worn work boots, he looked like an older, more sun-grizzled and life-worn version of Cole. He still had a full head of hair, though it had gone mostly silver and was cut considerably closer than Cole's. He was squarely built, still muscular in his fifties. His dark eyes were deeply set, and the lines of his weathered face seemed to have settled into a permanent scowl.

Wiping his hands on a shop towel, he greeted his son without obvious signs of surprise or pleasure. "Cole."

"How's it going, Dad?"

"Can't complain. You?"

"I'm good." Cole drew Stevie forward. "There's someone I want you to meet. This is my wife, Stevie. Stevie, meet my father, Jim McKellar."

"It's a pleasure to meet you, Mr. McKellar." She gave him a warm smile and held out her right hand.

She might have expected him to show some surprise, but his expression didn't change when he glanced at her outstretched hand then back up at her face. "I'm covered in oil," he said, still scrubbing at his hands with the towel. "Good to meet you, though. When was the wedding?"

If he was hurt that he'd been neither informed ahead of time nor invited to attend, he kept the feeling well hidden. It wasn't hard to figure out where Cole had learned to mask his emotions.

"We were married Friday," Cole replied. "We're on our way home from a short honeymoon in Branson. I thought you'd like to meet Stevie while we were in the area. Is Peggy here? Stevie should meet her, too."

"Peg's gone to some sort of program at her church. Won't be home for a couple hours yet."

"Next time then."

Jim looked around uncomfortably. "You, uh, want some coffee or something? Got some left in the office."

"Not for me. Stevie?"

She shook her head. "No, thank you."

"Guess we could go in the house and sit down," Jim said, though he glanced tellingly at the car he'd been working on.

"We can't stay, Dad. Stevie and I both have to work tomorrow, so we should head on home."

Something flitted briefly across the older man's face in response to Cole's reply, but Stevie wasn't sure if it was relief or a touch of regret. Maybe a complicated mixture of both. Before she could decide, he spoke again. "Glad you stopped by. Congratulations on the marriage. I'll tell Peg you said hello."

Cole nodded. "Yeah, give her our best."

Blinking, Stevie looked in disbelief from son to father and back again. That was it? No hugs or hearty slaps on the back? No questions about how she and Cole had met or when they'd decided to marry? About future plans or current activities? Just "hey, how's it going, see you later?"

She tossed back her hair and spoke up in a bright tone. "Maybe you and your wife can visit us in Little Rock soon, Mr. McKellar. I'd love to meet her. We could treat you to a nice dinner out, get to know each other better."

Her determined friendliness seemed to startle him a little. "We, uh, don't get down that way very often. Guess you can see I've got a lot of jobs going. These folks want their cars back as soon as we can get 'em finished." He cleared his throat, then seemed to feel something more was expected from him. "But y'all can stop by any time. I'm sure Peggy'd like to meet you."

"We'll try to get back soon," Cole said, his tone as stiltedly cordial—and as emotionally distant—as his father's. "We're both pretty busy with work for the next few months, which is why we had so little time for a honeymoon. Stevie owns her own kitchen design business and she's made quite a name for herself in Little Rock."

Jim nodded, though he didn't look notably impressed. She suspected he was one of those men who couldn't imagine there was much more to kitchen design than deciding where to put the refrigerator. He glanced at Cole before asking gruffly, "You still playing around with computers?"

Stevie saw a muscle tighten in Cole's jaw, but he replied evenly, as if the question was one he'd heard too many times to take offense. "Yeah, pretty much."

"That was all the boy was ever interested in," Jim said as an aside to Stevie. "Holin' up in his room with computer games and such. Couldn't get him interested in sports or hunting or fishing, and he sure wasn't getting his hands dirty under the hood of a car."

Cole placed a hand on Stevie's arm, though she wasn't certain if it was for her benefit or his own. "I doubt Stevie wants to hear a list of your disappointments with me, Dad. It's getting dark, so we'd better get back on the road. I'm sure you want to get back to your work."

Jim's eyes narrowed with what might have been a flash of irritation, but he merely nodded and said, "Yeah, I'm trying to finish this one tonight. Y'all take care now." He turned and picked up a wrench.

Cole turned toward the exit, nudging Stevie to move along with him. She looked back over her shoulder as they walked out, but Jim was hidden behind the car hood again.

They were on the road again for less than ten minutes when Cole sighed gustily. "Okay. Let's hear it. You're obviously bursting to express your opinion."

She'd been all but squirming in her seat, her mind whirling with all the things she wanted to say but wasn't sure how to articulate. In response to his urging, the words gushed from her in a flood of exasperation. "Are you kidding me? That's the way you announce to your father that you've gotten married? That's the way he responds? What on earth is wrong with you two?"

Cole didn't look at all surprised by her outburst. "I gave up trying to answer that question a long time ago. I guess Dad and I are just too different to be close. Not that anyone gets close to my dad. He and Peggy get along well enough, but I'd hardly call their relationship a warm and cozy one. She takes care of the house and stays busy with her church. He works, eats the meals she makes him and watches a little TV before he starts again at daylight the next day. The guys who work for him call him a grouch and a perfectionist, but he pays well enough that most of them have been with him quite a while."

"So he's a difficult man. That doesn't mean you should stop trying to have a relationship with him."

"I do try, Stevie." Cole spoke just a bit more sharply this time. "Why the hell do you think I stopped by to introduce you to him? You saw how he acted. Like we were an interruption he had to tolerate before he could get back to work. He couldn't have cared less."

She twisted a curl around one finger, growing

thoughtful as she replayed the awkward encounter in her mind. "I'm not entirely sure that's true. I think he did care. And I think maybe he was gruff because his feelings were a little hurt."

The SUV swerved just a fraction on the road, a clear indication of Cole's surprise. He gripped the wheel more tightly and focused hard on the road ahead. "You're way off base there. Why would his feelings, if he had any, be hurt? He was the first person we told about our marriage, wasn't he?"

"Well, you didn't mention that to him," she reminded him. "For all he was aware, he was the last to know."

"You didn't hear him ask, did you?"

"No. He probably has too much pride for that. That wall between you has gotten so thick I don't think either of you knows how to break through it. Even how to start."

"I did my part. I reached out a hand and as usual, he basically slapped it away because he considers it too clean to be a real man's hand."

For just that moment, Cole's composure slipped enough for her to catch a fleeting glimpse of the old pain that he kept deeply hidden, but he recovered almost instantly. "Let's not talk about this now. It's not the way I want to end our weekend. I'll just assure you that you don't have to worry I'll be anything like my father when it comes to being a dad. He's taught me everything not to do."

She still believed Cole would be a wonderful father. Which didn't mean he wouldn't still carry the scars from his past. Or that those old wounds might not open up again someday in the future, to the detriment of himself and anyone close to him.

Because she could sense it would do no good to keep

pushing him now while the disappointing visit was still so fresh and raw in his mind, she let it go, changing the subject to their upcoming week's schedule, instead. But she was going to think about this quite a bit more, she vowed silently. And maybe she'd figure out a way to help Cole and his dad build a door in that stubborn, pride-strengthened wall.

There was a moment of awkwardness a while later when Cole turned onto the street where they lived. They'd stopped for a nice dinner when they'd arrived in Little Rock because he'd said they were both too tired to cook after the trip. Now that they'd finally arrived home, he didn't seem sure whether to pull into her driveway or his own garage.

"I'll carry the baby things into your house first," he decided, parking in front of her house.

Faced again with the reality of their new living—and sleeping—arrangements, Stevie tried to hide her own attack of nerves behind practicality. "We should go check on Dusty. Do you think she'd adapt to living in my house with us? I don't think cats like change, do they?"

"Beats me. I've never actually owned a cat before. Or should I say, I've never been owned by a cat before."

She laughed. "She does get her wishes across, doesn't she? Let's bring her over and see if she finds my house suitable."

Dusty seemed a bit wary of the move at first, nervously exploring the house while making sure both Stevie and Cole remained nearby. Stevie set up the litter box in the easily accessible laundry area and the food and water bowls in the kitchen, then showed both to the cat, slipping her a couple of treats in the process. Afterward, Cole sat in an armchair in the living room and patted his knee. Dusty jumped up, curled up on his lap and promptly went to sleep, apparently exhausted by the change but content to be back in her favorite place. Her rumbling purr was audible even halfway across the room to Stevie.

"She's a demanding little diva, isn't she?" Cole asked, fondly rubbing his pet's ears. "I'll help put things away in a bit. Just let me sit here with her for a few minutes to reassure her."

She was suddenly a little jealous of the cat. She wouldn't at all mind sitting in Cole's lap and being petted by him. With a wry smile and shake of her head, Stevie turned toward her bedroom. "Take your time and relax. You did all the driving this weekend. I'll just unpack my bag."

Usually, entering her impeccably decorated bedroom was like escaping to a peaceful retreat. This lovely and understated room soothed her, gave her busy mind a rest from the creative demands of her job, from hectic schedules and complex relationships.

She hadn't shared this bed often. Joe had rented a loft downtown, which had suited him better than this sedate, family-friendly neighborhood. He'd called her place boring, his tastes leaning to modern industrial—soaring ceilings, open pipes, exposed bricks and numerous musical instruments.

Shaking her head to clear her mind of the past, she unpacked her bag and put away her things, then combined a couple of drawers to make space for Cole. It would take a while to get everything arranged, of course, but she wanted him to feel immediately welcome.

She walked back into the living room only to stop

short in the doorway to admire the appealing scene that greeted her. Cole was sound asleep in the chair, one hand still resting on the cat dozing in his lap. His hair was rumpled around his face and he looked younger and more unguarded than usual. She had no doubt he would be on his feet instantly if she said his name, but she tiptoed out of the room, leaving him to rest.

The past two days had been as eventful for Cole as they'd been for her, she mused, trying to put herself in his shoes for a moment. Did he feel the weight of his actions on his shoulders, the responsibilities of the promises he'd made to her and her child? Of course he did. That was just who he was. He was going to have to learn to let someone else take care of him occasionally, she thought firmly. Because that was just who *she* was.

Moving as quietly as possible, she settled at the kitchen table with a cup of herbal tea while she checked email and texts on her phone. The phone vibrated in her hand and she checked the caller ID. Seeing one of her two best friends' names on the screen, she moistened her lips. She didn't want to break her big news on the phone, but she didn't want to lie to her friend, either. She hoped neither option would be necessary as she said, "Hi, Tess. What's up?"

"Just checking in. Scott and I just got back from a weekend in New Orleans."

Stevie was a little surprised. "I didn't know you'd planned a New Orleans weekend."

Tess sighed happily. "He surprised me after we left the office Friday by driving straight to the airport for a Valentine's Day getaway. He'd been planning it secretly for weeks, with the help of his brothers' wives. We spent two nights in a lovely hotel in the French Quarter and we hardly mentioned work all weekend. Even though it was a little chilly and it rained quite a bit it was heavenly to get away for a couple of days."

"Nice." And an illustration of how much workaholic Scott's priorities had changed since he'd become engaged to Tess. A whole weekend away from the busy, successful construction business that meant so much to him was definitely a demonstration of his commitment to his bride-to-be. "I'm glad you had fun."

"Now I'm looking forward to our honeymoon," Tess admitted with a laugh. "I can't wait to get on that warm beach in the Cayman Islands after this cold, dreary winter."

Tess and Scott were to be married in mid-June on the spreading back lawn of his parents' West Little Rock home. Their guest list would be as small as they could politely manage, their theme restrained and elegant. A sweet, simple wedding, as Tess frequently described, was her preference. But "simple" was a matter of perspective, Stevie thought wryly, remembering her own little ceremony with Pastor Dave and Luanne.

"Tess…"

Oh, goodness, how to even start?

"Yes?" her friend prodded after a moment.

On a sudden inspiration, Stevie blurted, "Can you come to my place tomorrow evening? Around seven? I know it's short notice, but it won't take long if you have other things you need to do. I'm going to ask Jenny, too."

"A girls' night?" Tess asked after a momentary hesitation that indicated she'd heard something odd in Stevie's voice.

"Not exactly. I'll explain tomorrow, okay? It'll be easier in person. Can you come?"

"I'll make time. Stevie…is something wrong?"

"Everything's good," Stevie assured her. "We'll talk tomorrow."

Her call with Tess completed, she shot a quick text invitation to Jenny, who accepted immediately.

"Everything okay?" Cole asked from the doorway.

She looked up from her phone to find him studying her expression in concern. "I've invited Tess and Jenny to drop by tomorrow evening at seven. I'll tell them everything then."

"Sounds like a good plan. I'll do some work over at my place while they're here to give you privacy for your talk."

Grateful for his understanding, she nodded. "I'll text you after I've explained everything to them. I want you to meet them."

She wasn't sure why he'd never met Jenny and Tess. They'd heard her talk about her neighbor and knew Stevie and Cole had become friends, but they'd never all been in the same place at the same time for introductions. In a way, it was almost as if she'd been keeping her friendship with Cole to herself. Those pleasant evenings over tea with him and his cat—they'd been special to her, she admitted now. She could never have dreamed then where they'd lead, but she'd privately treasured them.

And now it was time to bring those separate components of her life together.

"What about you?" she asked Cole. "Do you have friends you'll want to bring together for the big announcement?"

He shrugged. "I'll spread the word among my friends in the next week or so. I have a few local buddies, but no one as close as Jenny and Tess are to you. I need to call my mother, but I'll wait until the morning since it's an hour later in Florida."

"I should call my mom, too. It's still early enough in Hawaii for me to call her now. I'll send a text to my brother later. He's not much for talking on the phone."

"Sorry I conked out on you in there. Dusty's snoring put me to sleep."

She chuckled. "No problem. You're tired. Where is… oh, here she is."

She reached down to stroke the cat winding around her ankles. Dusty was beginning to look more comfortable in her new quarters now that she'd been reassured her beloved Cole had come with her.

"I emptied a couple of drawers for you on the right side of the dresser. We'll have to rearrange the closet to fit your things, but we can do that later. It's a big walk-in and there's plenty of room for your stuff."

"Thanks. I'll unpack while you call your mom."

Drawing a deep breath for fortitude, she called her mom as soon as she was alone in the kitchen again. Her mother had plans for the evening but she made time to take her daughter's call. Stevie barely gave her mom time to say hello before she burst into a nervous speech. Her words all but tripped over each other as she explained that she had eloped with her next-door neighbor and was expecting a child in August and that she and Cole were looking forward to sharing childcare duties and expected to have a long, successful marriage.

Her mother interrupted only a couple of times to ask her to slow down, but she handled the news with typical equanimity. The baby's parentage didn't come up, not that Stevie had expected it to with her nontraditional mom.

"So you chose to marry," her mom said when she finally had a chance to speak. "That's cool, though you know how I feel about the institution. You're keeping your own name, right? Holding on to your business and your financial independence? Do you have a prenup?"

"Don't worry, Mom," Stevie replied with a wry smile. "It's a completely modern marriage."

"There's no such thing," her mother replied brusquely.

"You'll like Cole, Mom. He's a great guy. And he has a very successful career and owns his own house," she added pointedly.

"That sounds promising," her mother conceded grudgingly. "I hope you'll be happy. And make sure you have a good lawyer."

"Yes, Mother," Stevie said with a grin that had to be audible in her voice.

Her mom's musical laughter came through the phone. "Now you're just being sassy."

"Look who raised me," Stevie retorted affectionately. "You're going to be such a fun grandma."

"Oh, God, don't call me that. Your child can call me Bonnie. Or maybe BonBon. That's cute, right?"

"We'll discuss it. Enjoy your evening."

"Oh, I will. Aloha, sweetie."

"Aloha, Mom."

Cole joined her again a few minutes later, pausing in the doorway to make sure the call was concluded before he walked into the room. "How did your call go?"

"Mom wished us well and told me to keep a good lawyer on call. Oh, and she wants to be called BonBon, not grandma."

He smiled, unoffended by the message. "I have to admit, I'm looking forward to meeting your mother."

"She wants to meet you, too. Would you like some tea?"

"Sounds good, but I'll make it. Why don't you stay off your feet for a while. It's been a long day."

At least he'd had the tact not to tell her she looked tired, though she felt a bit bedraggled. "Tea bags are in the pantry, cups in that cabinet," she said, pointing.

He turned her toward the living room. "I'll find what I need. Go rest."

"You talked me into it."

She told herself she was only going to lie down for a few minutes. She curled on the couch with a throw pillow beneath her head, her legs drawn up in front of her. She was just drifting off when a warm little body settled beside her and a deep, steady purr lulled her to sleep.

She wasn't sure what time it was when Cole woke her with a gentle hand on her shoulder. "It's getting late, Stevie. Want to turn in?"

She opened her eyes, noting that he'd dimmed the lights. The cat wasn't beside her now. "What time is it?"

"After ten. I've been working on my laptop, but I think I'll get some sleep. How are you feeling?"

She yawned. "Okay. Just tired."

"Should I carry you to bed?"

Laughing softly, she climbed to her feet. "As manly and sexy as that sounds, I'll walk."

He rested a hand at the small of her back. "You think I'm manly and sexy?"

"Well, of course." She reached up to pat his cheek sleepily. "Not to mention a cutie."

He grunted. "Let's just leave it at manly and sexy, okay?"

She giggled.

A short while later Cole climbed into her bed beside her and reached out to turn off the bedside lamp. He paused for just a moment with his hand on the switch. "Stevie?"

"Mmm?"

"Have I told you how much I like the way you've decorated your house? Especially this bedroom. It's nice."

The light went out, leaving her to lie awake for a few minutes in the dark, thinking about how funny life could be sometimes.

An unexpected life, she thought, glancing in the direction of her jewelry box. She was certainly living up to that fortune cookie's prediction.

Fortunately, Tess and Jenny arrived together the next evening so Stevie didn't have to go through explanations twice. Cold air swirled into the house with the new arrivals, and they gathered around the crackling fireplace to shed their coats and scarves, which Stevie stashed in the front bedroom before returning to her friends. Her stomach was tied in knots as she wondered what they'd say in response to her news.

"How are you feeling?" she asked Jenny, shamelessly stalling for a moment.

With a little groan and a rueful expression, Jenny pressed her hand to her tummy. "Okay now, but the mornings are bad. I have to downplay how sick I feel, though, because poor Gavin gets so distraught."

That didn't surprise Stevie. She knew how overprotective Jenny's husband was. Jenny and Gavin had been sweethearts at the university all three of them had attended, though a bitter, youthful breakup had separated them for a decade. Stevie had been delighted when fate had brought the couple back together. And now they were married and having a baby together. *Way to go, fate.*

Tess smiled sympathetically, though her expression made Stevie wonder if Tess, too, was imagining a day when she and Scott would welcome a child. Ironically, Stevie was the only one of the three friends who'd been in no particular hurry to have a baby, until that capricious fate had stepped in to change her status.

Her friends were both so blissfully in love. Yet, having seen the pain both had gone through during rocky patches in their courtships, Stevie was relieved that she and Cole were being more practical with their relationship. Going into marriage and parenthood the way she and Cole had, with clearly defined boundaries and goals and expectations, should certainly minimize any chance of heartbreak for either of them. There would be challenges, of course, some disappointments and annoyances. She was quite sure she'd irritate the hell out of him at times, though she wasn't sure he'd tell her if she did. But they would make it work.

She hoped Jenny and Tess would see the logic of those arguments even if they worried that she had been recklessly impulsive again.

She poured tea all around and waited until the others were seated before clearing her throat in preparation to speak. She was a little surprised that neither of her usually sharp-eyed friends had noticed her new rings, but that only showed how distracted they were with their own lives.

So much had changed in the past year, she thought a bit wistfully. So many changes still lay ahead.

Jenny and Tess were looking at her now as if they sensed something momentous was coming. Before she could speak, a plaintive meow sounded from the doorway and Dusty padded warily into the room. The cat had dashed off to hide when the doorbell rang, nervous about the new arrivals. Dusty wasn't accustomed to company, having lived for a year with her somewhat reclusive owner. But she was too needy to remain hidden away for long when there were potential ear rubs waiting in here.

"Stevie, you got a cat?" Tess asked in surprise, holding out a hand to the little tabby who sniffed it with interest. "She's a pretty little thing, isn't she? Er, he?"

"She." Stevie watched with a faint smile as the cat leaped lightly onto the couch between her friends, regally allowing herself to be stroked and admired.

"What's her name?" Jenny asked.

"Dusty."

Jenny's eyebrows rose. "Your neighbor's cat?" she asked, having heard Stevie mention her cat-sitting sessions. "You're keeping her here when he's away now?"

"He isn't away. Dusty lives here now. And, um, so does Cole."

A startled silence followed her revelation. Jenny and Tess looked at her as if neither was quite sure she'd heard correctly.

Jenny recovered first. "Cole lives here? Since when?"

Stevie held up her left hand to display the glittering rings. "Since we eloped Friday afternoon. We got married."

Chapter Six

The quiet in the room was deafening. Stevie could almost hear her own rapid heartbeat as she waited for her friends' reactions. Of all their possible responses, silence was the last thing she expected.

It seemed minutes before Tess roused first from the temporary paralysis. "You're *married*?"

"Yes. For three whole days now." With a look of apology, she sought out the gaze of her oldest friend. "I'm sorry I didn't tell you before. It's just…well, it all happened very fast."

Setting aside her teacup, Jenny rose slowly to her feet. "I can't believe this, Stevie. It's…it's just…I can't believe you're married."

"When did all this come about?" Tess nudged the cat gently out of the way and stood. "You never even hinted that you and Cole were seeing each other."

Stevie twisted her hands in front of her. "It's sort of a

long story. I was going to tell you part of it when we got together last week, but it was the night you announced your pregnancy, Jen. I didn't want to steal your thunder or worry either of you. Cole and I agreed it might be easier for us to elope and tell you everything afterward. Please don't be hurt that I didn't tell you first. As I said, this all came about very quickly, and there was hardly time to make any calls. I didn't even tell my mom until after the wedding."

She watched as her friends exchanged glances that held all the doubts and concerns she'd braced for. "You don't have to look so worried. I knew what I was doing, and I gave it careful consideration."

Okay, maybe she'd given it all of five minutes consideration before she'd accepted Cole's proposal, she thought with a slight wince of memory. Perhaps it would be best not to mention that just now.

"Forgive us for being skeptical," Jenny said slowly, "but, Stevie…have you lost your mind?"

Stevie didn't take offense. She might have said exactly the same thing if the tables had been turned. "No. I have my reasons, Jen, and I think when you hear them you'll agree they're good ones."

"The only valid reason to marry is for love," Jenny retorted flatly. "Aren't you the one who made that declaration repeatedly when I was considering Thad's proposal? You were never enthusiastic about my relationship with him because you said it was too calculated and dispassionate. You were all for me getting back with Gavin despite our differences, because you knew I had always loved him."

"And didn't you nag me to make sure Scott and I were getting married for the right reasons?" Tess chimed in. "You said marriage should be more than a practical business arrangement. You were so insistent that I actually broke off our engagement until Scott was able to convince me he was in love with me. So I hope you have a very good reason for eloping with your neighbor."

"I did marry Cole for love," Stevie assured them, her hand on her stomach. She loved this baby enough to give him or her as many advantages as she could provide, including a man who would dedicate himself to being a wonderful father. She thought her friends would agree there was nothing cold-blooded or calculated about this marriage, despite its functional foundation.

Jenny knew her too well and for too long to simply accept those words at face value. She took a step closer and frowned intently into Stevie's eyes. "You broke up with Joe only three months ago. I knew you weren't particularly heartbroken by that split—and frankly, I thought it was well past time—but you never said a word about having feelings for anyone else. This wasn't a rebound thing, was it? Or were you involved with Cole even then?"

Again, Stevie wasn't insulted by Jenny's personal questions. As both her friends had just reminded her, she'd butted her nose into their affairs a few times, always with the best intentions. Just as they held now toward her. "No. At the time, Cole and I were simply good friends."

"When did that change?"

She drew a deep breath, then confessed, "When I told him I was pregnant and that I was nervous about trying to raise the child alone."

Tess sank abruptly back down onto the couch, as if

this newest surprise had taken the stiffening right out of her knees. "You're pregnant?"

"Yes." She aimed another look of apology toward Jenny. "Now do you understand why it was so hard to tell you on the same night you told us about your baby? You were so thrilled and excited, and I was so happy for you and Gavin. I knew there would be time to share my own news later."

Jenny gripped Stevie's arm as if she couldn't restrain herself any longer. She looked from her face to her waistline and back again, her expression almost comically conflicted. "You're pregnant? You're sure? How far along are you? Do you feel okay? Is Cole happy about the baby?"

A laugh escaping her, Stevie covered Jenny's hand with her own and rested her cheek for a moment against her friend's shoulder in a little hug. "Yes, I'm absolutely sure, and I'm fine. I've only been sick once, and that was this past weekend, probably from too much rich food. Cole is very excited about the baby. He'll be a good dad. He's a great guy, Jen. Smart and dependable and kind, with a dry sense of humor and a generous heart. You'll like him, I promise."

"Where is he?"

"He went next door to his house to give us some privacy for this talk. I told him I'd text him when you were ready to meet him."

"Well, call him over." Jenny bounced a couple of times on the balls of her feet, her lips pursed in what was meant to be an intimidating frown. "I want to get a look at this guy. Maybe rake him over the coals a little to make sure he's worthy of you."

As she texted him, Stevie laughed softly, grateful that Jenny was trying to make the best of this admittedly awkward situation. "Good luck with that. You'll find my husband is not easy to rattle."

"Your husband." Holding the cat now, who'd taken a strong liking to her, Tess still looked dazed. "This is a lot to process in one night. So both my bridesmaids will be in maternity dresses for the wedding."

Relieved that most of the confessions were out of the way—with one notable exception—Stevie nodded. "Looks that way."

"Well, at least that loose, comfortable style I requested should work for both of us," Jenny said with a strained little smile. "We'd better get busy finding the perfect dress that will suit whichever shape Stevie and I happen to be in June."

The opposite of a demanding diva bride, Tess waved a hand. "Pick whatever dress you and Stevie like. As long as it works with the colors I've chosen, I trust your judgment on style."

Jenny nodded. "I'll check with my suppliers and see what I can find in the time we have."

"Yes, well, you and Gavin had a very short engagement, and you thought *my* wedding was short notice," Tess commented with a little laugh. "I'd say Stevie wins this one. She skipped all the wedding prep entirely."

"Cole took care of everything," Stevie admitted. "We had a lovely little Valentine's Day wedding at a cute chapel in the Ozarks. I have a disc of photos that was part of the wedding package. I want to have them printed in one of those glossy photo books when I have time to deal with them."

"I can't wait to see them," Tess said.

Tess was obviously trying hard to show support for Stevie's decision, to look happy about the developments despite whatever concerns she wasn't voicing. Stevie appreciated that, though she wasn't sure she deserved it after keeping her friends in the dark all this time.

Jenny examined Stevie's middle again. "When is your due date? Maybe it's the same as mine. Wouldn't that be something?"

"Um, no." Stevie moistened her lips. "I'm a little farther along than you. I'm due in early August. My tentative due date is August 10."

Jenny looked confused. "August? But that makes you—"

"Three months pregnant."

"Three months," Tess murmured, staring at Stevie's waistline in disbelief. "But you aren't showing."

"I'm getting a little thicker around the middle. I'm wearing loose clothes so it's hard to tell. But I haven't gained much weight yet, though my doctor assured me the baby is developing as it should be."

Comprehension dawned slowly but inevitably on her friends' faces. "But three months ago…"

Stevie held Jenny's gaze without looking away. "That was just before Joe moved to Austin."

"So Joe is…?"

"Out of the picture. Permanently."

Jenny digested that for a moment, then asked quietly, "Does he know?"

"Yes. But it doesn't make a difference. He made his choice. I made mine. I don't think either of us will have any regrets."

"Cole doesn't mind…?"

"Like I said, Cole's looking forward to being a dad to this baby. I married my very good friend, Jen, and we're going to raise a child together. We'll make it work."

"I have no doubt of that," Jenny murmured, her eyes suddenly liquid. "But will you be happy, Stevie? Truly happy? I always thought you'd be crazy in love when you married."

Stevie managed a smile. "You know me. I'm always happy. I'm confident I could have handled all this on my own, just like my mother did, but I'm very fortunate that I'll have a helpmate. That my child, like yours, will have a dad to love and encourage him. Or her."

"It doesn't surprise me that you'd sacrifice everything for your child. That's just so you."

"I don't think of it that way at all," Stevie assured her, equally softly. "Cole is fully committed to this partnership, and I'm so grateful to him. I just hope he doesn't feel that he's the one making the sacrifice."

"I don't."

Stevie almost gasped in response to the deep voice from the doorway leading into the kitchen. She looked around to see Cole standing there, his eyes locked with hers, his expression somber.

"I didn't hear you come in," she said.

"I came in through the back door."

She moved to draw him into the room, standing beside him as they faced her friends. "Jenny, Tess, I'd like you to meet my husband, Cole McKellar."

"Oh, my God." Cole draped himself over a living room chair, his limbs hanging bonelessly, his hair rumpled from being scraped through with both hands. "I've had job interviews complete with FBI background checks that were less grueling."

Reclined on the couch, Stevie laughed. "It wasn't that bad."

"It was that bad. I had the feeling that if I gave one wrong answer, your friend Jenny would throw me out on my ear."

"Just give her a little time to adjust. You have to admit I sort of sprang all this on them."

He opened one eye to look at her. "You think she will? Adjust, I mean?"

"Of course. She already likes you. I could tell, and I know Jen better than anyone. She's just a little worried."

He grew serious. "Your friends seem nice. I figured they would be, from everything you've told me about them."

"You'll like their guys, too. You and Scott have quite a bit in common, actually. He's into tech stuff, too. Always buying new computer equipment for his commercial construction business. Gavin's more into sports and cop stuff, but he's a great guy."

"Cop stuff, huh?"

She shrugged.

"I'll try to find things to talk about with him. Something tells me we'll be spending time with them since you girls are so tight."

"I'd like to meet your friends, too. We haven't talked about them much. Who's your best friend?"

"Probably Joel Bradley. He's an engineer, living and working in Dubai at the moment. He's the one I told you about, my friend from school who was adopted?"

"Of course I remember." He'd said his friend was closer to his adopted family than Cole was to his biological one. Having seen Cole with his Dad, Stevie didn't find that hard to believe now. "Do you hear from Joel much?"

"We stay in touch. Through computers, of course," he added with a wry smile. "It's been a while since we've touched base, but we'll talk again soon."

"And what about your friends here?"

"Sometimes I meet up with a couple of guys from

my gym for beers and conversation. And I'm still tight with some friends from the dojo where I trained for a while. We try to get together once a month for some friendly sparring or *gomoku* tournaments."

"Go—?"

"Gomoku. It's a traditional Japanese board game played with black and white stones. My friends and I are kind of nerdy," he confessed with a chuckle that made no apologies.

Fascinated by this new glimpse into his private life, she prodded, "You said you met at a dojo? You trained in martial arts?"

"Yes."

In the year she'd known him, it was the first she'd heard about this. Swinging her feet to the floor, she studied his face. "What kind?"

"Karate."

"How high did you advance? The belt color thing, I mean?"

"I have a black belt. Second degree."

She felt her jaw drop a little. So that explained why he was in such good shape! "I thought you weren't into sports."

He spread his hands. "Not football or basketball or other organized team sports, particularly, though I've been known to attend a game occasionally with friends. I look at karate more as a way to stay in shape than as a sport. After all, I sit at a computer all day."

She wondered if his father knew about Cole's accomplishment. Jim had been so dismissive of Cole's job and interests, implying that they weren't "manly" enough—but surely a second degree black belt in karate was macho enough to satisfy even Jim McKellar's old-fashioned gender expectations. More than likely

Cole hadn't mentioned it. He didn't seem to need to prove anything to his hard-to-please dad, nor need to defend his masculinity. He'd never even mentioned his accomplishments to her.

"Can you break a stack of boards with your fist?"

He smiled. "I've been known to split a few."

She cocked her head and pictured him barefoot in the traditional white wrap jacket and loose pants, a black belt wrapped around his taut waist, his hair and face damp with sweat as he squared off against an opponent. A jolt of sexual attraction shot through her in response to the image. Interesting. And unexpected, considering what she'd once considered her "type." She'd certainly never before envisioned her quiet, cat-owning, math-whiz neighbor as a tough, sweaty warrior.

He frowned. "Why are you staring at me as if you've never seen me before?"

"Sorry, was I? You're just turning out to be full of surprises, Cole Douglas McKellar."

His lips quirked into a half smile. "Just trying to stay healthy."

"Do you still train?"

"Other than the casual sparring, no. I wasn't interested in competing in tournaments and that would be the next step."

"I'll have to work off the baby weight after Peanut arrives. Maybe I should take up karate."

His grin made her wonder just what amused him so much. Couldn't short, busty women wear white pajamas and kick things?

But he changed the subject before she could challenge him. "By the way, I finally connected with my mom this afternoon. Told her we were married and expecting a kid."

The latter fact was one he'd neglected to mention to his father, she remembered. "How did your mom react?"

"She's pleased with the prospect of being a grandmother. She said she and Ned would head this way in a few months to visit, once the weather gets warmer."

"She didn't mind that she wasn't invited to the wedding?"

"No. Not when I told her no one else was there, either."

"Good." She'd have hated to get off on the wrong foot with her mother-in-law.

He rubbed his chin. "Your friend Tess is planning a big wedding, isn't she?"

"They're trying to keep it contained, but Scott has a big family and a ton of business associates. Tess's family is smaller, but her friends and relatives want to be there, too."

After a moment, he asked, "Are you sorry you didn't have a more traditional wedding so your friends could stand up with you?"

"No," she said and hoped he believed her. "I much prefer our sweet little ceremony. I wouldn't have minded having Tess and Jenny there, but if we'd invited them, others might have been hurt, so it's best we kept it just the two of us."

"I just don't want you to feel that I prevented you from having the wedding you wanted."

"You didn't talk me into anything I didn't want to do," she said, meeting his eyes. "I'd think you should know by now that I make my own choices."

He conceded with a nod, though he didn't look particularly gratified.

An uncomfortable stillness fell over the room. Stevie felt as if there were more things he wanted to say.

More things she perhaps needed to say. She just couldn't think of them at the moment.

She pushed herself to her feet. "I have a meeting with a client tomorrow afternoon. I think I'll go over my notes for a while. Unless you need something?"

"You don't have to entertain me, Stevie. I live here now, remember? I have some reading to do. Might watch some TV for a while. We're good."

We're good.

For some reason those two words made her feel somewhat better as she moved into her office.

Cole couldn't focus on either work or television for the next hour, though both the TV and computer screens flickered in front of him. His thoughts were focused on Stevie and on the snippet of conversation he'd heard earlier.

He hadn't liked Jenny's suggestion that Stevie had sacrificed herself for her child's sake by marrying him. He thought they were doing very well so far. He enjoyed having meals with her, planning a future with her, waking up beside her. He especially liked making love with her. He was already starting to picture himself teaching their kid about science, math and computers, about classic sci-fi and the basics of martial arts training. All the "nerdy" things he longed to share. Stevie would impart her love of music, her creativity, her humor and joyous spontaneity, her people skills and business acumen. Between the two of them, the kid would have a well-rounded foundation.

He was even starting to feel less guilty—a little— that he was moving on in his life, putting past regrets behind him and looking forward to a new, rewarding future.

* * *

Pepper Rose was rapidly becoming one of Stevie's all-time favorite design clients. Despite the name Pepper herself cheerfully termed a "classic stripper name," she was a brilliant and highly respected neuropsychiatrist affiliated with the medical school in Little Rock. Sixty years old, defiantly flame-haired, a few pounds overweight but energetic and light on her feet, Pepper had insisted on the use of first names as their collaboration continued.

"Just don't call me Dr. Pepper," she'd added with a weary smile. "You have no idea how tired I get of that particular joke."

"I can imagine," Stevie had responded with a laugh.

Married to a cardiologist, Pepper had recently cut back on her formerly grueling work schedule and was now involved in remodeling the home she and her husband had purchased a few months earlier. Built on a tall bluff with a breathtaking view of the Arkansas River below and the distant rolling hills beyond, the house was luxurious but a bit sterile in decor, especially in the white-on-white-on-stainless contemporary kitchen.

"Color," Pepper had said when Stevie asked the first thing she wanted changed. "Please give me some color. I don't care about trends or fashion, I just don't want to feel like I'm still in a hospital setting when I walk into my kitchen in the morning."

Stevie had embraced the challenge of designing a kitchen that was functional, fashionable and still incorporated Pepper's love of color—most particularly, the color purple.

"Oh, Stevie, you've found it!" Pepper exclaimed at this meeting in her home late Tuesday afternoon. "This is the ideal granite for my countertops. I can't believe it."

Almost smugly, Stevie patted the granite sample she'd brought with her. Mottled shades of gray with a subtle purple veining, the granite hadn't been easy to locate, but she'd known when she'd found it that it was exactly what Pepper wanted. Though Pepper had tentatively approved a blueprint for the remodel, the multitude of other choices had been put on hold until Stevie located the perfect granite.

"We can keep the backsplash neutral or pull out more of the purple. I've also located a set of pendant lights for over the island that I think you'll love, but we'll have to order them quickly if you want them. They're a little pricey, but still just within the lighting budget." She turned her tablet toward her client to better display the photo of the unique pendants formed of hand-blown purple glass.

"They're gorgeous. Order them." Typically, cost meant little to Pepper, though she and her husband had determined a top dollar for the remodel project. "Stevie...is there something you haven't told me?"

Looking up from the tablet screen, Stevie searched her mind for any other kitchen item she'd forgotten. "What do you mean?"

Pepper reached out to touch Stevie's left hand. "I don't remember seeing these before."

Her gaze drawn to the rings, Stevie nodded in comprehension. She felt her cheeks warm a little. "Oh. Yes, I was married last Friday."

"And you're working today?" Pepper clicked her tongue in disapproval.

"We're delaying our honeymoon for now," she answered lightly. "It's a busy time for both of us in our careers."

"Congratulations on your marriage. I hope you'll be very happy. And I hope he knows how lucky he is."

Stevie smiled. "Thank you, Pepper."

"Philip and I will celebrate our thirty-fifth anniversary next month. We were both still in medical school when we married. It's hard to believe the time has passed so quickly."

"Congratulations to you, too. That's quite a milestone."

Thirty-five years. She couldn't even imagine that far ahead in her own marriage.

Pepper gave a little shrug. "I won't pretend we never had a rough time keeping it together. It wasn't always easy balancing two very demanding careers and two inflated egos, along with the challenges of marriage and raising our two daughters. We were fortunate to be able to hire nannies and housekeepers to assist us, but there were plenty of times when I was ready to pull out my artificially red hair," she added cheerfully. "Philip didn't have enough left to pull by the time he was thirty."

Stevie laughed softly. "It's still quite an accomplishment to have a successful career and a successful marriage."

"I'm glad we made it through. Now that our daughters are grown and we've started spending a few less hours at work, there are quite a few things we'd like to do together. Visit our little grandson in Tucson. Travel around Europe. See Australia and New Zealand. We've just never had the time."

"That all sounds wonderful." She wondered if she and Cole would do things like that someday. After this baby was out of the nest, would they be a couple who wanted to share adventures together? Or would they be more like Cole's father and stepmother—he still immersed in his solitary work, she pursuing her own interests for the most part? She didn't like that option. Could either of them really be happy settling for that?

"Stevie? Is everything okay?"

She schooled her expression quickly, reminding herself of her client's profession. It wasn't easy to fool a psychiatrist, especially for someone like her who wore her emotions close to the surface, anyway. "Yes, thank you. It's all still very new, of course, so we have some adjustments to make, but Cole and I are looking forward to setting up our household and starting our family. We've, um, actually gotten an early start on that. I'm expecting a baby in August."

"Well, congratulations again." Pepper looked genuinely delighted. "You'll be a wonderful mother."

"You think so?"

"I know so." Pepper patted her hand again. Then, seeming to sense that Stevie wanted to change the subject, she reached for the tablet. "Now, about these cabinets. Paint or wash?"

Relieved to be brought back into her area of expertise, Stevie pushed her concerns to the back of her mind and focused on her business.

Breathing heavily, Cole tugged off his head gear and ran a hand through his sweat-dampened hair before mopping at his face with a small towel. His friend Russ Krupistsky dropped to the mat at Cole's feet, dragging in breath as he rested with his knees drawn up in front of him. "Good match, Cole," he said, his voice still raspy from exertion.

"Yeah, you, too." Cole reached down to shake Russ's outstretched hand.

He'd met with five others for the monthly meeting

at the dojo where he'd studied karate. It was Thursday evening, and the place was closed for lessons, but the owner encouraged these gatherings of former and current students who wanted to stay in touch. They chipped in to compensate Sensei Tim, deeming the exercise and fellowship worth the nominal cost.

Having refereed the bout and declaring Cole the winner, though by only a very slim margin, Tim gave him a couple of hearty pats on the back. "Good job, Cole. You're staying in good shape for a computer guy."

Cole laughed. "Thanks, Sensei. I do my best."

His broad, dark face creased with a grin, black eyes glinting with humor, Tim reached down a hand to help Russ to his feet, already making a few suggestions for Russ's next bout. When he wasn't formally teaching, Tim was easygoing and jovial. Put him at the head of a class, though, and he barked out orders and corrections with the sharp precision of the army drill sergeant he'd once been.

"Hey, Cole." Her white gi belted snugly around her, Jessica Lopez touched his arm to get his attention. Her brown ponytail hung limply and her cheeks glistened from exertion, but she was smiling. "That was a nice side kick that took Russ down."

"Thanks. I saw you sparring with Gabriel. Looked like you were holding your own."

Jessica, who was somewhere in her late twenties, chuckled wryly. "Considering he's nearly a decade younger and a helluva lot faster than I am, holding my own was the best I could do. But he took it easy on me and I had fun."

"That's what we're here for, isn't it?"

She nodded, ponytail bobbing. "So, Cole... Gabe and Russ and Nick and I thought we'd go have a burger or something when we're done here. We've worked off the calories, right?"

She laughed and he smiled in response, preparing for the inevitable next question.

"Would you like to join us?"

It wasn't the first time in the past few months that he'd suspected Jessica was interested in him, and not just as another member of the gang. He was kind of dense at times when it came to social signals, but even he recognized when a woman was letting him know she wouldn't mind spending time with him.

"Thanks, but I'll have to pass this time. My wife is waiting at home for me."

My wife. The words still felt a little odd on his tongue, even though he'd been married before. It was just taking a little time to grow accustomed to thinking of Stevie in that way.

Jessica's eyes widened dramatically. "Your wife?"

"Dude, you got married?" Russ asked, overhearing. "When did this happen?"

"Last week." He draped his towel around his neck, subtly flashing his wedding band in the process.

As he accepted the surprised congratulations from his friends, he was glad he'd come tonight. He'd only done so, though, because Stevie had a meeting and he'd figured he might as well stick to his regular schedule.

She wasn't yet home when he let himself in. He dropped his keys in a little basket she used for that purpose and wiped his feet carefully on the mat leading in from the garage before bending down to greet Dusty with a pat.

Stevie kept her house impeccably neat. When he'd first met her, he'd have assumed she lived in cheery chaos. His own housekeeping skills were limited to

keeping things mostly in their place and wielding a
mop once a week or so, but he made sure not to make
a mess here. Not that Stevie would have minded. As
tidy as she was, she made her home a comfortable, welcoming place, and she didn't seem bothered by Dusty's
toys that popped up all over the house, or the occasional
scattered kibble or rare, but inevitable, hairballs. She
wouldn't fret about kid's toys spread across the living
room floor, either, he thought, picturing just that as he
moved through the living room toward the bedroom.

He was freshly showered and dressed in a T-shirt
and pajama pants when she arrived an hour later. She
hung up her coat. "Sorry I'm so late. The meeting ran
over. How was your evening?"

"Not bad. Sparred a couple of times. Won the second time. Got my butt handed to me in the first bout."

She laughed and moved to pat his cheek. "Someone
beat up my hubby? Should I be incensed?"

Catching her hand, he leaned his head down to kiss
her lingeringly. "I'll recover," he said when he released
her.

Her cheeks looking a little flushed now, she cleared
her throat. "Glad to hear it. Do you ever have spectators at monthly sparring things? I'd like to watch you
sometime."

"Occasionally someone tags along, but we're not really performing for an audience. Just trying to stay in
shape."

"Still. I'd like to see you being all manly and sexy."

He laughed in response to the teasing phrase she'd
used before. "As long as you don't call me a 'cutie' in
front of my opponents," he said, remembering the addition she'd tacked on last time.

Giggling, she moved toward the bedroom, looking

over her shoulder. "I'm sure they're already aware of that."

He lasted all of a full second before he gave in to that beckoning look and followed her.

Chapter Seven

Along with Jenny and Gavin, Stevie and Cole were invited to a Sunday potluck lunch in the sprawling home Tess shared with her fiancé, Scott Prince. The cozy gathering was a celebration of Stevie and Cole's new marriage, and a chance for Cole to meet the other men.

It was still too cold to lunch out on the patio, so they ate in the dining room. They lingered a long time over the meal of side dishes they'd all contributed and succulent short ribs Scott had cooked on his beloved fancy grill. There was no lull in the conversation, of course. Stevie and her girlfriends never had trouble filling a silence. The men were a little quieter at first—possibly because they didn't have much chance to speak—but she was glad that Cole was soon involved in conversations with them.

"They seem to be getting along well," Tess commented while she and Jenny and Stevie prepared coffee and scooped blackberry cobbler into bowls after lunch.

The men were outside admiring the barbecue kitchen that was Scott's pride and joy. Stevie could see Cole through the patio doors, and he looked relaxed and comfortable. Despite the cold, none of them seemed in a hurry to come back in. Maybe they were enjoying a few minutes of quiet out there, she thought with an understanding smile. But they came in eagerly after being summoned for dessert.

"Oh, wow, Jen, this is good," Scott said, attacking his cobbler with enthusiasm.

She beamed. "Thanks. It's my grandmother's recipe. We won't mention calories, since this is a celebration party."

"Speaking of which…" Tess stood and dashed from the room for a moment, returning shortly afterward with a couple of large, beautifully wrapped gifts that she placed in front of Stevie and Cole.

"This seems like a good time for you to open these," she said, her smile including both of them. "This one is from Jenny and Gavin and this one is from Scott and me."

Stevie gasped in pleasure. "Oh, how sweet."

Cole looked startled by the unexpected gifts. "It was nice, but you didn't have to—"

Stevie elbowed him teasingly into silence. "Hush, before they decide to take them back," she chided and reached out to open the nearest package.

Obviously, Jenny and Tess had shopped together because the gifts were coordinated—a gorgeous porcelain tea service and a matching set of dessert plates featuring the sage green that was Stevie's favorite color.

"I know they're a little feminine, but we figured you'd enjoy eating sweets and drinking tea from them," Jenny said to Cole.

"They're great," he assured her. "Thanks, everyone."

Gavin gave a rough laugh and held up his hands. "To be strictly honest, I didn't even know what we'd gotten. But congratulations, anyway. You're a lucky man."

"Yes," Cole agreed with a glance at Stevie. "I know."

"And," Jenny said, her eyes glowing, "our kids can grow up together, just as Stevie and I did. They'll probably think of themselves as cousins."

"Makes sense, with you and Stevie as close as sisters," her doting husband commented. He glanced at Cole then. "How are your diapering skills, Cole? As for me, I've got a lot to learn yet."

"Same here," Cole admitted with a faint smile. "But I'm looking forward to the experience."

Stevie was sure Gavin and Scott had been filled in on the details of her pregnancy. It pleased her that they were treating it with such equanimity. For Cole's sake, especially, she was relieved that there was no awkwardness in the discussion of impending parenthood.

"We've already started working on our nursery," Jenny said, reaching out to take Gavin's hand. "We know we have plenty of time yet, but there's quite a bit to do. With our busy schedules, we'll have to work on it whenever we get a little extra time. Fortunately, Gavin's very handy around the house. All that work he's done at his fishing cabin has given him a lot of carpentry experience."

"What about you, Stevie?" Tess asked. "Have you thought about your nursery yet?"

"Yes." She mentioned the bedroom she'd decided upon. Familiar with her house, everyone nodded in approval. "Cole and I are still working out details. We'd like to have a guest room, but I'm using the third bedroom for an office. Cole is having to use the office at his house next door, which is inconvenient and impractical. It's possible we'll sell both our houses and try to find one that will better accommodate our needs."

Scott frowned thoughtfully. "You have a great house—classic mid-50s bungalow. And the neighborhood is good. If you want to stay there, you should consider some renovations. You could remodel the attic into two decent-sized home offices with plenty of built-in storage. I have a few connections in residential work if you want to proceed. I could have my architect draw up a plan and an estimate for you."

Intrigued, Stevie glanced at Cole, who gave her a gesture that told her he considered this more her decision than his. She frowned, but smoothed the expression quickly. True, it was still technically her house, but a remodel like this would certainly affect him, too.

For some reason, she thought of that tense moment in the baby store in Branson, when she'd been so determined to assert her financial independence. Had that moment of obstinacy really been for his sake—or for her own? They'd never talked about the incident afterward. Had she gone too far with her insistence that she hadn't married him for monetary assistance? Had he taken away the message that she wanted him to be hands-off in other areas of their lives, as well? Their home—even this child? That hadn't been her intention at all. She'd have to find the right time to have that discussion with him, and she'd have to do a better job of expressing her concerns without hurting his male pride.

"I'd like to think about it," she said, looking at Scott again. "It's definitely a possibility and one I hadn't yet considered. Thanks for the suggestion."

"How long would a renovation like that take?" Cole

asked, and Stevie was pleased he seemed interested, at least.

"From plans to completion, maybe six, seven weeks, assuming everything goes smoothly."

"So it could be finished before August?"

Scott considered a moment, then shrugged lightly. "I should think so."

Cole nodded. "Definitely something to think about."

The conversation moved on, skipping from renovations and babies to wedding plans. Gavin was still on night shift rotation, so he had to leave not long afterward, and the party came to an end with hugs and kisses all around and promises to get together often. Stevie thought Jenny and Tess looked a bit more reassured about her marriage to Cole now that they'd spent more time with him, but she knew they still worried. They loved her. They wanted her to be happy. They wished for her what they'd found for themselves, even though she had assured them she was content with what she'd found.

She frowned. The word didn't feel quite right in her mind. Was "contentment" all she truly wanted with him? Or—she swallowed—was it the best she could expect?

A short while later, she and Cole walked into their home, placing their gifts on the kitchen counter to be put away later.

"Well?" Stevie said, reaching down to pick up Dusty and snuggle her beneath her chin, asking Cole, "You liked Scott and Gavin, huh?"

"Sure. They seem like great guys."

"Did I hear that you and Gavin have some mutual friends?"

"Yeah, through the gym and dojo. Not that big a surprise. For a medium-sized city, Little Rock's a small world in some ways. I'm sure Scott and I would find a mutual acquaintance or two if we put our heads to it hard enough."

"Probably." Feeling suddenly overwarm, she put down the cat and tugged off the oversized cardigan she'd worn over a black shirt and leggings. She pressed a hand to her middle. "I think maybe I ate a little too much today. Peanut's not used to so much good food at once."

Cole stepped toward her, searching her face. "Are you ill?"

She held him off with one raised hand. "No. Just a little unsettled, that's all."

"I'll make you some peppermint tea."

"That sounds good, but I can—" Too late. He was already headed for the stove.

Shaking her head, she went into the bedroom to hang up her sweater. She was tempted to put on her pj's and get comfortable since she had no intention of leaving the house again that day, but it was still a little early. Not even dinnertime yet. If Cole weren't there, she'd say the heck with the time and "jammie," anyway, but...

She growled as she realized the direction her thoughts had drifted. Why was she treating him like a guest in the home she'd thought of as his, too, only an hour or so earlier? If she wanted to wear pajamas before dinner, she should do so. She wasn't going to walk around in tatters, but she had some cute lounging clothes, and darn if she wasn't going to get comfortable in her own—in *their* own home.

"Your tea is ready." Cole stood in the doorway a few minutes later, watching her as she examined herself in the full-length mirror. "Are you okay?"

"Yes." She'd donned a long-sleeved purple top with purple and green plaid dorm pants and fuzzy pink socks. "I decided to get comfy for the evening. My clothes were feeling a little tight."

"Your tea is ready."

"What did you think about Scott's idea of renovating the attic?" she asked, following him to the kitchen.

He poured the tea and handed her one of the mugs. "Sounded promising. Now you'll just have to decide if you want to remodel and stay here or look elsewhere for more space."

"I do love this house," she said, gazing wistfully around the kitchen she'd poured her heart, soul and savings into.

"Then maybe you should consider Scott's suggestions."

Cupping her mug between her hands, she leaned back against the counter and studied him gravely. "I have one major concern about that plan."

"Oh? What's that?"

"You."

Taken by surprise, he lowered his mug with a little cough. "Me? Why?"

"I worry that as long as we live here, you'll think of yourself as a guest in my home. That's not what I want. Maybe if we sell both houses and invest in someplace new, it will feel like ours rather than mine."

"Stevie." Setting his mug on the counter, he rested a hand lightly on her shoulder. "I appreciate your concern, really. And I'll admit this is all taking some getting used to mentally. That's only natural. I'm already feeling more at home here. If we set up an office upstairs so I'm not running next door for most of the day, it'll feel even more like my place, too."

Running a fingertip around the rim of her cup, she eyed him through her lashes. "You really didn't mind moving in here rather than your house?"

He shrugged. "I like my house fine, but I have no particular emotional attachment to it. I've only lived there a year. You grew up in this one. I can sell my place and put some of the profit toward the upstairs re-model, or we can hang on to it as rental property, if we want to deal with the occasional annoyances of being landlords. Doesn't really matter to me."

He really didn't seem to have much of a connection to his house. To him, it was just a place to live and work, a roof over his head. Of course, he'd never shared that home with anyone but his cat. Would that have made a difference? Did he still have warm feelings about whatever home he'd shared with his late wife, or had he seen that place, too, as just basic shelter? Maybe it really didn't matter to him where they lived, and she could feel less conflicted about staying in this house she didn't want to leave.

"Okay, we'll look at the figures Scott works up for us," she said. "But we'll make sure there's plenty of room for you to work up there. I don't need much space, just a cubbyhole for a desk and computer and maybe some built-in shelves."

"You pretty much described all I need, as well. I think we'll get by just fine here."

Get by. He probably hadn't intended for that phrase to sound so lackluster. He'd simply been agreeing that Scott's idea had been a good one.

A workable plan for a growing family in a house she loved and that he considered adequate for their needs. What more could she possibly want?

* * *

They settled into more of a routine during the next three weeks. Every morning, Cole kissed her after breakfast and headed next door to work as she left for her midtown office or job sites. Most afternoons he visited his gym for an hour or so, then put in a couple hours more work before dinner. He insisted on helping her with food prep and cleanup and he did his share of housework. More than his share, perhaps, she thought with a shake of her head.

Unless one of them had an appointment, they spent most evenings at home. Sometimes they played board games, though Cole quickly despaired of teaching her the finer points of Japanese strategy games, for which she had little patience. Conversation was never a challenge. They chatted about work and friends and current events, about politics and religion and philosophy, about literature, music and hobbies they'd sampled over the years. They didn't always agree, but she found the workings of his mind fascinating, and he seemed to value her opinions in a respectful way that was rather new to her coming from the man in her life.

During those three weeks, they got to know each other in other ways, as well. Stevie was delighted by the increasing awareness that Cole was the best lover she'd ever known. In the bedroom, too, Cole respected her and encouraged her, making her feel beautiful and desirable and sensual. He didn't play emotional games or try to manipulate her; he simply stated what he liked and expected the same of her. He didn't use flowery words, of course. No cutesy nicknames. That was so not Cole. He merely murmured her name, and something about hearing it in his deep, rumbly voice affected her in a way no poetry ever had.

She told herself she should be more content than she'd ever been. But an annoying little voice deep inside her whispered that something was still missing. And it still seemed to have something to do with that word…*content*.

She wished she could say for certain how Cole felt. He appeared to be—she grimaced in response to the word that popped into her mind—content. But was that enough for him? For either of them?

Physically—well, she had no doubt that neither of them had complaints in that area. They were dynamite in bed. Their explosive chemistry had proven a delightful surprise for her, and he'd made it very clear he felt the same. But was he really happy with the way things were going for them otherwise? No secret regrets? They were both mature enough to understand the difference between physical attraction and true love. Was the life they were making for themselves anything at all like what he'd shared with Natasha?

As subtly as possible for her, she'd tried a couple of times to coax him to talk about his first marriage. After all, that had been a significant part of her husband's past. Yet every time she'd brought it up, he'd changed the subject. She'd gotten the message that he didn't want to talk about his late wife. Was it still too painful for him? She couldn't help wondering wistfully if she would ever measure up to his memories of Natasha. What worried her even more was that someday, even as generous and considerate as he'd been, she wouldn't be quite as satisfied with what Cole had left for her. Telling herself to stop being greedy and focus on gratitude instead, she pushed those concerns to the back of her mind each time they tried to creep forward.

She met her friends for lunch the third Tuesday in

March. As usual, they launched straight into conversation, catching up on everything that had happened since they'd last talked.

"So, anyway, I told Gavin that he absolutely had to back off or I'm going to lose my mind long before this baby ever arrives," Jenny said, continuing a diatribe to her sympathetic friends. "I told him to save all that helpful hovering for the last few weeks of the pregnancy when I'll be all bloated and surly and unable to get around easily. I don't want him burning out on caregiving this early in the process."

Tess laughed. "How did he react to that?"

"Oh, you know Gavin. He pouted for a while, then he apologized and promised he'd tone it down. I told him I thought it was sweet that he wants to take care of me, and I know he isn't sure what he's supposed to be doing at this early stage, but geez."

After Stevie and Tess laughed, Tess looked toward Stevie. "What about Cole? Is he prone to hovering?"

"No, that's not his style. He's just reliably there for me. He tells me occasionally to be careful, and he's made me assure him I won't hesitate to ask for anything I need, but he isn't a hoverer."

She was aware that both her best friends eyed her closely as she talked about her husband. She knew she'd been a bit circumspect in discussing her marriage with them. She didn't know why, exactly, because she'd been prone to share even intimate details of her previous romances. But Cole was a private man, and she respected his comfort zone too much to breach his trust.

"Okay, I just told you that Scott and I butted heads over something at work this morning, and Jen told us about her confrontation with Gavin last night," Tess recapped. "So what do you and Cole fuss about?"

Stevie blinked, then spread her hands. "Nothing."

Jenny snorted skeptically. "Nothing? Seriously? I think I know you better than that, Stevie."

She understood why Jenny would question her. It wasn't that she had a bad temper, but she wasn't one to hold back her feelings, either. She got mad, she expressed it, then she just as quickly forgave and moved on. The closest she'd come to quarreling with Cole had been when she'd snapped at him in the baby store on their honeymoon, she realized now. He hadn't gotten angry in return, and had seemed to go out of his way not to step on her toes since. She bit her lower lip. Was that a healthy thing?

"You said he's in Chicago this week?" Tess inquired.

Stevie heard her own little wistful sigh before she replied, "Yes. He left this morning. He'll be back Friday. He doesn't usually have to travel as much as he has the past couple of months, but there've been issues with a conversion to some sort of new data system that's totally beyond my comprehension."

Jenny toyed with her food, but her gaze was still focused on Stevie. "So you have the house to yourself again for a few days."

"Yes. I have to admit it already feels a little odd not to have him there." She laughed quietly. "Dusty isn't much of a conversationalist, though she is good company."

Jenny allowed the full measure of her concern to show on her face. "So you're happy with Cole?"

"I'm happy," she said firmly. "We're getting along very well and we're both looking forward to the baby. We love the plans Scott's architect drew up for our attic renovation and the estimate was very reasonable, so we're excited about moving forward with that, too."

Maybe "excited" wasn't the best adjective to describe Cole's satisfaction with the plan, but close enough, she decided. "We've agreed it will be better to stay at his place while the staircase construction is underway. Once we're settled again, we'll decide whether to sell or rent out his house."

"Sounds like you have your future all planned out," Tess remarked.

"As much as anyone can plan for the future."

"Do you think you and Cole will have more children?" Tess asked artlessly.

Stevie blinked, caught off-guard by the question that hadn't even occurred to her until now. "We haven't had this one yet," she said, resting a hand on the more noticeable bulge of her tummy.

"But you *are* sleeping together?" Jenny asked bluntly. "And by sleeping, of course, I mean—"

"Jen," Tess murmured, apparently deciding the questioning had gone just a bit too far with that one.

Jenny's expression was a mixture of apology and defiance. She spoke quietly, her words audible only to Stevie and Tess in their corner booth. "She understands why I'd ask. We've known each other since we were kids, right, Stevie? I knew the day you had your first period. The day you got your first of several broken hearts. I know you lost your virginity after senior prom to the first of those heartbreakers. You knew when Gavin became my first, something you recognized the minute I walked into our dorm room afterward. I'm fully aware this is none of my business. You can tell me to jump into a lake and I won't get mad, because you have every right to do so. But you know I love you, and I worry about you. And you have to admit you've never been shy about expressing your opinions when you were concerned about me."

There was no way Stevie could hold out against that heartfelt speech. For one thing, every word of it was true.

She drew a deep, steadying breath. "Cole and I married for the sake of this child neither of us was expecting but both of us want," she said, paraphrasing something he'd once said to her. "And yes, it is a real marriage in every way. It's a win-win-win situation. The baby gets a father, I get a partner in raising the child and Cole gets a family. It's what we both want. Thank you for caring. I love you both, and I'm glad all of us are happy now. I'm looking forward to raising our kids together, backyard barbecues and birthday parties, being eccentric old lady friends who get together and brag about our grandchildren. I know I didn't go about this marriage in a typical manner...but when have I ever been typical?"

Her eyes suspiciously liquid, Jenny managed a watery smile. "Never. And I wouldn't change a thing about you."

"That goes both ways," Stevie said gruffly, returning the smile.

"So could I ask just one more question?"

Stevie growled humorously, wondering when she and Jenny had swapped personalities. This sounded exactly like a conversation they'd have had in the past, only with roles reversed. "What the hell. Ask."

"Is there any chance you're falling in love with Cole?"

"I—" Stevie took a quick sip of her water to loosen her suddenly tight throat. "Cole is a sweet, kind, very special man. Of course I love him."

"I asked if you're *in* love with him. But never mind."

Jenny shook her head, her expression genuinely apologetic now. "You're right, Stevie, I'm stepping way over the line here. Let's just change the subject, okay? It's almost time for us all to get back to work, anyway."

Stevie nodded gratefully.

"For what it's worth, I think Cole knows how lucky he is," Tess said, speaking quickly to defuse the tension before they moved on. "He hardly took his eyes off you when we gathered at our house. I bet he's missing you while he's away."

She hoped he did miss her a little, Stevie thought as she sat on the couch later that evening, the dozing cat curled in her lap. Funny how quiet and empty the house seemed now without him in it, especially considering he wasn't one to make much noise when he was there. It was just that she'd become accustomed to his quiet presence. His warmth beside her in her bed at night. And she missed him.

Dusty mewed and looked up at her. Stevie scratched the cat's ears in the way she'd seen Cole do numerous times, and the cat purred with pleasure.

"You miss him, too, don't you?" she asked the tabby, who arched her neck for better access.

"I do love him, of course. We've had such a special friendship. It meant a great deal to me, even before we took this step."

Dusty sneezed.

"And would it really be such a bad thing if I do fall in love with my husband? Seems to me that would be something to be desired. And hardly a risk for heartbreak since we're already married and we plan to stay together."

No heartbreak from a breakup, anyway, she couldn't help adding silently, looking away from the unconcerned cat. But how would it feel to realize she was head over heels in love with a man who was merely fond of her? How much would it hurt to know that while she was sitting here missing him so much, he'd hardly given her a thought?

Her phone rang and she jumped, startling the cat who leapt down to the floor. Seeing Cole's number on her screen, she cleared her throat before answering. "How's Chicago?"

"Let's just say I'm looking forward to being home."

"Good. Dusty and I miss you," she said lightly.

"I miss you guys, too. How are things there?"

It was hardly a yearning declaration, but she'd take it. "Everything's fine. I had a few complications come up with Pepper Rose's kitchen redesign, but I think we've taken care of them."

"Nothing major?"

"Not in this case. Just a frustrating back order situation. It'll work out."

"Good. How's Peanut?"

"Growing. I had to change my mind about an outfit this morning because I couldn't button the shirt. By the way, I'd almost forgotten that I have a doctor's appointment next week. Would you like to go with me?"

"Absolutely." He sounded pleased that she'd asked.

"Okay, then. I'll introduce you to my doctor. You'll like her."

"I'm sure I will. Didn't you mention you were having lunch with Tess and Jenny today?"

"Yes, I did. They send their regards."

"So you had a good visit?"

"Yes, it was very nice."

He seemed to sense something beneath her words,

proving once again that Cole was just a little too perceptive when it came to her. "Is anything wrong?"

"I'm just a little tired, I guess. Long day."

"I'll let you rest. But if you fall asleep on the couch, you'll have to depend on Dusty to wake you to go to bed."

She laughed. "I'll let her know. Good night, Cole."

"'Night, Stevie."

He disconnected without further delay.

She looked at the silent phone. "Hurry home," she said.

The aroma of spices and peppers greeted Cole when he walked into the house early Friday evening. Stevie had ordered him not to eat at the airport. Judging by the scents and the clues on the kitchen counter, she'd prepared Tex-Mex. His stomach was already growling in response. She wasn't in the kitchen, so he moved toward the doorway to find her.

Dusty appeared and meowed in welcome. Setting down his bag, he bent to greet her, then picked up his bag again and headed for the doorway. He found Stevie in the bedroom, fluffing her hair at the mirror, seemingly unaware he was home yet. Was she primping for his arrival? The possibility pleased him, for some reason. Not that she needed enhancement. She wore something blue and floaty over black leggings with black slippers. Nearly the same color as her eyes, her blouse draped appealingly over her full bust and fell loosely to her hips, almost but not quite concealing the little bulge at her middle.

She looked beautiful.

Sensing his presence, she turned to look his way. Her

face lit up, her brilliant blue eyes glowing with pleasure. "Cole! You're home."

She launched herself at him and he dropped his bag with a laugh to catch her. His lips found hers in a kiss that made him all but forget his hunger for food.

As he'd expected, it felt damned good to be welcomed home this way, he thought as Dusty wound around their ankles. He never wanted to go back to always returning to a dark, quiet house.

Yet he, better than most people, knew how capricious life could be, how quickly circumstances could change. His arms tightened reflexively around Stevie, as if he could keep her safe and satisfied simply by holding her close.

Chapter Eight

"Anyway, we finally got the materials for Pepper's backsplash, and the plumber finally got the pipes in the right place. Honestly, that man can be so dense sometimes. Now that that job is moving along, the Blankenship remodel is about to make me pull my hair out. If Mindy changes her mind one more time about where she wants her refrigerator, I'm going to give her deposit back and tell her to draw up her own plans. Or tell her good luck finding someone to help her make a decision that comes with a guarantee of one hundred percent long-term satisfaction, which is more than I can seem to do for a woman who changes her vision of what she wants every morning when she wakes up. Heck, she changes her mind half a dozen times before lunch every day! Honestly, Cole, sometimes I wonder—"

He cleared his throat to break into the animated monologue. "Excuse me, Stevie, I'm paying attention to what you're saying, but is there any more of that salsa?"

She was startled into momentary silence before bursting into a peal of rueful laughter. "Poor Cole. I've been talking your ears off, haven't I? I guess I had a lot of words saved up for you. Yes, there's more salsa in the fridge. I'll—"

"Sit," he said when she started to rise. "I'll get it. Go on with what you were saying. Do you think you'll ever be able to please Mrs. Blankenship?"

"I'm sure I will. Maybe. With luck."

After returning to the table, he leaned down to brush a kiss at the corner of her mouth, his lips warm and spicy against her skin. She all but shivered in response to his touch. It seemed like more than a mere few days since she'd felt it.

He gave her shoulder a little squeeze before releasing her to take his seat. "I like hearing your stories. And knowing that maybe you missed me a little while I was away."

"More than a little." She hoped her smile looked natural. "Like that old song says, I've grown accustomed to your face."

He laughed, and as always the sound pleased her. "I'm glad." He dipped a tortilla chip into the spicy homemade salsa. "I've gotten pretty accustomed to yours, too. So, what's the next step with Mrs. Blankenship?"

As far as romantic exchanges went, that one had hardly been the most lyrical she'd ever participated in. Yet still she'd taken it to heart. Which only showed how little it took to please her when it came to Cole. What, exactly, did that say about her growing feelings for him? And how could she tell if he felt the same when he kept his emotions so very well concealed behind that sexy, unrevealing smile?

A couple hours later she watched with a thrill of anticipation as he emerged from the master bathroom and into the bedroom where she waited for him. She'd turned off the overhead light, leaving the room lit only by the lamp on the nightstand. Cole's bare chest gleamed in that soft glow as he approached the bed wearing only boxer shorts. His broad shoulders and firm muscles were outlined by shadows, and his dark eyes glittered like polished onyx as he studied her with a smile.

He turned out the light before climbing in beside her, plunging the room into darkness but leaving that image of him very clear in her mind. She folded herself into his eager arms, her mouth meeting his in a kiss that clearly established how much she'd missed him in their bed as well as at their dinner table. And though Cole wasn't one to express himself with words, he was breathtakingly efficient at conveying with his hands and lips how pleased he was to be back.

He trailed a string of openmouthed kisses from her mouth to her temple, from the soft indention behind her ear to the pulsing hollow of her throat. His big, warm hand cupped her left breast through her thin nightgown, his thumb rotating lazily over the nipple. She arched in reaction.

"Too sensitive?" he asked in a low rumble, lifting his thumb.

Catching his hand, she pressed it down again. "Feels good," she murmured, tangling her smooth legs with his longer, hair-roughened limbs.

He lowered his head, tugging the deep neckline of the gown out of the way so his mouth could find that achingly distended nub. With exquisite tenderness, he caressed it with his lips and with strokes of his tongue drew it into his mouth, then released it and soothed it with a rub of his closed mouth before he turned his attention to its jealous twin. His hand slid down her side, appreciatively shaping her changing form before finding the hem of her gown and slipping beneath it to stroke the heated depths he discovered there.

She gasped and plunged her hands into his hair. His thick, springy, beautiful hair. She held his head at her breasts, parted her legs to allow him full access to her secrets, lifted herself against him in a way that made it very clear how much she wanted him. She'd never been shy about her sexuality, but Cole had a talent for taking her to heights of sensation she'd never imagined, and she was impatient to find out just how high they could climb together.

When the last shred of patience evaporated, she shoved at his shoulders until he tumbled laughing on his bed against the pillows. Boxers and nightgown hit the floor and she straddled him, bracing herself with her hands on his solid shoulders. Her eyes had adjusted to the darkness now and she could just see him there against the white linens, grinning up at her with a flash of white teeth that gave her a glimpse of the warrior hidden deep inside this self-proclaimed computer nerd. And as always, that tantalizing peek made her even hungrier for more.

His hands on her hips, her hair falling around them, their moans and murmurs blending as their bodies merged, they reached that dazzling summit together, clinging there for as long as they could draw it out before they plunged almost simultaneously over the edge into a maelstrom of mindless sensation. Collapsing into his strong arms afterward, she wasn't sure she'd ever catch another full breath or form another coherent sentence, but at the moment, she just didn't care.

She was so glad to have him back home.

The doctor's appointment the following Monday went well. With the exception of slightly elevated blood pressure, Stevie was pronounced healthy, as was the baby. Though she'd been seeing the doctor only once a month until then, she was instructed to come in every other week from that point on. Dr. Prescott didn't seem overly concerned about the blood pressure reading, but she said they should monitor it closely just to be on the safe side. Stevie didn't argue.

"You were right," Cole said as he drove them away from the appointment. "I liked your doctor very much."

"I thought you would. She's great."

He was frowning a little when he asked, "Do you have a history of high blood pressure?"

"No. But it's okay. She said it's probably nothing to worry about, remember? It wasn't much higher than usual. How cool was it when she said those funny little feelings I've noticed during the past week are probably the baby kicking? I mean, I thought it could be, but they were just little flutters, not like real kicks yet, so I wasn't completely sure. But she said it's very likely that's what I'm feeling and it should start getting strong and it won't be long until you'll be able to feel it from the outside. And they're doing the next ultrasound in just four more weeks and we should be able to tell the gender by then so we can start narrowing down our list of names and it's all just so exciting."

He chuckled and she realized she'd let her enthusiasm carry her away for the moment. "Sorry. I know you heard her say all of that. I'm just glad the checkup went well. I get nervous every time beforehand."

"I noticed," he said, and she made a little face as she remembered how restless she'd been that morning, pacing through the house and checking the clock every few minutes until it was time to leave. "You were too nervous to eat much this morning. Want to stop for a bite somewhere?"

She tilted her head in consideration, then nodded. "Actually, I'm starving. You know what sounds good? Sushi."

"Aren't you supposed to avoid—"

"I know, raw fish is a bad idea in pregnancy. So maybe I'll just have udon noodles with chicken. That's sort of like sushi, right?"

He laughed. "That's nothing like sushi, other than being from the same country, but okay. We'll find udon noodles. Whatever you want."

Whatever you want. He said those words a lot, she mused, thoughtfully twisting a lock of hair. Sometimes she still felt as if their relationship was very uneven, as though she were the one getting most of the benefits while he was the one doing the bulk of the giving. That was still hard for her to get used to.

Someday, she promised herself, she'd find a way to do something special for Cole, other than preparing good meals for him and trying to make a nice home with him.

They chose to dine at a small Asian fusion chain restaurant located in a midtown shopping center. It was a popular destination for workday lunch crowds, and though it was a bit later than the work rush, the place was still busy. They'd just spotted an available two-top and Cole had pulled out a chair for Stevie when a woman said his name.

"Cole? I thought that was you."

The woman was tall and fit, her skin lightly tanned and her brown hair sun-streaked as if she spent a lot of time outdoors. Something about the way she smiled at Cole made Stevie's feminine nerve endings tingle in awareness. She had to resist an urge to take a step closer to him. She'd never in her life been the possessive or jealous type. She wondered in bewilderment if pregnancy hormones were messing with her again.

"Oh, hi, Jessica. Nice to see you," Cole said cordially, his hands still on the back of the chair.

"Sorry you didn't make it for sparring last week," she commented. "We missed you there."

"I was out of town on business. I'll try to make it next time. Oh, uh, Jessica Lopez, this is my wife, Stevie."

Stevie noted that the other woman's gaze slid down to her little baby bump, paused there a moment, then lifted back to her face. Jessica definitely had had a little crush on Cole, and was fully resigned now that nothing would ever come of it.

Because Stevie couldn't blame any woman for being drawn to Cole, she added a bit more warmth to her voice when she said, "It's very nice to meet you."

"Yeah, you, too. See you, Cole."

Cole motioned Stevie into the chair he still held for her. Drinks were self-serve at this ultracasual place, so he asked what she wanted then went to fetch it while she thought about the little encounter with Jessica.

She doubted Jessica was the only woman who'd been drawn to Cole during the past few years. She was sure he met nice women at his gym, on his business trips, in other everyday pursuits. He'd said he liked being married, but he'd apparently made no effort to court anyone during the five years he'd been single, not until her own situation had spurred him into action. So had he really been satisfied living on his own—or had no one lived up to his memories?

He'd implied on their wedding night that he'd been attracted to her for a while, though he'd done a good job of masking it during their year of platonic friendship. Would he ever have acted on that attraction had it not been for her pregnancy? Could she take encouragement in the fact that he'd chosen to finally change his single status for her, even though it had taken a fairly significant development to prod him into it?

He returned with their drinks and a couple of fortune cookies for after the meal. Their food arrived at almost the same time. Stevie picked up her chopsticks and dug in enthusiastically, making Cole chuckle at her eagerness. "How is it?"

"It's not sushi, but it's good, anyway."

He laughed and picked up his own chopsticks. Maybe for Cole, what they had was all he needed.

Maybe she should take a lesson from him.

They were able to start on the renovations the Thursday after the doctor's appointment. Spring was trying its best to shoulder winter out of the way, leading to noisy thunderstorms and one night of severe weather warnings. Considering they lived in the middle of "tornado alley," they'd decided to install a safe room in the garage while they were remodeling. The addition would add a week to the process but would provide a safe place for their little family to gather in dangerous weather. The shelter was Cole's idea initially, but Stevie heartily agreed. She'd spent too many nights in her lifetime huddling in a hallway or bathroom waiting for the tornado sirens to stop wailing.

She got a little taste of how he must have felt for the past six weeks when they moved into his house to avoid the mess created by the staircase reconstruction in her hallway. She didn't know where everything was, she bumped her shins on the furniture when the lights were off, the mattress on his bed felt different and her clothes were crowded into the extra space he made for her. It was a nice house, but it wasn't home. Maybe it was a good thing Cole didn't get attached to houses and possessions, she reflected ruefully. He'd adjusted much more easily to being surrounded by someone else's things than she would have. Even Dusty seemed to handle displacement better!

"When we get settled back into our house," she said as she and Cole sat at the kitchen table for dinner the second night, "we need to integrate your things there more. Are there any special pieces of furniture you want to move over? I'm sure we can make a place for anything you'd like to keep."

He glanced around as if the option had never occurred to him. "I'll keep my desk and office chair, of course. But all my work stuff will fit into the new office."

"What about any other furniture you particularly like?" He didn't possess more than the basics, and she hadn't noticed anything that looked as though it might be an heirloom, but maybe there was something that had sentimental attachment to him.

"Not really, no. Your stuff is nicer. We can have a tag sale with mine or rent the house furnished."

"You don't have any mementos from childhood or

college stashed in boxes somewhere? Things you want to keep?"

"I have a box in my closet with a few things like that," he said, slicing into the smothered pork chop she'd cooked for him. "It's not very big. I'll keep it in the closet of the new office."

She suspected those private treasures were things that had belonged to Natasha. She certainly didn't mind him hanging on to them. She would never be so petty that she would want him to forget his first wife or the few years he'd been allowed with her. It occurred to her that she'd never even seen a photograph of Natasha. Cole kept no framed photos out for display.

Had there been passion in his marriage? Had he and Natasha ever lost their tempers or even quarreled? He'd said she was very ill for some time. Had forewarning eased his loss, or had the grief been raw and devastating? Did it still tear at him sometimes, or had he packed those emotions away with that box in his closet?

"Stevie?" She glanced up to find him watching her quizzically from the other side of the table. "What's wrong? Are you feeling okay?"

She smiled reassuringly. "I'm fine. Just thinking about all we have to do during the next few weeks."

"Oh." That seemed to satisfy him. "Don't worry, it'll get done. I've got some free time tomorrow. Thought I'd work in the nursery while the crew's dealing with the staircase."

He'd volunteered to take care of emptying the small bedroom in preparation for the new nursery furniture they'd ordered. The walls had a few dents and nail holes to patch and the trim needed to be taped off before he could apply the rich cream color she'd chosen for the walls.

"Isn't there anything I can do for you here?" she asked. "Things I can pack or sort or something? I want to help as much as possible with this transition."

Finishing his dinner, he carried his dishes to the sink, collecting hers on the way. "I guess you could sort my closet some if you get bored. It's been a while since I've been through my wardrobe and I suspect some of the stuff in there needs to go straight into a donations bin."

From what she'd seen, his wardrobe consisted mostly of pullovers and jeans for working at home, with a couple of sport coats and dress shirts and slacks—and a few of the hated ties, she thought with a smile. "I'll look through your things and make a pile of items that could be questionable, though I'd never get rid of anything without checking with you."

He shrugged. "Wouldn't bother me. If you'd be embarrassed to be seen with me wearing anything you find in there, toss it."

"I'd never be embarrassed to be seen with you," she assured him, rising to refill her water glass.

"Oh, yeah? Not even if I do this?" He mugged a classic horror-movie-Igor pose, hunching a shoulder, dragging an arm, making a silly face.

Delighted with his rare lapse into absurdity, she gave a peal of laughter and tousled his hair. "Not even then. You're such a cutie."

Growling, he straightened and caught her in his arms. "There's that word again. I keep telling you, I'd rather you see me as manly and sexy."

He never forgot anything, she thought with another laugh. Wrapping her arms around his neck, she went up on tiptoes and brushed a kiss over his smiling mouth. "What a coincidence," she murmured. "That's exactly the way I see you. Most of the time."

Chuckling, he drew her into a heated kiss that definitely made this one of those times.

The first Sunday in April was Easter, and the day dawned clear and pleasantly moderate. Stevie dressed for church in a shades-of-purple graphic print dress, then checked her reflection. She was quite obviously pregnant now and made no effort to hide it. Actually, it was a relief that she was blossoming so quickly, as it meant her little Peanut was growing and thriving. The baby's movements were more frequent and noticeable now and she looked forward to Cole feeling the baby kick for the first time.

Everything seemed to be going so well that she was almost afraid she'd do something to jinx her good fortune. She wasn't used to feeling so relaxed in a relationship. She didn't have to walk on eggshells around Cole's ego, didn't have to second-guess her decisions or worry about plans being canceled last-minute or agreements being carelessly broken. When Cole said he'd do something or be somewhere, she could place a sizable bet on it.

She slid her feet into low-heeled shoes, her thoughts still focused on her marriage. She had to admit that so far it was going even better than she'd imagined it would the day they'd exchanged their vows. She wouldn't change a thing about their relationship. Except, perhaps…

No. Stop this, Stevie, before you jinx it, after all.

Ironically enough, she was aware that her biggest concern about her marriage was that it was too pleasant. And that Cole seemed to be trying too hard to keep it that way.

She'd never seen Cole come even close to losing control of his emotions, she thought, twisting a strand of hair. Her own had always been so close to the surface that she couldn't imagine how he managed. He was certainly passionate here in the bedroom, but even then his lovemaking always focused as much on her pleasure as his. She'd seen irritation—with his father, with annoying business associates—but never temper. Was it because he didn't feel things as intensely as she did, or had his childhood with a critical and emotionally distant father convinced Cole that a "real man" didn't acknowledge vulnerability?

Wouldn't it be only natural for him to get mad once in a while? Was it healthy, either emotionally or physically, for him to suppress anger if he felt it? Jenny and Tess certainly spatted occasionally with their guys, yet there was no doubt they were deeply in love and blissfully happy.

In love. She winced at the phrase. She wasn't comparing her relationship with those of her friends, of course. She and Cole had come at this with different needs than theirs. She simply wanted to make sure all his needs were being fulfilled. He was certainly taking care of hers.

"Stevie?"

In response to his voice from the doorway, she roused from her thoughts and turned toward him with a bright smile. "I'm ready."

Something about his expression made her stop and tilt her head to study him more closely. He looked great in the jacket and tie he'd donned for the holiday. But one hand was hidden behind his back and his face was as close to sheepish as she'd ever seen it.

"What is it?" she asked curiously. "Have you changed

your mind about going to church with me? Because that's certainly—"

"No, I want to go. I just—" Shaking his head a little, he brought his hand around. "I know it's a little silly, but I thought you might like this."

A little green wicker basket decorated with a green-and-white gingham bow dangled from his big fingers. Within the basket, a white stuffed bunny with floppy ears, big feet and an adorably sweet face sat on top of an assortment of her favorite specialty chocolates.

Stevie found it suddenly difficult to talk around a hard lump in her throat. Still, she managed to ask, "You brought me an Easter basket?"

"Yes. With your house all torn up and your schedule disrupted, I thought you'd like a little treat for Easter. I know you like these chocolates, so…"

His uncharacteristically self-conscious words faded into silence, leaving him looking almost shy as he held out the little basket to her. Stevie blinked back a film of tears when she accepted it from him. If she burst into sobs over his gesture, she was sure he would blame it on pregnancy hormones, and he would probably be right, for the most part. But it really was so sweet that her heart ached a bit.

"Can you see it?" Holding a cold metal wand pressed to Stevie's tummy, the sonographer looked with an indulgent smile from Stevie on the bed to Cole standing beside her. "Do you need me to show you?"

As curious as Cole was about what he'd see on the monitor, he was unable for a moment to tear his gaze away from Stevie's face. Her eyes looked bigger and bluer than ever, her beautiful mouth was curved into a smile of such joy he felt his throat tighten in response.

She was beautiful. And she was his, he thought with a surge of utterly male satisfaction.

She looked quickly from the screen to him and then back again. Her voice was breathy with excitement when she asked, "That's— It's a boy, right? That's a boy?"

The sonographer laughed, obviously enjoying her job no matter how many times she'd watched this reveal. "Yes, it's a boy. And he looks very healthy. Congratulations."

Stevie looked at Cole again with an expression radiant with wonder. "A boy, Cole. We're having a boy!"

He squeezed her hand, then impulsively raised it to his lips. Her fingers curled tightly around his. A hard knot formed in his throat when he looked back at the monitor with a knot in his throat.

A boy. For some reason, he'd been absolutely certain that Stevie was having a girl. As the past few weeks had swept by in a daze of work, construction, plans and commitments, the image had grown stronger in his mind of a little blonde girl with big blue eyes and a dimpled smile, a tiny clone of Stevie. He was very comfortable picturing himself as the father of that little girl. Helping her learn to walk. Holding her steady as she rode her first bike. Showing her constellations and planets, bugs and microbes. Teaching her how to drive, scowling off would-be suitors, maybe someday walking her down the aisle as no one had been there to do for Stevie. But a boy...

He studied the face in the ultrasound image, wondering if this little guy would have Stevie's curly hair and blue eyes. Looks didn't matter so much to him. He was more concerned with overcoming his own complex father-son issues and forming a bond with this boy. And for the first time in weeks, he was beset by doubts of his qualifications for the job.

"So now we're going to have to decide on a boy's name," Stevie announced happily when they were buckled into the car and he drove out of the clinic parking lot. "I've got a list started, but it has like fifty names on it already and every time I think I've narrowed it down a little I hear another name that's interesting enough to add to the list, so it's just getting longer instead of shorter. I've been keeping the nursery as neutral as possible with the classic children's tales artwork and the sage-and-cream color scheme, so nothing changes there, but now we can buy a few outfits because as much as I believe in equality, I just can't put a little boy in a lacy dress. I think in some ways I always knew he was a boy, even back when I first started calling him Peanut, which of course I won't do after we choose a name because heaven knows he wouldn't want that nickname to stick."

"No, he probably—"

"I have to text Jenny and Tess. I told them I'd let them know as soon as we left the clinic. They're almost as excited as we are to find out. And my mom and my brother want to know as soon as possible and I know your mother is eager to hear the news, so we'll have to make lots of calls and texts this evening. What about your dad? Are you going to call him?"

Cole's fingers tightened around the steering wheel. "Probably not."

She squirmed around in her seat to face him, surprise breaking into her excitement-fueled chattering. "You don't think he'd want to know the baby's gender?"

"Who knows with my dad?"

"You have told him I'm pregnant, haven't you?"

He cleared his throat. "I've only talked to him once

since we dropped by there in February, just for a routine six-week check to see how he's doing. The subject didn't come up."

There was a moment of shocked silence, and then her snort made her exasperation quite clear. "Honestly, Cole, you're almost as stubborn as he is. I know your dad was hard on you with his strict, narrow definition of masculinity, but has it occurred to you that maybe the prospect of being a grandfather would soften him up a little? That happens, you know, even with grumpy old men. It should especially please him that he'll have a grandson."

"So he can browbeat the boy the way he did me? Sigh at him when he cries or scowl at him if he doesn't want to tramp through the woods to kill a deer? I'm not going to let those things happen to this kid."

"We'd never let him do that. But if we establish clear boundaries and your dad follows them, maybe it would be good for both of them. I never knew my paternal grandfather and my mother's dad died when I was too young to remember him, but I always wished I had a grandpa if I couldn't have a dad. You and I could give our son both. You said you were close with your grandfather, and I'm sure he was pretty old-fashioned, too."

"He was," Cole conceded, thinking back to his hardworking, cattle farmer Pops. "He was strict, gave me plenty of rules and chores, but he wasn't as hard to please as my dad. Pops and I got along pretty well for the most part."

"And how was his relationship with his son?"

"Strained," Cole admitted slowly. "He got along better with his younger son, my uncle Bob. Pops didn't approve of Dad's marriage to my mother—rightly so, as it turned out—and he wasn't a fan of the way they kept putting me in the middle of their fights. He wasn't tactful with my father about his opinions, and Dad never took criticism well."

"Maybe your dad will find a soft spot for this little boy. Shouldn't we at least try to find out?"

"I'll think about it," he conceded grudgingly. "But frankly I'm tired of being the one to do all the reaching out. Dad knows my number. Wouldn't hurt him to call me every once in a while just to see if I'm still alive."

He shook his head before she could argue more. "Let's not talk about Dad now. This is too special a day. Why don't we celebrate this news by stopping by the baby store and picking up some more things for the kid? We're still looking for a stroller, right? Have you decided whether you want a three-wheel or four-wheel model?"

They'd done hours of research together on nearly everything they'd purchased to this point, reading all the safety records and brand comparisons they could find. He was pleased that Stevie wanted his opinions. Granted, he didn't know much about baby stuff, but he was damned good at research.

Stevie was enthused about shopping for the baby now that she knew more about him, and Cole was glad he'd made the suggestion. It was a sunny, warm spring day. He and Stevie had both been working so hard lately that it was nice to have a couple of daylight hours just to relax together. Maybe he'd talk her into a milkshake, which probably wouldn't be hard. She had a notorious weakness for chocolate milkshakes, and couldn't imagine why anyone—specifically, he—would want to ruin a perfectly good cup of ice cream with chunks of pineapple.

He was glad to see her happily chattering and laughing, so excited about learning more about the baby who'd be joining them in just over three months. She'd been a little more subdued than usual for the past few weeks—since Easter, really. He blamed it on all the turmoil in their lives. Stevie was accustomed to construction snafus and delays on her design jobs, but having the same things going on in her own home was more stressful, especially combined with the emotional roller coaster of pregnancy.

It still bemused him that she had such a strong attachment to her house. The place was certainly adequate for their needs, increasingly so as the attic renovation and storm shelter came closer to being finished, but he figured they'd have been able to find plenty of other houses just as functional. Maybe it was because he'd been shuttled so often from house to house as a kid that he didn't have as strong a sense of "home" as she did. For him, home was now wherever Stevie was. Didn't matter much where that happened to be. At least he had the satisfaction of knowing she missed him now when he wasn't in her beloved house with her.

"Are you sure you'll be okay when I'm away next week?" he asked as he parked in front of the baby store. "I can always try to change the meetings to conference calls if you—"

"Cole," she interrupted with a laugh and an affectionate pat on his arm. "You're starting to sound like Gavin. I'll be fine for a few days on my own, I promise."

He regretted missing next week's doctor's appointment, but this trip was rather important. He'd already made it clear to all involved that he wouldn't be traveling for a couple months after the baby arrived, so he was trying to take care of some things ahead of time. "You'll let me know if your blood pressure has gone up again? You'll tell the doctor you've had a couple of headaches in the past week?"

"Both of which occurred when I got busy and forgot to eat lunch on time," she reminded him. "Totally my fault. And I've been paying more attention to my schedule now that you set my phone to nag me about lunchtime. Haven't had a headache since. And my blood pressure has been stable the last two visits, so I think you can stop worrying about that, too."

He nodded slowly as he opened his door. Her blood pressure hadn't gone back down to prepregnancy levels, but it wasn't rising, either, so he guessed that was good. But that wouldn't stop him from worrying. Nothing would.

Chapter Nine

It was almost five p.m. when Stevie parked in front of McKellar Auto Service on the following Wednesday afternoon. She'd made the drive on one of her rash impulses and she was absolutely certain her husband would not approve had he known about it. But he was out of town, and she'd fought the urge as long as she could before heading north when she'd left a kitchen remodel job an hour earlier.

She might finally see her husband angry after this, she thought wryly as she climbed out of her car. But she'd been trying to think of something important to do for Cole ever since they'd gotten married. She hoped the result of this reckless mission would be worth incurring his initial anger.

There was more activity around the place than during her last brief visit, though she could tell it was nearing closing time. Several of the bay doors were open and she could see both mechanics and customers milling inside. Perhaps this hadn't been the best time to come by. Would Jim find her visit more intrusive than welcome?

She let herself into the door marked Office, finding only one person inside the cramped room. The broad-hipped, plain-faced woman at the paper-cluttered desk appeared to be about the same age as Jim. She wore a flowered T-shirt, faded jeans and sneakers, and her gray-streaked dishwater blond hair was tied back in a low ponytail. Was this Jim's wife?

"What can I do for you?" the woman asked in a broad country drawl. "Are you picking up a car?"

"Actually, I'd like to see Mr. McKellar, if he can spare just a few minutes."

The woman eyed her through red plastic-framed glasses. "Can I say who's calling?"

"I'm his daughter-in-law. My name is Stevie."

The older woman walked slowly around the end of the counter-styled desk. "You're Cole's wife?"

"Yes."

"I'm Peggy. Cole's stepmama." She directed a look at Stevie's middle, then glanced back up at her face. "Nice to meet you. I was sorry I missed you when you stopped by before."

So at least Jim had mentioned their visit. "It's very nice to meet you, too, Mrs. McKellar," she said warmly.

"Call me Peggy. Nothing's wrong with Cole, is there? He's okay?"

"Cole's fine. He's out of state on a business trip but he'll be back in a couple of days."

Peggy's eyebrows rose. "Does he know you're here?"

Making a little face, Stevie shook her head. "No."

"I'll get Jim. Move that parts catalog and sit in that chair if you need to take a load off your feet."

"I'm fine, thank you. I can't stay long."

Perhaps five minutes passed before Jim stepped in, closing the door behind him. He was wiping his hands on a shop towel, something Stevie now suspected was a habit to keep him from having to shake hands. She didn't bother to offer hers this time, though she gave him her most winning smile. "Hi, Mr. McKellar. It's good to see you again."

He nodded curtly. "What can I do for you?"

She felt her smile dim a little. To be honest, she was so accustomed to rather easily disarming people that she was a little startled Jim was not particularly receptive to her. "I just wanted a few words with you, if you have a couple of minutes."

"Did Cole send you?"

"No. He's away on a business trip. He doesn't know I'm here. It was sort of an impulsive visit."

"Hmph." Jim swept her with a look. "When are you due?"

"Early August. It's a boy. I thought you'd like to know."

The math was simple enough. He grunted, his face showing no particular emotional reaction to the news that he would have a grandson. Was he really so cold, or was he even better than his son at masking his thoughts?

"So that explains the quickie marriage. One of them 'have to' situations, huh?"

"No one 'has to' get married these days, Mr. McKellar. Cole and I chose to marry." For purposes that were none of his business, she added silently.

He shrugged. "I understand he makes good money doing whatever it is he does with computers."

For a moment she didn't follow him. The comment seemed to be a non sequitur. When it suddenly occurred to her what he was suggesting, she drew back with a frown. "I certainly didn't 'trap' Cole into marriage, if that's what you're implying."

Jim shook his head. Apparently her words had left him unconvinced. "That boy has always been a sucker for a woman in trouble. He married that last girl knowing she was likely going to die, but she didn't have anyone else to care for her at the time, coming from the worthless family she had. I didn't see any reason for him to put himself through that, but he never would listen to my advice. I know he went into debt paying her medical bills. Not that he ever asked for a penny from me, I'll give him that. So if you think he's got a bunch of money stashed away somewhere, I'd imagine you're wrong."

"Mr. McKellar—"

Either he didn't notice the signs of her mounting temper or he waved them off as insignificant. "And don't think you're going to get anything here, either. Everything I got is sunk into this place. The boy could have had this business given to him outright someday, but he always thought he was too good for dirty mechanic work," he added bitterly. "Instead, he holes up with his computer and spends all his money helping the women who marry him because they need someone to take care of them."

Furious now, Stevie drew herself up to her full five feet two inches, clenching her hands at her sides. "You might be my father-in-law, Mr. McKellar, but I've got to tell you… You're a—a…" A word Cole wryly used after frustrating business transactions popped into her head, and she applied it with no trace of humor. "A moron."

His brows lowered into a deep V of disbelief. "What did you—"

"I did not come here to ask you for money," she said, cutting him off. "And how dare you make that assumption?"

"Then why would you come here behind Cole's back?"

"Because I'm a moron, too," she replied with a bitter shake of her head. "I didn't come to ask for anything. I came to offer something. I stupidly thought I could charm you into making a new start with your son. It never even occurred to me that a kind, honorable, courteous man like Cole would come from a father who is so rude and…and just mean."

"Look, I—"

She swept on, her hands fluttering in agitation. "You're intentionally blind if you can't see what a fine man your son has turned out to be. He works very hard and he has gained a great deal of respect from people who recognize his intelligence and competence. You should be proud of what he's accomplished rather than trying to make him feel guilty because he didn't want to take over this business. He never thought he was too good for mechanic work. That's not the kind of man he is. He simply pursued the work that best suited him and that made him happy, which is what any parent should want for his child. And by the way, he obviously respects you more than you do him. He told me that you're a damned good mechanic, that there's not an engine in existence you can't tear down and rebuild, and that you've invested very wisely in your business and have been very successful with it."

"He said that?"

She was on a roll and in no mood to listen now. "He didn't tell you about the baby because he didn't think you'd care. I thought maybe he was wrong. I thought maybe you'd like the chance to be a granddad to this little boy. Despite the appalling example you've set, Cole will make a wonderful father. This child and I are very lucky to have him in our lives. You're the one who's losing out. So, here's the deal, Mr. McKellar. If you have even a lick of sense inside that stubborn head of yours, you'll apologize to your son and try to repair some of the damage your stubborn pride has done to your relationship."

She could tell by the stunned look in his dark eyes that gruff, stern Jim McKellar was not accustomed to being talked to in that manner. Did no one ever stand up to him when he acted like a total jackass? If not, it was past time someone did.

"I'm leaving," she said, moving to the door with as much dignity as she could manage in her condition. "I assume you have your son's telephone number if you come to your senses."

She didn't give him a chance to reply before she let herself out and stalked to her car.

Her seething resentment on Cole's behalf lasted until she'd arrived home. She stamped into the house that still smelled of fresh paint and sawdust. The staircase to the second floor was now completed, leading to a small landing that branched into a nearly completed office on either side. She thought she could work quite comfortably in hers and Cole had assured her he felt the same way about the one he'd helped design for himself. It wasn't like having an entire house to himself, of course, but it would be very nice, she assured herself in an attempt to assuage a sudden, inexplicable ripple of guilt.

That boy has always been a sucker for a woman in trouble.

He spends all his money helping the women who

marry him because they need someone to take care of them.

Jim's acrimonious comments echoed in her mind as she walked through the empty house.

As often as she tried to convince herself that Cole had gained as much from their marriage as she, there was always a niggling suspicion that he was giving the most. She'd wanted to believe his wants were simple— a compatible wife, a family, a nice home to return to from his business trips. But she was tormented by the feeling that there was something more he needed, even if he wasn't aware of it himself. She'd thought reconciling him with his father would be a gift she could give to him, but now she wondered if maybe she'd just made everything worse.

She groaned and pushed her hands through her hair. She only hoped Cole wouldn't someday regret the day he'd ever moved next door to her.

As Stevie had predicted, Cole was not thrilled when he found out what she'd done. Still, he seemed as annoyed with her for making the drive by herself as he was for interfering with his family.

"That was reckless," he said, his tone as critical as it had ever been with her. "What were you thinking?"

She shook her head impatiently. She'd understand if he was angry. She'd even been prepared for a flash of previously unseen temper, but not for this reason. "Obviously, I'm perfectly capable of making an hour's drive. I'm trying to apologize for butting into your affairs without checking with you first."

"It was a two-hour drive round trip," he reminded her. "And anything could have gone wrong. You don't need to be taking chances at this stage in your pregnancy."

Was he redirecting his irritation at her for speaking with his father into a less complicated and slightly more justifiable, in his mind at least, annoyance with her for risking her health?

"I drove carefully and, of course, I had my phone with me. It's not as if your father lives on a different continent, though you wouldn't know it from the way you two behave."

He drew a deep breath and she wondered if he was mentally counting to ten.

"Say what you need to say, Cole."

Another ten-count and he finally spoke, though he kept both the words and the tone coolly controlled. "I appreciate what you were trying to do, Stevie. You just wanted to help."

Taken by surprise, she frowned. "It's okay if you're mad. You can tell me. I know I stepped over the line."

He shrugged, his dark eyes revealing nothing. "Like I said, you were trying to help. You just didn't realize what you'd married into when it comes to your father-in-law."

She hadn't told him everything because she didn't want Cole to become too outraged on her behalf in case the two men mended their bridges in the future. She'd said only that his father hadn't seemed pleased by her visit, nor had he shown particular enthusiasm for a grandchild.

Cole didn't bother with further chastisements. He merely drew a long, deep breath and then said, "In the future, maybe it would be best if we discuss things like this first, though you hardly need my permission to do anything. Just be careful, okay?"

She blinked rapidly. Seriously? That was it? "I'm just saying, it's okay if you're angry. You don't have to walk on eggshells around me."

Squeezing the back of his neck, he looked at her with an expression that bewildered her. Was he actually amused now? "Honestly, Stevie, do you *want* me to be mad? I mean, if it's important to you, I'll try to work up some righteous indignation, but I'd rather have dinner, if it's all the same to you. That chili smells really good."

Of course she didn't want him to be mad, she fumed as she turned to finish preparing the meal. He was absolutely correct that she'd meant well, that she'd tried to reach out to his father for Cole's sake. She'd been fully prepared to make those arguments if he'd scolded her. So why did it perturb her that he'd made her case for her, instead?

She just wanted him to feel free to be himself with her, she thought with a sigh. She didn't want to be seen as a damsel in distress. She wanted him to know she was here for him, too, if ever he happened to be the one in distress.

Would calm, controlled, utterly self-sufficient Cole ever need anything from her? And if he did, would he ever have enough faith in her to show it?

A week later the home offices were ready for occupation. It had taken only five weeks from clearing the attic to the last touches of paint. Stevie was delighted to have the construction out of the way so they could move Cole's things over, finish the nursery and set up the guest room. Meanwhile they'd decided to sell his house, agreeing that what had been Stevie's home would now serve their needs well for many years to come.

They took a weekend off work to move boxes into the

new offices and unpack. Cole had taken advantage of her design experience to help him with his space. He'd told her what he liked and approved the plan she'd then created for him. She'd made use of artwork and other items from his house mixed with a few new pieces she'd bought, keeping the color palette warm and earthy. Her office, of course, was a mix of the grays and greens she loved with corkboard on the walls for the notes and photos and inspiration pages that she always seemed to collect.

Dusty insisted on "helping" with the office setup, winding around their ankles, rubbing her cheek against everything she could reach to make sure it was marked with her scent. Stevie petted the cat fondly, thinking this was as much her home now as it was theirs.

"Here?" Cole asked, holding a framed print of an antique map up against the wall opposite the dormer window.

Stevie tilted her head and studied it with narrowed eyes. "Just a little lower. There. Hang it right there."

He marked the spot with a pencil, then reached for a hammer and nail. Stevie arranged two small bronze figurines of samurai warriors on a shelf above his computer monitor, smiling at the whimsy of them. Cole had only a few personal treasures he cared to display, but he'd shown a fondness for this set, which he said had been a gift. He didn't elaborate and she didn't ask for details, but she took care in finding just the right spot to display them.

Satisfied, she opened another box while he hung the print. A framed photograph smiled up at her when she looked into the box. It rested on several other frames and what might have been a couple of photo albums and scrapbooks. "Oh, I'm sorry. This looks like personal rather than business stuff."

He glanced over his shoulder and went still. "I'm not planning to unpack that box."

She couldn't resist taking out the 5"×7" frame, gripping it carefully between her hands as she studied the woman in the photograph. She wasn't beautiful, not even pretty, exactly, but she had a sweet, pleasant face and a generous smile. Her hair and eyes were brown, her skin tone slightly olive. Though this was only a headshot, cropped just below the shoulders, Stevie got the impression she'd been very thin. The expression in her eyes spoke of warmth and kindness underlain with difficult experience, or maybe Stevie was just projecting what little she'd heard about her. "This is Natasha?"

"Yes."

"She looks amazing," she said sincerely.

"She was. You'd have liked her."

"I'm sure I would have."

Replacing the photo in the box, she closed the lid gently. Cole lifted it onto the top shelf in the big storage closet, then closed the shutter-style door.

Settling on the floor in front of his desk to start connecting wires, he glanced up at her as she stood there watching him. "You can ask," he said, either reading her expression or knowing her so well.

"Only a couple of questions," she promised.

He nodded.

"How did you meet her?"

"We met in high school. She was born with a heart condition and she was sick a lot. One of our teachers asked if I would tutor her in math to help her keep up. We became friends. Lord knows she needed a friend then."

"Why?"

He reached beneath the desk, his voice muffled when he said, "Bad family life. Alcoholic parents, couple of troublemaker brothers. My dad didn't like me hanging around her because he didn't approve of her family— not that anyone else did, either. Even outside of that, everyone treated her differently because they thought of her as sickly. Which I guess she was, but she had a sharp, creative mind and she was trapped in a family that didn't much value academic accomplishments."

Like his own father? Had that lack of parental bonding drawn Natasha and him together?

"Anyway," he continued, emerging with a surge protector cord in hand, "her health got better after high school and she was able to attend college on a full scholarship. Then one of her brothers went to jail and her dad got sick. Her mother tried to talk her into quitting college and moving home to serve as a live-in cook and maidservant, despite Tasha's own health issues. She refused and was forbidden to come home after that, even on holidays. She didn't mind too much since her family's idea of celebrating a holiday was drinking too much and getting into a brawl."

"How on earth did she turn out so well coming from that background?"

He shrugged. "We always joked about it being a recessive gene. She didn't think she was better than her family," he clarified, "but they led a life that didn't interest her, and they couldn't accept her for being different."

That statement seemed to Stevie to even more strongly reinforce her feeling that Cole and Natasha had connected over their similar family issues, though Cole had been spared the alcoholic parents and criminal brothers.

"Anyway, Natasha and I got married not long after college graduation. It seemed like the right move at the time for both of us."

"Your father didn't approve." That wasn't a guess, of course, since Jim had made it clear enough.

"No. Our relationship, which was already strained by my choice to study computer science rather than car mechanics, has been even more distant since. I entered grad school and Tasha got a desk job processing insurance claims. We had almost six years together. Her health was stable enough for the first few years that we were encouraged to start planning a future. We talked about maybe adopting a child—but then, five years ago, she caught pneumonia. She was never able to recover fully, and it was too much for her weak heart to take."

She searched his face. Though he wore no particular expression, his eyes looked dark and clouded. "I'm sorry," she whispered.

He nodded and plugged in another piece of equipment.

She leaned down to brush a light kiss against his cheek. "Thank you for sharing that with me. And now I should probably start dinner."

He pushed himself to his feet and brushed off his hands. "Why don't we go out tonight? We've been working so hard today there's no need for either of us to cook. How about Italian?"

"That sounds perfect. Just let me freshen up and I'll be ready to go."

Minutes later, when she smoothed her hair in front of her bathroom mirror, she saw how tired she looked. No doubt her sharp-eyed husband had noticed. He would feed her and bring her home and make sure she rested.

She had no doubt Cole was very fond of her. Why couldn't that be enough for her?

Her hand fell slowly to her side as the answer hit with a jolt. Despite all her resolutions against fairy tales and unrealistic expectations, her foolish heart had led her into trouble again. She'd fallen head over heels in love—perhaps really in love for the first time in her life—with a man who was fully deserving of her heart. And yet, still a man who couldn't give her what she'd always longed for.

Chapter Ten

The wedding for Tess and Scott was beautiful, the party afterward noisy and fun. Scott's six-year-old twin nieces served as flower girls. They dashed around the grounds of Scott's parents' lovely home after the ceremony, twirling in their pretty yellow dresses splashed with red poppies and tied with long red sashes. Tess's small family mingled easily with Scott's larger one, everyone looking happy to be there to celebrate.

There'd been quite a bit of teasing at the reception about Tess's two pregnant bridesmaids. Jenny was already almost as big as Stevie. Wearing floating knee-length dresses and carrying poppy bouquets, they'd smiled and perhaps sniffled a bit as their friend had exchanged vows with her love.

"You should sit down," Cole suggested as the warm June afternoon wore on. "You're starting to look a little strained."

Acknowledging the logic in his advice, she found a seat at one of the yellow-draped tables set up beneath a fluttering canopy. "I have a touch of a headache," she admitted in a low voice. "It's not bad, just a little annoying. I guess it's from the heat."

He frowned in concern. "Do you want to leave?"

"Not just yet." She looked around the milling, laughing crowd who seemed in no hurry to break up the party. Scott and Tess were obviously having just as much fun, neither of them looking impatient to cut their special event short. "Soon."

"Let me get you something cold to drink, then."

She smiled up at him. "Thank you, Cole."

"He's certainly attentive this afternoon," Jenny commented, sinking gratefully into a chair close to Stevie's.

Realizing she'd been rubbing her temple, Stevie dropped her hand and nodded. "Yes. Not quite to Gavin's levels of hovering, but I'd say I'm being well cared for."

Jenny laughed ruefully. "I made the mistake of mentioning last night that my back hurt a little and Gavin asked if we needed to call his EMT buddy to take me to the hospital. I swear, if he doesn't have a nervous breakdown before this baby gets here, it will be a miracle."

Stevie laughed. "It's probably only going to get worse after your daughter arrives. I can't stop giggling when I think about Gavin with a daughter."

Her hand resting affectionately on her swollen middle, Jenny made a face, though a smile lit her eyes. "He's been in a daze ever since we found out it's a girl. Our poor daughter is going to have a cop dad who'll scare off all the boys who even look at her. I'm sure I'll do my share of refereeing between them in about fourteen years, though something tells me Gavin and his daughter are going to adore each other despite the inevitable clashes."

"I have no doubt," Stevie agreed in amusement.

She glanced across the lawn toward the food tables, where Cole had been detained in a conversation with Gavin. Probably comparing notes on living with pregnant wives, she thought with a chuckle. Her gaze lingered on her husband's face. He seemed to enjoy the gathering of her friends, but she knew he'd be glad to get back home. He had a big work project underway and he would probably put in a few extra hours that evening. He would likely stay up a couple hours after she turned in, then he'd try not to disturb her as he slid into bed. She would rouse when he joined her, as she usually did, and would nestle against him in the cozy sleeping arrangement they'd settled into. She always slept better now when he was there, the room seeming empty and somehow darker when he was away.

"Are you still trying to pretend you don't absolutely adore your husband?" Jenny asked quietly, her gaze focused on Stevie's expression with the wisdom of more than two decades of friendship.

Stevie latched automatically onto a strand of hair, winding it slowly around one finger. "Cole is a very special man," she said after a moment.

"And you're in love with him."

She shrugged helplessly, feeling her eyes burn with a prickle of tears she refused to release. She could never deceive her oldest friend. "How could I not be?"

"And Cole?"

"Is very fond of me. *Very* fond of me," she emphasized. "We have a good life. We've had a great time getting the house ready for the baby and talking about the future. We were good friends for a year before we married, of course, and we've only gotten closer since."

She knew there was no call to justify her marriage to Jenny, but for some reason she wanted to emphasize her good fortune.

"You have seemed happy," Jenny conceded slowly, her brow creased with concern.

Stevie forced a smile. "I know how lucky I am. Really, Jen, don't worry about me. I couldn't ask for anything more."

What more could she expect, anyway? Passionate, flowery words? That would never be Cole's style. Guarantees that he would never desert her or this child? She was confident that would never happen. Promises that he would always be a loyal and faithful husband? Knowing this innately honorable man as well as she did, that was a given. Assurances that he appreciated her mind, her competence, her talents and her body? He made those things known in a myriad of ways every day, not always in words but certainly through action.

Which meant that she just needed to grow up and learn to be satisfied with what she had.

He and Gavin approached the table together. Cole handed Stevie her cold beverage, then rested a hand lightly on her shoulder as he asked her friend, "How are you holding up, Jenny?"

"I'm fine, thank you," she assured him, accepting a glass from Gavin. "I'm having a wonderful time."

"This time next year our babies will be babbling together when we sit around a table." Stevie smiled as she envisioned many pleasant future gatherings.

"Hmph," Gavin grumbled, though he was obviously suppressing a grin when he pointed a finger at them.

"I'm going to be keeping an eye on that boy of yours around our daughter."

"Just so that daughter of yours doesn't break our boy's heart," Cole shot back with a smile.

Stevie reached out to pat her husband's cheek as the others laughed. "Isn't he a cutie?"

Cole growled, but she could tell he didn't really mind her teasing. He was getting used to it by now.

Though large social gatherings with a lot of strangers weren't really his style, Cole had a good time at the wedding. It helped that it wasn't a stuffy, formal affair and that he already knew Stevie's closest friends. He enjoyed watching her with them. The bond between the three women was so strong it was almost visible. Their men fit in well enough, but that special friendship was the heart of the group, the glue that would hold them all together in the future.

He knew these people would be part of his life now, but he didn't mind. They had accepted him warmly despite the early doubts he'd sensed in Jenny and Tess. He believed he'd convinced them that he would never intentionally hurt their friend. His wife.

He'd sat in a folding chair among the rest of the audience as Tess and Scott exchanged their vows, though it had been hard for him to take his eyes off Stevie. She'd looked so pretty standing up there in her bridesmaid dress, her blond curls falling soft and loose to her shoulders, her big blue eyes luminous with emotion. Even round with pregnancy, she was beautiful. He was always proud—and a little amazed—to be seen with her.

He knew she would honor the vows they'd exchanged in their own wedding ceremony. Maybe he wasn't her

Prince Charming, but she seemed satisfied with a knight in practical armor.

Satisfied. For some reason, the word made him wince, though he couldn't quite explain why.

Just what would happen if Stevie's satisfaction ever waned, if she decided he wasn't what she wanted, after all? She was a woman of her word, but he'd never want to hold her to it if she truly longed to leave. Would he ever know for certain if her mother's restlessness nagged at her, too?

For only a moment as she chatted and laughed with her friends, he imagined how it would feel to go back to the life he'd had before they'd eloped. Just him and his cat alone in a comfortable, quiet house. He'd thought himself happy enough at the time, but now the vision made his chest muscles tighten painfully.

Impatient with himself for wasting even a minute of this nice afternoon with pointless imaginings, he shook off the odd mood and focused again on his determination to make sure Stevie had a good time. He couldn't even speculate about returning to a life without Stevie in it. Just thinking about it made his heart hurt—and this was neither the time nor place to analyze his convoluted feelings for his wife.

Two weeks before her due date, Stevie stood in the center of the sage-and-cream nursery, looking around in satisfaction. Everything was in place and waiting to welcome the baby, whose name was still to be determined. She had to admit she was the holdup in that respect. Cole had made several suggestions and had liked several of her recommendations, but she simply couldn't make up her mind on this momentous decision.

She smiled a little as she remembered how tactfully he'd vetoed a few of her more fanciful brainstorms.

"I'm not saying the kid would get beat up on the playground if you give him that name," he'd said about one of them, "but maybe we'd better start martial arts training early."

Laughing, she'd agreed with him that maybe it wasn't the best choice for an Arkansas boy, and had gone back to her research.

She rubbed her temple against another dull headache as she absently repositioned a striped-shade ceramic lamp on the antique nightstand she'd found in a dusty resale shop. The turtle night-light sat beside the lamp, smiling blandly up at her. The pretty little bassinet from Branson was displayed in the center of the room. Next to the new crib sat an overstuffed nursing chair and ottoman—a joint gift from Tess, Jenny and their spouses. It still brought a lump to her throat to admire it, and she knew she would think of her dear friends every time she rocked her baby there.

Straightening the soft hand-knit throw draped over the back of the chair, she thought about resting there for a few minutes now. Her head was really starting to hurt and her back ached. Maybe she needed a nap. Though it was a Saturday, she'd tried to work a little that morning upstairs in her office, and maybe she'd simply sat too long in an uncomfortable position. Not that there was any truly comfortable position these days.

"Stevie?" Cole strolled into the room with a package in his hands. He'd been outside on this hot, late July Saturday and his face was still a little flushed from the humid heat, his hair rumpled the way she liked it best.

Already in a sentimental mood, she felt her heart swell even more at the sight of him. She loved him so much. Lately she'd been thinking she should just tell him how she felt. She'd almost done so a time or two, but something had always held her back. Perhaps the fear of making him uncomfortable, of creating awkwardness between them as the baby's arrival grew ever closer. Maybe even the nagging fear that he would smile indulgently and pat her arm as if writing off her feelings to those annoying pregnancy hormones. It wasn't like her to be shy with her feelings, but in her current vulnerable state, she thought it might break her heart if he didn't believe her.

Unaware of her inner conflict, he said absently, "Looks like maybe another baby gift. The return address on this package says it's from a P. Rose."

"Pepper Rose," she said with a quick smile of delight. "The client I told you about."

"Oh, yeah. You did her kitchen a while ago, right? Big job up on River Ridge?"

"Yes, that's the one. She's such a sweetheart. It was nice of her to—Oh, God."

The pain ripped through her skull like a nail driven into her temple. She put both hands to her head, squeezing her eyes shut against a flash of light, fighting down a wave of nausea.

She heard a soft thud as the package hit the carpeted floor, and then Cole was beside her, his hands on her upper arms. "Stevie? What's wrong?"

"My head," she gasped just before her knees buckled.

He caught her—as she knew he always would.

The pain was overwhelming. "Cole?"

He gathered her close. "I'm here."

"Don't leave me."

"Never. Let's get you to the hospital."

* * *

Time passed in a haze of pain and fear. Stevie was rushed straight into an emergency exam room, her clothes stripped away, IVs and monitors quickly attached to her. She clung tightly to Cole's hand when he was allowed near her.

"I'm here, Stevie." His voice was hardly recognizable.

She gazed up at him through pain-clouded eyes. For the first time since she'd met him, she saw Cole's face raw with emotions—fear, compassion, helplessness. She thought his hand trembled around hers, though it was hard to distinguish her own unsteadiness from his.

"Tell the doctor…" She recoiled against another wave of pain, then forced out the words. "Tell them to save the baby."

"Stevie…"

"Mr. McKellar? You need to step out now," a nurse said, her voice kind but firm. "You can sit in the waiting room. We'll keep you updated."

His hand tightened on Stevie's as if he wanted nothing more than to refuse to leave her, but he nodded grimly and leaned over to press a gentle kiss on her lips. "You remember the bet we made at the mini golf course on our honeymoon?"

She forced an answer through another wave of pain. "I—I remember."

"I never collected on that bet," he reminded her, his tone intensely serious. "I'm naming the prize now. I want a Valentine dance with you at our golden wedding anniversary celebration. You got that, Stevie? You have to pay up, you promised."

A low moan escaped her despite her efforts to swallow it. She managed a nod and a whispered, "I promise."

"Mr. McKellar?"

Groaning in frustration, he straightened and released her hand. "I'm going. You take care of my wife, you hear? Whatever it takes, you save her."

"I love you, Cole," Stevie croaked but she didn't think he heard her. Didn't even know if he was still in the room. She closed her eyes and gave herself over to the medical personnel surrounding her.

She woke much later in a narrow hospital bed, still hooked to IVs and monitors but mercifully free of pain. She sensed the discomfort lurking just outside the range of the medicines controlling it, but for now she was okay, just still very sleepy. The overhead lights were dimmed and the hallways quiet outside the room, so she guessed it was nighttime, perhaps quite late. She vaguely remembered that she was in an ICU unit being closely watched by medical staff. For the moment, however, no one hovered over her bed, which was a relief.

Her restless hand fell on her noticeably flatter stomach and she gasped in sudden fear. The baby?

"He's fine. I have him."

Cole's reassuring voice came from close by. She turned her head to see him settled in a visitors' chair with a snugly wrapped bundle in his arms. An empty portable plastic bassinet sat beside him. He glanced back down with a ridiculously besotted—and absolutely heart-melting—expression on his face. "Looks like Mom's awake," he said softly.

Her heart tightened.

Cole stood and carried the baby to the bed, looking so big and strong in contrast. "He's doing great. The nurse will be back in a couple minutes to check on you both, but so far everything is good."

Her gaze focused without blinking on that little bundle, the beautiful little pink face topped with a blue knit cap. "He's—he's okay?"

"He's perfect. I don't know how much you remember, but he weighed six pounds, one ounce, and he's seventeen inches long. Little, but healthy. He's got quite a set of lungs on him. I heard him protesting an exam a little while ago. Both of you will be staying a few nights here, but everything looks good. Ready to hold him?"

"Oh, yes."

Smiling in response to her fervency, Cole shifted her loose hospital gown to uncover an expanse of skin on which to carefully lay the baby. Cheek to breast, the baby nuzzled instinctively but didn't awaken. Cole rested a hand on the little back. "He's worn out from that fit he threw, I guess."

Stevie could hardly speak. The feel of the warm, damp little face against her skin was incredible. Her heart was so full of love she could barely breathe. She felt a jerk of nerves as she cradled him against her, cupping his little head through the snug cap. He was so tiny. So fragile. So totally dependent.

Something made her look up at Cole then, and she heard the fierceness of her own voice when she said, "I could do this alone if I had to. I could take care of him and support him. My mom did it. Twice. Lots of single mothers do it every day. I could handle it."

He took a step back from the bed, looking almost as if she'd slapped him. He schooled his expression quickly. "I have no doubt you could handle it. Are you telling me that's what you want?"

Her eyes were so heavy, her thoughts clouded. "I just…needed you to know," she murmured, snuggling the warm, sleeping baby as she drifted on a cloud of exhaustion and medication.

"Get some rest, Stevie," Cole said quietly. "I'll be here to watch over you. For as long as you want me."

There was more she needed to say, but her mouth simply wouldn't form the words. She slept, knowing he would be there when she woke.

Cole had believed his inner barriers had been so heavily reinforced during his youth that words could never hurt him now. He'd thought he'd learned years ago to keep his emotions protected, never expecting too much so he wouldn't be disappointed by rejection.

He'd loved Natasha, but he realized now that even with her he'd always held back a small piece of his heart. He'd grieved when he'd lost her, but it hadn't destroyed him.

It had taken Stephanie Joan McLane to storm those old barriers and lay claim to every molecule inside him. He wasn't sure how. Wasn't certain when the walls had fallen. But the events of this day had left him emotionally battered and bleeding.

Seeing the faces of the medical staff who'd attended to Stevie upon arrival, he'd immediately understood the gravity of her situation. Unable to think clearly enough even to make phone calls to her friends, he'd been almost paralyzed with shock, finding it hard to believe he was facing this tragedy again. He'd been wracked with fear of losing the baby. Of losing Stevie. Even knowing now that she would recover, he felt his throat tighten painfully just at the memory of that nightmarish hour.

Though her blood pressure had been carefully monitored during her pregnancy, it had soared rapidly and unexpectedly today. Pregnancy-induced hypertension.

Had she not gotten medical assistance in time, it could have led to seizures, a possible stroke—or even worse, he thought with a hard swallow as he tried to remember everything her doctor had said. Now that the baby had been delivered, Stevie would be fine, though she would remain under watchful care for a few weeks. The doctor had added that future pregnancies were not ruled out, though even more precautions would have to be taken. He couldn't even begin to think that far ahead. Especially without knowing exactly what Stevie had meant when she'd informed him she could raise this child on her own.

His gaze moved from the woman sleeping in the bed to the swaddled child dozing in his arms, Rocking the baby afterward had brought him back to sanity. he'd felt his world slowly begin to right itself again. Maybe his eyes had been damp and his throat dry, but his heart had returned to a strong, steady beat. He'd told himself that everything was going to be all right.

And then Stevie had woken to tell him she didn't need him, after all. He'd always been aware of that, but he'd thought they'd become a well-oiled team, each with strengths to bring to the union. He'd thought she could overlook his flaws, his messed up family, his sometimes-obsessive commitment to his work, in return for the parenting partnership she'd thought she wanted.

He should have known better. He shouldn't have fooled himself that the bubbly, indomitable, fearless Stevie needed anyone, much less him. Maybe she was more like her mother than she had realized, too restless and free-spirited to be tied to anyone other than the child she would certainly adore. How idiotic had he been to think an impulsive elopement based on her uncertainties and his loneliness would last a lifetime?

He'd promised himself he wouldn't try to hold her if she wanted her freedom. He could go back to the way things had been before. But while his job, his routines, his home might eventually be the same again, there would always be something missing. As uncharacteristically maudlin as it sounded, he would always know that he'd left his broken heart in Stevie's small, capable hands.

He settled back in the ICU visitor chair to keep watch over his wife for the remainder of the night. He tried not to think about what might come with morning.

Though sore from her C-section and still easily tired, Stevie felt much better the next afternoon. After a few nerve-racking initial attempts, she and the baby were both finally getting the hang of breast-feeding. She'd texted photos of the baby to her mother, brother and friends, the latter of whom were giving her a couple of days to recover before descending on her, though she knew they were impatient to meet little Liam.

She'd been moved out of ICU and into a regular room, though she would have to remain in the hospital for a couple more nights. Flowers, balloons and stuffed animals from family and friends surrounded her, but she had eyes only for the rosy-cheeked infant sleeping in a plastic bassinet drawn up next to the cushioned chair in which she sat. She wanted to regain her strength quickly and she couldn't do that lying in bed.

Every time she heard footsteps in the hall, she perked up, thinking it might be Cole. She'd sent him home a few hours earlier to get some rest and feed the cat. He'd been so tired from sitting up with her all night that his unshaven face had been a little pale. She'd slept a lot after the delivery, but every time she'd been awakened to tend to the baby, Cole had been there keeping watch, sometimes holding Liam with such tenderness that her heart had melted. He'd said very little this morning. She'd figured that in addition to exhaustion, he was understandably overwhelmed with everything that had happened yesterday.

She smiled brightly when the door opened and Cole came in, a vase of cheery yellow roses in one hand, the bag of personal items she'd requested in his other. "They're beautiful," she said as he made a place for the roses among the other gifts.

Looking a little sheepish, he all but shuffled his feet. "I thought you might like them. You've gotten quite a few deliveries while I was gone, I see."

"Yes, I have. But your roses are the prettiest."

She thought he might smile at that. He didn't. In fact, he looked entirely too serious as he went to look down into the bassinet. "How's he doing?"

"He's perfect," she said with a happy sigh. "He had a good feeding half an hour ago, and he's been sleeping like an angel ever since."

"And you?"

"I'll be glad to get rid of this thing," she said, waving a hand to indicate the IV line still taped into her arm. "I'm uncomfortable, of course, but it's not too bad."

"You wouldn't complain even if it was."

She shrugged, still studying his face. "Cole? Are you okay? Did you get enough rest?"

He sat on the edge of the rumpled bed, facing her chair. "I'm fine."

He didn't look fine. She tried again to get him to smile. "I've finally decided on my choice for Liam's middle name."

They'd agreed on Liam for a first name, but the mid-

dle name had been more difficult for her. Cole had left
the choice to her, saying he had no real preference other
than the first name they both liked. She'd known since
this morning exactly what name best suited her son. "I
want his name to be Liam Douglas McKellar."

A muscle twitched in Cole's jaw. He turned his head,
but not before she saw a flash of emotion cross his face.
Was he touched that she wanted to name her son after
him? Happy? Sad? What?

"You aren't saying much today," she said, her eyes
fixed on his somber profile.

He pushed a hand through his already tousled hair.
"Look, Stevie. I just want you to know that whatever
you need, whatever Liam needs, I will always be here
for you. You have my word on that. But—"

He paused to clear his husky throat.

But? She didn't like the sound of that.

Her throat closed and she felt her hands begin to
shake. Was Cole… Surely he wasn't trying to tell her
he'd changed his mind about being married to her! Had
the reality of actually seeing the baby, the physical reminder of the huge responsibility involved in caring for
this tiny, totally dependent person, made him reevalu-
ate the promises he'd offered so impulsively? Or had
he realized he didn't want to raise another man's baby,
after all? She was pretty sure she could actually feel
her heart breaking at the very thought.

"Cole?" she whispered. "What are you trying to tell
me?"

He took a deep breath. "I know you don't need me to
help you raise him. So, if you've decided you'd rather
do it on your own, if you've come to the conclusion that
you married too quickly and for the wrong reasons, I

won't stand in your way. I'll always be your friend, no matter what. I just want you to be happy."

Her heart started to beat again, slowly, tentatively, as she deciphered what she thought, what she hoped, he meant. She vaguely remembered the fiercely assertive speech she'd made to him while floating on pain meds and shock. "You think I want out of our marriage?"

He pushed his hands down his thighs as if drying nervous palms. "I know you weren't thinking clearly yesterday, but you said—"

That fleeting glimpse of emotion gave her encouragement to break in. "You misunderstood my point, Cole. I'm sure I was babbling, so I might not have made a lot of sense, but I'd have hoped you'd gotten to understand me a little better than this."

He raised his eyes to meet hers. For the first time since she'd known him, she saw self-doubt there. He'd always seemed so quietly competent, so relaxed and assured. But now he looked…almost afraid, she realized with a twist of her heart.

"You said you didn't need me."

Had he really believed she would stay with him only if he made himself indispensable to her? "What I was trying to say was that I could get by without your help, if necessary. I have other options. Family and friends. A nice home and a good job."

He nodded grimly. "I know. But I thought—"

Stevie had always been willing to risk everything for anyone important to her—family, friends, boyfriends. Only with Cole had she tried to be cautious, to put her fear of being hurt above those all-or-nothing instincts. Now she realized how foolish she'd been. What she'd found with him was worth more to her than any relationship she'd ever had before. This was not the time to become shy about expressing her feelings.

She met his eyes squarely. "I'm not staying with you because I need to, Cole. As grateful as I am to you for everything you've done, everything you've promised, that isn't why I want to be with you. I married you because I care very deeply about you. Maybe I didn't even understand how much at the time. During these past six months, I've come to realize that you've always been more than a friend to me. Even when I thought you weren't interested, even when I tried to convince myself I wasn't falling in love with you, I was fighting a losing battle. I won't stay with you because I need to, Cole, but because I want to. If you want me, too, that is."

"I want you," he said almost before she finished her speech. He surged off the bed and leaned over her chair, his glittering dark eyes locked with hers. "And though I know you don't really need me, I need you. I need your laughter, your passion, the color and energy you bring into my life. I don't want to give that up. Not now, not ever. When the doctors told me how much trouble you were in when we arrived at the hospital yesterday, I nearly lost my mind. I couldn't handle the possibility of losing you." He swallowed hard before he asked, "Will you stay married to me? Please?"

She reached up an unsteady hand to cup his firm cheek. "Yes."

Not even bothering to blink away her tears, she gave him a watery smile. "I made a promise to you on Valentine's Day in front of Pastor Dave and Luanne. I knew even then it was for a lifetime. Besides, I owe you a dance, remember? I would never renege on a bet."

"Damn straight," he murmured as he swooped down to claim her lips.

He drew back after a thorough kiss that only left her wanting more. "I'm going to do my damnedest to make sure you're never sorry, Stevie."

She shook her head in fond exasperation. She heard a little catch in her throat as she replied. "You don't have to earn my love. You have it. And I'm confident you care about me, too," she added bravely.

It would be enough, she told herself. She would never have to doubt Cole's loyalty and affection.

"I do care about you, Stevie. But I am also completely, totally in love with you."

She felt her eyes go wide, her lips part in surprise. "You—you are? Since when?"

"Since approximately the day I met you," he answered. "I didn't think I was your type. Wasn't sure I had anything to offer…until I found an excuse to make my move." He gave her a glimmer of a smile. "And then you'll notice I didn't waste any time."

She blinked rapidly against an incipient flood of tears. The last thing she wanted right now was to embarrass him. "I wasn't sure you… I mean, I know you loved Natasha…"

Her voice trailed off uncertainly.

That cheek muscle twitched again, but he spoke evenly. "Natasha was a special woman. I loved her for her courage, for her determination, for her intelligence and grace. I grieved for her when she died, and I felt guilty as hell that I didn't see how critical she was those last few days, even though I know she deliberately hid her pain from me. Then I fell for you, and to be honest, the guilt came back for a while when I thought about what a great life I'd have with you and Liam. Maybe that kept me from showing you just how much you'd come to mean to me. I won't hold back anymore. I love you, Stevie."

"I love you, too." Her voice was thick, but she managed to contain the tears to a mere trickle. "And I'm glad you don't feel guilty now. I'm sure Natasha would have wanted you to be happy. To have a family who loves you and makes you happy."

"She would have," he agreed. "So...don't scare me again the way you did yesterday, okay? When I thought I was going to lose you, too—" Emotion choked his voice, bringing a fresh film of tears to her eyes.

"I'm not going anywhere. I'm so blessed to have you for my husband. And our baby," she added, stressing the *our*, "is the luckiest little boy in the world to have you for a daddy."

He kissed her again as their son gave a little purr of contentment in the bassinet.

Epilogue

The nursery was quiet, all the lights out except for the glowing turtle on the nightstand. Stevie and Cole stood side by side next to the crib, holding hands as they gazed down at the angelic six-week-old baby sleeping soundly on his back. The fuzzy little tiger Cole had purchased on their honeymoon in Branson sat on a nearby shelf next to the floppy-eared Easter bunny, both faithfully on guard against bumps in the night. Cole had given Liam the new Stripy the day he'd come home.

"I'm glad the baptism this afternoon went so well," Stevie murmured. "And that everyone we love managed to be there with us."

The church had been filled with friends and family. Stevie's mother had spent the past week in their guest-room getting to know her grandson. Tom had made the drive to join them today, and had then taken their mom to spend a few days in Tennessee with him before she flew back to Hawaii. Cole's mother and stepfather had traveled from Florida and were staying in a nearby hotel for a few days. Even Cole's favorite uncle Bob had made a rare trip to Arkansas from his Wyoming ranch, where he'd lived for the past twenty years.

But it was the couple who'd arrived at the last minute before the service started that had most startled Cole.

"I have to admit," he said now, "I nearly fell over in surprise when Dad and Peggy walked into that church. I didn't know you'd even sent them an invitation."

She smiled faintly. "I didn't want you to be hurt again if it didn't work out, but Peggy and I conspired to make it happen. She's as fed up with the rift between you and your dad as I am. She told me your father regretted it, too, but he's just been too bullheaded to admit it. Now he can use getting to know Liam as an excuse to spend time getting to know his son again."

"He and Mom were almost civil to each other." Cole shook his head in amazement. "That's near miraculous in itself."

"I think Peggy warned your father that I would be very displeased with him if he wasn't on his best behavior," Stevie said with a little giggle.

Cole's grin flashed white in the shadowy room. "I'd say you definitely got your bluff in on him. Dad looked like he was taking no chances of triggering your temper again."

"I think underneath that gruff, prickly exterior, he might be softening a bit with age. I saw him tickling Liam's cheek and looking very pleased to get a smile in reward."

Not that anyone could resist this beautiful baby's sweet smiles, she thought without even trying to be objective.

Growing serious for a moment, Cole rested a hand on her shoulder. "Don't get too carried away, Stevie. Though I'll do my best to keep the goodwill going, I doubt the relationship between my dad and me will ever be warm and fuzzy."

She nodded. "Just as long as there is a relationship. Family is important. I want Liam to grow up surrounded by people who love him."

He wrapped his arm around her shoulders, murmuring, "There is definitely love in the home we've made for him here. He'll never have to doubt that."

"Yes, there is." She tugged his head down for a long, slow kiss to demonstrate just how much she loved and appreciated him.

Cole took a step backward and held out a hand to her. "Now that we've gotten the all clear from your doctor, I'm looking forward to showing you exactly how much I love you."

Confident that her romantic heart was finally safe in the place where it belonged, Stevie followed him with eager anticipation.

* * * * *

KEEPING HER
BABY'S SECRET

RAYE MORGAN

This book is dedicated to the Mother Lode and all the wonderful towns along Highway 49.

CHAPTER ONE

DIANA COLLINS woke with a start and lay very still, her heart beating hard in her chest. She stared into the dark room. She'd heard something. She was sure of it.

It was midsummer and her windows were all open. That was nice for ventilation, but not so wise for safety, even out here in the country. Silently she railed at herself. She'd known she should do something about getting bars on the windows or...

But wait. There it was again. The intruder wasn't stumbling around in her little turn-of-the-century cottage. He was still outside. He was...singing.

Slowly she lifted her head. She knew that song. She knew that voice.

"Cam," she whispered, and now a different brand of adrenaline was shooting through her veins. She smiled.

"Cam, you idiot!"

Slipping out of bed, she went to the window and looked down toward the lake. She could just make out a dark figure lounging on the pier. The moonlight glinted on a bottle he was holding as he leaned back to let out a wobbly high note.

"Oh, Cam," she said despairingly, but she was laughing. It must have been ten years since she'd last seen him. Joy flashed through her as she dashed around the room, searching for a robe to throw over her light nightgown—and to conceal, at least for the moment, her rounded belly.

Everything was going to be…well, not okay, but better. Cam was back.

Cameron Garfield Wellington Van Kirk the third was feeling no pain. There was no denying it—he'd been indulging. And since he almost never had more than a single glass of wine at dinner these days, he'd been affected more quickly and more thoroughly than he'd expected. He wondered, fleetingly, why he seemed to be bobbing in a warm, mellow glow. It was unusual, but rather nice.

"Maybe a little too nice," he muttered to himself in a Sam Spade accent, trying to look fierce and world-weary at the same time. It didn't really work. But did that matter when there was no one here to witness it anyway?

Never mind. He was going to sing again. Just one more swig from this nice bottle and he was going to sing that song about Diana.

"'I'm so young, and you're…'" he began tunefully, then stopped, frowning. "Wait a minute. I'm older than she is. This song doesn't make any sense."

An owl called from across the water, then swooped by, its wings hissing in the air.

He turned and there she was, coming down toward the pier, dressed in lacy white and looking like something ethereal, magic—from another world. He squinted, trying to see her better. He wasn't used to thinking of her as part angel, part enchantress. The Diana he'd known was a girl who had both feet firmly placed in a particularly earthy sort of reality. At least, that was the way he remembered it.

"Diana?" he whispered loudly. After all, he didn't want to wake anybody up. "Is that you?"

She came closer and he watched, fascinated, then blinked hard and shook his head. It was his old friend Diana all right but it looked like she was floating. Were her feet even touching the ground? Her cloud of blond hair shimmered around her and the gown billowed in a gust of wind and he felt a catch in his breathing. She was so beautiful. How was it that he'd managed to stay away this long?

"Cam?" she said, her voice as clear as the lake water. "Is that really you?"

He stared at her without answering. "If this is heaven," he mumbled as he watched her, enchanted and weaving dangerously right next to the water, "it's more than I deserve."

"It's Apache Lake, silly," she said as she came onto the pier and headed right for him. "Heaven is still to come."

"For you, maybe," he muttered, shaking his head as he looked her over.

She might look magical but she was all woman now—no longer the barefoot girl with the ragged cutoffs and the skimpy cropped top and a belly-button ring—

and like as not a set of bruises administered by her bully of a father. That was the Diana he'd left behind.

This new Diana was going to take some getting used to. He made no move to give her a hug or a kiss in greeting. Maybe that was because he wanted to with a sudden intensity that set up warning flares. And maybe it was because he'd had too much to drink and didn't trust himself to keep it simple.

"Some of us are still holding our options open," he added irrelevantly.

Her answering laugh was no more relevant, but it didn't matter. She was laughing from the pure joy of seeing him again. She looked up at him, still searching his face as though needing to find bits and pieces of the Cam she remembered. She noted how he was still fighting back the tendency to curl in his almost-black hair. And there were his startlingly blue eyes, crinkling with a hint of laughter. That was still the same. But there was a wary reserve that hadn't been there before. He was harder now, tougher looking. The sweetness of the boy had been sloughed away and in its place there was a cool, manly sort of strength.

For just a moment, her confidence faltered. He was large and impressive in a way she didn't recognize. Maybe he'd changed more than she was going to like. Maybe he'd become someone else, a stranger.

Oh, she hoped not, but her heart was in her throat.

"Hey," he said.

"Hey yourself," she said back softly, her dark eyes luminous in the gloom as she searched for clues in the set of his shoulders, the lines of his face. "What are you doing here?"

He frowned, trying to remember. Everything seemed to have fuzzy edges right now. He'd been on his way home—if you could call the house where his parents and grandfather lived his home. Yeah, that was it. He'd been on his way home, and then, he'd taken a detour....

Suddenly the answer was clear. He'd thought he was just stopping by to say hello to an old friend, putting off the homecoming he had waiting for him at the Van Kirk family mansion on the hill not too far from here. But now he knew there was a flaw in his thinking. There had been another motivation all along. He just hadn't realized it. He'd come to find the person he'd missed most all these years. And here she was, not quite the same, but good enough.

He looked down at her, needing nothing more than the Diana she was today. He soaked her in as though he'd been lost in the desert and dying of thirst. She promised to be something better and more satisfying than mere alcohol could ever be.

They said you can't go home again, and maybe that was true. Things could never be the way they'd been before he left. But that was okay. The way Diana had turned out, things might just be better.

"What am I doing here?" he repeated softly, still struggling with blurry thinking. "Looking for you."

"For me?" She laughed dismissively, looking over his shoulder at the moon. "I think you're looking for someone who isn't here anymore."

"You'll do," he said simply.

They stared into each other's eyes for a long moment, their memories and emotions awakening and connecting in a way their words could never quite explain.

"I thought you weren't ever coming back," she said at last, and her voice had a catch in it that made her wince. Tears of raw feeling were very near the surface and she couldn't let them show. But to see him here, standing on her pier, just as he had in those bygone days, sent her heart soaring.

She looked at him, looked at his open shirt and wide belt, his attractively tight jeans and slim hips, the way his short sleeves revealed nicely swelling biceps and she shook her head. He was so like the young man she'd known, and yet so different. The dark hair was shorter and cut more neatly, though it was mussed a bit now and a spray of it still fell over his eyes, just like always. The face was harder, creases where dimples used to be. But the gorgeous eyes were just as brilliantly blue, sparkling like star-fire in the moonlight.

For so long, she'd been afraid his last declaration to her would come true. Even after all these years, the memory of those final words had the capacity to sting deep down in her heart.

"I'm out of here, and I'm never coming back."

She'd thought her world had melted down that day. And now here he was, back after all.

"Naw," he said carelessly. "I never meant it. Not really."

She nodded. She accepted that. She'd waited for a long time for him to show up again. She'd been so sure he would, despite what he'd said. But after years, when it didn't happen, she'd finally started to lose faith.

She remembered when he'd left. She'd been an angry and confused eighteen-year-old, trapped in a broken home, grasping for a reason to thrive. For so long, he'd been her anchor to all that was good in life. And then he'd left and she'd felt adrift in a world without signs or shelter. She'd been so very all alone.

"What I can't understand is why you're still here," he said.

She lifted her chin. "Where did you think I'd be?"

He shrugged. "I don't know. San Francisco maybe. Becoming sophisticated." He half grinned. "Gettin' swanky."

"Swanky?" She laughed. "That'll be the day."

As if on cue, he began to softly sing the Buddy Holly song of the same name, still staring soulfully into her eyes.

"You're drunk," she accused him, shaking her head as though despairing of him.

He stopped short and grimaced. "No. Impossible." He stared hard, actually trying to convince her. "You can ask anyone. I don't drink."

"Cam!" She looked pointedly at the bottle in his hand.

He looked at it, too, then quickly looked away. "Hey, anyone," he called out a bit groggily across the lake, forgetting all about keeping it quiet. "Tell her. She needs to hear it from a neutral source."

She bit her lip, trying not to laugh at the picture he made. "There's no one out there," she told him simply.

"Sure there is." He turned his heavy-lidded gaze on her. "Look closely, now. Can't you see them?"

Turning to lean on the railing, she looked out across the lake to the stand of pines and cottonwoods shivering in the breeze. It was so good to be here in the night with Cam, almost as though a missing part of her was back in place, where it should be.

"See who?"

"Us." He moved closer and spoke very near her ear. "Cam and Di. The boy and girl we used to be. The ghosts are out there."

She could feel his warm breath on her skin. It made her pulse beat just a little faster and she was enjoying it, for now.

It had been so long.

She'd tried asking about him over the years, first in the village, then at the Van Kirk mansion when she'd been there in connection to her job, and the response she had was minimal. She'd told herself that it looked like he was gone for good, that he'd had some sort of rift with his family that couldn't be repaired—that he was never coming back. She'd tried to convince herself to forget about him. But his influence on her was embedded in her soul. She couldn't shake him loose, no matter what.

And at the same time, she'd always known that she could never really have him. But that was a tragic fact of life, something she'd accepted as a given.

She turned and looked at him. "I don't see anything," she told him, determined to be the realist to his crazy dreamer. "There's nobody out there."

"Sure there is." He frowned as though it was a puzzle that needed solving. "Maybe you should have some of this," he said, brandishing the bottle and looked at her hopefully. "Your vision might get better."

She shook her head, rolling her eyes as she did so. He looked at the bottle, drained it, then frowned, silently reproaching himself. She had a right to hate drinking. She'd certainly suffered enough from the stuff.

"Okay. I'll get rid of it." Easy enough for him to say. The bottle was empty now.

"Wait!" She stopped him from sending it sailing out into the water, snatching it from his hand. "Don't litter in my lake. I'll put it in the trash can."

He blinked at her but didn't protest, leaning back on the railing with his elbows and watching her with the trace of a smile on his handsome face. She tossed the bottle and turned back to him. Her heart lurched at the picture he made in the moonlight, part the man he was now, part the memory of the boy. There had been a time when she would have done anything for him. And now? Hopefully she knew better now.

Looking out across the water again, she pretended to squint and peer into the moonlight. "Wait a minute," she said, looking hard. "I think I see them now. Two crazy kids stomping around in the mud."

"That's them," he said approvingly, then looked down at her. "Or more accurately, that's us."

Us. Yes, they had spent time together on that side of the lake. How could she forget? Some of the best moments of her life had been spent there.

Cam was always fighting with his grandfather in those days. After a particularly bad argument, she would often find him down at the far side of Apache Lake, fishing for rainbow trout. She would sit and watch and he would tell her stories about the valley's history or his sister's latest exploit or…sometimes, what he wanted to do with his life. His dreams involved big things far away from gold country. Whenever he talked about them, she felt a sense of sad emptiness inside. She knew she would never be a part of that world.

He always used catch and release, and she would watch regretfully as he threw the shiny, silvery fish back in and they watched it swim away. He didn't realize that she could have used it for dinner. More often than not, the refrigerator at her house was bare and her father was off somewhere burning through the money that should have gone to food, pouring it down his throat in the form of bargain wine. But she never said a word to Cam. She was too embarrassed to let him know her dinner would be a cheap candy bar that night.

Such things were not a problem any longer. She had a nice little business that kept her comfortable, if not exactly rolling in wealth. These days she was more likely to try to cut down on calories than to need to scrounge for protein.

Times had changed. She'd traded a rough childhood for an adulthood that was a lot nicer. She'd been a damaged person then. She was okay now.

Her hands tightened on the railing and she bit down on her lower lip to keep it from trembling. Who was she trying to kid? A woman who was content with her life didn't take the steps to change things that she had recently done.

He hadn't noticed yet. She resisted the urge to pull her robe more carefully over her slightly rounded belly. He was going to have to know the truth some time and it might as well be now.

Well, maybe not now. But very soon.

"Remember the night before I left?" he was saying, his voice low and slightly hoarse. "Remember…?"

He let his voice trail off and she closed her eyes. She remembered all right. She would never forget. It was the one and only time he'd ever kissed her. It wasn't much of a kiss—not at all the kind of kiss she'd yearned for. His lips had barely touched hers. But she still considered it the best kiss she'd ever had.

She felt him touching her hair and she sighed. If she turned to look at him, would he kiss her again? She tried it, moving slowly, opening her eyes to look up into his face. For just a moment, she thought he might do it. But then a look of regret came into his eyes and he turned from her, moving restlessly.

Her heart sank, but she scolded herself at the same time. What was she thinking? A romance with Cam was not in the cards—never had been.

"So where have you been all this time?" she probed to get her mind on other things.

He shrugged. "Pretty much everywhere. Served a few years in the Navy. Worked on an oilrig in the Gulf. Spent some time as a bodyguard in Thailand. The usual stuff."

She nodded. This was definitely not the sort of thing his mother would have bragged about. If he'd been at law school on law review, spent time working as an aide to the governor, or made a pile of money on Wall Street, she would have made sure the local paper covered it in minute detail. Cam had always had a tendency to turn away from the upper class path to respect and follow his own route to…what? That had often been a bone of contention between him and his family.

But who was she to complain? It was exactly that inclination that had led him to be her protector for those early years. Their friendship had started when she was in Middle School. Her father was the town drunk and that meant she was the object of vile names and other indignities that adolescent boys seemed compelled to visit upon those weaker than themselves. Cam was a couple of years older. He saw immediately what was going on in her life and he stepped in to make it stop.

That first time had been like magic. She'd gone for a swim at the park pool. None of her friends had shown up and suddenly, she'd been surrounded by a group of boys who had begun to taunt her, circling and snapping at her like a pack of wolves. She knew she could hold her own against one boy, or even two or three, but there were too many this time and she panicked. She tried to run, which only egged them on, and just when she thought she was going to be taken down like a frightened deer, Cam appeared on the scene.

He was only a few years older than the boys, but his sense of strength and authority gave him the upper hand

and they scattered as soon as he challenged them. He picked her up, dusted her off and took her for ice cream. And that began a friendship that lasted all through her school years. He was her protector, the force behind the calm, the one who made everything okay.

Even when he'd gone away to university, he'd checked on her whenever he came home. He treated her like a big brother. The only problem was, she'd never been able to completely think of him that way.

No, from the start, she'd had a major crush on him. It hadn't been easy to hide. And the effects had lingered long after he'd skipped town and left her behind. In fact, she knew very well it was her feelings for him that had ruined every relationship she'd attempted ever since.

"So you've pretty much been bumming around the world for ten years?" she asked, frowning as she looked at him again. Whatever he'd been doing, it actually looked to be profitable. Now that she noticed, his clothing was rumpled, but top-of-the-line. And that watch he wore looked like it could be traded in for a down payment on a small house.

"Not really," he told her. "The first five years, maybe. But then I sort of fell into a pretty lucrative situation." He shrugged. "I started my own business in San Diego and I've done pretty well."

"Good for you."

He shrugged again. "I've been lucky."

She knew it was more than that. He was quick, smart, competent. Whatever that business was, he was evidently successful at it.

"And all that time, you never thought a simple phone call might have been in order?" she asked lightly. "A letter, maybe? Just some sign that you were still alive and well?"

She bit her lip again. Was she whining? Better to drop it.

He shook his head. "I figured a clean break was the best way," he said softly.

She winced. That was exactly what he'd said that night, after he'd kissed her. But she wasn't going to complain anymore. It wasn't like he owed her anything. When you came right down to it, he'd done more for her than anyone else ever had. What more could she ask for?

That was a dangerous question and she shied away from it quickly.

"So what brought you back?" she asked. "Are you back for good?" The words were out of her mouth before she could stop them and she made a face, knowing she had sounded altogether too hopeful.

He looked at her, then at the moon. "Hard to tell at this point," he muttered. Turning, he looked back toward the little house she lived in. She'd done something to it. Even in the dark, it didn't look so much like a shack anymore.

"Your old man still around?" he asked.

"He died a few years ago," she told him. "Complications from pneumonia."

Complications from being a rotten drunk was what she could have said, he thought bitterly. She was better off without him. But that being said, you didn't get to choose your relatives and he *was* her father.

"Sorry," he muttered, looking away.

"Thanks," she said shortly. "For all the grief he gave me, he did manage to hang onto this little piece of property, so it's mine now. All five acres of it."

He nodded, then smiled, happy to think of her having something like this for her own. Whenever he'd thought of her over the years, he'd pictured her here, at the lake. It was so much a part of her.

"I had a funeral for him," she went on. "At the little chapel on Main. I thought it would just be me and him." She shook her head, remembering. "Do you know, most of the town came? I couldn't believe it." She grinned. "I even had a cousin I'd never met before show up, Ben Lanker. He's an attorney in Sacramento and he wanted to go over the will for me, to see if all was okay." She laughed shortly. "I think he was hoping to find a flaw, to see if there was some way he could get his hands on this property. But I'd had everything nailed down clear and legal when I was dating a lawyer in San Francisco, so he was out of luck."

He laughed along with her, pleased to know she was taking care of herself these days. Looking at her, he couldn't imagine her being a victim in any way.

"So tell me, Cam," she said. "The truth this time. I'm still waiting to hear the answer to my question. What brings you back to your ancestral home?"

He sighed. "It's a fairly easy answer. I'm just embarrassed to tell you."

That made her laugh again. "Oh, now I *have* to hear it. Come on. The raw, unvarnished truth. Give it up." She smiled at him. "What did you come home for?"

Giving her a sheepish look, he grimaced.

"Okay. You asked for it."

She waited expectantly. He took a deep breath, as though this was really tough to admit.

"I came home to get married."

CHAPTER TWO

THE smile froze on Diana's face. She blinked a few times, but she didn't say anything. Still, it felt as though Cam had shot an arrow through her heart.

It shouldn't have. She had no right to feel that way. But rights didn't wait on feelings. She stared at him, numb.

"Married!" she finally managed to say in a voice that was almost normal. "You?"

He coughed discreetly. "Well, that's not actually technically true."

She blinked. "Cam!"

One dark eyebrow rose provocatively. "Take it as a metaphor."

"A metaphor!"

He was driving her crazy. She shook her head. It was too early in the morning for mind games.

"Will you tell me what is really going on?"

He sighed. "Let's just say my mother has plans. She thinks it's time I settled down."

"Really." Diana took a deep breath. So…was he getting married or wasn't he? She was completely confused and beginning to get annoyed. "Who's the lucky girl?"

He looked at her blearily. "What girl?"

She wanted to throw something at him and it took all her strength not to snap back through clenched teeth. "The girl your mother wants you to marry."

"Oh." He frowned as though he didn't see how this mattered. "There's no specific girl. More like a category of women." He shrugged and raked fingers through his tousled hair, adding to his slightly bewildered look. "She has a whole roster picked out. She's ready to toss them at me, one at a time, and I'm supposed to catch one of them in the end."

Diana took a deep breath. This had been the most maddening conversation she'd had in a long time. The strongest impulse she had right now was to push him into the lake. How dare he come back here this way, raising old emotions, raising old hopeless dreams, and then slapping her back down with vague news of pending nuptials? Was this a joke? Or was he just trying to torture her?

But she knew that wasn't really it. He didn't have a clue how she had always felt about him, did he? Well, despite the position it put her in, that was probably a good thing.

Holding all that in as best she could, she looked out at the moonlight on the lake. Funny. Cam had come home and within minutes she had reverted back to being the little raggedy urchin who saw him as her white knight. For years she'd clung to his protection, dreaming that one day, when she was older, he would notice that she wasn't a little girl anymore, that she'd grown into a woman.

She sighed softly. It had always been a stupid goal, and still was. He was from a different world and only visited hers when it suited him. He wasn't available, in other words. And even if he were, what she'd done to her own situation alone would rule out any hopes she might have. She should know better by now. A little toughness of her own was in order. No more shabby girl with her nose pressed to the windowpane.

She tilted her head to the side, a bemused look on her face as she worked on developing a bit of inner strength.

"Let me get this straight," she challenged. "You came back because your mother wanted you to?"

He blinked at her groggily. "Sort of," he admitted.

She shook her head, eyes flashing. "Who are you and what have you done with the real Cam Van Kirk?" she demanded.

"You don't buy it, huh?" He looked at her, trying to be earnest but too groggy to manage it well. The swath of dark hair that had fallen down over his eyes wasn't helping. He was looking more vulnerable than she'd ever imagined he could look.

"Actually," he murmured, "neither do I."

"What does that mean?"

"Come on, Di, you know how it is. You grow up. You begin to realize what is really important in life. And you do things you never thought you would."

Sure, she knew how it was. But she couldn't quite believe it. Not Cam. Not the young rebel she'd idolized for so many years.

"What happened to you, Cam?" she asked softly, searching his face.

He moved toward her, his hand reaching in to slide along her chin and cup her cheek. She pulled back, looking surprised at his touch and pushing his hand away.

And as she did so, she forgot to hold her robe closed and it fell open. Her rounded belly was obvious.

"Whoa," he said, jerking back and staring at it, then looking up at her face. He shook his head as though trying to clear it so that he could deal with this new development. "What happened to *you?*"

"It's not that big a mystery," she said quickly, pulling the robe back. "It happens a lot, in case you hadn't noticed."

He stared at her for a moment, his brow furled, and moved a bit further away, purposefully keeping his eyes averted from her midsection.

"Did you go and get married or something?" he muttered uncomfortably.

She looked away and he frowned. The downside of that possibility was suddenly clear to him. He didn't want her to be married. Given a choice, he would rather she wasn't pregnant, either. But that was clearly settled and he could have no influence on it. But the married part—no, if she were married he was going to have to leave pretty quickly and probably not come back.

Why hadn't he considered this possibility? Somehow it had seemed natural to find her here, just where he'd left her. But of course things had changed. It had been ten years, after all.

"No, Cam," she said calmly. She pulled the robe in closer and looked out at the lake. "I'm not married."

Was he supposed to feel relief at that? Probably not. It was pretty selfish of him. But he couldn't help it. Still, it left a few problems behind. There had to be a man involved in this situation. Cam blinked hard and tried to act sober.

"Who's the daddy? Anyone I know?"

She shook her head. "It doesn't matter."

He shrugged. "Your call. So I guess you're doing this on your own, huh? Are you ready for that?"

She gave him a quick, fleeting smile. "I'm fine, Cam. I can handle this."

Something stirred inside him. Was it admiration? Or regret? He was a bit too groggy to tell. But the Diana he'd left behind had seemed to need him in so many ways. This one, not so much. That was probably a good thing. Wasn't it? If only he could think clearly, he might even be able to tell.

"Well, you know, if you need any help…" he began.

She turned on him, ready to be defensively self-reliant, and that was when she saw what looked like blood. It was trickling down out of his dark hair, making a rivulet in front of his ear. She gasped, then looked more closely, detecting a lot more that had started to dry against the collar of his shirt.

"Cam! What's this?" She touched it and showed him.

"Oh, just a little blood." He pulled out a handkerchief and dabbed at it.

"Blood!"

He gave her a melancholy smile. "I had a little accident. Just a little one."

She stared. "With your car?"

He nodded. "The car wouldn't go where I tried to get it to go. I kept pulling on the wheel and saying, 'Come on, car, we've got to get to the Van Kirk mansion,' and the stupid car kept saying, 'You know you'd rather go see Diana.'" He looked at her with mock earnestness. "So we crashed." He waved toward the woods. "We smashed right into a tree."

"Cam!"

"Just a little one. But I hit my head pretty hard. Didn't you hear it?"

She stared at him, shaking her head. "Oh, Cam."

"It wasn't very far away." He frowned. "I'm surprised you didn't hear it."

"I was asleep."

"Oh." He sighed and stretched out his arms, yawning. "Sleep, huh? I used to do that."

She noticed the dark circles under his eyes. For all his handsome features, he did look tired. "Maybe you shouldn't drink when you drive," she pointed out sharply.

"I didn't." He shook his head. "The drinking came later."

"Oh."

He shrugged. "Just a bottle I found in the trunk after the crash. I brought it along to tide me over while I waited on your pier for the sun to come up." He looked forlorn. "I was planning to invite myself for breakfast."

How did he manage to look so darn lovable in this ridiculous state?

"It's still a little early for breakfast." She sighed, then reached out and took his hand. "Come on."

"Okay," he said, and started off with her. "Where are we going?"

"Where else would the prodigal son go? I'm going to take you home."

The drive up to the Van Kirk mansion was steep and winding. Diana had made it often over the last few years in her little business van. Alice Van Kirk, Cam's mother, had been one of the first people to hire her fledgling floral styling company to provide fresh arrangements for the house once a week back when she'd originally started it.

The sky had begun to lighten, but true dawn lurked at least a half hour away. Still, there was enough light to let her see the turrets and spirals of the Van Kirk mansion ahead, reaching up over the tops of the eucalyptus trees, shrouded in the wisps of morning fog. As a child, she'd thought of the house as an enchanted castle where royalty lived high above the mundane lives of the valley people, and it looked very much like that now.

"Are they expecting you today?" she asked.

When she didn't get an answer, she glanced at Cam in the passenger's seat. He was drifting off to sleep.

"Hey!" She poked at him with her elbow. "I don't think you should let yourself sleep until you see a doctor. You might have a concussion or something."

"Hmm?" he responded, looking at her through mere slits where alert eyes should be.

"Cam, don't fall asleep," she ordered.

"Okay," he said, and his eyes immediately closed all the way.

"Oh!" she said, exasperated and poking him with her elbow again. "Here we are. Which door do you want?" She grimaced. "I don't suppose you have a key, though, do you?"

He didn't answer and his body looked as relaxed as a rag doll. With a sigh, she pulled into the back entrance, using the route she was used to. The servants' entrance she supposed they probably called it. The tradesmen's gate? Whatever, it was just off the kitchen and gave handy access to the parts of the house where she brought flower arrangements once a week. She rarely ran into any of the Van Kirks when she came. She usually dealt with Rosa Munez, the housekeeper. Rosa was a conscientious employee, but she doubted the woman would be up this early.

"How am I going to get you in there?" she asked, shaking her head as she gazed at the dark house. Turning, she reached out and pushed his dark hair back off his forehead. His face was so handsome, his features so classically perfect. For just a moment, she ached, longing to find a place in his arms. But she couldn't do that. She had to be tough.

"Cam," she said firmly, shaking his shoulder. "Come on, wake up."

"Okay," he murmured, but his eyes didn't open.

This made things a bit awkward.

Slipping out of the car, she went to the door and looked at the brass handle, loath to try it. She knew it would be locked, and she assumed there was a security system on the house. Everyone was obviously still asleep. What the heck was she going to do?

Stepping back, she looked up at the windows, wondering if she could climb up and get in that way, then picturing the embarrassment as she hung from a drainpipe, nightgown billowing in the breeze, while alarm bells went off all through the house. Not a good bet.

Turning, she went back to the car and slid into the driver's seat.

"Cam, I don't know what we're going to do," she said.

He was sound asleep and didn't even bother to twitch. She sighed with resignation. She was going to have to wake up the whole house, wasn't she? Now she regretted having come without changing into day clothes. But she hadn't been sure she could keep Cam in one place if she left him to go change, and she'd thought she would just drop him at his doorway and make a run for home. She should have known nothing was ever that easy.

"Okay. If I've got to do it, I might as well get it over with," she said, leaving the car again and going back to the door. Her finger was hovering half an inch from the doorbell and she was bracing for the sound explosion she was about to unleash on the unsuspecting occupants, when the door suddenly opened and she found herself face-to-face with Cam's sister, Janey.

"Diana? What in the world are you doing here?" she demanded.

"Janey!" Diana was immediately aware of how odd she must look standing on the Van Kirk doorstep in her filmy nightgown and fluffy white robe. The shabby slippers didn't help, either.

Janey, on the other hand, looked trendy and stylish in high end jogging togs. A tall, pretty woman about a year younger than Diana, she was evidently up for an early morning run and determined to look chic about it. Diana couldn't help but have a quick catty thought wondering which of the local squirrels and chipmunks she might be trying to impress. But she pushed that aside and felt nothing but relief to have a member of the family appear at the door.

She and Cam's sister had known each other forever but had never been friends. Janey had been aware of the close ties between Diana and her brother, and she'd made it very clear in very public ways that she didn't approve. But that was years ago. When they saw each other now, they weren't exactly warm, but they were perfectly civil.

"Janey," Diana said, sighing with relief. "I've got Cam in the car. He was in an accident."

"What?"

"Not too bad," she reassured her quickly. "He seems to be basically okay, but I think a doctor ought to look him over. And…well…" She winced. "He's been drinking so…"

"You're kidding." Janey followed her to the car and then they were both fussing over her brother.

"Cam, you blockhead, wake up," Janey ordered, shaking his shoulder. "We haven't seen you in years and this is the way you arrive?"

He opened one eye. "Janey? I thought I recognized your dulcet tones."

She shook her head. "Come on. I'll help you up to your room. I'm sure Mother will want to call Dr. Timmer."

"I don't need Dr. Timmer," he grumbled, though he did begin to leverage himself out of the car. "If Diana can take care of herself, I can take care of myself." He tried to pound his own chest and missed. "We're a pair of independents, Diana and I."

Janey gave him her arm and a quizzical look. "I have no idea what you're talking about," she said crisply. "Come on. We'll let your friend get back to her…whatever."

"Diana is my best friend," he murmured, sounding almost melancholy. "My favorite person in this valley. Always has been."

Janey chose that moment to notice Diana's baby bulge. Stopping short, she gasped. "Cam! Oh, no!"

Despite his condition, he immediately recognized the way her mind was trending and he groaned. "Listen, Janey, I just got into town at about 2:00 a.m. Not even I could get a lady with child that fast."

"*Humph*," she harrumphed, throwing Diana a look that took in everything about her pregnancy and the fact that she was running around the countryside in her nightgown, delivering a rather inebriated Cam to his old homestead. It was obvious all this looked pretty darn fishy to her.

Diana almost laughed aloud. If Janey only knew the irony involved here. "Can you handle him without me?" she asked the other woman. "I'd like to get home and try to get some sleep. I do have an appointment back here with your mother at eleven."

"Go, go," Janey said, waving a hand dismissively and turning away.

But Cam didn't turn with her. He stayed where he was, looking back at Diana. "I was just getting used to having you around again, Di," he said. "A little later, when I've had some sleep…"

"You'll be busy getting caught up on all the family news," Janey said quickly. "And learning to give up living like a drifter."

"Like a drifter?" Cam looked up as though that reminded him of something and Diana laughed.

"Watch out, or he'll break out into song on you," she warned his sister as she turned for her car. As she walked away, she heard the Cam's voice warbling, "'Here I go again…'" She grinned.

Cam was back. What did this mean? Right now, it meant she was full of sadness and happiness at the same time.

"The thrill of victory and the agony of defeat," she murmured nonsensically as she began the drive down the hill. A moment later, tears were streaming down her face and she had no idea why.

But Cam was back. Good or bad, things were going to change. She could feel it in the air.

CHAPTER THREE

CAM woke to a pounding headache and a bunch of bad memories. It didn't help to open his bleary eyes and find the view the same as it had been when he was in high school. That made him want to close the world out and go back to sleep again. Maybe he would wake up in a better place.

No such luck. He opened his eyes again a few minutes later and nothing had changed. He was still a wimp for having let himself be talked into coming back here. Still an unfit driver for having crashed his car just because of a freak tire blowout. Still an idiot for having had too much to drink and letting it show.

And still bummed at finding Diana more appealing than ever and at the same time, totally unavailable. Life wasn't exactly glowing with happy discovery for him right now.

Then there had been the humiliating way he'd returned to the green green grass of home. His mother had tried to pretend he was fine and gave him the usual hugs and kisses a mother would bestow upon a returning miscreant. But, his father barely acknowledged his return. And Janey was plotting ways to undermine him and making no bones about it. He groaned. The outlook wasn't bright.

There was one more gauntlet to brave—the most important one right now—his grandfather. There was no point in putting it off any longer.

He made the water in his shower as cold and stinging as he could stand. He needed to wash away the previous day and start over. Maybe if he could just start fresh…

But he already knew it was going to take all his will to be able to stay and do what he'd promised he would do—save the family business, and in so doing, hopefully, save the family.

Funny that it would be up to him. When he'd left ten years before, his grandfather had just disowned him and his father had refused to take his side. His mother was upset about his choice of friends, and his sister was angling to take over his position in the family. To some extent, a somewhat typical twenty-one-year-old experience. But it had all been a culmination of years of unhappiness and bad relations, and something had snapped inside him. He'd had enough. He was going and he was never coming back.

Leaving Diana behind had been the only hard part. At eighteen, she'd still been gawky, a coltlike girl whose antics made him laugh with quick affection. She thought she needed him, though he knew very well she was strong enough to handle things on her own. She was fun and interesting and she was also the only person who seemed to understand what he was talking about most of the time.

But that was then. Things were different now. Diana had proven she could make it on her own, no problem. She'd done just fine without him. And she now belonged to somebody else. She could deny it, but the facts were right there, front and center. She was pregnant. That meant there was a man in her life. Even if he was out of the picture for the moment, he was there. How could it be any other way?

And all that was just as well, actually. Without that complication, he knew he could have easily fallen in love with her. He'd known that from the moment he saw her coming down to the lake, looking like an angel. He responded to her in a way he never did with other women, a combination of past experiences and current attraction. Yes, he could fall hard. And falling in love was something he was determined never to do again.

For just a moment he thought about Gina, the woman he'd lived with for two years and had almost married. But thoughts of Gina only brought pain, so he shrugged them away.

He needed to focus on the purpose of his return. He needed to get ready to face his grandfather.

Diana parked in the same spot she'd used earlier that morning. This time there was a buzz of activity all around the compound. Workmen were putting new doors on the multiple garages and a painter was freshening up the long white fence that edged the driveway. Across the patio, two men were digging postholes for what looked to be a new barbecue center. With all this action, she could see she wasn't going to need to contemplate a break-in this time. Sighing with satisfaction, she slid out of the car and made her way to the back entrance.

She'd traded in her nightgown for a sleek pantsuit she'd picked up in Carmel a few months before. Luckily she could still fit into it. She'd chosen it out of her closet specifically to rival anything Janey might be wearing. It had a high collar and a loose jacket that hid her belly and she knew she looked pretty good in it—always a confidence booster.

The back door was propped open and she went on into the huge kitchen, where Rosa, elbow deep in flour, waved at her from across the room.

"Mrs. Van Kirk is out in the rose garden," she called. "She asked that you meet her out there to go over some new plans."

"Fine." She waved back at the cheery woman and headed into the house. She'd been here often enough lately to know her way around. This place that had seemed so special to her as a child, and then so scary when she was friends with Cam but never invited in, was now a part of her workspace.

Walking down the long hall, gleaming with Brazilian cherry hardwood, she glanced into the library, and then the parlor, to check on the large arrangements she'd brought just a few days before. Both looked pretty good.

Ever since she'd stressed to Rosa that the stems could use a trim and fresh water every few days, her master-pieces were holding up better than they had before.

The Van Kirk mansion was beautiful in a way few houses could be. The quality of the original materials and workmanship shone through. The rich past and full history just added luster. It made her happy and proud just to be here, walking its beautiful halls.

As she rounded the stairwell to head into the dining room and out the French doors, Cam surprised her by arriving down the stairs and stopping right in front of her.

"Good morning, Miss Collins," he said smoothly. "You're back."

She cocked her head to the side and looked him over, fighting hard to suppress her reaction as her heart began a frantic dance in her chest. Here he was. It was really true. She hadn't dreamed what had happened the night before. Cam was back in her life, just when she'd thought it could never be.

He looked so good. Morning sunlight was even more flattering to his handsome face than starlight had been. Dressed in khakis and a blue polo shirt that matched his eyes, he looked hard and muscular as an athlete but gentle as a lover at the same time.

The perfect man—hadn't that always been the problem? She'd never found anyone better. It made her half-angry, half-thrilled, and practically hopeless. Now that he was back, what was going to happen to her peace of mind?

One casual meeting and she was already straying into

thoughts she'd vowed to stay away from. A simple look into that silver-blue gaze and her breath was harder to find and she was thinking moonlight and satin sheets and violins on the terrace. Given half a chance, she would be sliding into his arms, raising her lips for kisses….

No! She couldn't let that happen.

Very quickly, so quickly she hoped he didn't even notice, she pulled herself up short and forced a refocus. Cam was a friend and that was all he could ever be.

So think friend, she ordered herself. Lover thoughts are not allowed.

"Yes," she agreed, putting steel in her spine. "I'm… I'm back."

His gaze swept over her. "You're looking particularly lovely today," he noted, a slight smile softening the corners of his wide mouth.

The corners of her own mouth quirked. "As opposed to what I looked like yesterday, after midnight?" she said, half teasing.

His grin was crooked. "Oh, no. After midnight you looked even better. Only…"

"Did you see a doctor last night?" she broke in quickly, eager to forestall any flirting he might have in mind. They had to keep their relationship on a certain level and she was bound and determined she would be the watchdog of that if he wouldn't be.

"I guess so." He shrugged. "I was pretty much out of it."

"Yes, you were."

Looking chagrined, he put his hand over his heart and

gazed earnestly into her eyes. "I don't drink, you know. Not really. Hardly ever."

If she wasn't careful, he was going to make her laugh, and that was almost as dangerous as making her swoon.

"So you said."

"And it's true. If I'd found a box of crackers in the trunk of the car instead of a bottle of booze, I'd have been all crumbs last night, instead of the sauced serenader I devolved into."

She choked and his eyes sparkled with amusement at his own joke.

"But I do want to apologize. I was rude last night. I took over your lake and ruined your sleep and generally made myself into a damned nuisance."

He meant it. He was really apologizing. She met his gaze in solemn candor. "You did."

"And I'm sorry." His blue eyes were filled with tragic regret.

She laughed softly, shaking her head. She'd missed him, missed his candor, missed his teasing and missed what often actually seemed to be his sincere sensitivity to what she was feeling. But she had to admit, that sensitivity could sometimes slosh over into a subtle mockery and she was afraid he might be working his way in that general direction right now.

Still, they were friends, weren't they? She was allowed to act like a friend, at least.

"I'm not," she said firmly. "I'm not a bit sorry." She smiled up into his face. "Despite everything, it is good to have you back in the neighborhood."

"'Despite everything,' you say." He looked skeptical. "Seriously?"

Her smile deepened. "Of course."

The warmth between them began to sizzle and she knew it was time to pull back. But it felt like resisting quicksand to do it. If only she could allow herself this small island of pleasure. Soon enough she would leave and hopefully wall off any further contact with Cam, except the most casual and occasional kind. Would it really ruin everything to let herself enjoy him, just for this warm spring morning?

Yes. He was looking at her mouth and it sent shivers all through her. She couldn't risk even a tiny moment or two of weakness. Determined, she pulled away.

"I drove by to look at your car this morning," she said over her shoulder as she started to walk toward the French doors that opened onto the gardens.

"How's it doing?" he asked, walking with her.

She glanced at him sideways. "You didn't tell me you'd had a tire blow out."

"Didn't I?"

"No." She stopped in the doorway, turning to face him again. "It's too bad. I sort of liked your story about fighting the wheel in order to get to my place."

He snapped his fingers. "That was exactly what I was doing when the blowout occurred."

She grinned. "Right."

Mrs. Van Kirk, wearing a wide-brimmed sun hat and carrying a basket filled with cut flowers, was out among her prized rosebushes and as she turned, she spotted the two of them and began to wave. "Yoo-hoo! My dear, I'm over here."

Diana lifted her hand to wave back and said out of the corner of her mouth, "Who's she talking to, you or me?"

He stood beside her in the doorway, looking out. "I'd say it's a toss-up."

She glanced at him. "She's your mother."

His eyes narrowed suspiciously as he looked out at where she stood, waving at them. "Sometimes I wonder," he muttered.

Diana didn't wonder. In fact, she didn't have a doubt. Cam looked so much like his mother, it was cute—or frightening, depending on how you looked at it.

"Well, I'm going to go to her," Diana said, turning to leave.

He hung back. "I'm not coming with you. I've got a command audience with my grandfather."

"Oh, no." Stopping, she looked back at him. "Is this the first you've seen him since you came back?"

He nodded, a faraway look in his eyes. "This should be interesting."

To say the least. Diana winced, remembering all those old, painful arguments with the old man when he was younger. She could see by the look on his face that he wasn't as optimistic about the coming meeting as he might pretend.

"I'm surprised you're not taking in a bodyguard," she said lightly, only half joking. "I remember those sessions you used to have with him." Her eyes widened as she recalled some especially wild fights they'd had and she shuddered. "He put you through the wringer."

Cam nodded and he didn't smile. "That he did." His gaze skimmed over her face. "You want to come with me?"

She reared back. "Not on your life. When I was suggesting a bodyguard, I was thinking more along the lines of one of those burly fellows digging posts for the new barbecue center out back."

He laughed. "I think I can handle my grandfather," he said. "I'm older now. Wiser." He cocked an eyebrow. "More agile."

Diana shook her head, suppressing a grin. "And besides," she reminded him. "From what I hear, he's often bedridden. I guess that would give you an advantage."

He laughed again. "Exactly."

Word was that his grandfather was in rapidly failing health. With Cam's father spending most of his time at spa resorts that specialized in "rest cures" and his sister reportedly caught up in playing musical husbands, that left Cam to support his mother and help make some decisions. She was beginning to realize that those circumstances were probably part of the reason he'd agreed to come back home.

"I'll come out and join you if I survive."

"Okay." She winced as she started out through the rosebushes. She shouldn't be encouraging any of this "joining" or chatting or anything else with Cam. Her goal coming in had been to have the meeting with Mrs. Van Kirk and then get out of here as quickly as possible.

It was becoming more and more clear that staying away from Cam had to be her first priority.

The older woman came toward her, smiling.

"Oh, my dear, I'm so glad to see you. Thank you so much for coming by. Come sit with me in the garden and Rosa will bring us some nice tea."

Diana smiled back and followed her to the little gazebo at the far side of the flower garden. Her relationship with Cam's mother had undergone a complete transformation in the last few years. When she was a teenager, she knew very well the woman had considered her a guttersnipe who would contaminate her son if she didn't keep a constant vigil. The one time Cam had tried to bring her into the house, Mrs. Van Kirk had practically barred the door with her own plump body.

Years later, after Cam was long gone and Diana had started her flower business, the woman had hired her periodically, acting rather suspicious at first, but warming to her little by little as the quality of her work became apparent. By now, her affection for the girl she used to scorn was amazingly obvious to everyone—and sometimes resented by Janey.

But Diana was comfortable meeting with her, and she settled into a chair across from her in the gazebo, thinking once again how similar some of her features were to Cam's. She'd been a beautiful woman and was still very attractive in a plush sort of way. Her hair was auburn where Cam's was almost black, and her look was soft rather than hard, but she had the same blue eyes and sweet smile he did.

"I want to tell you how much I appreciate you bringing my son home last night after that terrible accident," Mrs. Van Kirk began. "He was certainly out of sorts for a while, but Dr. Timmer assures us there will be no lasting injuries. He was so fortunate it happened so close to your place." Her gaze sharpened and she frowned. "How exactly did you know the accident had happened?"

"Just lucky I guess," Diana said breezily. This was not the time to go into reasons why Cam felt at home enough on her property to use it as a refuge. "I was glad to be able to help."

"Yes," she said, gazing at Diana as though seeing her with new eyes. "Well, anyway, we'll have tea." She signaled toward the kitchen, where Rosa had appeared at the door. The housekeeper waved that she understood, and Mrs. Van Kirk turned back to the subject at hand.

"Now, I want you to take a look at my new roses." She pointed out a pair of new English heirlooms. "What do you think of them?"

"Oh, they're lovely. That soft violet color is just brilliant."

She looked pleased. "Yes, I've hired a new rose expert to come in twice a week and advise me. I want to make sure I'm getting the right nutrients to my little babies. He's very expensive but I'm so pleased with his work." She looked up. "Perhaps you know him. Andre Degregor?"

Diana nodded. "Yes, he's quite good." And an internationally recognized rose expert. "Expensive" was probably putting it mildly.

"You seem to be doing a lot of work on the estate," she noted, giving the older woman an opening to get the conversation back on track.

"Yes." She settled down in her seat and gave Diana a significant smile. "And that's why I wanted to see you. I'm going to begin a major project. And I want you to take a primary role in the preparations."

"A project?" she echoed brightly. What type of project would involve a flower stylist? She was beginning to feel a faint thread of trepidation about this. "What sort of project?"

"It's something I've been thinking about for a long time." Her eyes were shining with excitement. "I'm planning a whole series of various social gatherings—teas, dinner parties, barbecues, card parties—all culminating in a major ball at the end of next month."

"Oh my," Diana said faintly.

"On top of that, we'll be hosting quite a few guests between functions. I've hired a wonderful caterer from San Francisco—for the whole month!" She laughed with delight at the thought. "And I want to hire you for the decorating. If all goes as planned, this will be quite an undertaking."

"It certainly sounds like it."

"Now, I'm going to want you to put some extra effort into your weekly arrangements and prepare to work up an entire decorating plan for the various parties."

"Really." Diana's smile felt stiff and artificial as she began to mull over the implications. She had a very bad feeling about this. Ordinarily she would be welcoming the new business, but something told her she wasn't going to like this once she got the full picture.

Rosa arrived with a tray containing a sterling silver teapot and two lovely, egg-shell thin porcelain cups with saucers, along with a plate of crisp, slender cookies. Out of the corner of her eye, Diana could see Janey making her way into the garden and she offered up a fervent prayer that the young woman would find her way out again before stopping in to see them. She had enough to deal with here without Janey's caustic comments.

"You have such a good eye for decorating, Diana. I'm really going to be counting on you to help make this very special."

"What is the theme going to be?" she asked as Rosa poured the tea.

"Well, what could be more obvious?" She waved a hand dramatically and leaned forward. "I'm planning to introduce Cam back into the society he should have been a part of all these years," she said emphatically. "That's the theme."

"The theme," Janey said, flouncing into the gazebo and flopping down into a wicker chair, "is that Mother wants to marry Cam off to the most important socialite she can find for him, and preferably the one with the most money. He's raw meat for the voracious upper crust marriage market."

Her words stung, but Diana kept smiling. After all, she'd known this was coming, hadn't she? Cam had said as much, though he'd tried to take it back. He'd come back home to get married.

"Janey!" Mrs. Van Kirk said sharply.

Her daughter shrugged. "It's true, Mother, and you know it. We need the money."

The woman's sense of decorum was being challenged by her daughter's gloomy vision of reality and she didn't like it at all.

"Janey, I will thank you to keep your acid tongue to yourself. We have no financial problems. We've always been able to live just the way we've wanted to live. We're going to be just fine."

"Dream on, Mom." Janey looked at Diana and shrugged. "She won't look out and see the tsunami coming. But you might as well know it's on its way."

The older woman pretended not to hear. "Now, I want you to think this over, Diana. I'm hoping you'll be free." She sighed happily. "Such a lot of activity! It will be just like the old days."

"What old days are those, Mother?" Janey asked, the tiniest hint of sarcasm edging her tone.

"Oh, I don't know." Her mother frowned at her. "Things were more hectic when you children were younger. We had parties. Remember all those picnics we had when you were sixteen? It's been a long time since we've had an actual event here. It's exciting, don't you think?"

Diana was torn. On the one hand, she liked Cam's mother, despite her eccentricities—or maybe because of them. On the other hand, she didn't want to be involved in roping Cam into a marriage—any marriage, good or not. The very thought was darn depressing. It would be awful to see him make a bad marriage just for his mother's sake, but it would be almost worse to see him falling in love with some beautiful young debutante.

Either way, Diana would be the loser.

But that was crazy and she knew it. Cam would marry someone. He had to. It was only natural. She only wished he would do it far away where she didn't have to know about it.

"Poor Cam is going to be sold off to the highest bidder," Janey said. "I wish him better luck in marriage than I've had. But then, I tend to marry penniless jerks, so there you go."

"Janey, please," Mrs. Van Kirk said icily. She'd had enough. "I'd like to talk to Diana alone. We need to plan."

For a moment, Diana thought Janey was going to refuse to leave, but she finally rolled her eyes and rose with a look of disdain on her face. Diana watched her go and for once, she wished she could go along.

How was she going to tell Cam's mother that she couldn't do this? She hated to disappoint her, especially when she was so excited about her project. But the situation was downright impossible. She was going to have to find the right words…somehow.

And in the meantime, she was going to have to find a way to keep Cam at a distance.

CHAPTER FOUR

FILLED with comforting tea and discomforting misgivings, Diana skirted the house as she made her way back toward her car, hoping to avoid seeing Cam.

No such luck. He came around a corner of the house and met her under the vine-covered pergola.

"Hey," he said, looking surprised.

"Hay is for horses," she said back tersely, giving him barely a glance and trying to pass him.

"Channeling our school days, are we?" He managed to fill the passageway, giving her no room to flee. "I guess the meeting didn't go so well."

She looked up at him and sighed. "Oh, it went fine. I'm just a little jumpy today." She made a show of looking at her watch. "I've really got to go. I'm late."

He didn't buy it. Folding his arms across his chest, he cocked his head to the side and regarded her narrowly. "Late for what?"

She hesitated, not ready to make something up on the fly. "None of your business," she said instead. "I just need to go."

He stepped forward, suddenly looking concerned, glancing down at her slightly protruding belly. "Are you okay? Do you need help?"

He was being too darn nice. Her eyes stung. If he kept this up, she might end up crying, and that would be a disaster. Shaking her head, she sighed again and decided she might as well tell him the truth. Lifting her chin resolutely, she forced herself to meet his gaze.

"I'm going to be perfectly honest, Cam. I…I need to keep my distance from you. With all these plans and all that's going on, I can't spend time with you. It just won't work."

He looked completely baffled. "What are you talking about?"

She took a deep breath and plunged in. "Your mother just spent an hour telling me all about the plans to find you a wife. She wants me to help." She took a deep breath, praying her voice wouldn't break. "I don't think I can be involved in that."

"Diana, it's not a problem." His laugh was short and humorless. "She can look all she wants. I'm not getting married."

She blinked up at him, not sure why he would say such a thing. "But you said last night…"

He gave her his famously crooked grin. "I think I said a lot of crazy things last night. Don't hold me to any of them."

"Cam…"

"I'll tell you one thing." He grimaced and raked his fingers through his dark hair, making it stand on end in a way she found eminently endearing. "I'm never going to drink alcohol again."

"Good. You'll live longer and be healthier." She shook her head. She wasn't really worried about that. "Why did you say you'd come back to get married if you don't mean to do it? Maybe the alcohol brought out your true feelings."

He groaned. "What are you now, a psychologist in your spare time? Forget it. This is a 'don't try this at home' situation." He shook his head, looking at her earnestly. "Diana, my mother has been trying to get me to come home and get married for years. I've resisted. I'm still resisting. But she's still trying. That's all there is to it."

She frowned suspiciously. "Okay, you're saying you didn't come home to get married?"

"Of course not."

She waved a hand in the air. "But then why is your mother planning all this?"

"She's always planning things. That's how she lives her life." He shrugged. "Let her go on planning. It'll keep her busy and out of the way."

She frowned, not sure she could accept that. "I don't know."

Reaching out, he took hold of her shoulders, fingers curling around her upper arms, and stared down into her face. "Okay, Diana, here's the honest truth. My mother can make all kinds of plans, for all kinds of parties. She can even plan a wedding if she wants to. But I'm not marrying anybody." His added emphatically, "Anybody. Ever."

Anybody…ever…

The words echoed in her head but it was hard to think straight with his warm hands holding her and his hard body so close. A breeze tumbled through the yard and a cloud of pink bougainvillea blossoms showered down around them. She looked up into his starry blue eyes and had to resist getting lost there.

"What happened to you, Cam?" She heard the words as though from far away and it took a moment to realize the voice was her own.

He hesitated, staring down into her eyes as though he didn't want to let her go. The warning signs were there. She had to pull away. And yet, it seemed almost impossible. When her body wouldn't react, she had only her voice to reach for as a defensive weapon.

"Cam, what is it? What do you have against marriage?"

Her words seemed to startle him and his head went back. He stared at her for a few seconds, then grimaced.

"Once bitten, twice shy," he muttered, releasing her and making a half turn away from where she stood, shoving his hands down into his pockets.

Watching him, shock shot through her system and she barely avoided gasping. What was he saying? Did he really mean what it seemed he meant?

"You've been married?" she said, coming down to earth with a thump.

"No," he responded, looking back at her, his eyes hard. "But I did come close. Not a pretty story, and I'm not about to tell it. Just understand I've been inoculated. I've stared into the abyss and I've learned from that. I won't need another warning."

She didn't know why she was so disturbed by what he was saying. He was a normal man, after all. No, strike that, he was an abnormally attractive man, but with a normal man's needs and desires. Of course he'd had women in his life these last ten years. Naturally he'd been in love. What could be more ordinary? Just because *she* was a nut case and couldn't forget Cam for long enough to have a relationship with another man didn't have any bearing on his experiences. Some amateur psychologist she was; she couldn't even fix her own life, much less dabble in his.

"Well, if that's true, you'd better tell your mother," she said, grasping at the remnants of their conversation to steady herself on. "It's not fair to let her give parties and invite people."

"I said we should let her make plans. I never said she could put on any parties."

She shook her head. "That doesn't make a lot of sense."

"Don't you think I know that?"

He looked so troubled, she wanted to reach out and comfort him. If only she had the right to do it. But then she remembered—even if she had that right, she would have had to stop herself. She couldn't risk doing anything that might draw them closer. She had to think of her child.

"I've got to go," she said, turning and starting toward where her car was parked.

"I'll walk you out to your car," he said, coming along with her.

She walked quickly, hoping to stay at least an arm's length from him. She just had to get away.

"Diana's Floral Creations," he said aloud, reading the sign painted in pretty calligraphy on the side of her tiny little van. "Interesting name."

She threw him a look over her shoulder. "It's pretty generic, I know. I'm creative with flowers, not with words."

"No, I meant it. I like it. It suits you."

She hesitated, wanting to get into her car and go, but at the same time, not wanting to leave him.

"What made you go into this flower business stuff?" he asked her, actually seeming interested.

She smiled. This was a subject she loved. She was on firmer footing here. "I've always been good with plants. And I needed something to do on my own. I took horticulture classes in college so I had some background in it. Then I worked in a flower shop part-time for a couple of years."

He nodded, his gaze skimming over her and his admiration for her obvious. That gave her the impetuous to go on, tell him more.

"It's really a wonderful line of work. Flowers are so special, and used for such special occasions. We use them to celebrate a birthday, or a baby being born or two people getting married—or even the life of someone who has died. They add something to the most emotional times of our lives. And that interests and excites me."

"And also just to decorate a room," he reminded her, since that was what she was doing here at his house.

"Yes," she agreed. "But usually flowers are used to represent an emotion. They're symbols of feelings people have a hard time expressing in words." She stopped, coloring a bit, not used to being so effusive about her line of work. For some reason, she'd felt the need to tell him, explain. Well, now she had. She turned to her car, ready to make her escape.

But he stopped her once again.

"I'm glad you have something you love so much," he told her. "The business I've been running is a bit more prosaic." He hesitated, then grimaced.

"Okay, Di," he said, looking down at her. "I might as well get this off my chest. Here it is. The real reason I came home, the reason behind everything I'm going to be doing for the foreseeable future."

She waited, heart beating, wondering if she really wanted to hear this. She knew instinctively that whatever it was he was about to reveal would have the effect of tying her more closely to this family—this crazy outlandish bunch of people who had once scorned her and her family. And now he was going to tell her something that would make her care about them. It didn't seem altogether fair. But then, life wasn't often fair, was it?

He turned from her, flexed his shoulders and then turned back.

"There won't be any parties. There can't be any parties. The fact is, there's no money."

Diana heard what he said, but she couldn't quite digest it. Janey had said things that had let her know money was probably a consideration, even a concern, but to say there wasn't any... That just seemed crazy.

These were the Van Kirks. They had always been the richest family in town.

"What? What are you saying?"

"I've just been talking to Grandfather, finding out how bad it is. He already outlined the situation to me over the phone a few weeks ago. That's why I came home. And now I know the rest of the story." He took a deep breath and a pained expression flashed across his face. "My family is on the verge of losing everything."

Her head came up. Despite the things his sister had said, she would never have dreamed it could come to this. "You mean bankruptcy?"

He nodded. "I came home for one reason, Di. I came home to try to save my parents from losing their home."

"Oh, Cam, no."

He went on, detailing where the problems lay and how long they had festered, but Diana was thinking about his mother and remembering how she'd seemed oblivious to the dangers as Janey had taunted her with them. She'd thought Cam's sister was exaggerating, but it seemed she was wrong.

She knew without having him explain it that the issue went back years and years. Many of those old fights Cam had with his grandfather centered around the old man's fear that Cam would end up being a drone like his father was. She'd been vaguely aware at the time that Cam's dad had tried running the family affairs and had failed miserably, mostly through his own weaknesses. The grandfather had been trying to groom Cam to be a better manager. Even though Cam hadn't stayed here to take his father's place, it seemed he'd found his way in the world and made something of himself. And now it was Cam whom the grandfather had turned to in hopes of getting the family out of this mess. She wondered if he really had the experience. She knew he had the family background for it. And with his grandfather as his mentor, surely there would be hope that he could use his younger energy to turn things around.

No wonder Cam had been called back. Someone had to rescue the family, she supposed. Why he'd decided to let them pull him back, after all he'd said when he left, was another question, one she couldn't answer.

But there was no doubt the situation was dire. Bankruptcy sounded so radical. And the Van Kirks not living in the Van Kirk mansion? Unthinkable.

Still, this couldn't be her problem. She couldn't let it be. The more Cam talked, the more she wanted to go to him, to throw herself into his arms, to tell him she would help in any way she could. But she couldn't do that. She had to get out of this situation. Her baby had to be the main focus of her life, the reason for living. She couldn't get distracted by old longings. She had to get out of here and leave temptation behind. And that meant leaving Cam behind.

"I'm sorry all this is happening," she told him, trying to be firm. "But I really can't be involved. Do you understand?" She gazed up at him earnestly.

He nodded slowly. "Sure. Of course. You have your baby to think of. You need a calm environment. Don't worry about Mother. I'll explain things to her."

A few minutes later, she was in her car and heading for home again, only this time she wasn't crying. Her face was set with determination. She was going to be strong if it killed her.

Diana was up a tree—quite literally—a black oak to be exact. It wasn't something she usually did and that was probably why she seemed to be so bad at it. It was a typical well-meaning rescue mission gone awry.

She been jolted awake early that morning by small, piercing cries from outside. When she'd wrapped herself in a blanket and stepped out to find what tiny creature was in distress, she'd been led, step by step, to the big old black oak. Looking up, she saw the cutest little black kitten staring down at her with huge golden eyes.

"Oh, no, you don't," she'd grumbled at the time, turning back toward the house. "I know very well you'll have an easier time getting down from there than I would in going up. You can do it. You just have to try." She glanced over her shoulder at the little one as she returned to the house. "And then I hope you'll go back wherever you came from."

That had been hours earlier. In the meantime she'd made herself breakfast, taken the time to do a bit of book-keeping for her business and returned some phone calls, including one from her attorney cousin Ben Lanker in Sacramento. It seemed their uncle Luke, the last survivor from the older generation, had died a week before and left a piece of property in the mountains to the two of them, jointly, as the only remaining descendants in their family. She'd received something in the mail that she hadn't understood, but Ben explained what was going on and suggested they get together and talk it over.

She was tempted to put him off. She already had the only piece of land she'd ever wanted and from what Ben said, the inheritance from Uncle Luke might turn out to be more trouble than it was worth.

But then she remembered that she'd been suspicious of her cousin in the past and she decided maybe she'd better look into the facts.

"One shouldn't look an inheritance in the mouth, I suppose," she muttered to herself.

It could just be that Ben was trying to pull a fast one. He had that slippery lawyer way about him. So she told him she would get back to him soon and find a time when they could get together and go over the situation to see what would be best.

In the meantime, the little cries had grown more pitiful with time, wearing away at her like water torture. When storm clouds began to threaten, she finally decided she had to bite the bullet and climb up or she wouldn't be able to live with herself when the worst happened. She kept picturing the exhausted kitten losing all strength and falling to its death through the gnarled branches.

"I'm coming," she said reassuringly as she hoisted herself up with a foothold on the first major branch, regretting that she didn't have any ladders tall enough to do this job. "Just hold on."

It had been a while, but she'd climbed this very tree often when she was young. The only problem was, she wasn't all that young anymore. Muscles and instincts she'd had at that age—not to mention the fearlessness—seemed to be gone. And the tree was a lot bigger. And she was pregnant. To her surprise, that threw her balance off in ways she hadn't expected. But she kept climbing, reaching for the kitten. And every time her fingers almost touched it, the silly little bugger backed away and climbed higher.

"This is not going to work," she said aloud, staring up at the infuriating cat. "I'm not going any farther. You're going to have to come to me."

Fat chance. The golden eyes just got bigger and the cries just got more pathetic.

"Oh, never mind," Diana said, turning away and giving up. And then she looked down.

Somehow, she'd come further than she'd thought. The ground looked very far away. And as she clung to a space between a branch and the trunk, she began to realize she was going to have a heck of a time getting down.

And the kitten was still crying.

"You little brat," Diana muttered to herself. "Look what you've done. You've got me up a tree. How am I going to get down?"

"Meow," the kitten chirped.

And the rain began.

"I can't believe this," she moaned as drops began to spatter all around her. "Why is everything going wrong at once?"

And that was when she heard Cam's car arrive.

"Oh, no!"

She hadn't seen him for the last two days. She'd almost begun to think he might have taken her last words to heart and might just let her be alone, not try to pull her into his life again. But here he was, so she supposed that had been a bad guess.

She sat very still and watched as he turned off the engine and slipped out of the car. He looked around at the trees and the lake, but his gaze didn't rise high enough to notice her and she kept quiet while he went to the front door and knocked. The rain was still light, but it was beginning to make rivulets down her neck.

"Diana?" he called. "You home?"

Now it was time to make a decision. What was she going to do—let him know she was stuck in a tree? Or just sit here and let him drive away again and try to figure out how she was going to get down on her own in a rainstorm?

It was a rather big decision. She felt like a fool sitting here. And yet, she was liable to break her neck if she tried to get down by herself. It was pretty obvious what her decision was going to have to be, but she put it off as long as possible. She couldn't even imagine the humiliation she was going to feel when she began to call out to him, pitiful as the little animal scrabbling around on the branch above her.

Luckily she didn't have to do that. He heard the kitten screeching and finally looked up into the tree on his own. She looked down. He looked up. He fought hard to hold back a big old grin that threatened to take over his handsome face. She tried hard not to stick her tongue out at him. They both failed.

He came over and stood right under where she was. "Good view of the valley from up there?" he asked.

"The best," she answered, her nose in the air. "I come up here all the time."

"Do you?" He bit back a short laugh. "I see you have your faithful feline companion with you. What's the kitty's name?"

"Once you name them, you own them," she warned. For some unknown reason, she was unable to keep the annoyance from her tone. "Do you need a kitten? I'm putting this one up for adoption." She tried to move a bit without losing her footing. "The only catch is, you have to climb up here and get her."

"Well, I don't need a cat," he admitted. "At least not today. But I will help you down."

"I don't need any help," she said quickly, then bit her lower lip. What was she saying?

"You can get down by yourself?" He just couldn't hold the grin back and that was infuriating.

"Of course."

He shrugged. "Okay then. I'll just leave you to your own devices." He turned as though to head for his car.

"Cam! Come back here." She shivered. She was really getting wet. "Of course I need help getting down. Why do you think I'm sitting here like a lump of coal?"

He tried to control the chuckle that was fighting its way out. "A little humility is a wonderful thing," he noted.

She glared at him, but followed his instructions and

a moment later, she took the last leap of faith and ended up in his arms. He held her for a moment, her feet just off the ground, and looked down into her wet face.

"Why is it that every time I see you I want to smile?" he asked.

She tried to glare at him. "You're probably laughing at me."

"No." He shook his head, and his eyes darkened as he looked at her lips. "That's not it."

She drew her breath in and pulled away, regaining her footing and turning toward her little house. "Let's get out of this rain," she said, and as if on cue, it began to pour. They'd barely made the porch when she remembered something.

"Oh, wait! We forgot the kitten!"

"No problem," he said, pointing just behind her.

She whirled. There it was, looking like a drowned rat and staring up at her with those big golden eyes. Despite everything, she laughed. "You little faker! I knew you could get down if you tried."

"I guess you could call this a mission accomplished," Cam said as he opened the door and they all rushed into the warmth of the little house.

"I'll get towels," she said, reaching into her tiny bathroom. "We'd better dry off kitty first. She's liable to catch pneumonia, poor little thing."

Her gaze flickered over Cam as she spoke and she couldn't help but notice the rain had plastered his shirt nicely against the spectacular muscles of his wonderful chest. Why that should give her a sinking feeling in the pit of her stomach she couldn't imagine, and she looked away quickly.

"Here," she said, handing him a towel. "You take this one."

She caught the kitten as it tried to make a dash for the underside of her couch, toweled it down and then let it go. It quickly scampered into the next room.

"I ought to put her out so she can find her way home," she said, shaking her head. "But how can I put her out in the rain?"

"I think you just got yourself a cat," Cam noted, slinging the towel around his neck after rubbing his thick hair with it. "Here. You need a little drying off yourself."

She opened her mouth to protest, but he was already applying a fluffy fresh towel to her wild hair.

"I can do it," she said, reaching for the towel.

"Hold still," he ordered, not letting it go.

She gave in, lifting her face and closing her eyes as he carefully dabbed at the raindrops on her nose. He smiled, remembering the time he'd had to clean her up in similar fashion after a messy exploding bubble gum incident. She'd had more freckles then, but otherwise she looked very much the same.

Then she opened her eyes and the memory of Diana as a young girl faded. She was anything but a young girl now. She was a warm-blooded angel just as he'd seen her the other night. As he gazed down into her dark eyes, he had the sense that his larger vision was picking up details so sharp, so clear, that he could see everything about her—the tiny curls at her hairline, the long, full sweep of her eyelashes, the translucent shimmer of her skin, the clear outline of her beautiful lips. She was a woman—a beautiful, desirable woman, a woman he had known most of his life and loved just as long—loved as a friend, but the affection was very strong just the same.

And yet this was different. This was something more. A jolt of arousal went through him and he drew back quickly, as though he'd touched a live wire. But he didn't turn away. He stood where he was, watching her as she reached for the fluffy towel and began to rub her hair with it.

He knew he'd had indications of this sort of response to her ever since he'd come back, but this time it was so strong, he couldn't pretend to himself that it was anything but exactly what it was. That presented a bit of a problem, a bit of a conflict. He considered her his best friend, but the way he was feeling today was light years beyond friendship. Did he have a right to feel this way? Or was this a big mistake?

She dropped the towel onto the couch and looked at him, a challenge in her dark eyes, as though she had a sense of what he was feeling and wanted to warn him off. He felt clumsy and that wasn't like him. He just wasn't sure…

"Why did you come here today?" she asked him.

He raised one eyebrow, startled at her question. "I wanted to see how you're doing."

"I'm doing fine." She said it crisply, as though that ought to take care of the matter, and he might as well be going.

But that only put his back up and meant he was going to be staying all the longer.

"Actually I haven't been around for the last few days," he went on, "I was down in L.A. talking to some money people, bankers I've got contacts with, trying to work out some sort of deal to stay afloat, at least for now."

The challenge faded from her gaze and a look of concern began to take its place. That reassured him. The Diana he knew was still in there somewhere.

"Any luck?" she asked.

"Marginal luck." He hesitated, then went on. "I did talk to a real estate broker about selling the house."

"Oh." Her hands went to her mouth and her eyes took on a look of tragedy. "That would flat out kill your mother."

"I know."

"You didn't…?"

"Not yet. I'm hoping to avoid it."

She sighed and nodded. "Have you told her there won't be any parties yet?"

He grimaced uncomfortably and didn't meet her gaze for a moment. "Not totally."

"Cam!"

"It's making her so happy to plan." He looked back at her ruefully. "I hate to burst the bubble on her dream."

"But she's hiring people like Andre Degregor and the caterer from San Francisco. You've got to stop her."

He knew that. He had to do something very soon. But right now all he could think about was how this new electricity he felt between the two of them was working out. Not well, he took it, from the look on her face. She was wary and guarded and wanted him to leave. He rubbed the back of his neck and frowned thoughtfully, about to ask her why. But the kitten was back, looking for attention.

"Oh, kitty, what am I going to do with you?" she said, smiling down at it. "I don't need a kitten. I'm having a baby."

His immediate sense was that she'd said that as a reminder to him, and he took it to heart. He knew she was having a baby. That very fact made the way his feelings toward her were evolving all the more problematic.

"What you do need," he said to her, "living out here on your own, is a dog. Whatever happened to Max?"

"Max?" She smiled, thinking of the golden retriever she'd grown up with. "Max died years ago. He was really a great dog, wasn't he?"

Cam nodded, remembering. There was a time when Max had been part of the whole picture, always bounding out to meet him when he came to fish or to see Diana. Realizing he was gone left an empty spot. Nothing lasted forever. Everything changed.

Moving restlessly, he turned and looked around the room.

"You know, I've never been in here before."

She looked surprised, then nodded. "No one was allowed in here while Jed was alive."

His mouth twisted as he remembered. "Your father was something of a barnyard dog around this place, wasn't he?"

"That he was."

He turned back to look at her. She hadn't invited him to sit down. She hadn't offered a drink or something to eat. She wanted him to go, didn't she? He frowned. Funny, but he didn't want to leave. Everything in him rebelled at the thought.

"I came close once," he pointed out. "I came over here full of righteous anger and tried to come in to talk to him."

She looked up, curious. "What about?"

"You. I came to tell him to stop using you for a punching bag."

She flushed and shook her head. "I'm sure he agreed immediately, once you explained to him how naughty it was to beat up on your teenage daughter," she said dryly.

"He pulled out his shotgun." Cam grinned, remembering. "I took off like a scalded cat." He glanced down at the kitten, now wrapped around Diana's ankles.

"No offense intended, kitty," he said glibly before raising his gaze to meet Diana's. Their gazes caught and held for a beat too long, and then she pulled away and turned to pick up the kitten and carry it into the kitchen where she put down a tiny dish of milk from the refrigerator.

He watched, thinking about that time he'd come looking for Jed. He'd called the older man out and told him if he hit her again, he'd take her away from here. She'd told him again and again not to do it, that it would only make things worse for her. But when he found her with bruises on her upper arms and a swollen knot below her blackened eye that day, he'd raged with anger. He'd had enough.

"You do it one more time and I'll take her with me," he'd yelled at Jed. "You won't see her again."

"Where do you think you're going to take her?" Jed had jeered back at him. "Won't nobody take her in."

"I'll take her to my house. We'll take care of her."

Jed had laughed in his face. "You can't take her to your house. Your mother would die before she'd let a little white trash girl like my daughter in on her nice clean floor. Your mother has higher standards, son. You're living in a dream world."

And that was when he'd come out with the shotgun.

Cam had gone home. He told his mother his idea. Funny thing. He'd been so sure his mother would prove Jed wrong. But the man had turned out to have a keener understanding of how things really worked than he did. His mother had been horrified at the idea. She wanted no part of his crazy scheme. Her reaction had been part of what had motivated him to leave home.

Strange how that had changed. Now Diana was one of his mother's favorite people.

She came back out of the little kitchen and looked at him questioningly, as though not really sure why he was still here. But Cam was still lost in the past, mulling over what had happened with her father in the old days.

"When exactly did your dad die?" he asked her.

She told him and he nodded. "Your dad had a grudge against the world and he set about trying to drink himself to death just to spite us all."

She looked troubled and he added, "I suppose your mother dying pretty much threw him for a loop at some point, didn't it?"

Her gaze rose to meet his again. "My mother didn't die. She left when I was six years old."

That sent a shock through him. "I thought she died."

She nodded. Turning from him, she began to collect the towels. "That was what he wanted everyone to think. But the truth was, she couldn't take it anymore and she headed out. Leaving me behind."

Cam felt a wave of sympathy. He could hear the barely concealed heartbreak in her voice. He started to reach for her, but the moment he made a move, he could see her back stiffen, so he dropped his hand back to his side.

"Have you ever heard from her?"

"No." Her chin rose. "And I don't want to."

"I would think you would want to reconnect, especially now with the baby coming."

She whirled, glaring at him. "You know what? My pregnancy is not up for discussion in any way."

"Oh. Okay."

He frowned. His first impulse was to let her set the rules. After all, she was the one who was pregnant. Pregnant women needed extra care, extra tolerance, extra understanding, from what he'd heard. But the more he thought about it, the more he realized he was bending over backward a bit too much. This was getting a little perverse, wasn't it? He turned back and faced her.

"You mean I'm supposed to ignore your baby and pretend it doesn't exist? Is that what you're asking?"

Her face was set as she went on folding the towels and she didn't answer.

Being purposefully defiant, he asked, "So how far along are you, anyway?"

"Cam!" She glared at him, pressing the stack of towels to her chest. "I will not discuss this with you."

He shook his head. "Sorry, Di, that's not going to fly any longer. I need to know what's going on with you and I need to know now."

CHAPTER FIVE

"DIANA, tell me about your baby."

She stared up at him, holding his gaze with her own for a long moment, then she turned and began to march from the room.

He caught up with her, took her by the shoulders and turned her back.

"Come on, Di," he said, carefully being as gentle as he could be, especially in his tone. "You can't run away from it. Tell me."

"Why?" She looked up but her eyes looked more lost than angry. "There's nothing to tell."

He shook his head and his hands caressed her shoulders. "You can't do this. You can't keep it all wrapped up inside you."

She looked almost tearful. "You don't know what you're talking about."

"That's just it. I'm trying. But you've got to let me in."

She shook her head, her hair flying wildly around her face.

"Come on, Diana. We're friends. Remember? We need to stand together."

She looked up, still shaking her head, but slowly. "Cam…"

"It's me, Cam. You can count on me. But you've got to trust me first."

She sighed and he smiled, coaxing her.

"What are you going to name your baby, Di? Have you picked anything out yet? Tell me. Please?"

She swallowed hard and looked away. When you came right down to it, there was no one else in the world she trusted like she trusted Cam. That was just a fact of life and she couldn't deny it.

"I'm going to call her Mia," she said softly. "My mother's name was Mia."

At any other time, Cam would have been horrified to feel his own eyes stinging, but for once, he didn't care. "Oh, Di," he said with all the affection he had at his disposal. "Oh, sweetheart." And he pulled her close against him. "That's a beautiful name."

Her arms came up, and for just a moment, she clung to him. He pressed a kiss into her hair and held her close. And then she pulled away, all stiff again, and took a step back.

"When is Mia due?" he asked, hoping to keep the connection from breaking again.

But she shook her head and looked as though she regretted what she'd already told him.

"What are your plans? How are you doing physically? Diana, what can I do to help you?"

She took another step away from him. "I'm fine," she said shortly. "Just leave it at that, Cam. I'm doing fine."

He shook his head. "Don't lock me out, Diana."

She stared at him for a long moment, then sighed and said, "Don't you see? I have to lock you out. If I don't…"

"What?" He shook his head. He didn't see at all. "What will happen if you don't?"

She swallowed hard, as though this was very difficult, but she held her shoulders high and went on quickly.

"Here's the deal, Cam. You were my savior when I was a kid. You defended me from the bullies. You made life seem worthwhile. I was going through a pretty rough time where it looked like the world was against me. And then you came."

She closed her eyes for a moment, remembering that day. "And suddenly I had a champion. It made a huge difference in my life and I thank you for it to this day. But…"

He sighed. "Oh, yes, I thought I could sense a 'but' coming."

"In some ways you ruined me."

He stared at her, shocked. "Ruined you?"

"This is how. My expectations in what a man should be, in what I wanted in a man to share my life, became unrealistic. You raised the bar so darn high, I couldn't find a man who could clear it."

He looked at her in complete bewilderment and was close to laughing, but he knew that would be the kiss of death.

"That's nuts."

"No, it's true. I'm serious." She shrugged and sighed.

"I don't know if it was the real you or my enhanced imaginary you."

He groaned. "You make me sound like an action figure."

"But that image was hard for any man to overcome." She bit her lip and then went on. "I tried. For years, I tried. But I couldn't get you out of my mind." She hesitated, wanting to leave it at that. Going any further would be getting a bit risky. But she knew there was a bit more that she had to say.

"So I finally took some affirmative steps and moved forward. I had to. And now suddenly, here you are." She shook her head and looked at him as though pleading for his understanding. "I can't let myself slide back to being that dependent little girl I was in the past. I just can't let that happen."

"I understand that," he said, though it was only partly true. "I respect you for it."

She searched his eyes. "But do you understand that I can't be around you? You distort my reality."

He hesitated, wishing he knew how best to deal with this. Bottom line, he didn't want to take himself completely out of her life. He just couldn't imagine that happening. And he still didn't really believe in all this on a certain level. "That can be fixed."

"No, it can't." She took a step back away from him, as though she'd begun to realize he didn't really understand at all. "I have a baby to think about now. She has to be my focus. Cam, I just can't be around you. I can't live my life hoping to see you smile, hoping to have a minute with you, watching as you go on with what you do. Don't you see that?"

She meant it. He could see it in her face. He rubbed his neck and frowned at her. "This is crazy."

"It only seems crazy to you because you haven't thought about it like I have. Believe me, I've lived it for years. I think I have a better grasp of what I have going on inside, in my heart and soul, than you do. I know what I'm talking about." She looked so earnest. "Please, Cam. Don't come here anymore."

Now that was just too much. "What are you talking about?"

"I need you to leave me alone."

He shook his head, still avoiding the implications of her insistence. "So you're telling me…"

"I'm telling you I need space. This is a hard time for me right now and I need space away from you while I learn what I can do, and what I need."

He felt very much at sea. On one hand, he could understand that she might have had some problems. She was raised to have problems. How could she have avoided it? But he didn't see why she was taking it all so seriously. The problems all seemed repairable to him. If he wasn't around, if they were never together, how could these things be fixed? No, her insistence that he stay away didn't seem reasonable.

There was only one explanation he could think of, one factor that might make her so adamant about keeping him out of her life, and she wasn't bringing it up at all. Turning slowly, he asked the pertinent question.

"Is the baby's father liable to show up anytime soon?" he asked.

Something changed in her face. Turning on a dime, she strode to the door and threw it open.

"Go," she said.

And there was just enough anger brewing in him by that time to do exactly what she said without another word.

It was two days later before Diana saw Cam again.

Thursday was her regular day to change the flower arrangements at the Van Kirk mansion. She usually went in the afternoon, but once she found out that Mrs. Van Kirk was going to a garden club lecture at 10:00 a.m., she slipped in early in hopes of missing her. The last thing she wanted was to have the woman try to pin her down on when she would be available to begin work on the "project."

From what Cam had told her, she assumed the project was as good as dead. Though she felt sorry for Cam's mother, that did get her off the hook as far as having to come up with an excuse as to why she couldn't partici-pate. It just wasn't clear when Cam would finally tell his mother the truth. She was going to have to have some sort of conversation about it sooner or later, but hopefully things would be settled down before that came about.

She parked in her usual spot and saw none of the usual family cars. Good. That meant she had the house to herself—except for Rosa, of course. And then there was the grandfather.

She'd never had a conversation with the old man, though she'd seen him out in the gazebo a time or two when she'd come to change the flowers. Funny, for a man who had been such an influence on the valley, and had made such an impression on Cam's life, he was almost invisible these days. As far as she knew, he spent most of his time in his room in a far wing of the house. Even though she would be working in the house for the next hour or so, she didn't expect to run into him.

She replaced the sagging gladiolas in the library with a fresh assortment of spring flowers and moved on into the dining room where she began weeding out lackluster roses and replacing them with a huge glass bowl holding a mix of yellow tulips and deep purple Dutch irises. At the last minute, she pulled out a few extras and a couple of bud vases and headed for the stairs. She always liked to put a small arrangement in Mrs. Van Kirk's sitting room, and while she was at it, she might as well surprise Cam with a small vase, too. Just because she didn't want to meet him face-to-face didn't mean she wasn't thinking about him.

Thinking about him—hah! She was obsessing on him and she knew it had to stop. But ignoring him when she was handing out flowers wasn't going to fix that problem.

She dropped off one vase in Mrs. Van Kirk's room, then went down the hall to where she thought Cam's room must be. The door was slightly ajar and she knocked softly, then pushed it open enough to confirm her assumption. There was a large bed and a bedside table and cabinets against one wall. Banners and sports items from ten years before filled the other wall. Nobody had made the bed yet and the covers were thrown back casually.

"Naughty Cam," she murmured to herself. What was he waiting for, maid service? He should make his own bed.

She set the small vase with one yellow tulip and one blue iris on the stand beside the bed, then stood back to admire it. Her gaze strayed to the bed itself, and she noted the impression on the pillow where his head had been, then groaned at the way it warmed her just to think of him asleep. She really was a sucker for romance—as long as Cam was the man in the fantasy.

A noise from the hallway turned her head and in that same moment, the door to the attached bathroom opened and Cam came out wearing nothing but a very skimpy towel.

She froze, mouth open, disbelief paralyzing her. In the split second it took to recognize him, he erased the distance between them with one long step, grabbed her and put a hand over her mouth. She gasped as he pulled her tight against him and nudged the door closed with his foot.

"Shh," he whispered against her ear. "Someone's in the hall."

She only struggled for a second or two before she realized that he was just trying to keep her from speaking out loud and making it obvious to whomever was out there that she was in here with a nearly naked Cam. She nodded and then she sagged into his arms and he slipped his hand from her mouth and just held her. The voices went past the room slowly. She thought she recognized Janey's voice, but not the woman with her.

But it hardly mattered. By the time the voices faded, she was lost in a dream. She was in Cam's arms. Hadn't she always imagined it would feel this way? She looked up into Cam's face. His eyes were brimming with laughter, but as she met his gaze, the humor evaporated quickly, as though he could see what she was feeling, and his arms tightened around her.

She had to pull away, she had to stop this, but for some reason, she couldn't. Every muscle she possessed was in rebellion. She felt like she was trying to move in honey—she couldn't do it. Her body, her mind, her soul, all wanted to stay right there and be held by Cam.

His eyes darkened and a sense of something new seemed to throb between them. And then he was bending closer and she gasped just before his mouth covered hers. At that point, she gave up trying. Her own lips parted and her body seemed to melt into his. She accepted him as though she'd been waiting for this all her life.

And she had.

Cam hadn't exactly planned to do this. In fact, he'd been pretty rough on himself, swearing he wouldn't do this or anything like it in rather strong terms. All those things she'd said had been rattling around in his head for the last two days. The more he thought about it the more they didn't make any sense to him—and his own reaction to them made even less sense. He'd always known she had a bit of a crush on him, but he hadn't taken it seriously. That had been long ago—kid's stuff. Things had changed. He'd changed. That was just the point.

So had she changed, too? Were his instincts right? Had her crush turned into something stronger? And if so, what was stopping her from following her instincts and responding to these new currents between them?

The baby's father, of course. What else could it be?

On a certain level, he had to respect that. The bond between a woman and the father of her baby was sacred, even if there were problems between them. He had to stay back, out of the way, and let her deal with the things she needed to deal with.

On the other hand, where the hell was the guy? What kind of a jerk was he? How could he leave Di alone to handle all these life changes on her own? She needed support. She needed her friends around her, if nothing else. As a good friend, how could he ignore that?

But she'd asked him to stay away. Reluctantly he would do the honorable thing and keep his distance, leave her alone.

But, dammit, how could he do that if she showed up in his bedroom like this? *Game over, Diana!*

He had her in his arms and he wanted her there. He had her fresh, sweet scent in his head and the excitement of her touch on his skin and the feel of her soft, rounded body against him and he wanted to drown himself in her body. There was no going back now.

Diana was finally beginning to gather the strength to resist where this was going. It was so hard to push away the man she'd wanted close for most of her life but she knew she had to do it. She couldn't believe, after all she'd been through, after all the serious thinking she'd done on the subject and all the serious preparations she'd made to resist her feelings toward him, here she was, lost in his kiss and loving it. How could this be?

Maybe her response to the temptation that was Cam was so strong because it had been so long since a man had held her and kissed her…but no, it wasn't a man's touch she craved. It was Cam's touch. Only Cam.

She finally mustered the force to pull away from him, leaning back, still in his arms.

"Oh, Cam," she said in despair, her gaze taking in his beautiful face and loving it.

"Hush," he whispered, leaning forward to drop a kiss on her neck. "Unless you want Janey bursting in here to demand an explanation."

She sighed, shaking her head. "Admit it. This isn't working."

He kissed her collarbone. "What isn't working?"

Reaching up, she pushed hard to make him release her. "Our plan to stay away from each other."

He looked amused. "Hey, don't try to pin that plan on me. I never liked it much anyway."

Her sigh was a heartfelt sign of regret. "I thought once I told you face-to-face…"

"That didn't work, did it? Want to try something else?"

"What?"

"This." He leaned closer again and began to nibble on her ear.

She pushed him away. "No! Cam, we have to try harder."

"Hold on." He shook his head, looking down at her in disbelief. "Di, you need to decide what you really want. You order me out of your life, then show up in my bedroom. Either you've developed a split personality, or you're conflicted in some way."

"I was just delivering flowers," she said plaintively, knowing it wasn't going to fly as a serious defense.

"Ah, the old delivering flowers ploy."

"Cam, I didn't mean to start anything like this."

"Didn't you?"

"I thought you were gone."

"You were wrong."

"Obviously." She managed to get a little more space between them, her gaze lingering on his wide shoulders and the beautiful planes of his naked chest. Just looking at him made her stomach do a flip and made her knees begin to tremble. She had to get away from him quickly or she was going to be lost. She closed her eyes and pressed her lips together, then opened them again with more determination. "Now how am I going to get out of here without running into your sister?"

"I heard her go back downstairs a minute ago. You should be in the clear."

She stared at him. She hadn't heard anyone go by again. She'd been deep into kissing him, too deep to be able to process anything else. But he hadn't been, had he? That was something to keep in mind.

Turning away from him, she gathered her supplies,

her hands shaking and fingers trembling, and headed for the door. He pulled it open for her and smiled.

"Give me a minute and I'll get dressed and…"

"No." She shook her head. "I'm going, Cam. This doesn't change anything."

His eyes darkened. "The hell it doesn't," he muttered.

She shook her head again, looking out into the hall to make sure it was clear. "Goodbye," she said. Avoiding his gaze, she hurried away.

She made a quick trip through the first floor rooms, giving her arrangements a last-minute check, then turned to leave and almost ran into Janey.

"Hello." Cam's sister was dressed in a black leotard with a bright pink sweatshirt worn over it. Her hair was up in foil, being colorized. Diana quickly made the assessment that the voice she'd heard in the hallway was her hairdresser. She knew the woman came to the house on a weekly basis.

"I saw your car," Janey said. "I was wondering where you were."

"I was putting flowers in a number of rooms," Diana said, trying hard to sound innocent and casual. "And I'm running late."

Janey's green eyes flickered. "Well, how's that baby coming?" she asked.

Something in her tone put Diana on alert. "Just fine, thank you," she said, looking at Janey hard before starting for the kitchen.

To her surprise, Janey stepped forward and blocked the doorway, looking at her speculatively. "You know, there are people who have practically come out and asked me if Cam is the father."

Diana's heart lurched but she stood her ground. "How interesting. Too bad you don't know the answer, isn't it?" She felt a twinge of regret. Why didn't she just tell the woman Cam wasn't the father and put the question to bed? But hadn't Cam already tried to do that? Janey wouldn't believe her no matter what she said.

"Mother is still planning her parties," Janey said coolly, her eyes flashing. "You do understand what these parties are about, don't you?"

"I think I have a vague idea."

Janey nodded. "We need Cam to marry a rich girl. That's pretty much our only hope of getting out of our current financial difficulties."

Diana held her anger in check, but it wasn't easy. "Good luck to you," she said, and stepped forward in a way that signaled she wanted to go through the doorway.

Janey didn't move out of the way, but her eyes narrowed. "So tell me, how does that fit in with your plans, exactly?"

She glanced down at Diana's rounded belly, making it very clear what she was talking about. She was worried that Diana was going to try to snag Cam for herself. Diana's anger was truly simmering now. How dare she! Well, she could just go on wondering. No matter what she was told, she wasn't going to believe it.

"I don't have any plans, Janey," she said, meeting the other woman's gaze with her own clear vision.

Janey arched an eyebrow. "Don't you?"

"No." She arched an eyebrow in return. "In fact, the parties are going to have to go on without me. I'm going out of town for a while. So you're going to have to find someone else to try to bully." With one firm hand, she gently pushed a surprised Janey out of the doorway and made it past her. "So long."

She walked quickly through the kitchen and out to her car, swearing softly to herself as she went. That woman!

It wasn't until she was in the driver's seat and starting the engine that she remembered what she'd said to her and she half laughed.

So she was going out of town. Funny, she hadn't realized she had a trip in her future until she'd told Janey. But now that it was out in the open, she was glad she'd thought of it. It was probably her only hope to stay away from Cam. And with a little distance and a bit of perspective, she might even think of a way to fall out of love with him.

CHAPTER SIX

DIANA was back in town.

She'd been gone a little over a week. She'd left her occasional assistant, Penny, in charge of supplying arrangements to her weekly clients, and she'd spent a few days in San Francisco with her old roommates.

She'd made a run up to Sacramento as well, hoping to catch her cousin, Ben, but he was gone on business, so she missed him. They had since connected by phone and he was coming to Gold Dust today so they could meet. He had some things to show her.

She was very curious as to what he was up to. Having her uncle leave them a piece of property together was interesting but she wasn't sure if that wasn't going to be more trouble than it was worth. Hopefully Ben would clear some of this up when he arrived.

They were meeting at Dorry's Café on Main and she was on her way there now. She lucked into a good parking place in front of the library under a big old magnolia tree. It was a short walk to the café, but she needed the exercise.

She had a lot of things on her mind, but mostly, she was thinking about Cam. Had absence made the heart grow fonder? Not really. She couldn't get much fonder. But there definitely had been no "out of sight, out of mind" involved, either. Thinking about Cam sometimes seemed to be her main state of being. She was getting better and better at it. And it had to stop.

But there was something else on her mind as well— or should she say someone else? She could feel Mia move, just a flutter, like a butterfly caught in a magic net, but that tiny bit of movement made all the difference. Mia was real to her now like she hadn't been before. Mia was her baby, her child, the center of her future and that meant that Mia was all the world to her.

She was definitely showing, and proud of it. But that made for a different atmosphere as she walked down the streets of the little Sierra town she'd lived in all her life and interacted with the people. Strangely she felt almost as though someone had painted a big red A on her chest when she wasn't paying attention. Suddenly everyone was noticing that she was carrying a child, and most of the looks she was getting were not sympathetic.

Still, what she saw wasn't really old-fashioned small town disapproval. What she had to face every day was even more annoying—blatant curiosity. Everyone wanted to know who the father was. They all knew very well that she hadn't dated anyone for over a year. She had taken a few trips to San Francisco, but other than that, she was busy working with her flowers and hanging out at her lake, with nary a male in sight.

Of course, things were different now. Cam was back.

And it seemed Janey wasn't the only one with suspicions. It was amazing how many ways people could contort a simple conversation into hinting around at the question—*was the baby Cam's?*

Everyone knew that Cam had been her champion once upon a time. Now she was pregnant—and he was back. Was there a connection? It was difficult to find a way to come right out and tell them there was nothing to the rumors when they never actually put the darn thing into words she could refute. They just said something here and left a little hint there and gave her looks that spoke volumes.

She was working on a way to deal with the problem without getting too rude, but as time passed and more and more people got bolder and bolder with their probing, she was beginning to think rude might be the only way to go.

But she smiled and nodded to passersby as she made her way to Dorry's. Maybe this was just the price you had to pay for living in a small town. And bottom line— she loved it here.

Cam saw her going into Dorry's and he stopped on the street to have a two-minute argument with himself. He knew she didn't want to see him or talk to him, but the fact was, he wanted very much to see her and they had plenty of things to discuss. She'd been gone for a week and he'd missed her. That morning in his bedroom had proven one thing—she wanted him. The fact that he wanted her was a given. But no matter how she protested, she'd let the cat out of the bag, so to speak. Left to its own devices, her body would take him in a New York minute. It was just her heart and mind he had to convince.

Just thinking about that morning made him throb and he knew it was going to be very hard to stay away from her. He wanted to talk to her. Hell, he wanted to be with her. Should he leave her alone, give her a few more days of peace? Or should he get on with this?

They were friends, first and foremost. He valued her like he had valued few others in his life. And from the moment he'd seen her the other night, a new element had been added. Of course she knew that. He hadn't been very subtle about it. She attracted him in every way possible.

But he wasn't a nut case. He knew she was out of bounds right now and he respected her need to stay away from him most of the time. He didn't agree with it and he didn't like it, but he had every intention of keeping his distance—for the moment. Until he convinced her it was pointless.

But did running into her here in town count? Not at all, he decided at last. After all, this was casual and public and totally nonthreatening. So he might as well go on in and say hello.

Great. That was settled. He strode confidently toward the café and went in, waving to plump, friendly Dorry with her head of gray curls and nodding to Jim, the tall, skinny mechanic who had worked on fixing his car and was now up to his elbows in a big, juicy cheeseburger. But all the time, he was searching for a familiar looking blonde.

And there she was.

"Hey, good-lookin'," he said, sliding into the booth across from her and smiling.

She looked up and winced. It was like looking into the sun. The light from the big bay window shone all around him, giving him a halo effect. That, along with his dazzling smile, sent her reeling for a split second or two. He was too gorgeous to be real. Maybe she'd just invented him in her head.

Everything about him looked smooth and clean, from the tanned skin showed off by his open shirt, to his beautiful, long-fingered hands. For a moment, she thought she'd lost the ability to breathe. Whenever she saw him unprepared, he made her react this way. No other man had ever affected her like this. Why oh why? It just wasn't fair.

"Go away," she said hopefully, but there was no strength of will behind her words.

"No," he said calmly. "You've admitted that we are friends. Old friends. Dear friends. And friends get together now and then and shoot the breeze. That's what we're doing here."

She raised her gaze to the ceiling and said plaintively, "It would be better if you would go away."

"We're adults, Di," he said pleasantly as he reached across and took a bread stick from the basket the waitress had put on the table. "We can sit in a café and talk."

She looked worried. "Can we?"

He grinned and waved the bread stick at her. "You bet."

Diana shivered and shook her head, trying to ground

herself and get back to reality. "Some other time, maybe," she said, and as she said it she seemed to pick up confidence. "I don't have time today. I'm meeting someone."

"Oh?" He tensed and his sense of humor seemed to evaporate without a trace. Suddenly he was very guarded.

"You'll have to leave before he gets here."

So the person she was waiting for was male, was he? Cam stared across the table at her. She looked nervous. Her usual calm was not evident and her hands were fluttering as they pushed her hair back behind her ear, then reached for her glass of water, then dropped back into her lap. Was he making her nervous? Or was it the pending arrival of her visitor?

He went very still and stared at the wall. His first guess was that this was the father of her baby whom she was meeting in this public place. Had to be. In which case he wasn't leaving until he got a good look at him.

He turned his gaze back and met hers squarely. "Diana, I'm going to be up-front about this. My instincts are to throw you over my shoulder and run off to a cave for the duration."

Diana had unfortunately just taken a drink of water and she nearly spewed it across the room. "What are you talking about?" she sputtered hoarsely, still choking on the water as she leaned across the table in hopes no one else would hear this.

"I'm serious." He leaned forward, too, speaking as softly as he could, but with definite emphasis, and gazing at her intently. "I want to take care of you. I want to protect you. I want to make sure you and your baby are okay." He grabbed her hand and held it. "Everything in me is aching to do that. And I have to know." He grimaced. "Are you going to marry this guy?"

She blinked at him. "What guy?" she asked in bewilderment.

"The father of your baby. Mia's father."

"Mia's... Oh, Cam." She almost laughed, but not quite, and her fingers curled around his and then her eyes were suddenly shimmering with unshed tears. "You're crazy."

His hand tightened on hers. "That doesn't answer my question."

"Who says I have to give you an answer?" She smiled through her tears. "But I will. No, I'm not going to marry anyone. I'm like you. No wedding in my future."

He set his jaw with resolution and looked deep into her eyes. "Okay," he said. "Then I'm warning you, I'm going to do what I have to do."

"As long as you leave me with my feet on the ground," she teased him. "And no caves, okay?"

He shrugged. "Like I said, I'll do what I have to."

The waitress arriving with the salad she'd ordered saved Diana from having to respond to that. She drew back and sat up straight and looked across the table at Cam. She couldn't help but love him for his concern for her and her baby. Still, that didn't change anything.

But this was no place to have that argument. As soon as the waitress was gone again, she picked up a fork and began to pick at her food, and meanwhile, she changed the subject.

"Your mother was on my answering machine twice in the last few days. I'm going to have to call her back eventually. What am I going to say to her?"

His wide mouth twisted. "A warm hello would be nice, I suppose."

She studied his face. "Have you told her yet? Does she understand that you aren't going to be doing the parties?"

Leaning back, he sighed and looked troubled. "I have told her as firmly as I can muster. What she understands and doesn't understand is another matter."

"Meaning?"

"Meaning she is so deep in denial…" He straightened and rubbed his neck. "Well, I did try to have it out with her yesterday. I'm afraid there was a little yelling."

She put down her fork and stared at him. "You didn't yell at your mother!"

He grimaced. "Just a little bit." He definitely looked sheepish. "She drives me crazy. She just won't face reality."

"Didn't you show her some documentation? Facts and figures? Spreadsheets and accounting forms?"

He nodded. "Even an eviction notice."

"What?"

"For one of our warehouses in Sacramento."

"Oh." She sagged with relief. The picture of Mrs. Van Kirk being carted out of her home by the sheriff with an eviction notice was a nightmare scenario she didn't want to see played out in the flesh.

"But I showed it to her to try to convince her of how serious this is. Well, she got a little hysterical and ran out to go to her precious rose garden and fell right down the garden steps."

Diana's hands went to her face in horror. "No! How is she?"

Cam was looking so guilty, she couldn't help but feel sorry for him, even though she knew his mother probably deserved the pity more.

"She was pretty shaken up." He sighed with regret. "And she broke her ankle."

"What?"

He shook his head, his eyes filled with tragedy. "All my fault, of course."

"Oh, poor thing."

He gave her a halfhearted smile. "I knew you would understand."

"Not you! Your mother." But she knew he was only trying to lighten the mood with a joke, and his quick grin confirmed that.

"Don't worry. It's a hairline fracture sort of thing. The orthopedist said she'll be better in about a month and good as new by Christmas."

Diana groaned. "She's got a hard row to hoe," she said. "It's hard sitting still when you're used to being busy all the time."

"True." He looked at her speculatively. "So now we're reversing a lot of plans," he went on more seriously. "We're firing a lot of the workmen she hired and we're letting the caterer from San Francisco go. And the rose expert. And the barbecue center will have to wait for flusher times."

Diana sighed, shaking her head. "I suppose you'll be laying off the floral stylist as well, won't you?"

"Is that what you call yourself?"

She nodded.

He grinned without much humor. "Yup, she's a goner."

Diana sighed again. "Your mother's been my best account."

He gave her his finest cynical sneer. "Such are the ripples in a stagnating pond."

She laughed. "Now that's just downright silly," she told him. "The Van Kirks are not stagnating. I thought you were going to see to that."

He nodded, his eyes brimming with laughter. That was one thing he loved about her, she seemed to get his silly jokes and actually to enjoy them. Not many people could say that.

"I'm doing what I can. I still can't say we've saved the house. But I'm working at it."

"I'm sure you are." She gave him a quelling look. "Now if you would just buckle down and marry some rich gal, all would be forgiven."

"Right."

"But if you're not going to have the parties…"

He frowned uncomfortably. "Well, about the parties…"

"Yes?" she said, one eyebrow arched in surprise.

He made a face. "We're sort of compromising."

"What does that mean?"

"She was so devastated, I had to give her something. So there will just be one party. A simple party. No fancy chefs, no rose experts."

"I see."

"Mother, Janey and Rosa are going to have to do most of the work themselves." He hesitated, narrowed his eyes and gazed at her as though evaluating her mood. "But since she's flat on her back right now, we need a coordinator to take charge."

Diana's head rose. Why hadn't she seen this coming from farther away? She knew she was staring at him like a deer in the headlights. She was thinking as fast as she could to find excuses for saying no to him. She had to say no. A yes would be emotional suicide.

She could just imagine what it would be like, watching beautiful young, rich ladies from the foremost families in the foothills, dressed in skimpy summer frocks, vying for Cam's attention while she was dressed like a French maid, passing the crudités. No, thank you!

"Janey could do it," she suggested quickly.

"Sure she could," he said out of the corner of his mouth. "If we want a disaster to rival the Titanic. She'll undermine it all she can." He gave her a significant look. "There's only one person Mother would trust to handle this."

She stared back at him. "You can't be thinking what I'm thinking you're thinking."

He shrugged and looked hopeful. "Why not?"

Slowly she began to shake her head. "You couldn't pay me enough. And anyway, didn't you say you were broke?"

He nodded. "That's why I'm hoping you'll do it for free."

She laughed aloud at his raw audacity. "There is no

way I'm going to do this at all. Save your breath, Mr. Van Kirk. I refuse to have anything to do with the whole thing."

This could have gone on and on if it hadn't been for the arrival of Diana's visitor. He stopped by their booth, a tall man, handsome in a gaunt way, just starting to gray at the temples, and dressed in an expensive suit. Cam hated him on sight.

"Hello, Diana," he said, smiling coolly.

"Oh." Diana had to readjust quickly. "Hi, Ben. Uh, this is my friend Cam." She threw out a pointed glance. "He was just leaving."

Cam didn't budge. He made a show of looking at his watch. "Actually I think I've got a little more time."

"Cam!"

"And I've got a sudden yen for a piece of Dorry's apple pie. It's been ten years, but I can still remember that delicate crust she used to make."

She glared at him, and so did Ben, but Cam smiled sunnily and went on as though he hadn't noticed the bad vibes, chattering about pie and apples and good old home cookin'.

"Cam," Diana said firmly at last. "Ben and I have something personal to discuss. You've got to go."

He gazed at her intently. "Are you sure?" he said softly, searching her eyes. He wanted to make certain she really meant it, that she didn't want him to stay and act as a buffer for her.

She gave him a look that should have warned him that she was losing patience. "I'm sure. Please go."

He rose reluctantly and flashed her friend a sharp

look, just to let him know he was going to be keeping an eye on him.

"Okay," he said. "I'll be over there in the corner, eating apple pie. In case you need me."

She closed her eyes and waited for him to go. Ben looked bored. Cam went.

But he didn't go far and he kept up his survey of what was going on from a pretty good vantagepoint. They were talking earnestly, leaning so that their heads were close together over the table. It tore him up to watch them. If this was really the guy…

Their meeting didn't last very long. Ben pulled out a portfolio of papers that he showed her, but he packed most of them away again and was obviously preparing to leave. Cam felt a sense of relief. There had been nothing warm between them, none of the sort of gestures people who had an emotional bond might display. If there had ever been anything between them, he would say it was pretty much dead now. In fact, Diana looked almost hostile as Ben rose to leave. And as soon as he was out of sight, she looked up and nodded to Cam, as though to beckon to him. He was already up and moving and he went to her immediately, sliding in where the other man had been sitting.

"I need your help," she said without preamble. She had one piece of paper that he'd left behind sitting on the table in front of her. "Because I don't know how to do this."

"Do what?" he asked. "Sue the guy? Charge him with abandonment? Get some money out of him for child care?"

She was shaking her head, wearing a puzzled frown. "What are you talking about?"

He blinked. "That wasn't the father of your baby?"

She threw her head back. "Oh, Cam, for heaven's sake! Ben is my cousin. I told you about him."

"You did?" Her cousin. It figured. The body language had been all wrong for lovers, or even current enemies who were past lovers. He should have known. Feeling a little foolish, but even more relieved, he took a deep breath and calmed down. "Oh. Maybe you did."

"Never mind that," she said, staring down at the paper. "Here's the deal. Ben's a lawyer. He always seems to be looking for a weak spot to exploit." She looked up, wrinkling her nose. "You know what I mean? Our uncle Luke, my father's older brother, died last week. I met him a few times years ago and he came to my father's funeral. But to my shock, he had a little piece of land in the mountains and he left it to Ben and me."

"The two of you together?" That could be a seemingly lucky break but with a sword of Damocles hanging over it.

"Yes. I assume he thought we would sell it and share the revenue or one would buy the other out. Whatever."

"Okay. What's the problem?"

She frowned, chewing her lip. "Ben wants to buy me out. But…" She made a face, thought for a moment, then leaned closer, speaking softly. "I know this is going to sound really horrible, but I don't trust him. Everything he says seems logical enough and it sounds good and all. But, well, he tried to find a way to get a piece of my lake property when my dad died. He wasn't all that open about it, but I could tell he was snooping around here for a purpose. And now I just can't help but wonder…"

"Better safe than sorry," he agreed. "Where's the land?"

"That's just it. He seems a little vague about that. He does say it's out in the sticks, far from any amenities and there seem to be some encumbrances on it that are going to make things difficult. I did get something in the mail myself, something from my uncle's lawyer, but I couldn't make heads nor tails of it and when I tried to call him, the number didn't seem to work. Ben gave me this paper with the parcel number and coordinates, but as far as a map on how to get there, he was very unhelpful."

"Has he been out to take a look at it?"

"He says he has. He says it's pretty barren. Flatland with not even a lot of vegetation. No views. Nothing."

Cam nodded, thinking that over. "So you're a bit skeptical."

She made a face. "I hate to say it, but yes. Color me skeptical."

"And you would like to go take a look for yourself." He nodded again, assessing things. "I think that's good. You need to know a little more about where it is and what condition it's in before you make any drastic moves."

"I think so," she said. "For all I know, it's a garden paradise or a great site to build a house on." She squinted at him hopefully. "I just thought you might know what state or county agencies to go to and things like that. Or maybe you have connections in the Forest Service?"

"I know some people who might be able to help." He

looked over the paper for another moment. "Can I take this with me?"

"Of course."

"Good." He folded it and put it in his pocket, then gave her a sardonic look. "I'm going to have to pull some strings, you know. I might have to call in some favors. Use my family's influence." His smile was suddenly wicked. "And after I've done all that, going out of my way, putting my reputation on the line, going all out to do something for you…" His shrug was teasingly significant. "Well, I'm sure you're going to be more open to doing a favor for me in return."

It was obvious he was still trying to get her to manage the party for his mother—the last thing on earth she wanted to do.

"Cam!"

His wide mouth turned down at the corners for just a moment. "Just think about it. That's all I ask." He patted the paper in his pocket. "I'll get back to you on this." His smile returned to being warm and natural. "You'll trust me?"

"Of course I'll trust you." She smiled back at him. It just wasn't possible not to. "Now go away," she said.

Actually he was late for a meeting at the mayor's office, so for once he obeyed her. But first, he leaned forward, caught her hand in his and brought it to his lips, kissing her palm.

"See you later," he promised, giving her a melting look.

She shook her head, half-laughing at him as he slid out and left the café. But as she looked around the room at the glances she was getting, her face got very hot. It was obvious a lot of people had witnessed that hand kissing thing and could hardly wait to get on their cell phones to tell their friends what they'd seen.

Small towns!

CHAPTER SEVEN

IT ONLY took Cam two days to get all the information Diana needed to make a trek up to see the land. She was thrilled when he called her with the news. So now she'd fed the kitten and watered her flower garden and dressed herself in hiking clothes and was ready to go. This was totally an adventure and she was looking forward to it. She just had to wait for Cam to show up with the map of the location of where she was going.

She knew she was not acting according to plan. She'd sworn she was going to stay away from Cam—far, far away. She wasn't going to risk falling back into the patterns that had ruled her life for so long. She was a grown woman with a child on the way and she couldn't afford to act like a lovesick teenager.

She knew asking for his help put her in a weaker position in refusing to help his mother, and yet, she'd done it anyway. Somehow Cam kept weaving his way through the threads of her days, finding a reason here, an excuse there, and before she knew it, she was almost back in the fold, tangled in his life, loving him again, unable to imagine a future without him.

It had to stop. Right after he gave her the map. She had the grace to laugh out loud as she had that thought. What a ridiculous fool she was!

She heard his car and hurried out to meet him, hoping to get the map and send him on his way. He got out of the car and leaned against it, watching her come toward him with a look of pleasure on his face. She couldn't help but smile.

"Oh, Cam, don't do that."

"Don't do what? Enjoy you?"

She gave him a look. "Do you have the map?"

"Yes, I do."

She looked at him. Both hands were empty.

"Where is it?"

"In the car."

"Oh." She tried to look around him. "May I have it?"

"No."

She stared at him. "What do you mean?"

His eyes sparkled in the sun. "I'm the keeper of the map. I'll handle all navigational duties."

She put her hands on her hips and gave him a mock glare. "That'll be a little hard to do, since you'll be here and I'll be the one approaching the site," she said crisply.

"Au contraire," he countered smugly. "Since we're going in my car…"

"No way!"

"And I have the picnic prepared by Rosa this very

morning and packed away in an awesome picnic basket, with accoutrements for two."

She drew in a quick breath. "I never said you could come with me."

He gave her the patented lopsided grin that so often had young ladies swooning in the aisles. "That's right, you never did. But I'm coming anyway."

Fighting this was probably a losing battle and not worth the effort as it stood, but still, she frowned, trying to think of a way out. "Can I just see the map?"

"Sure. But I'll hold it."

She groaned at his lack of trust, but that was forgotten as he spread out the map and showed her where her property lay.

"Ohmigosh, that's really far from any main roads. I thought it would be closer to Lake Tahoe."

"It's uncharted territory. Just be glad it's not winter. Think about the Donner party."

She shuddered. "No, thanks." She frowned at him, trying to be fierce. "Now if you'll just give me the map."

He smiled and dropped a sudden, unexpected kiss on her forehead. "I go with the map. Take it or leave it."

She shook her head, but a slight smile was teasing her lips and her heart was beating just a little faster. "What a bully you are."

"Guilty as charged. Let's go."

They went.

It was a lovely drive through the foothills and then into the taller mountains. They passed through small idyllic towns on the way, and little enclaves of farm or ranch houses. Cows, horses and alpacas seemed to be grazing everywhere on the still-green grasses. They talked and laughed and pointed out the sights, and all in all, had a very good time. The final segment was a fifteen-mile ride on a dirt road and that was another story. For almost half an hour, they were bouncing so hard, conversation was impossible.

And then they arrived. Cam brought the car to a stop in a cloud of dust and they both sat there, staring out at the open area. For a moment or two, neither said a word.

Finally Diana asked pitifully, "Are you sure this is it?"

"Afraid so," he said.

She turned to gaze at him, a look of irony in her eyes. "I don't think there could be an uglier patch of land in all the Sierras, do you?"

"It's definitely an ugly little spud," he said out of the side of his mouth, shaking his head. "I don't think anyone is going to want to build here. There are no trees, no view, no nothing."

"No paved road," she pointed out, wincing as she looked back at all the rocks and gullies they were going to have to go back through. "Looks like the best thing to do would be to take Ben up on his offer and let him buy me out."

"Maybe." Cam frowned, leaning forward on the steering wheel. "Though I can't help wondering why he wants it—or whom he's going to sell it to. I can't see one redeeming element here."

She let out a sigh. "Darn. I was hoping for a bit of good luck for a change."

"Ya gotta make your own luck, sweetheart," Cam said in his best Sam Spade imitation. "That's the way the game is played."

She made a face at him and admitted, "I don't even see a place to have a picnic here. And we passed a nice park about thirty minutes ago. Shall we go back?"

The ride back wasn't any better than the ride out had been, but they found their way to the nice park and sighed with relief when they got there. The park had tables with built-in benches and they set up their feast on a nice one under an oak, in full view of the small river that ran through the area. Rosa's lunch was delicious. They ate and talked softly in the noon day sunshine. A group of children played tag a short distance away. Mothers with strollers passed, cooing to their babies.

Diana took a bite of her chicken salad sandwich as she watched the passing parade. "Funny how, once you're pregnant, you suddenly notice all the babies that pop up everywhere."

He gave her a covert look. She'd brought up her pregnancy on her own. Did this mean that the moratorium on mentioning it was lifted? Just in case, he made sure to tread softly.

"You're going to make a great mom," he noted.

She flashed him a look and for a moment, he thought he was going to get his head handed to him. But then her face softened and she almost smiled.

"What makes you say that?" she asked.

"I get a clear vibe from you that seems encouraging,"

he said. "You seem to be settling into this new role you're about to play in the world."

Now a smile was definitely tugging at the corners of her mouth. "It's funny, but it has taken me a while to fully realize what I've done, what I'm about to do. Mia seems very real to me now. I can hardly wait to hold her in my arms. I only hope I'll be a good mother to her."

"I have no doubts. I remember how you took care of your father."

"Do you?" She looked at him in surprise, then with growing appreciation. "I don't think most people remember that, or even noticed at the time." She shook her head. She'd spent too much of her young life taking care of him and getting little thanks for it. But she'd done it out of duty and a feeling of compassion for the man. And though she'd gone off to the big city as soon as she could, to leave all that behind her, she'd come back when her father needed her and no one else would have taken care of him as he lay dying. So she did it.

Funny. She'd left Gold Dust because of her father and then she'd returned for the same reason.

"He needed someone to take care of him. It was a cinch he couldn't take care of himself."

He waved a carrot stick at her. "You were taking care of him when you were too young to be taking care of anything more than whether your socks matched."

She smiled. Trust Cam to have paid attention and to have realized how difficult it was for her when she was young. How could you not fall for a guy like that?

She was quiet for a moment, then said softly, "I loved him, you know."

He looked at her and saw the clouds in her eyes. He wanted to take her in his arms, but he held off, knowing how she felt about the situation.

"Of course you did. He was your father." He shifted in his seat. "Did you ever know your mother at all?"

"Not much." She shook her head. "She took off before I was six years old and never looked back."

"That's a shame."

She tilted her head back and smoothed her hair off her face. "I'm not so sure. If she was worth knowing, she'd have made a point of letting me know her." Her laugh was short and spiked with irony. "At least my father stuck around."

They packed away the remnants of their lunch, put things into the car, and walked down to watch the river roll by. There were just enough boulders and flat rocks in the river's path to make for a pretty spectacular water show. They followed the river for a bit, then sat on a large rock and listened to the rushing sound.

"You need something like this at your place," he told her. "Your lake could use some shaking up."

"I've got a nice stream," she protested. "That's more my sort of excitement. Something manageable and contained."

He laughed, leaning back beside her and tossing a flat pebble into the river. "That's all you want out of life, is it? Something manageable?"

"What's wrong with that?"

"Not a thing." He tossed another pebble. "But back about the time I left, I thought you had plans to go to the city and become a model." He shifted so that she could lean back against his shoulder instead of the hard rock. "What happened to that?"

She hesitated, then gave in to temptation and let her body snuggle in against his. "Kid dreams," she said airily.

He turned his head, savoring the feel of her against him. A sudden breeze tossed her hair against his face and he breathed in her spicy scent. "You would've been good," he said, closing his eyes as he took in the sense of her.

"No."

"Why not?" Opening his eyes again, he was almost indignant. "You've got the bones for it. You could be a model." Reaching out, he touched her hair, then turned his hand, gathering up the strands like reins on a wonderful pony. "You...Diana, you're beautiful."

He said it as though it were the revelation of the ages. She smiled wryly, appreciating his passion but knowing it was just a bit biased.

"I'm not cut out for that sort of life," she said simply.

"Chicken."

She shook her head. "No. It's not that."

He went very still for a moment, thinking over her situation. "Maybe you should have gone for it anyway," he said softly.

She moved impatiently, turning to look at him. "You don't understand. I know more about it than you think I do. I lived in San Francisco for a couple of years after college. I did all those things you do when you live in

San Francisco. I went to parties in bay-view penthouses, danced in sleazy discos, dated young account executives and overworked law students. Climbed halfway to the stars in little cable cars. Lived on a houseboat in Sausalito for a few months. Worked at a boring job. Had my car broken into. Had my apartment robbed. Had a lot of fun but finally I'd had enough and I wanted to come home. To me cities are kind of those 'great to visit but don't make me live there' sorts of places."

He smiled, enjoying how caught up in her subject she'd become. Reaching up, he touched her cheek. "You're just a small town girl at heart."

"I guess so. I love it in Gold Dust." She threw her head back, thinking of it. "I love to wake up in the morning and see the breeze ruffling the surface of the lake. I love the wind high up in the pines and the fresh smell after a rainstorm. I love that feeling of calm as the sun sinks behind the mountaintops and changes the atmosphere into a magic twilight."

"I understand," he said. "That's part of what pulled at me to come back." He hesitated only a few beats. "That…and you."

The moment he said it, he knew it was true. Through all the turmoil, all the hell he'd gone through with Gina, Diana had always been in the back of his mind, a calm, rational presence, an angel of mercy whose care could heal his soul. He'd always pushed the memories away, thinking they were a crutch he'd held on to in order to comfort himself, like a favorite fantasy. But now he knew it was much more. What he felt for Diana might be fairly hopeless, but it was real and true and strong inside him. It was more real than any other part of his life had ever been. His gaze slid over her, searching the shadowed areas along her neckline, her collarbone, the upper swell of her breasts.

She turned toward him slowly, as though in a dream. She knew he was going to kiss her. She heard it in his voice. Her heart was thumping so loud, she wasn't sure if she could breathe. He was going to kiss her and once again, just for this moment, she was going to kiss him back.

She didn't wait, but leaned toward him, her lips already parted, and his arms came around her and she clung to him, moving in a cloud of sensual happiness. Was this real? Was that really Cam's body that felt so warm and wonderful against hers?

It was over too soon. She sighed as he pulled back, then smiled up at him.

"How can I miss you if you won't go away?" she murmured, half-laughing.

"What is that supposed to mean?" he asked, touching her cheek with his forefinger.

"It means you're always there," she said, straightening and moving away from him. "You're either in my life or in my dreams. I can't get rid of you." She said it lightly, as though teasing, but she meant every word.

He watched her through narrowed eyes, wondering why she appealed to him more than any other woman he'd ever known. Holding her felt natural, kissing her had been magic. He wanted her in his bed, in his life. But what did that signify? Right now, it was just confusing.

It was later, as they winged their way home, that he brought up the topic she'd been dreading all along.

"You haven't been over to the house for a while."

"No. I was gone and then…" She let her voice taper off because she knew there was no good excuse for her sending Penny to take care of the arrangements at the Van Kirk mansion one more time, even though she herself was back in town.

"My mother is asking that you come see her," he said, glancing at her sideways.

"Oh, no," Diana said, her eyes full of dread. "She's going to beg me to take over the party plans, isn't she?"

He nodded. "Yes."

She wrinkled her nose. "Tell her I've got the flu."

This time his look was on the scathing side. "I make it a practice never to lie to women," he said, and she wasn't sure if he was joking or not.

She smiled sadly just the same. "Only to men, huh?"

He suppressed a quick grin. "Of course. A man can handle a lie. Likely as not, he'll appreciate a well-told one. Might even appropriate it for his own use in the future, and thank you for it, besides."

"Unlike a woman," she countered teasingly.

"Women only appreciate lies about themselves, and then only if they're complimentary."

She stared at him, struck by how serious he sounded all of a sudden. "What made you so cynical about the human race?" she asked him.

For just a moment he was tempted to tell her about Gina, the only other woman he'd been close to loving over the last ten years, about how she'd nearly pulled him into an ugly trap, teaching him a lesson about feminine lying he would never forget. But at the last moment, he decided it was a story best kept to himself and he passed over it. It was all very well to use episodes from the past as lessons in guarding one's trust like a stingy uncle, but to inflict those stories on others was probably too much.

"Life does take its toll," he said lightly instead.

"Are you done?" she asked.

He glanced at her in surprise. "Done doing what?"

"Done running around the world looking for affirmation."

He gave a cough of laughter. "Is that what I've been doing? And here I thought I was looking for adventure all this time."

She shrugged, loving the way his hair curled around his ear, loving the line of his profile, loving him in every way she possibly could. She'd missed him so. She would miss him again when he left. And she was sure his leaving was inevitable. She didn't know when, but she knew he would go. And this time, she refused to let her heart break over it.

"Tell me why you went in the first place? The real reason."

"You mean, beyond the fight with my grandfather? It's pretty simple. The age-old story." He maneuvered through a traffic circle in the little city they were passing through. "I had to go to see if I could make it on my own without the Van Kirk name boosting me along. I didn't want to end up like my father. And I didn't much want to end up like my grandfather, either. I wanted to be me."

She nodded. That was pretty much what she'd expected. "And now?"

He grinned. "Now I'm thinking my grandfather isn't such a bad model after all."

"Interesting." She thought about that for a moment, then went on. "Has anyone ever told you that a lot of people thought you left because of Lulu?" she informed him, watching for his reaction.

He looked blank. "Lulu?"

"Lulu. Lulu Borden. You remember her." She hid her smile.

"Oh, sure. Tall, curvy girl. Lots of red hair. Nice smile. Kind of flirty."

"That's Lulu."

He shrugged. "What does Lulu have to do with me?"

"Well…" She gave him an arch look. "She started showing right about the time you disappeared. A lot of people figured you were the one who got her that way. And that was why you took off."

"What?" He gaped at her in horror until she reminded him to keep his eyes on the road. "If a lot of people thought that a lot of people were wrong."

She nodded happily. "I was pretty sure of that, but it's good to hear you confirm it."

He frowned, still bothered by the charge against him. "What did Lulu have to say about it?"

"She married Tommy Hunsucker, so she's not sayin' much."

"Geesh." He shook his head with a look of infinite sadness. "Maligned in my own hometown."

"Sure," she said cheerfully. "Where better to have your reputation besmirched?"

"And now they think I'm a daddy again, don't they?" he said cynically, looking at her growing tummy. "At least the town has a lot of faith in my potency."

She grinned. "Legends speak louder than facts sometimes," she admitted.

"Speaking of legends…" He hesitated, then went on bravely. "Tell me why you aren't going to marry the father of your baby."

All the humor drained from her face and she seemed to freeze. "That is not up for discussion."

He turned to look at her. "Di…"

"No. I'm not going to tell you anything." She shook her head emphatically and her tone was more than firm. "This is my baby. The father has nothing to do with it."

He winced. "That's not true."

"It is true," she insisted fiercely. "That's it." She held her hand up. "End of discussion."

He didn't press it any further, but he thought about it all the rest of the way home.

It was late afternoon before they turned onto the Gold Dust Road and came in sight of her little house by the lake.

"Getting back to the point," he said as he pulled up before her gate. "Will you go to see my mother?"

"Wow, that was a subject I thought we'd left in the dust way back there somewhere. Or at least we should have."

She thought for a moment before answering. She

wanted to give him the benefit of the doubt, an even chance, a fair hearing, and all those other tired clichés that meant he probably had a point to make and she ought to let him make it.

He moved impatiently. He obviously thought she'd taken enough time to come up with a fair decision and he was beginning to think she was dragging her feet.

"Listen, Di. I owe my mother something. I owe her quite a bit, in fact. I wasted a lot of time trying to figure out what life was about and what my place was in the general scheme of things. By the time I'd sorted it all out, I was back where I'd started. But by then, I realized family was more important than anything else. And I needed to make up for some things with mine. So that's why I came back. Unfortunately they're in more trouble than I can easily deal with. But this, at least, I can do for her. I can let her have her party. And she needs help to do it."

Diana listened to him and agreed with just about everything he said. He was a good son after all. And she knew she could help. She sighed.

"All right, Cam. I'll go to see your mother." She shook her head. "But I can't go tomorrow. I've got a doctor's appointment in the morning and I won't be back in time."

"Here in town?"

"No." She looked at him speculatively, then amplified a bit. "I decided from the first that I'd better go to a clinic down in Sacramento. I found a good doctor there. And I didn't want everyone in town knowing all about my pregnancy."

He nodded. "Probably a wise move," he said.

"So I'll plan to come by and see her Friday," she went on. "I'll talk to her." She winced. "But I'm afraid I'm only going to disappoint her."

He grunted and she couldn't tell if he was agreeing with her or dissenting.

"I still don't feel comfortable being a part of the great wife search," she told him, "especially if you plan to thwart your mother on it. If you really mean it, that you won't marry anyone, I hope you're planning to tell her the truth from the beginning."

"She knows how I feel."

"Does she?" Somehow, doubts lingered. "Cam, let's be honest. Your mother is looking for a bride for you, like it or not. It's not exactly fun for me to be a part of that."

"Why is that?" He gazed challengingly into her eyes. "Tell me what bothers you about that?"

Her lower lip came out. "You know very well what it is," she said in a low, grating voice. "It's not really fair of you to make me say it. You know exactly what it is and you know there's no cure for it."

With that, she grabbed her map and slipped out of the car, heading for her little lonely house.

Cam sat for a long time, not moving, not reaching for the ignition, just staring at the moon. And then, finally, he headed home.

CHAPTER EIGHT

DIANA dreamed about Cam, about his kiss and how lovely it was to be in his arms. And then she woke up and there he was on her doorstep.

"Doughnuts," he said, holding out a sack of them like a peace offering. "For your breakfast."

"Thank you," she said, taking the bag and closing the door right in front of him.

"Hey," he protested, and she opened the door again, pretending to scowl at him.

"Too early," she said. "You're not even supposed to see me like this."

"I'll close my eyes," he lied. "I came early because I didn't want to be too late to take you to the doctor."

She stared at him, and slowly, she opened the door wider for him to come in. Turning, she looked up at him. "I don't need anyone to take me to the doctor," she said stiffly.

"I'm not trying to horn in on your private business," he assured her. "In fact, if you want me to, I'll wait in the car. But I think you ought to have someone with you, just in case. And since the baby's father isn't around to help you, you can count on me. I'll be around in case something happens, or whatever."

You can count on me—the words echoed in her head. She knew he meant it, but she also knew he couldn't promise anything of the sort. "Cam, I really don't need help."

He stared down into her wide eyes. "Yes, you do," he said firmly. "Di, I know you can do this on your own. You're very brave and you've tried your whole life to do everything on your own. I know you don't actually, physically, need any help. You're strong. You've done it all on your own forever."

Reaching out, his hands slid into her hair, holding her face up toward him. "But everyone needs somebody. No one can chart his own course forever. I'm here now. I can help you. I can give you some support and be around in case you need a shoulder to lean on. You don't have to be alone."

To her horror, her eyes were filling with tears. She fought them back. The tears were a sign of weakness, and she couldn't afford to show that side to anyone. But as she fought for control, he was kissing her lips, moving slowly, touching gently, giving comfort and affection and a sense of protection that left her defenses crumbling on the floor. She swayed toward him like a reed in the wind. He was so wonderful. How could she resist him? A part of her wanted to do whatever he said, anytime, anywhere. And that was exactly the part she had to fight against.

He pulled back to look at her, his gaze moving slowly over her face, a slight smile on his own.

"Please, Diana," he said softly. "Let me be there for you. I'm not asking for anything else. Just let me be there."

She was really crying now. Deep sobs were coming up from all her past pain, all her loneliness, and she was helpless in his arms. He pulled her up against his chest and stroked her hair. When she could finally speak again, she pulled back and looked at him. How was she going to make him understand?

"Cam, don't you see? I can't start to depend on you. If I do that…"

"I'm not asking for a long-term commitment and I'm not offering one," he insisted, holding her loosely, looking down into her wet, sleepy face and loving it. "But I am here now. I can help you. You could use a friend. I want to be that friend. That's all."

She closed her eyes. Didn't he understand how dangerous this was for her? Didn't he see how much she loved him? She had to send him away. It was the only chance she had for strength and sanity.

She felt him move to the side and heard paper rustling and she slowly opened her eyes and then her mouth to tell him to go, but before she got a word out, he popped a piece of doughnut inside it.

"Let's eat," he said cheerfully, and his comical look made her laugh through her tears. She chewed on the delicious confection and laughed at his antics and somehow her resolutions got forgotten for the time being.

But she knew this wasn't the end of the matter. She

might let her guard down for now, but very soon, she would have to erect it again. She knew that from experience. So she would let him come with her to her doctor's appointment and she would be with him for another day. And she would love doing it. But it couldn't last and she couldn't let herself be lulled into thinking that.

"If I were one to sing old Elvis songs," Diana muttered to herself the next afternoon. "I'd be singing that 'caught in a trap' song right now."

She was going to help Cam's mother. She'd always known, deep down, that she would end up doing it. The mystery was why she'd tried to fight it for so long. A lot of needless Sturm und Drang, she supposed. She was a pushover in the end.

"You're completely spineless, aren't you?" she accused herself in the hallway mirror. "Shame on you!"

Mrs. Van Kirk had looked so pathetic lying back on her chaise lounge overlooking her rose garden, and she'd been so complimentary about Diana's talents on all scores—and when you came right down to it, Diana liked her a lot. She felt sorry for her, wanted to help her have her silly parties, wanted to make her happy. So in the end, she agreed to take over all the planning for the event. She was to be totally in charge of it all.

So now she was enlisted to help find Cam a bride— what fun.

There was still the problem of how she would be paid. She'd assumed Cam was serious when he'd teased her about doing it for free, but he assured her she would be paid for her work—someday.

"How's this?" he said. "You'll have the first option on our future earnings."

"What earnings?" She knew he was working hard on setting things to rights, and she supposed there was income from the Van Kirk ranch to throw into the mix, plus some of his funds borrowed from his own business. But it all seemed like slim pickings so far.

He gave her a grand shrug. "We may just go in the black someday."

She rolled her eyes. "Great. I'll be looking forward to it."

"Seriously, Di," he said, catching hold of her shoulders to keep her from running off. "I'm going to make sure you get compensated. Just as soon as I've saved this house and have a little spare cash to take care of things like that."

She looked up at him and barely kept herself from swooning. He looked so handsome, his blue eyes clear and earnest, rimmed with dark lashes that made them look huge, his dark hair falling over his forehead in a particularly enticing way. She could feel his affection for her shining through it all. He was hers—in a way—for the next few days, at any rate. Then, if his mother's plans came to fruition, he would be some other woman's. And Diana would be left with nothing but memories.

"Forget it," she said, shaking her head, pushing away her dour thoughts. "I'm doing this for your mother. And that's it."

Of course, it turned out to be even more work than she'd thought it would be. There was so much to do. The event itself was to be called a Midsummer Garden Party to welcome Cam back to the foothills and from what they'd heard, it was already stirring interest all over the valley and environs far and wide.

"Everyone from the Five Families will be attending," Mrs. Van Kirk told her matter-of-factly.

Diana knew who the Five Families were and it made her cringe a little. The Van Kirks were one of those five, though they might be clinging to that distinction by their fingernails at the moment, hanging by the thread of their past reputation. They were all descendants of five Kentucky miners who'd come here together in the nineteenth century as forty-niners, discovered gold in these hills, settled the land and established the town of Gold Dust. They were the aristocracy of the area now, the movers and shakers of local affairs all through the valley, the main landowners and definitely the richest people around.

It was only natural that Cam's mother wanted him to marry one of the young women from that group. Why not? Not only did they have the money, they had the background to rule the area. And Cam was a natural leader as far as that went. So here she was, working hard to help him take his rightful place—at the top of the social ladder and right beside some simpering debutante.

Well, maybe she wouldn't be simpering. In all fairness, the women from the Five Families spent a lot of time doing charity activities and working on cleaning up the environment. But still, they were eligible to marry Cam and she wasn't. So a little resentment didn't seem so out of line, did it?

But she had to shove that aside and concentrate on the work at hand. Establishing a theme came first. They needed something that would allow them to make cheap, easy party dishes instead of the gourmet selections that had been the choice when the fancy chef was being engaged.

She gathered Cam and Janey together and the four of them brainstormed and what they finally came up with was a Hawaiian theme.

"Hawaiian?" Janey wailed. "That's so retro."

"Exactly the point," Diana said. "That way we don't have to spend money on fancy decor items. We can use flowers from both your gardens and my fields. We'll string leis as party favors and have flowers to clip in the hair of ladies who want that. We'll have rose petals floating in the pool."

"But the food," Janey moaned.

"Don't worry, it'll be fine—very colorful and much cheaper. Things like bowls of cut up fruit will serve two purposes—decorating as well as eating. And as for the more substantial items, I have a friend, Mahi Liama, who runs a Polynesian restaurant in Sacramento. I'm sure he'd do a lot of the food for us. Maybe some pit roasted pork and chicken long-rice and poi. The rest will be mostly finger food that we're going to be fixing ahead and freezing and popping in the ovens at the last minute."

Janey groaned. "What a drag. I like it when we hire the work out a lot better."

Diana gave her a pasted on smile. "It'll be great. Just you wait and see."

The invitations came next. They couldn't afford to have any printed up, so Diana scavenged up some lovely notepaper she found in the bottom drawer of a beautiful carved desk in the den and put Mrs. Van Kirk to work doing them by hand. That was something she could do sitting down and it turned out she had gorgeous penmanship.

"The trick is to make it look like we are taking advantage of your handwriting skills and creating something unique without letting on that it's an economy measure," she told the older woman.

"Shall I add a little Hawaiian looking flower, like this?" Mrs. Van Kirk suggested, proving to have drawing talent as well.

"Perfect," Diana said, pleased as punch. "These will be so special, people will save them as keepsakes."

Buoyed by all the praise, Mrs. Van Kirk got busy and had a dozen done by noon on the first day.

Diana conferred with Cam about the seating arrangements. It turned out that he had rummaged in the storage sheds and found at least twenty round tables and a huge group of wooden folding chair to go with them, supplies obviously used for parties years ago. They needed cleaning up and some repair, and probably a coat of spray paint, but it seemed doable and he was already on the job.

There was a large patio suitable for dancing. With a few potted plants arranged along the outer perimeter and a few trellises and arbors set up, it could look stunning.

Diana was beginning to take heart. It looked like things were falling into place pretty easily. The whole family was involved, including a few cousins who stopped by occasionally, and despite the whining from some quarters, she generally thought that a good thing.

She was especially glad to find a way to get Janey to help out. Once she remembered that Cam's sister had been quite a musician in her younger days, she knew exactly how she could use her talents.

"Here's what you do," she told her. "I've called the high school. They have a small jazz combo, a pianist and a couple of different choral groups. I think one's a cappella. Hopefully they can do some low-key Hawaiian tunes. Their music director says they need the experience in playing in front of audiences, so I think we could get them really cheap and they could trade off, one group playing during the opening cocktails, another during the meal, another for the dancing, etc. You go talk to them and see what you can arrange. You'll be in charge of picking out the music. It's all yours."

"You know what?" Janey said, actually interested for once. "Adam, the man I've been dating, has a teenage son who does that Djaying thing at dance clubs to make a little extra money. Maybe he would help out."

"That would be great." She made a face as she had a thought. "Just make sure you have right of approval on everything he's going to play first. We don't want any of the raunchy stuff some of the kids like these days."

"Indeed," Janey said, drawing herself up. "Wouldn't fit the Van Kirk image."

Diana grinned at her. "You got it."

And for the first time in memory, Janey smiled back.

They had been working on party plans for three days when Diana got a present she wasn't expecting—and wasn't too sure she wanted. She was out in the garden cutting back a rosebush in order to encourage a few blooms that looked about to break out, when she noticed a strange sound coming from the toolshed. It sounded as though an animal had been locked in by mistake.

Rising with a sigh, she went to the door and opened it. Inside she found a small caramel-colored ball of fluffy fur. The puppy looked up at her and wriggled happily.

"Well, who are you, you little cutie?" she said.

Kneeling down beside him, she pulled out the tag tied around his neck. "Hi," the tag said. "I'm Billy and I belong to Diana and Mia Collins, only they don't know it yet."

"What?"

She rose, staring down at the dog as Cam came into the shed.

"What do you think?" he asked, a smile in his voice if not on his face.

She whirled to meet him.

"*You* did this," she said accusingly.

He put a hand over his heart. "Guilty as charged." He wiggled his eyebrows at her. "A friend of mine had a whole litter of these cute little guys. I picked out the best one for you."

She frowned, feeling frazzled. "Cam, I can't take care of a puppy."

"Sure you can. I'll help you."

She sputtered, outraged that he would take it upon himself to do this to her. He looked at her earnestly.

"Di, calm down," he said. "You know very well you need a dog. This little fellow is going to grow up to be a good watchdog. He'll be there to protect you and the baby when…well, when I can't."

She understood the theory behind the gift. She just wasn't sure she appreciated the motives.

"Cam," she said stubbornly, "if I decided I needed a dog, I could get one for myself. And right now, I don't need a dog."

He didn't budge an inch, either. "You need the protection. Living alone like you do, out there in the sticks, it's too dangerous." He gave her a trace of his lopsided grin. "You never know what sort of madman might show up drunk on your pier in the middle of the night."

She turned away. So that was it. The dog was supposed to take his place. Was he just trying to ease his guilt over the fact that he was not going to be there for her when she needed him in the very near future? She could never have him, but she could have his dog. How thoughtful of him. She was tempted to turn on her heel and leave him here with his bogus little animal.

But she looked down and saw a pair of huge brown eyes staring up at her, a little tail wagging hopefully, a tongue lolling, and she fell in puppy love.

"What am I going to do with you?" she asked the pup.

Billy barked. It was a cute bark. An endearing bark. And it cemented the future for Billy. He was going home with her. There was no doubt about that. Still, there were problems and concerns attached to this gift.

She frowned, biting her lip and thinking over the logistics of the situation. "But I'm over here all day. I can't just leave him alone at the lake, not at this age."

"I agree," Cam said. "That's why I rigged up a dog run alongside the shed. You can have him here with you in the daytime. He'll go home with you at night."

Cam had thought of everything. She looked at him, loving him and resenting him at the same time. Slowly she shook her head. "I don't know what my little black kitten is going to think of this," she said.

"They're both young. They should be able to adjust to each other quickly."

She looked up at Cam. A few weeks before she hadn't had anything. Now she had a baby and she had a kitten and she had a dog. The only thing she still lacked was a man of her own. But you couldn't have everything, could you?

She shook her head, looking at him, loving him. He shrugged, his arms wide, all innocence. And she laughed softly, then walked over and gave him a hug.

"Thank you," she whispered, eyes shining.

He dropped a kiss on her lips, a soft kiss, barely a gesture of affection, and turned to leave before she could say any more.

* * *

It was at the beginning of her second week of work on the party that Diana came face-to-face with Cam's grandfather for the first time. She'd been working hard on all aspects of the preparations and she'd gone into the house to get out of the sun and found herself in the cool library with its tall ceilings and glass-fronted book-cases. It felt so good, she lowered herself into a huge leather chair and leaned back, closing her eyes.

At times like this she was getting used to communing silently with baby Mia, giving her words of encourage-ment, teaching her about what life was going to be like once she emerged from her protected cave and came into the real world. She knew the baby couldn't really hear her thoughts, but she also knew that something was com-municated through an emotional connection that was getting stronger every day. Hopefully it was the love.

The minutes stretched and she fell asleep, her hands on her rounded belly. The next thing she knew, there was an elderly man standing over her, peering down as if to figure out who she was and just exactly why she was sleeping in his chair.

"Oh!" she cried, and she jumped up as smoothly as she could with the extra weight she was carrying. "I'm sorry, I…"

"Sit down, sit down." He waved his cane at her sternly. "Just sit down there and let me look at you, girl."

She glanced toward the exit, wishing she could take it, but reluctantly, she sank back down into the chair and tried to smile. She knew right away who this was, and if she hadn't known, she would have guessed. She could see hints lurking behind the age-ravaged face of a man who had once looked a lot like Cam, blue eyes and all.

"So you're Jed Collins's daughter, are you?" he growled. "You sure do look like your mom. She was one of the prettiest gals in the valley in those days."

"Th…thank you," she said, still unsettled by this chance encounter. "I think."

He nodded. "She ran off when you were a little one, didn't she? Ever find out what happened to her?"

Diana bristled a bit at the sense that he seemed to think he had a right to delve into her family matters at will. But she reminded herself that he probably thought of himself as a sort of elder statesman of the community, and she held back her resentment, shaking her head. "No, sir. Never did."

"You ought to get Cam to look for her. He could find her. That boy can do just about anything."

"I don't want to find her."

He stared at her for a moment and then gave a short shout of laughter.

"You're as tough as she was, aren't you? Good. Your dad was weak and he couldn't hold on to her. But who'd have thought she was tough enough to go off and leave her baby girl behind like she did? I'm telling you, nobody expected that one."

His casual assumptions outraged her. Who did he think he was to make these judgments on her family members? And yet, he was bringing up issues no one ever dared talk about in front of her. So in a way, it was sort of refreshing to get things out in the open. She'd never really had a chance to give her thoughts on the situation before, with everyone tiptoeing around it. Now was her chance, and she took it.

"You call that being tough?" she challenged, trying to ignore the lump that was rising in her throat. "For a woman to leave her six-year-old daughter behind in the care of a man who had no ability to handle it?" Her eyes flashed with anger, and that was reassuring. She would rather have anger than tears. "I call it being selfish and cruel."

He reared back and considered what she had to say as though he wasn't used to people disagreeing with his proclamations.

"Well, you would I suppose. But you don't know why she did it, do you? You're judging results, not motives."

She drew in a sharp breath. "You're darn right I'm judging results. I'm living the results."

He chuckled. "You've got fire in you, I'll say that," he said gruffly. "I know that grandson of mine has always had a special place in his heart for you." He frowned, looking at her. "But we all have to make sacrifices."

"Do we?"

"Damn right we do." He waved his cane at her again. "He promised me years ago he would marry one of the gals from the Five Families. I had everything set up and ready to go when he lit out on me. Left that poor little girl in the lurch."

He stamped his cane on the ground and suddenly he looked exhausted, leaning on it.

"Now he's going to have to make up for it." He shook

his shaggy head. "He's a good boy. I knew he'd come through in the end. Not like his worthless father."

Diana stared at him. This was all news to her. "Cam was set to marry someone when he left ten years ago?" she asked softly, heart sinking. That would explain a lot. And make things murkier in other ways.

"Darn right he was. Little Missy Sinclair. Now he'll finally get the job done."

Cam appeared in the doorway before the old man could go on with his ramblings.

"Here you are," he said to his grandfather. "I didn't know you'd come all the way downstairs." He threw Diana a glance as he came up and took the old man's arm. "Come on. I'll help you back to your room."

"I'm okay, I'm okay," the older man grumbled. "I've just been talking to the Collins girl here. Pretty little thing, isn't she? Just like her mama."

"That she is," Cam agreed with a grin her way. "And the more you get to know her, the more you're going to like her."

"Well, I don't know about that," he muttered as his grandson led him away. "We'll see, I suppose."

Diana sat where she was as they disappeared down the hallway. She would wait. She knew Cam would come back down to talk to her. And she had some things she wanted to talk about—like secret engagements and leaving people in the lurch.

She looked up as he walked back into the room.

"Sorry about that," he told her with a quick smile. "He usually doesn't come downstairs these days. I hope

he didn't say anything…well, anything to upset you."
His gaze was bright as he looked at her and she had the
distinct impression he was afraid exactly that had
happened. And in a way, he was right.

"He did say something that surprised me," she told
him, wishing her tone didn't sound quite so bitter, but
not knowing how to soften it right now. "I didn't know
you were supposed to marry someone just before you
ran off to join the circus ten years ago."

He sat down on the arm of her large leather chair and
shook his head as he looked down at her. If her use of
that phrase for his leaving didn't show him that she still
harbored a grievance from those days, her tone would
have given him a clue.

"Di, come on. I didn't run off to join the circus."

"Well, you might as well have." She bit her lip, realizing she was revealing a reservoir of long pent-up anger
against him for doing what he'd done and leaving her
behind. Just like her mother had. Funny, but she'd never
connected those two events until today, when Cam's
grandfather had forced the issue.

"There were a lot of reasons behind my leaving at the
time," he told her, taking her hand up and holding it in his.

This was all old news as far as he was concerned.
He'd thought she understood all this. Of course, he had
to admit, he'd never told her about the arranged
marriage that never happened—mostly because he'd
always known he wouldn't go through with it. And so
had the so-called "bride." It had never been a major
issue in his thinking—except to avoid it.

"Mostly I needed to get out from under the suffocating influence of my grandfather. And part of what he was trying to force on me was a marriage to a girl I had no interest in marrying. But that was just part of it."

She nodded, digesting that. "Who was she?"

He hesitated, thinking. "Tell you the truth, I forget her name."

"Missy Sinclair?"

He looked at her penetratingly. "If you knew it, why did you ask?"

She shrugged. The turmoil inside her was making her nauseous. "Did you ask her to marry you at the time?"

"No." He began to play with her fingers as he talked. "It wasn't like that. Me marrying Missy was cooked up between my grandfather and Missy's grandfather about the time she was born. I had nothing to do with it and never actually agreed to it. Never."

Diana took in a deep breath, trying to stabilize her emotions. "Where is she now? Is she still waiting?"

"Are you kidding?" He laughed and went on, mockingly. "Selfish girl. She couldn't wait ten years. She went ahead and married some guy she actually loved. Strange, huh?"

She finally looked up and searched his blue eyes. "You didn't love her? Not even a little bit?"

He pressed her fingers to his lips and kissed them, holding her gaze with his own the whole time. "No, Diana, I didn't love her and she didn't love me. It was our grandfathers who loved the idea of us getting married. We both rebelled against it. The whole thing was dead on arrival from the beginning. The only one who even remembers the agreement is my grandfather. Forget about it. It meant nothing then and means nothing now."

She closed her eyes. She really had no right questioning him about this. What did she think she was doing? He had a right to get engaged to anyone he wanted. She had no hold on him, even though the things he did could hurt her more deeply than anything anyone else alive could do.

If only she had followed through on her original intention to stay away from Cam. Now it was too late. She was heading for heartbreak on a crazy train and there was no way to get off without crashing.

CHAPTER NINE

BABY MIA was moving all the time now. Diana was bursting with joy at the feeling. The tiny butterfly wing flapping sensations had grown into full-fledged kicks. She would feel Mia begin to move and she would bite her lip and her eyes would sparkle and she would think, "There you go, little girl! Stretch those little legs. You'll be running in no time."

It was hard feeling like she couldn't tell the people around her what was happening. One afternoon, she couldn't contain it any longer. Mia was kicking so hard, it was making her laugh. She sidled up to Cam, who was overseeing some workers who were building a trellis and whispered to him.

"Give me your hand."

He looked at her, surprised. He'd just come back from a meeting with some bankers, so he was in a business suit and sunglasses and looking particularly suave and sensational. But he did what she asked, and she placed his hand right on the pertinent part of her tummy.

He stood very still for a moment, then turned to her with wonder in his eyes.

"Oh my God. Is that…?"

"Yes." Her smile was all encompassing. "Isn't it funny?"

He stared at her, his blue eyes luminous. "It's like a miracle."

She nodded, filled with joy. He took her hand and pulled her behind the gazebo where they could have a bit of privacy.

"How amazing to feel a new life inside you," he said, flattening his hand on her stomach again with more hope than success. "Di, it's wonderful."

"I can't tell you how transporting it is," she agreed. "It's really true. I'm like a different person."

His smile grew and took in all of her. "No," he said, cupping her cheek with the palm of his hand. "You're the same person. You just have new parts of you blossoming."

She nodded happily. Impulsively she reached up and kissed him, then turned quickly and retreated, back to work. But his reaction had warmed her to the core. She loved her baby and having him appreciate that, even a little bit, was super. Just knowing she had her baby with her was enough to flood her with happiness. All the worries and cares of the day fell away as she concentrated on the baby she was bringing to the world.

She had some qualms about raising Mia alone, without a father figure to balance her life. She'd gone through a lot of soul searching before she'd taken the plunge into single motherhood. Was it fair to the child?

Would she be able to handle it? She knew she was taking a risk and that it would be very hard, but she also knew she would do what was best for her baby, no matter what. And once she'd taken the step, she hadn't looked back for one minute.

She'd begun to buy baby clothes and to plan what she was going to do with the second bedroom in her house, the one she was converting into a nursery.

"I'll paint it for you," Cam had offered. "You shouldn't be breathing in those paint fumes while you're carrying Mia."

She'd taken him up on that offer and they had spent a wonderful Saturday trading off work and playing with Billy and the kitten. While Cam painted the room pink, Diana made chocolate chip cookies and worked on a pet bed she was constructing for the puppy.

Afterward, they took fishing poles out to the far side of the lake and caught a few trout, just like they had in the old days, catch and release. Diana made a salad for their evening meal and afterward, Cam found her old guitar and sat on the couch, playing some old forgotten standards and singing along while she watched.

A perfect day—the sort of day she would want for her baby to grow up with, surrounded by happiness and love. If only she could find a way to have more of them.

She walked him out to his car as he was leaving. The crickets were chirping and the frogs were croaking. He kissed her lightly. She knew she shouldn't allow it, but it was so comforting, so sweet. She leaned against him and he held her loosely.

"What would your father say if he could see you now?" he wondered.

She thought for a moment. "If he could see me now, he'd be out here with a shotgun, warning you to go home," she said with a laugh.

"You're probably right," he said. "Maybe it's just as well he's gone."

"I do actually miss him sometimes," she said pensively. "And I know I'm going to wish he could see Mia once she's born."

"Better he's not here to make her life miserable, too," Cam said cynically.

She sighed, knowing he was right but wishing he wasn't. If only she could have had a normal father. But then, what was normal anyway?

"He apologized to me toward the end, you know," she told him.

"Did he?"

She nodded. "He told me a lot of things I hadn't known before, things that explained a lot, things about his own insecurities and how he regretted having treated my mother badly. It's taken me some time to assimilate that information and assign the bits and pieces their proper importance in my life. Just having him do that, filling in some gaps, put things into a whole new perspective for me."

"No matter what his excuses, it can't justify what he did to you," Cam said darkly. Anger burned in him when he remembered how those bruises had covered her arms at times.

"No, I know that. I want to forgive him, but it's hard. It's only been very recently that I've even been able to start trying to understand him…and my mother…and what they did."

He held her more closely. "You deserved better parents."

She sighed. "I'm trying to get beyond blaming them. In a way, they only did what they were capable of doing."

He didn't believe that, but he kept his dissent to himself. If she needed to forgive them to make her life easier, so be it. He had no problem with that. He only knew that *he* didn't forgive what they'd done to her and there was a part of him that would be working to make it up to her for the rest of his life.

Billy began to yip for attention back in the house. They laughed.

"I guess I'd better get going," he said.

He looked at her from under lowered lids, looked at her mouth, then let his gaze slide down to where her breasts pushed up against the opening of her shirt. His blood began to quicken, and then his pure male reaction began to stir, and he knew it was time to go.

She nodded, but she didn't turn away.

He wanted to kiss her. He wanted to do more than that and he knew it was folly to stay any longer. Steeling himself, he let her go and turned for the car. Reaching out, he opened the door, but before he dropped inside, he looked back. And that was his fatal error.

One look at her standing there, her hair blowing around her face, her lips barely parted, her eyes full of something smoky, and he was a goner. In two quick steps he erased the space between them, and before she could protest, he was kissing her, hard and hot.

She didn't push at him the way he thought she would. Instead her arms wrapped around his neck and she pressed her body to his. He kissed her again and this time the kiss deepened.

She drank him in as though he held the secret of life, and for her, in many ways, he did. His mouth moved on hers, his tongue seeking heat and depth, and she accepted him, at first gladly, then hungrily, and finally with nothing but pure sensual greed.

This was what he'd been waiting for, aching for, dying for. All the doubts about who she might really want in her life dried up and blew away. He had her in his arms and that was where she belonged. He was going to stake a claim now, and if any other man wanted to challenge it, he'd better bring weapons.

Diana gasped, writhing in his embrace and wondering where this passion had come from. It had her in its grip, lighting a fire inside that she'd never known before. Every part of her felt like butter, melting to his touch. She knew this was crazy, this was playing with fire, but she couldn't stop it now. She wanted more and she wanted it with a fever that consumed her.

Billy barked again, and just like that, the magic evaporated, leaving them both breathing hard and shocked at what they had just been through.

"Oh my," Diana said, her eyes wide with wonder as she stared at him.

"Wow," he agreed, holding her face with two hands, looking down into her eyes as though he'd found something precious there.

"You…you'd better go," she said, stepping back away from him and shaking her head as though that would ward off temptation.

He nodded. "Okay," he said reluctantly, his voice husky with the remnants of desire still smoldering. He didn't dare touch her again, but he blew her a kiss, and then he was in his car and gone.

Diana watched him until his taillights disappeared around the far bend. Then she bit her lip and wondered why she seemed to be into torturing herself.

"The more greedy you get," she told herself, "The more you're going to miss him when he's gone."

But she had to admit, right now, she didn't really care. Right now she had gathered another memory to live with. And she would surely hold it dear.

The work was going well and the party was only a couple of days away. Janey had thrown herself into picking the musicians and the music, auditioning all sorts of groups as well as the high school kids. Every spare moment was filled with food preparation, mostly of the finger food variety—lumpia, teriyaki chicken wings, pineapple meatballs, tempura shrimp, wontons and everything else they could think of. Rosa set out the ingredients and Diana and Janey began to cut and mix. Rosa manned the ovens. Janey cleaned the trays. And once each batch was cooked, it was filed away in one of the massive freezers the estate maintained.

Meanwhile Mrs. Van Kirk was busy going through the RSVP returns and setting up place cards for the tables.

"The Five Families are coming en masse," she announced to everyone, happily running through her cards. "The eligible young woman count is at eleven and rising fast. Once they find out Cameron is up for matrimonial grabs, they sign up without delay. He's quite popular among them, you know."

Diana didn't have to be told. She already knew and she was sick at heart about it. She knew this was the last gasp as far as her relationship with Cam went. His family wanted him to marry a rich lady and that was what he was going to have to do. He might not know it yet, but she did.

He felt guilty for leaving his family in the lurch ten years before. He was ready and ripe for the picking as far as expiating that guilt and doing what would make his family happy and solvent went. He was going to have to marry someone. He just hadn't faced it in a calm and rational way.

Her mind was made up. She was going to endure this party to the best she could and then she was going to head home and stay away from the Van Kirks for the rest of her life. Every one of them. She would have Penny come and do the weekly flower arrangements and she herself would have no further contact with these people. That was the only way to preserve her happiness and her sanity. It wasn't going to be easy, but she would keep her allegiance to her baby uppermost in her mind and she would fight through the pain. It had to be.

Cam sat in his car staring at the Van Kirk mansion. He'd been in Sacramento doing some research and he had some news for Diana, who was inside, working on party preparations. He wasn't sure how she was going to take it. He wasn't sure how he took it himself.

His grandfather had mentioned the fact that Di's mother left her at a young age and that no one knew exactly why she might have done such a thing. Was she running off with another man? Had she reached the end of her rope dealing with her drunk of a husband? But if that was the case, why did she leave her child behind? In this day and age, the answers to such questions were a lot easier to find than they had been in the old days before computers and public access to so much government information.

At first Cam had resisted looking into the matter. After all, if Di wanted to know these things, she could have instituted a search herself, years ago. To go ahead on his own was to intrude where he had no right to. And yet, once his grandfather had brought it up, the mystery had nagged at him until he'd had to find out for himself.

His dilemma now was whether or not to tell Diana that he'd done it. And whether or not to tell her what he'd found as a result. What made him think that she actually wanted to know?

But it had to be done. Swearing softly, he got out of the car and started into the house, ready to go looking for Diana. The time of reckoning was at hand.

"Hi," she said, looking harried. "Listen, I need to talk to you. Ben has been calling me."

He reacted quickly to that, turning his head to stare at her. "What for?"

"He wants me to commit to selling out my portion of the inherited land." She appealed to him, a worried look in her large dark eyes. "What do you think? Should I do it?"

He hesitated. He hadn't been able to find out anything that would make him counsel that she turn Ben down, but something about this whole deal didn't seem right to him.

"Maybe you ought to wait," he said.

Diana seemed impatient. "Wait for what? We saw the land. It's not worth much. And I could use the money." She patted her rounded tummy. "I've got a baby coming, you know."

"I know." He smiled at her obvious joy every time she thought of or mentioned her baby. "I've tried to find out if there is any reason he would be so hot to have it, but so far, I haven't found a whisper of anything that would lead in that direction."

He'd come looking for her to tell her what he'd found about her mother, but as he gazed at her now, he thought twice and decided to hold off. She had too many things on her mind as it was. This business about her mother would just add to her worries and she didn't need that. He thought for a moment, then shrugged.

"Oh, what the hell. Go ahead and sell to him. Why not?"

"Okay. I'll give him a call and tell him to write up

his proposal. He said he would send me a check once it was signed." She looked up at him, eyebrows raised in question. "Maybe you could use the money to help with…?"

"Forget it," he said, but he grinned at her. "The amount we need is way beyond what you'll be getting. But thanks for the thought. I appreciate it."

She nodded. "Okay then." She noted a worried look in his eyes and she frowned. "Cam, how's the search for funding going? Have you had any luck yet?"

He shook his head briefly and gave her a fleeting smile. "No. With the economy the way it is, no one wants to take a chance."

She hated to see defeat in his face. "What about your business in San Diego? Have you thought about…" She almost gulped before she dared say the word. "Selling it?"

"Don't you think I've tried that?" He ran a hand through his hair, regretting that his response had been a bit harsh. "Of course I've thought about it. I've even put it on the auction block. So far there have been no takers."

"Oh." She was beginning to realize that this was really not looking good. It just might be that the Van Kirks were going to lose their family home and all the land they'd held for over a hundred years.

Funny how that sent a shiver of dread through her. What did she care, after all? These were people who had scorned her and her family all her life, until very recently. While she and her father had scrimped and clawed their way to a bare bones existence, the Van Kirks had lived a wealthy life of ease and comfort.

Or so it had seemed from afar. Once she got to know them better, she realized they had their own problems, their own demons to deal with. With wealth, your priorities changed, but the obstacles were very much the same. Life was no bed of roses no matter what side of the fence you lived on.

"You mean that darned old Freddy Mercury knew what he was talking about?" Cam said when she tried to explain to him how her thinking was running.

"Only if the Van Kirks end up as champions," she retorted, giving him a snooty look. "No time for losers, after all."

He put his forefinger under her chin and lifted it, looking down into her face. "We're going to come out of this okay, Diana," he said firmly. "I promise. Somehow, someway, I'm going to save the family farm."

She couldn't help but believe him. He had always been her champion, after all.

It was two days later that Cam came to her in a hurry just as she arrived at the estate. She'd barely risen from her car when he came rushing up.

"Diana, I need your help," he said without preamble. "Please. Find Janey and get her to take my mother downtown."

"What for?" The request was a little surprising, as Mrs. Van Kirk hadn't set foot off the grounds since her accident.

"Find some excuse. We've got to get her out of here. We've got appraisers and bank people coming to take a look at the house. It'll kill her if she sees that. She'll put two and two together and get…zero."

"Why are they coming?" Diana asked, not too good at putting two and two together herself.

"Why do you think? They want to take measurements and do evaluations." He gave her a dark look as he turned away. "Let's just say the vultures are circling."

That was an ominous thing to say and she shuddered every time she thought of it. But she did find Janey and prompted her to convince her mother to go into town for a bit of window-shopping. The real thing was off the budget for the foreseeable future. She watched as they drove off in Janey's little sports car, Mrs. Van Kirk complaining about the tight fit all the way. Just as they disappeared down the driveway, a limousine drove up and disgorged a group of businessmen who reminded her of a scrum of ravenous sharks.

Cam went out to meet them and began to take them on a tour of the grounds, talking very fast all the while. She wondered just what line of fantasy he was trying to spin. Whatever it was, they seemed to be listening attentively.

It wasn't until he brought them into the house that she began to realize something was wrong. She heard shouting and as she ran toward the front of the house where the noise was coming from, she began to realize it was Cam's grandfather who was causing a ruckus.

Old-fashioned cuss words were flying as she burst into the library where Cam was trying to quiet the older man. The bankers and appraisers were shell-shocked, gathering against the far wall of the room like a school of frightened fish.

"Get out of my house," Cam's grandfather was yelling. "I won't have you bloodsuckers here. I'd rather die than give in to you thieves. Where's my shotgun?"

"Get them out of here," Cam told her as she skidded to a stop before him, pointing to the group of visitors. "I'm going to lock him in here."

She shooed the men away, then turned back. "I'll stay here with him," she heard herself say, then gaped in horror at her own suggestion. The last thing in the world she wanted to do was stay here with this raving madman, but at the same time, she couldn't see locking him in here all alone. He was too old and too honored a member of this family to be treated like that.

"Really?" Cam looked at the end of his rope. "Great. Thanks, Di. I'll make it up to you, somehow."

He took off after the others, locking the door behind him, and Diana turned to look at the grandfather.

He'd finally stopped yelling and he sagged down onto the couch, his face turning an ashen shade of gray. She quickly got a glass of water from the cooler in the corner and handed it to him. He took a long drink and seemed to revive somewhat. He turned to look at her and frowned.

"They want to take my house away," he told her shakily. "I can't let them do that."

"Cam is going to try to fix it," she said, wishing she had more faith in the fact that a fix was possible. "I think these men are just here to gather some data."

He didn't answer and for a moment, she thought he'd

forgotten she was there. Then he turned, gazing at her from under bushy eyebrows.

"Let me tell you a story, girl. A story about family and friendship and history."

She glanced toward the door. Surely Cam would be coming back to rescue her soon. "Well, if it's only a short one."

"Sit down."

He did have a way with words—a strong and scary way. She sat down.

"I'm sure you know all about the Five Families, how our ancestors all worked together to establish a decent community for our loved ones here. Those bonds were still strong back when I was young. Through the years, they've frayed a bit. But two of us remained true friends, me and Jasper Sinclair. Some called our friendship historic. We were the only remaining descendants in our generation of a group of close friends who had struck out together for the California gold fields in the mid-nineteenth century, men who found their fortunes, and founded a pair of towns rimming the Gold Dust Valley."

He shook his head, his foggy gaze obviously turned backward on ancient scenes.

"Me and Jasper, we were raised to feel it our duty to maintain area pride in that culture and history. The other families sort of dissolved for one reason or another. Oh, they're still around, but their kids don't really have the pride the way they should. The Van Kirks and the Sinclairs, though, we've still got that Gold Rush story running in the blood in our veins."

Diana nodded. She knew a lot of this already, and she knew that it was a Sinclair girl that Cam had been expected to marry ten years ago.

"Jasper's gone now, but he had a passel of grand-daughters. I always said, if Cam can't decide on one of those pretty girls, he just ain't the man I think he is. You see, I promised Jasper I would see to it that we kept the old ways alive. Traditions matter. That's what keeps a culture intact, keeps the home fires burning, so to speak."

Diana took a deep breath and made a stab at giving her own opinion on the subject. "You know, in this day and age, it's pretty hard to force that sort of arranged marriage on young people. It just doesn't fit with the way we live now."

He fixed her with a gimlet eye. "Some of those arranged marriages turn out better than the ones people fall into by themselves," he said gruffly. "Look at your own parents. They married for love. That didn't turn out so well, did it?"

Diana had just about had it with his casual interest in giving out his view of her family affairs.

"Mr. Van Kirk," she began stiffly.

But he didn't wait to hear what she had to say.

"Did you know that your dad and my son, Cam's father, were good friends back before the two of you were born? Drinking buddies, in fact."

That stopped her in her tracks. "No," she said softly. "No, I didn't know that."

He nodded solemnly. "I used to blame him. Your dad, I mean. But now I realize they were both weak, both with addictive problems. Funny, isn't it?"

"Tragic is more like it," she said, but the words were under her breath and he didn't hear them.

He glared at her. "Anyway, I just hope you understand that Cam has got to marry one of them girls. There's no other way. It's either that, or we are over as a family." He shrugged as though dismissing her. "Sorry, but that's the way it is."

Cam returned before he could go on and she rose gratefully, leaving him to take his grandfather back up to his room. She felt numb. She knew what the old man had been trying to say to her. He needn't have bothered. She knew Cam would never marry her. As far as he was concerned, she was pregnant with another man's child. Besides, he didn't want to marry anyone. Didn't the old man know that?

But if all that was true, why was she crying again?

Cam sat in the darkened library staring out at the moon and wondering how things had gotten so crazy. He held a crystal glass filled with golden liquid of a certain potent variety and imbibed from time to time. But mostly, he was lost in thought.

It was the night before the party. Everyone had worked long into the evening, and would be back first thing in the morning to finish preparations before the guests began to arrive. Cam felt tired down to his bones, but he knew it was more emotional than physical.

Tomorrow the grounds would be filled with party-goers. A lot of beautiful young women from eligible families would be showing off their pretty summer dresses. Most of them were just coming to have fun, to see friends, to be at a party. But he knew there were certain expectations, mostly from his own family, that he would choose one of them to court. Preferably one of the richest ones, preferably from one of the Five Families. Hopes were high that he would do something matrimonial to save his own family from being kicked out of their ancestral home.

That wasn't going to happen. Much as he wanted to do something to save his family from ruin, he couldn't marry someone he didn't love. And he couldn't stop loving someone he couldn't marry.

He groaned, stretching back in the leather chair and closing his eyes. He should never have let his mother have her way with this party. He should never have let any of them get their hopes up this way.

Janey had actually brought the subject up earlier that day.

"Look," she'd said, waving a paring knife his way as she took a break from fashioning vegetable decorations. "It's only obvious you're crazy for Diana. You don't want to marry any of those women who are coming. I'm not sure you even want to be here with us."

She waved the knife so dramatically, he'd actually stepped back to be sure he was out of range.

"Why don't you just grab Diana and go? Take off for parts unknown. Leave us behind. We'll sink or swim without you."

He shook his head. "I can't do that."

"Why not?"

"Because it turns out, though I tried for ten years to forget it, blood is thicker than water. I'm a part of this family and I do care what happens to it."

Janey looked at him as though he were demented. "You can't just go off and be happy with the girl you love?"

"No."

Janey looked at him for a long moment, then said, "More fool you," but her eyes were moist and she turned and gave him the first hug he'd had from her since they were children.

A part of what complicated things, of course, was that, even if he wanted to go off with Diana, he wasn't sure she would want to go off with him. He knew she had a lot of affection for him, knew that she'd missed him and resented that he had gone off and left her behind suddenly the way he had—and for so darn long.

But why wouldn't she tell him who Mia's father was? He didn't know anything about the man who had fathered her baby. There was only one reason he could think of for that. She must still love him, still hope to get him to return and take up his duties as her child's father. What else could it be? And if that was still her dream, how could he get in the way?

He wished he understood women better. Somehow their thought processes were such a mystery. Just when he thought he'd figured one of them out, he found she was off in outer space somewhere, running on completely different assumptions than he was.

Gina for instance, the woman he'd lived with for a substantial length of time two years before. He'd thought they had the perfect adult relationship—companionship and sex without strings. She was the one who had suggested it and he'd been glad to accept her conditions. Then, suddenly, she wanted to get married. That was a shocker. He very quickly realized he didn't love her and didn't want to spend his life with her. When he explained that to her, she left in a huff.

A few months later, she was back, claiming to be pregnant with his child. He'd felt trapped, threatened, but he wanted to do the right thing. They planned a wedding, but he was in torture the whole time, resenting her, resenting the coming child, and hating himself for feeling that way.

Out of the blue, she died in a car accident. He was even more miserable, sad for her and the baby, tortured with the way he'd acted. He wished he'd been kinder to her.

Then, when the medical reports came in, he found out that the baby wasn't his after all. The confusion that left him in lasted for months. He couldn't even think about dating again. He didn't trust any woman he met. He'd actually begun to wonder if he would ever feel comfortable with a woman again.

Then he'd come home and there was Diana. It didn't take long to realize he was probably in love with her and always had been. The fact that it was crazy and doomed didn't bother him. He was used to life not turning out the way he'd hoped it would.

A sound in the doorway made him open his eyes and sit up straighter. There was Diana, walking slowly into the room and finally spotting him as her eyes adjusted to the gloom.

"I thought you'd gone home," he said.

"I did, but I forgot to put some of the leis we strung together in cool storage. I didn't want to leave them out overnight."

He nodded. "Will you join me in a drink?" he offered.

"No, thanks." But she came close and perched on the arm of the overstuffed leather chair where he was sitting. "I've got to get on home. I just stopped in for a minute."

"I was just sitting here thinking about you. About us."

She sighed. "Cam, there is no 'us.'"

"I've noticed that, Diana. Tell me why that is."

She looked down at him, startled by his tone. "There's a party happening tomorrow that is supposed to result in you choosing a rich bride to save the family," she said crisply. "That pretty much takes care of any 'us' there might have been."

He shook his head and took a sip of his drink. "I'm not buying it, Di. There's a wall between us and I'm just beginning to realize you put it there."

"That's crazy. I didn't invent this commitment you have to your family. It's enshrined in your Van Kirk legacy. It's like a shield carved into your front door. You gotta do what you gotta do."

"No, I don't."

"Yes, you do. You know very well it's what called you back here. You are part of something you can't shake free of. Duty, responsibility, whatever you want to call it. It's part of you and you're going to do what they expect."

He stared at her in the darkness. Was she right? Was he really going to do this thing they wanted of him?

He loved his grandfather with a fierce devotion, but he'd always resented him and his manipulating ways with almost as much passion. The senior Van Kirk had constantly tried to guide his life, but in the past, he'd resisted, sometimes violently. That was what the whole mad dash to shake off the dust of this gold country town in the hills had been all about. So he'd gone off to get out from under his family's rules and make his fortune. And here he was, coming back into his family's sphere and acting like that had all been a huge mistake. Was he really ready to follow his grandfather's wishes this time?

No. The whole idea was insane.

"Diana, I've told you a thousand times, I'm not marrying anyone."

"Really?" She clutched at the hem of her blouse and twisted it nervously. "Well, I think you ought to revisit that statement."

He frowned up at her. "What are you talking about?"

"You made a promise a long time ago, from what your grandfather tells me. And now that your family needs you to put yourself on the line, I think you ought to fulfill that promise." She knew she was beginning to sound a little shrill, but she couldn't help it. Her emotions were very near the surface and she was having a hard time holding them back.

"You need to have a nice little Five Families baby with one of those super rich girls and save the house, save the legacy, save it all. It's your destiny. It's what you were raised to do."

He stared at her, aghast. "You've really drunk the Kool-Aid, haven't you?"

"I've listened to your grandfather, if that's what you mean. And I've realized you're going to hate yourself if you don't do what you've been raised to think is your duty. You can't fight it."

He swore softly, shaking his head, disbelief shuddering through him.

"Just like I was raised to be pretty much the opposite," she went on, her voice sure but a bit shaky. "That's what my father always used to tell me. 'You're just a white trash girl. Don't get no fancy ideas, running around with a Van Kirk boy. That bunch will never accept you.' That's what he used to say. I didn't believe him then, but now I see the wisdom in accepting the truth."

"Truth." He said the word scornfully. "That's not truth. That's someone's fantasy dressed up as faux reality. You've fallen down the rabbit hole, Di. Stop listening to the Mad Hatter."

She almost laughed. "Your grandfather?"

He nodded. "Despite everything, I love that old man." He shrugged. "And you're right, up to a point. I made certain promises. I've got certain responsibilities."

Reaching up, he caught hold of her and flipped her down into his lap, catching her by surprise and eliciting a shriek as she landed in his arms. "But one thing I won't do is marry a woman I don't love," he said. "And you can take that to the bank."

"Cam…" She tried to pull away but he was having none of it.

His body was hard, strong, inescapable and she knew right away she couldn't stop him. But she didn't really want to and when his mouth came down on hers, it felt so hot, she gasped. His ardor shocked her, but in a good way, and very quickly her own passion rose to meet it. The pressure of his mouth on hers was pure intoxication. She sank into the kiss like a swimmer in a warm, inviting whirlpool, and very soon she was spinning round and round, trying to get her head above water often enough to catch her breath, but strongly tempted to stay below where his smooth strength made her giddy with desire.

He'd wanted to do this for so long, his need was an urgent throb that pushed him to kiss her harder, deeper, and to take every part of her in his hands. He plunged beneath her clothes, craving the feel of her soft flesh, sliding his hands down the length of her, sailing on the sensation like an eagle on a burst of wind. In this moment, she was his and he had to take her or die trying.

The top buttons of her blouse were open and his hot mouth was on her breast, finding the nipple, his lips tugging, his tongue stroking, teasing senses cued to resonate to his will. She was writhing in his arms, begging for more with tiny whimpers, touching him as eagerly as he was touching her.

"More," was the only word that penetrated her heat. "More, please, more!"

All thoughts of duty and responsibility were forgotten.

Thought itself was banished. Feeling was king, and she felt an arousal so intense it scared her. She was his for the taking, his forever. Right and wrong had nothing to do with it. He was all she'd ever wanted. The rest was up to him.

And he pulled back.

She stared up at him, panting, almost begging to have him back against her, and he looked down at her dispassionately, all discipline and control.

"You see, Diana?" he said. "There *is* an 'us,' whether you want there to be or not. You can't deny it. And I can't marry anyone else when I want you more than I've ever wanted any other woman."

He set her back on the wide arm of the chair and rose while she pulled her clothes together.

"I'll see you in the morning," he said, and walked away.

Diana sat where she was, shaken to the core and still trembling like a leaf. She was putty in his hands. He could do anything he wanted with her and her body would respond in kind. She was helpless. Helplessly in love.

CHAPTER TEN

PARTY time!

The scene was being set for a wonderful party. Cam had recruited some old high school friends to come help him and they had strung lights everywhere throughout the yard. They had reactivated a man-made watercourse that had been built years before to run all through the gardens, and now water babbled happily, recreating the look of a mountain stream. Cam had even found a way to put lights just beneath the surface at random intervals, so the whole thing sparkled as though it was under perpetual sunlight.

Guests began to arrive at midafternoon. The sense of excitement was contagious and the air was filled with the scent of flowers and the sound of music. Diana knew very few of the people who arrived. Some were cousins of Cam's who had come by to help a time or two in the past few days. But most of the Five Families children went to private schools, so she hadn't had much occasion to cross paths with many of them, and some of the ones she did know didn't seem to recognize her.

One lucky result of the theme was that no one had even suggested she wear a French maid's costume while mixing with the guests as she had feared at the first. The Hawaiian decor meant that she could wear a beautiful long island dress and put flowers in her hair and look just as good as most of the visitors did.

"I can pretend, can't I?" she muttered to herself as she wove her way in and out of the crowd. Still, she was the one holding the tray with the wineglasses, though, wasn't she? That pretty much gave the game away.

"Oh my dear, you look wonderful!" Mrs. Van Kirk approved, nodding as she looked her over. "I love the garland of flowers you've put in your hair. You look like a fairy princess."

Mr. Van Kirk, Cam's father, was home on a rare visit, looking half soused, but pleasant. He nodded agreement with his wife but didn't say much, except, "Hey, I knew your dad. He was one of my best friends. God, I really miss those days."

And she didn't linger to hear his stories.

Everyone praised the wonderful stream and the lights and the music and once the cocktail hour began to blend into dinnertime, the food was center stage. Diana was so busy making sure there was enough and the access was ample that she hardly had time to notice anything else, but she did see Cam once in a while, and every time her wandering gaze found him, he was surrounded by women.

"I'm sure he's having the time of his life," Janey said, and for once she sounded amused rather than resentful. She had her latest date, Adam, with her. A rather

short man, he seemed to follow her dutifully everywhere she went, looking thoroughly smitten, and she
seemed to enjoy it.

While she was filling the punch bowl with a fresh
supply of green sherbet punch doused with rum and
meant to take the place of daiquiris, Janey came up and
elbowed her.

"Look at there, by the waterfall. Those three are the
prime candidates."

She lifted her head to look at the three beautiful
young women. "What do you mean?" she asked, though
she was very much afraid she already knew.

"We need Cam to pick one of them to marry. They
are the richest ones."

"And the most beautiful, too," she said, feeling just
a bit wistful.

"Well, the one on the right, Julie Ransom, is only
semibeautiful," Janey opined. "But she's got a wonderful personality."

"Oh, great. Better and better."

"What do you care? He's got to pick one of them."

"I know."

"Tina Justice, the redhead, is said to be a bit on the easy
side, but nice. And Grace Sinclair, the one in the middle,
is the younger sister of Missy, the one Cam was supposed
to marry years ago. She's considered just about the most
beautiful woman in the valley. Wouldn't you agree?"

"Oh, yes," she said, heart sinking as she looked at the
woman who was wearing a turquoise sari and standing
out in the crowd. "She's got that luminous quality."

"Yes. And I think Cam likes her pretty well. So let's work on getting the two of them together. Agreed?" Janey gave her an assessing look, as though wondering how she was going to react to that, but Diana didn't give her the satisfaction of letting on.

"You get busy on that," she said lightly. "I've got some crudités to crunch."

In some ways it was nice that Janey now considered her a coconspirator rather than an enemy, but this sort of scheming put her in a very awkward position. She didn't need it. She was going to keep her distance from actual matchmaking no matter what.

Just a few more hours, she told herself, and then you'll be free. You'll never have to look at this family again. But whether you can forget them—ah, there's the rub.

It was only a short time later that she found herself listening to the three prime candidates as they chatted about Cam, ignoring her completely. She was in the kitchen, taking cheese sticks out of the oven, when they came in to wash a spill out of the redheaded girl's dress at the sink.

"They say his mother is pushing hard to get him to pick a bride tonight," she was saying.

"Tonight?" Grace repeated, looking out the window to see if she could spot him.

"Yes! Have you danced with him yet?"

"Twice." Grace sighed, throwing her head back. "He is super dreamy. I just wanted to melt in his arms. If I can get him again, I'm going to find a way to maneuver him out into the trees so we can have a little make-out time. There's nothing like stirring up the old libido and then doing the old tease for arousing a man's interest in getting engaged. And if his mother is pushing…"

"I haven't had a go at him yet," Julie said with a pout. "You all just back off until I've had my turn."

The redhead frowned thoughtfully. "You know, they also say he's got a pregnant girlfriend in the valley."

Grace nodded. "Could you put up with that?"

Julie tossed her head. "I think I could hold my own against a little piece of valley fluff."

They all laughed and began to adjust their makeup at the kitchen mirror.

Diana looked at them with distaste. She wasn't sure if they'd seen her or not. Somehow she thought it wouldn't have mattered anyway. Thinking her a servant, they would likely have looked right through her. Nice girls.

She gathered some fruit on a platter, preparing to go out with it, but just for fun, she stopped by where they were primping.

"Would any of you ladies like some grapes?" she offered, pointing them out. "They're very sweet. Not a sour one in the bunch."

All three pairs of eyes stared at her, startled.

"No, thanks," one murmured, but it was obvious they didn't know what to make of her. She smiled and carried the tray out into the party area. But her heart was thumping and her adrenaline was up. Nice girls indeed!

The dancing seemed to go on forever. Diana managed to avoid Cam, although she saw him looking for her a time or two. She was not going to dance with him. After tonight, she was going to be a stranger. No sense in prolonging the agony.

Finally the night was drawing to a close. Adam's DJ son had taken over center stage and was announcing themes for dances. It was a cute gimmick and was keeping a lot of people on the dance floor who probably would have been on their way home by now if not for the encouragement from the DJ.

Diana was tired. She wanted to go home and put her feet up.

"The last dance," the DJ was saying on the loudspeaker. "And this one is special. Our host, Cameron Van Kirk, will pick out his chosen partner and then we will all drink a toast to the couple. Mr. Van Kirk. Will you please choose your partner?"

It was like a car crash, she couldn't look away. Which one of the beautiful young women who had come here to look him over and to be looked over would he pick? She peered out between two onlookers and there was Cam. He was searching the scene, scanning the entire assembly, and then he stepped down and began to walk into the crowd.

Suddenly she knew what he was doing. There was no doubt in her mind. He was looking for her.

Her heart began to bang against her chest like a big bass drum and she couldn't breathe. How did she know this? What made her so sure? She wasn't certain about that, but she did know as sure as she knew her own name that he was headed her way.

She turned, looking around frantically. Where could

she hide? He couldn't possibly do this—could he? It would be an insult to all those beautiful, wealthy women for him to pick the pregnant party planner as his special partner. She squeezed her way between a line of people and hurried toward the side exit. And ran right into Cam.

"There you are," he said, taking her hands before she could stop him. "Come with me. I can't do this alone."

"Can't do what alone?" she said robotically, still looking for a chance to escape. But with all eyes on her, she really couldn't push his hands away and she found herself walking with him to the middle of the dance floor.

"Please welcome Mr. Cameron Van Kirk," the DJ said, "and Miss Diana Collins. Give them a hand, ladies and gentlemen.'

The music began and Cam's arms came around her. She closed her eyes and swayed to the music, a hollow feeling in the pit of her stomach.

"You can't be surprised," he said very near her ear. "You know you're my choice. You always have been."

She pulled back so she could look into his face. "I know you think you made a great joke out of this, but…"

"Joke? Are you kidding?" He held her closer. "Diana, face it. I love you."

She closed her eyes again and willed this to be over. She knew he thought he loved her. And maybe he really did. But it was impossible. He couldn't do this.

The music ended and the applause was polite and the toast was pleasant. But people were somewhat puzzled. You could see it in their faces, hear it in their voices. This wasn't one of the girls he was supposed to pick.

Still, people gathered around for congratulations. And while Cam was involved in that, Diane slipped away. She headed for her car. She knew she was being a rat and leaving all the cleanup to others, but she couldn't help it. She had to get away. If she hadn't been here to confuse things, Cam would have been free to choose one of the rich girls. The only remedy she could think of was to clear the field and give him space to do what he needed to do. She had to get out of here.

She raced home, packed a bag in three minutes and called her assistant, Penny, and asked her to come house-sit, kitten-sit and dog-sit. That was a lot of sitting, but Penny was up for it. In no time at all she was on her way to San Francisco. It was going to be a long night.

Cam didn't know she was gone until the next morning when he got an e-mail from her. It was short and scary.

Cam, please go on with your life without me. I'm going to be gone for a week or two so that you can get used to it. When I come back, I don't want to see you. Please. Don't bother to reply, I won't be reading my e-mail. A clean break is the best way. Di.

He went straight to her house just in case and found Penny there.

"She said she had to go to San Francisco," Penny said when he demanded to know where Diana had gone. "I'm not sure where. She'll probably call me tonight to see how the animals are. Do you want me to give her a message?"

He shook his head. "I can't wait until tonight. You really can't give me any better clue than that?"

"Well… She did say something about staying where she stayed when she got pregnant with Mia. I think she wanted to revisit the base of her decision or something. She was muttering and I couldn't really catch her meaning."

His heart turned to stone in his chest. She was going to see Mia's father. He was sure of it. He should leave her alone. Maybe she could work something out with him. That would be best for Diana, best for Mia. Wouldn't it?

Everything in him rebelled at that thought. No! That was crazy. The man was obviously not right for either one of them—and anyway, he wasn't going to give up the woman that he loved without a fight. He was going to find her if he had to go door to door through the whole city.

But first he had to have a last meeting with his grandfather.

He took the stairs two at a time and raced down to the old man's wing of the house, entering his room with a preemptory knock.

"May I talk to you for a moment?"

The old man raised his shaggy head. "I was expecting you," he said simply.

Cam went in and began to pace.

"Grandfather, I've come to tell you that I've failed. I thought I had a line on some financing that might work out, but today I've been told that is no longer an option." He stopped and looked at his aged relative.

"Everything I've tried to set up has fallen through. I've come to the end of my bag of tricks. I don't know where to go from here." Taking a deep breath, he said the fatal words he'd hoped he would never have to say. "I'm afraid we're going to lose the house."

His grandfather frowned. "What about one of the Five Family girls? I saw some that looked interested last night. Don't tell me you're going to turn them down again."

Cam took a deep breath and let it out. "I think you know I can't do what you want, Grandfather. I can't do that to any of those girls. I can't do that to myself."

"Or to the Collins girl," his grandfather said angrily. "Isn't that the real problem?"

He hesitated, swore and turned on his heel toward the door.

"Hold it," the old man called. "Stop right there."

He turned back, eyes narrowed. "Grandfather…"

"You shut up," the older man cried, pointing at him. "I've got something to say."

Cam stood still, his jaw rigid, and his grandfather calmed himself down.

"Now, I know I've been a stickler for staying with the Five Families. Me and the old men of those families— we've always wanted to keep the old times alive by keeping our community together and close-knit. We figured it would be good to get the younger ones to marry in the group and keep us strong. Crazy, probably." Shaking his head, he shrugged. "Time moves on. You can't force these things on people. I know, I've tried to do it often enough."

Cam stood still, scowling.

"What I'm trying to say," the old man went on, "is that I understand. You love the Collins girl, don't you? Even if she's having someone else's baby. Even if it means we'll lose the house. You don't care. You just want her."

"I know that's how it looks to you," Cam said. "And I'm sorry. I've done everything I can to save the house, including putting my own business up for sale. But I can't do what can't be done."

"I know. I know." He sighed heavily. "Oh, hell, go marry your girl. Start over. We'll be okay. We'll get a little place in the hills and live simply. We've gone through hard times before. We can do it again."

Cam felt as though a weight had been lifted from his shoulders. "Grandfather…"

"Just go get her." He waved his gnarled hand. "Go."

Cam stepped forward, kissed the old man on the cheek and turned for the door. He was going to do what he had to do anyway, but having his grandfather's blessing made it so much easier.

Hopping into his car, he turned toward the city by the bay. Just as he was leaving, Penny called on his cell.

"I'm only telling you this because I know she's crazy about you," she told him. "She just called and gave me the number where she's staying. It's a landline. Maybe you can use it to find the address."

Of course he could. And he would.

His research led him to an unassuming row house at the top of a hill. Wearing snug jeans and a big leather jacket, he rang the bell, not knowing whether he would find her with a friend or with the man who'd fathered her baby. When a nice looking young woman answered the door, he was relieved, and it didn't take much fast talking to get past her and into the sitting room where Diana was curled up on the couch, her eyes red-rimmed, her hair a mass of yellow curls around her face.

"I'll leave you two alone," Di's friend said, but he hardly noticed. All he could see was Diana and the wary, tortured look in her dark eyes.

"I love you," he told her, loud and clear. "Di, I want to marry you."

She shook her head. "You can't," she said, her voice trembling. Tears were threatening. From the looks of it, she'd been doing a lot of that already.

He stared at her for a long moment, then looked around the room. "So where is he?" he asked shortly.

She blinked. "Where is who?"

"Mia's father." He looked at her. "Isn't that who you came to find? I want to meet this jerk."

She shook her head. "Why do you call him a jerk?" she asked. "What do you have against him?"

"He went off and left you, didn't he? He's never there when you need him the most."

She closed her eyes and swayed. "Oh, Cam."

He stood right in front of her.

"Diana, there are some things we need to get settled. The most important is whether Mia's father is going to be a part of your life or not. Is he going to be involved in raising her? I don't think you've told me the full truth about the situation yet." He shook his head, his frustration plain in his face. "I want to know who he is. I want to know where he lives. I want to know…if you love him. I want to know what place he is going to have in your life in the future. This is very important."

She raised her face to him. "Why?"

"Because I love you. Don't you get that? And, dammit all, I love Mia, even though she hasn't been born yet. I want to take care of you. I want to be with you. But I have to know…"

She began to laugh. He frowned, because her laughter didn't sound right. Was she getting hysterical? But no. Sobering, she rose from the couch.

"Come here," she said, leading him to a table at the end of the room. "I'll show you Mia's father."

She took out a loose-leaf binder and opened it to a page that displayed a filled-in form. He stepped closer. At the top of the page was the heading, a simple three digit number. Down the page he saw a list of attributes, including height, weight, hair color, personality traits, talents. As he read down the list, his frown grew deeper. It could have been someone listing items about him. Every detail was just like his.

"What is this?" he asked her.

"That is Mia's father," she said, holding her chin high with effort.

He shook his head. "It sounds like me."

She tried to smile. "You got it."

His bewilderment grew. "No, I don't get it."

She took a deep breath. "Cam, Mia's father was a

donor at an assisted reproduction clinic. I don't know him. I never met him. I only picked him out of a book of donors."

"What? That's crazy."

"Yes." She put a hand to her chest. "This is how crazy I am. I went to three different clinics and pored over charts of donors trying to find someone almost exactly like you. I couldn't have you so I tried to come as close as possible to recreating what we might have had together."

He could hardly believe what he was hearing. It sounded like a science fiction story to him. He shook his head as though to clear it. "Diana, I can't believe this."

Tears glittered in her eyes. "Do you hate me? I knew it was nuts. I felt like a criminal doing it. And…I sort of feel as though I was doing it to close that door, stop the yearning. I knew if I was going to do this, it would put a barrier between us that couldn't be overcome. But it didn't seem to matter, because there was less and less hope of ever seeing you again anyway." She took a deep breath and shook her head. "But I just had to go on with my life and stop waiting for you."

"So you got pregnant." He frowned, trying to assimilate this information. "Artificial insemination?"

"Yes."

"And then I came back."

She nodded. "How could I know you were ever going to come back? Cam, it had been ten years. Your family acted like you were dead. I had no way of knowing."

"Oh, Diana." Reaching out, he enfolded her in his

arms and began to laugh. "So you're telling me you're actually carrying my baby. Or a reasonable facsimile thereof. There is no other man involved. Just an anonymous donor."

"That's it."

He laughed again, then kissed her and looked down into her pretty face. "Let's get married."

"Wait, Cam…"

"I mean it, Di. We've already got our baby. All we need is a wedding ring."

"But what about your family?"

Quickly he told her about his conversation with his grandfather. "He basically gave me permission to marry you. Not that I was waiting on that. But it does make it less stressful."

She searched his eyes. "Are you sure?"

"I'm sure." He dropped another kiss on her lips. "Say 'yes'."

She smiled up at him. "Yes."

He whooped and danced her around the room. "I love you so much," he told her. "Last night when I made you dance with me, you looked so beautiful, I could hardly stand it."

"It was a nice party. Even if it didn't get you a wealthy bride."

"C'est la vie," he said, and reached down to pick up some papers that had fallen out of his jacket pocket when he'd danced her around the room.

"What are those?" she asked, her sharp eyes catching sight of her own name on one of them.

He hesitated, then nodded for her to sit down at the table. "I got this information a few days ago but I was holding off on telling you," he said. "You see, I did some research on what happened to your mother."

She went very still. "What?"

"And here's what I found." He spread some papers out in front of her and took another out of an envelope. "She died in a cancer clinic in Sacramento. The date makes it right around the time you were six years old."

Diana stared at the papers. "So what does that mean?"

"It's my guess, from all the records I could find and what I could piece together, that your mother got a diagnosis of stomach cancer and she went away to a cancer clinic where she could concentrate on fighting the disease."

"So she didn't run off with another man? She didn't just decide she hated us and couldn't stay with us anymore?" Suddenly Diana eyes were filled with tears again. "Oh, Cam, I don't know what to think. How do you know this? Why didn't my father ever tell me?"

"My guess is that she thought she would get well and come back and be taking care of you again. She thought she had a chance, but luck wasn't with her. She left because she couldn't take care of you and deal with your father while she was going through that."

Diana's brows knit together. "Do you think my father knew?"

"Who knows what he knew or didn't know. From what I hear, he was in pretty bad shape with the drinking around that time. She might have told him and he might have been too out of it to know what she was talking about."

"Or he might have been that way *because* of what she told him."

"True. I don't suppose we'll ever know the truth." He frowned. "So she had no living family, no one to leave you with?"

"Except my grandmother on my father's side. She was still alive. I spent a lot of time at her house in those days. But she died when I was ten."

"And she never said anything to you about your mother's absence?"

She shook her head. "Not that I remember. I was only six years old, you know. Maybe she told me something that I didn't understand at the time. Maybe she just avoided the issue. People of her generation tend to do that."

"True."

Diana drew in a shuddering breath. "It's going to take some time to understand this," she said. "To really take it all in. It's a relief to know she didn't just run off, but it's so sad at the same time, and I feel like it's sort of unreal right now. Like it's about somebody else."

He was frowning, looking at an envelope in the pile of papers he'd given her. "Wait a minute," he said. "What's this?"

He pulled it out. "Oh, I didn't know this had come. I requested some information from a friend about that land you inherited. The envelope must have been stuck in with this other stuff. I didn't see this before."

He slit it open and began to read. Without looking up, he grabbed her arm. "Diana, you didn't sign that contract with your cousin yet, did you?"

"Yes, I did," she said. "I just mailed it today."

He looked up, his eyes wide. "You've got to get it back. Where did you mail it?" He jumped up from his seat. "Quick! Where is it?"

"I put it outside for the mailman this morning. I doubt it will still be there." She had to call after Cam because he was already running to the front of the house. "What's the matter?"

The mailman was at the next house when Cam snatched the envelope from the box attached to the front of the house where she'd put it. He sucked in a deep breath and leaned against the building. "Wow," he said. "Just wow."

Turning slowly, he made his way back into the house where Diana was waiting.

"What's going on?" she said.

He waved the envelope at her. "My friend in Sacramento came through with some inside info. That piece of land? A major hotel chain is planning a huge resort there. That land will be worth twenty times what your cousin offered you for it. Whatever you do, hold on to that land."

"Wow." Diana said it, too. "Does this mean…I'm rich?"

"Pretty much."

A huge smile began to break over her face. "Then I guess you ended up with a rich girl after all, didn't you?"

He grinned and kissed her. "See? That was my plan from the first," he said. "I just had to wait until you were rich enough to help me save the farm."

"Will this do it? Seriously?"

He shrugged. "Hard to tell. But just having it means there are lenders who will give us extensions they wouldn't give us before. It'll certainly help."

"Good." Her bubbling laughter was infectious. "This is too much. I feel like I'm in the middle of an overload situation. Turn off the bubble machine."

"This is just the beginning," he told her, sweeping her up into his arms again. "You ain't seen nothing yet."

And he gave her a hard, deep kiss to seal the deal.

EPILOGUE

MORNING crept in on little dog feet but it was a cold black nose that woke Diana from her sleep. Then two doggy feet hit the mattress beside her head and she sighed. Those feet weren't really so little anymore.

"You monster," she said affectionately, and Billy panted happily, knowing love when he saw it. "Billy's here," she told Cam.

He turned and groaned, then rose from the bed.

"Come on you mangy mutt," he grumbled. "I'll let you out."

She watched him walk naked from the room, his beautiful body shining in the morning light, wondering how she had managed to be so lucky. All her dreams had come true. Did she really deserve this happiness? He was back in a moment and this time he closed the door with a decisive snap, then turned and reached for her before he'd even hit the bed. Making love was sweet and slow in the morning, warm affection building to hot urgency, then fading to the most intense love imaginable as the sensations melted away.

"That one's going to be our next baby," he said, letting his fingertips trail over her generous breasts.

"You think?"

"I know. I could tell."

"How?"

"Magic."

Mia's happy morning voice penetrated the closed door. She was singing to herself.

"She's awake."

"She's awake."

"You stay right here," he said. "I'll get her and bring her in bed with us."

She went up on one elbow as he rose from the bed. "Are you going to tell her?"

"Tell her what?"

She smiled lazily. "That she has a brother coming down the pike?"

He gave her his lopsided grin. "How do you know it's a boy?"

"I can feel it."

He frowned skeptically. "How?"

She smiled as though the world was paradise and she its ruler. "Magic."

He laughed and went to get their child. He agreed. Life was good. And Diana was magic.

A BABY FOR THE VILLAGE DOCTOR

ABIGAIL GORDON

**IN MEMORY OF MY FRIEND
IRENE SWARBRICK RNA SWWJ**

CHAPTER ONE

IT WAS a bright spring morning but as Georgina Adams drove along the rough track that led to the gamekeeper's cottage on the Derringham Estate she was oblivious to what was going on around her.

April was just around the corner and daffodils and narcissi were making bright splashes of colour in cottage gardens. Fresh green shoots were appearing in hedgerows and fields where lambs covered in pale wool tottered on straight little legs beside their mothers.

On a normal day she would have been entranced by the sights around her but today the beauty of the countryside in spring wasn't registering.

The only new life that Georgina was aware of was the one she was carrying inside her. She was pregnant and though there was joy in knowing that she was going to have a child, there were clouds in her sky.

Ben had never replied to the letter she'd sent, explaining that they needed to talk, and that she would travel to London to see him if he would let her know when it would be convenient. The weeks were going by and he didn't know about the baby.

She'd only written the once, and it had been very difficult, agonising over what to say and how to say it, because she wanted to tell him that he was going to be a
father again face to face. He was entitled to know that
he'd made her pregnant, and she needed to be there to
see his reaction.

In the end she'd written just a few bald sentences,
sealed the envelope before she changed her mind, and
gone straight away to post it to an address that she knew
as well as she knew her own name. He hadn't replied, and
it was now beginning to look as if that was the end of it.

The fact that the baby's father didn't know she was
pregnant was the biggest cloud in her sky, but the hurt
and loss from over three years ago had never gone
away. Remembering how Ben had been then, it wasn't
altogether surprising that he hadn't been in touch, but
she did wish he had.

Half of the time she was gearing herself up for the
role of single parent and for the rest she was battling
with the longing to have Ben beside her as she awaited
the birth of their second child.

At almost eight months pregnant there was no way
of concealing it and she was conscious all the time of
the curious stares of those she came into contact with.
She'd lived alone since she'd joined the village medical
practice three years ago as its only woman doctor and
had kept her private life strictly under wraps.

To her colleagues at the practice, her patients and the
friends she'd made since settling in the Cheshire village
of Willowmere, Georgina was pleasant and caring, but
that was as far as it went.

The only person locally who knew anything about what was going on in her life was James Bartlett, who was in charge of village health care and lived next door to the surgery with his two children.

He had told her that if she ever needed a friend, she could rely on him, and had left it at that. James hadn't asked who the father of her baby was, but she knew he would have seen her around the village with Nicholas during the weeks leading up to Christmas and it would have registered that he'd not been on the scene since the New Year.

Soon she and James would have to discuss her future role in the practice, but before that happened, replacements were required for two staff members who had recently gone to work in Africa.

When she stopped the car outside the grace-and-favour cottage of the woman she'd come to visit, the husband came striding out, dressed in a waterproof jacket with boots on his feet, a cap on his head and to complete the outfit he had a gun tucked under his arm.

Dennis Quarmby was gamekeeper for Lord Derringham, who owned Kestrel Court, the biggest residence in the area, and with it miles of the surrounding countryside. But at that moment the main concern of the man approaching was not grouse or pheasants, or those who came to poach them on his employer's estate.

His wife was far from well and on seeing that the lady doctor from the practice had arrived in answer to an urgent request, he waited for her to get out of the car before going on his way.

'Our eldest girl is with the missus,' he told her, his anxiety revealed in his expression. 'I wanted to be here when you came but Lord Derringham has just been on the phone to me because someone has been breaking down the fences up on the estate and he wants me there right away. He rang off before I could tell him I was waiting for a doctor to visit Christine. Her eyes and mouth are so dry she's in real distress, and with the rheumatoid arthritis, as well, she's feeling very low.'

Georgina nodded. She'd seen Christine Quarmby a few times recently and on one occasion had had to tell her that she was suffering from rheumatoid arthritis. Now there was this and there could be a connection that had serious implications.

When she went inside the cottage, the gamekeeper's wife said, 'Has my husband been telling you my tale of woe, Doctor? He does worry about me, though I have to admit I'm struggling at the moment. I'm having trouble swallowing, as well as everything else that is wrong with me.'

It was clear that the glands that produce tears and saliva weren't working, Georgina thought, in keeping with some sort of autoimmune disorder. But it required the opinion of a neurologist before she prescribed any medication and she told Christine, 'I'm going to make you an appointment to see a neurologist and the rheumatologist that you saw when we were trying to sort out the rheumatoid arthritis. We'll see what they come up with.'

'I know someone who has the lupus thing,' Christine said. 'You don't think it's that, do you, Doctor?'

'I wouldn't like to make a guess at this stage,' she told her, surprised that her patient had been thinking along the same lines. 'I'll ask for an urgent appointment and we'll take it from there.'

As she was leaving, Dennis returned and announced that as soon as he'd informed his employer that his wife was ill, he'd told him to forget the fences and come home.

'Christine will tell you what we've discussed, Mr Quarmby,' Georgina told him, 'and in the meantime send for me again if she gets any worse.'

'I'll do that, all right,' he promised. 'She plays everything down, having been made to suffer in silence when there was anything wrong with her when she was a kid, and thinks she shouldn't complain, which is not the case when there's anything wrong with me. I do that much moaning, everybody knows.'

'Yes, well, look after her. She needs some tender loving care,' she told him. 'I'm sending Christine to see two of the consultants at St Gabriel's and hopefully we'll have a clearer picture of what is wrong when she's been seen by them.'

When she returned to the practice in the main street of the village, it felt strange, as it had done for days with Anna and Glenn no longer there. Anna Bartlett was James's sister and had been one of the practice nurses.

On a snowy day in January she had married Glenn Hamilton, who'd been working at the surgery as a temporary locum, and in early March the newlyweds had gone to Africa to work with one of the aid programmes out there, before returning to Willowmere to settle down permanently.

They needed to be replaced and soon, or she and James would be overwhelmed by the demand for their services, and though she intended working until the baby was due, she would need time off afterwards. So some new faces were going to be needed around the surgery without delay.

It was lunchtime and James was having a quick bite when she appeared. 'The kettle has just boiled,' he told her. 'How did you find Christine Quarmby?'

Her expression was grave. 'Not too good, I'm afraid. There is something very worrying about her symptoms. Christine thinks she might have lupus, which as we know has connections with rheumatoid arthritis, and she could be right, though I do hope not. I'm referring her back to the rheumatologist she saw before and am going to arrange for her to see a neurologist, as well.'

'Hmm, there isn't much else you *can* do at this point,' he agreed. 'By the way, Georgina, I'm interviewing this evening for another doctor and a practice nurse. Beth Jackson is struggling single-handed in the nurses' room, and we haven't yet had anyone come in as another partner since the gap that was left when my father died.

'I would have liked Glenn to become permanent. He was an excellent doctor, like yourself, but it didn't work out that way. Do you want to sit in on the interviews, or will you have had enough by the end of afternoon surgery?'

'I'll give it a miss, if you don't mind,' she told him,

'unless you especially want me to be there.' She gave a wry smile, 'I'll be the next one to cause staffing problems, but not until after the baby is born.'

'Don't you worry about that,' he said. 'Just take care of yourself, Georgina. With regard to the interviews, I'll bring you up to date with what's gone on in the morning, so go and put your feet up when the surgery closes. It's only a fortnight to Easter. Why don't you go away for a few days?'

'I'll think about it,' she promised, and made a pot of tea to have with the sandwich she'd bought at the bakery across the road.

'How many applicants have you had for the two vacancies?' she questioned as he prepared to go back to his duties.

'There have been quite a few. I've sifted out the ones that sounded suitable and once the children are asleep, I'll be coming back for the interviews. Their daytime nanny finishes at half past six, which coincides with the end of my time here under normal circumstances, but Helen, my housekeeper, has offered to be there for Pollyanna and Jolyon tonight.'

When Georgina let herself into the cottage on a quiet lane at the far end of the village, it still felt empty without the lively presence of Nicholas. It had been nice to have her ex-husband's brother around for a while.

He'd been based in the United States since just after she and Ben had divorced. The offer of a job in aerodynamics that he'd long coveted had come up and he'd been torn between taking it and staying to help them sort out their lives. Both of them had insisted that *his* future mattered more than theirs and he'd gone, though reluctantly.

Nick had been back a few times and stayed with them both alternately. He'd done the same this last time when he'd come over to Manchester to arrange the U.K. side of the firm that employed him in Texas, staying with her during the week and spending his weekends with his brother in London as part of a situation where she and Ben never made any contact.

If she had ever felt the necessity to get in touch, as was now the case, Georgina knew where Ben could be found. It was she who had moved out of the house in a leafy London square all that time ago. A house where, in that other life, the two of them had lived blissfully with Jamie, their six-year-old son.

Jamie. It had been losing him that had taken the backbone out of their marriage and, like other loving parents before them, tragedy hadn't brought them closer, it had driven them apart.

She knew that Nicholas hated the situation he found himself in with the two people he cared for most in the world, yet he wasn't a go-between. Georgina had made him promise that he would never divulge her whereabouts to Ben without her permission. Even though she knew Ben was the last person who would come looking for her after all they had been through.

As she made a meal of sorts, Georgina was remembering how Nicholas had taken her to Willowmere's Mistletoe Ball in the marquee on the school sports

ground, and he'd gone with her to the gathering at
James's house on Christmas Eve when Anna and Glenn
had announced their engagement. So she supposed the
senior partner at the practice could be forgiven if he had
Nicholas down as the father of her baby.

It had been August when something she'd not been
prepared for had happened. She'd been at Jamie's
graveside, taking the wrapping off the white roses that
she always brought with her, when a voice had said
from behind, 'Hello, Georgina.'

She'd turned slowly and he'd been there, Ben
Allardyce, her ex-husband, the father of the cherished
child they'd lost.

He'd looked older, greying at the temples, and the
emptiness that had never left his eyes after Jamie had
been taken from them had still been there in the gaze
meeting hers. As she'd faced him, like a criminal caught
in the act, she'd known that no other man would ever
hold her heart as Ben had.

Nicholas had told her that Ben knew she visited the
grave, but during all the time they'd been apart she'd never
come across him until that day which had also been
Jamie's birthday.

She'd turned back to the labour of love that had brought
her there and was arranging the flowers with careful hands
on the white marble of their memorial to their son.

When it was done and she'd straightened up and
faced him again, he'd said, 'Nicholas tells me he's coming to the U.K. in October and is going to be here three
months. It will be good to see something of him.'

'Yes, it will,' she answered awkwardly, like a school-girl in front of the head teacher.

'Do you want to come back to the house for a drink before you drive back to wherever you've come from?' he asked in the same flat tone as when he'd greeted her. She observed him warily. 'It was just a thought,' he explained, and she wanted to weep because of the great divide that separated them.

'Yes, all right,' she heard a voice say, and couldn't believe it was hers. She turned back to the grave once more and dropped a kiss on the headstone, as she always did when leaving, and when she lifted her head, he was striding towards his car.

'You know the way, of course,' he said as she approached her own vehicle. She nodded, and without further comment from either of them they drove to the house that had once been their family home.

As she stepped inside, the sadness of what it had become hit her like a sledgehammer. The room began to spin and he caught her in his arms as she slumped towards him.

She rallied almost as soon as he'd reached out for her, but Ben didn't relax his hold. They were so close she felt his breath on her face as he said, 'You need to rest a while.' Picking her up in his arms, he carried her to the sofa in the sitting room and laid her on it.

When she tried to raise herself into a sitting position he told her, 'Stay where you are. I'll make some tea. A brandy would be the ideal thing but as you're driving…'

After he'd gone into the kitchen she looked around her and saw that nothing had changed in the place that had once been her home. Furniture, carpets, ornaments were all the same as she'd left them, and she thought numbly that it was them who had changed, Ben and herself, heartbreakingly and irrevocably.

Jamie had been taken from them in a tragic accident, and with his going their ways of grieving had not been the same. Hers had taken the form of a great sadness that she'd borne in silence, while Ben had been filled with anger at what he saw as the injustice of it, and it had turned him into someone she didn't recognise.

Instead of comforting each other, they had become suffering strangers and in the end, unable to bear it any longer, she'd asked for a divorce. Still fighting his despair, he'd agreed.

He'd offered her the house but she'd said no as it wasn't a home to her any more. She'd packed her bags and gone to take up a position as a GP in a pretty Cheshire village that was far away from the horror of those months after Jamie had drowned.

When Ben came back with the tea he put the cup and saucer down and, with his arm around her shoulders, bent to raise her upright. 'I never expected to see you actually here in the house again when I set off for the cemetery.'

'Neither did I,' she murmured, and as she looked up at him their gazes met and held, mirroring sadness, pain, confusion…and something else.

There was no sense or reason in what happened next. He bent and kissed her and after the first amazed moment she kissed him back, and then it became urgent, a tidal wave of emotion sweeping them along, and they made love on the sofa on a surreal August afternoon.

When it was over, he watched without speaking as she flung on her clothes, and when she rushed out of the house and into her car, he made no attempt to follow her.

It wasn't until after Nicholas had come to stay that Georgina had realised she was pregnant. She'd been feeling off colour for a while, nauseous and light-headed, but busy as ever at the practice hadn't thought much of missing her monthly cycle as she had always been irregular, initially putting it down to stress.

All the signs had been there—tender breasts, tired-ness, morning sickness—and she'd faced up to it with a mixture of dawning wonder and dismay while care-fully concealing it from her house guest. It hadn't been too difficult as, although she'd been five months along by the time he'd returned to America in the New Year, she'd barely shown at the time. Even James hadn't re-alised until she'd told him. Now, however, at eight months, her bump was there for all to see.

Knowing Nicholas, he would have felt he had to tell Ben if he'd found out about the baby, she'd thought, and she'd needed time to adjust to the situation that had come upon her so suddenly. Every time she thought about the wild, senseless passion that they'd given in to on that August afternoon, she wanted to weep. They'd lost a child born in love and gentleness. Under what circumstances had this one been conceived—loneliness, opportunism?

As the weeks had passed, the knowledge that she wasn't being fair to Ben had pressed down on her like a leaden weight until the night she'd written the letter. After that she'd felt better, and had begun the ritual of watching out for the postman every morning, but there'd been no reply.

She could have called him. It might have been easier. But she was afraid that she might give herself away on the phone, and she just *had* to tell him face to face. No matter how they'd parted after losing Jamie.

It had been Jamie's attachment to his football that had sent him careering over the edge of the riverbank. The ball had started to roll down the slope where she'd parked the car for the two of them to have a picnic.

She'd turned away to lift a folding chair out of the boot, and as she'd been erecting it had seen him, oblivious to danger and ignoring her warning to keep away from the edge, running towards the swollen river.

It had all happened in a matter of seconds and as she'd flung herself down the slope after him and shrieked for him to stop, he hadn't heard her above the noise of the fast-flowing water.

She'd nearly lost her life trying to save their son and when she'd been dragged half-dead from the river to discover that she was going to have to carry on living without him, she'd wished that she'd died, too.

Ben gazed at the letter in his hand. Each time Nicholas had visited since that August afternoon, he had asked him where he could find Georgina, but he'd reluctantly refused to tell, explaining that she'd made him promise never to pass on that information.

It hadn't been hard to believe when Ben recalled how she'd never come near the house apart from that one time when he'd found her at Jamie's grave. Whenever he'd seen fresh white roses on it he'd known that she'd been just a stone's throw away from the home they'd shared together, and the despair that had become more of a dull ache than the raw wound it had been during those first awful months would wash over him.

He'd thought bleakly that what had happened between them on the day he'd caught her unawares in the cemetery hadn't seemed to have made Georgina relent at all, and if Nicholas wasn't prepared to break his word to her, it was going to be stalemate.

On his last night in London his young brother had asked, 'Why are you so keen to find Georgina afer all this time?' And because there had been no way he was going to tell him what had happened, Ben had fobbed him off by telling him that some insurance in both their names had matured.

That had been in early January, and when Nicholas had flown back home Ben had gone to work in Scandinavia for a short while. He'd always been somewhat of a workaholic, even before their marriage had broken up, getting a lot of satisfaction out of helping sick children and being able to give Georgina and Jamie some of the good things in life at the same time.

When their life together had foundered after losing their son he'd immersed himself in his work more and more, and had spent less and less time at home. Without Jamie it wasn't a home any more.

When Georgina had asked for a divorce he'd agreed, because he'd felt their life together was over. They'd had no comfort to offer each other—he, because of the terrible bitterness inside him, and she because she felt responsible for what had happened.

But that day in August he'd discovered that their feelings weren't dead. There was still a spark there. It had been sweet anguish making love to the only woman he'd ever wanted, and he wasn't going to rest until he saw her again.

He'd gone to Scandinavia with less than his usual enthusiasm, because he was frustrated and miserable to think that she'd come back into his life and given him hope and then disappeared into the unknown once more.

Now he was home again, and amongst the mail that had accumulated during his absence was the envelope with Georgina's handwriting on it. With heartbeat quickening, he opened the letter.

The brief communication inside said that she needed to talk to him as soon as possible, and it went on to say that she would come to London if he wished. No way, he thought. He'd waited a long time to find out where she'd gone, and now the opportunity was here.

She hadn't used the word urgent, but there was something about the wording of the letter that conveyed it to him, and as the postmark on it was from weeks ago he immediately began planning how quickly he could get to this Willowmere place in Cheshire.

Ben was freelance, and not attached to any particular hospital, so there were no arrangements to make at his end. After a quick snack, and a phone call to arrange overnight accommodation at a place in Willowmere called the Pheasant, he was ready for the off, warning the landlord that he would be arriving in the early hours.

As she did on most evenings when she'd eaten, Georgina set off for a short stroll beside the river. A heron, king of the birdlife, familiar to all the village folk, was perched motionless on its favourite stone in the middle of the water when she got there, and she remembered how when she'd first moved to Willowmere she'd had to steel herself to look at the Goyt as it skipped along its stony bed.

As the last rays of the sun turned the skyline to gold she felt the child inside her move and wondered if it was going to be a son to follow the one they'd lost or a baby girl with the same dark hair and eyes as her parents.

She knew that under normal circumstances Ben would be over the moon at the thought of another child, but *normal* would have been as a brother or sister for Jamie and he was no longer with them.

They'd created a new life in those moments of wild abandon and it should be a source of joy for them both, but as it stood now *he* knew nothing about it.

She saw that the lights were on in the surgery as she walked back to the cottage and brought her thoughts back to the situation there. Would James find suitable replacements tonight for Anna and Glenn?

After a bath and a hot drink, she was tucked up in bed half an hour later and thinking drowsily that for half the population the night would only just be beginning, but tomorrow would be another busy day for her and James.

She awoke in the early hours to the noise of a car pulling up on the quiet lane below, but didn't get up to investigate. Instead she snuggled lower under the bed-covers with her eyes closed. The doors were locked, the burglar alarm on. Whoever it might be, she was too sleepy to check them out.

As he'd driven through the Cheshire countryside, Ben had thought wryly that Georgina had certainly intended to put some distance between them by coming here, and she'd also chosen a beautiful place to come to.

He'd seen a lake glinting through trees in the light of a full moon as he'd approached the village, and as he'd drawn nearer had seen that the main street was made up of cottages built from limestone next to quaint shops that made the present-day supermarket seem an uninteresting place by comparison.

He'd arrived earlier than expected, and had stopped briefly outside Georgina's cottage on a lane at the end of the village after receiving directions from an elderly man.

The curtains were drawn, for which he'd been thankful, as it was hardly the hour to be calling. After choking back the overwhelming feeling of regret for all the wasted years they'd spent, he'd driven off into the night to find his accommodation.

Knowing as he did so that ever since he'd found

Georgina in the cemetery and persuaded her to go back to the house, then made love to her like some madman, he'd been aching to see her again. Desperate to tell her how he regretted the way he'd behaved when they'd lost Jamie.

He'd been like someone demented and had vented his desolation on to her, as if she hadn't been suffering, too. If he'd been in charge, the tragedy would never have happened, he'd told her at times when he'd been at his lowest ebb, and it had been as if the love they'd shared had also died.

It hadn't been until in bitter despair she'd asked for a divorce and left because she'd been unable to stand it any more that he'd faced up to what he'd done to her.

He'd given her the divorce, couldn't for shame not to after the way he'd behaved, and ever since then had longed to have her back in his life. He wanted to tell her how sorry he was for forsaking her when she'd needed him, for being so selfishly wrapped up in his own grief without a thought for hers, and to explain how meeting her that day had brought all his longing to the surface in an enormous wave of passion.

There'd always been amazing sexual chemistry between them, but after losing Jamie they'd never made love, so estranged had they become. Now he was going to try to rebuild the marriage that had crumbled, and maybe Georgina wanting to talk was a step in the right direction.

CHAPTER TWO

WHEN Georgina looked through the window the next morning, there was no car to be seen so she concluded it must have driven off after stopping for a moment.

After a shower and a nourishing breakfast she was ready to leave, and with the car already outside from the previous day, she was about to slide into the driver's seat when she looked up and saw a man walking towards her along the deserted lane.

He was tall and dark-haired with a trim physique. As he approached she stared at him in disbelief and when he stopped at the bottom of her drive and said, 'Hello, Georgina,' in the same tone of voice as on that day in August, her legs turned to jelly.

'So did you get my letter?' she croaked from behind the car door.

'Yes, but only a few hours ago,' he said evenly. 'It had been lying unopened behind my door for weeks. I've been abroad recently. So what's the problem, Georgina? What do you want to talk to me about?'

So far the car door was concealing her pregnancy but

she couldn't stay behind it for ever, and with a sudden desire to shatter his calm she pushed it shut. Looking down at her spreading waistline, she said, 'I want to talk to you about this.'

It was Ben's turn to be dumbfounded. 'You're pregnant!' he gasped. 'Oh! My God! You're with someone else! Why didn't Nick tell me?'

'Nicholas didn't tell you because there was nothing to tell,' she informed him steadily. 'He doesn't know I'm pregnant, and as for the rest, there is no one else in my life. I am on my own and prefer it that way. You are the one who has made me pregnant, Ben. Maybe you recall an afternoon in August.'

Recall it? he thought raggedly. He would never forget it as long as he lived, the softness of her in his arms again, his mouth on hers, her desire matching his. Hope had been born in him that day.

It was why he had come to the place where Georgina had made a new life for herself, hoping that the matter she wanted to discuss was getting back together. Only here she was, carrying his child and making it very clear she hadn't been having any such thoughts. Yet nothing she said could take away the joy of knowing that those moments of madness were going to bring a new life into the world, another child to cherish. It wouldn't ever replace Jamie in his heart, but there would be no shortage of tenderness and love for this one…if he was given the chance.

'What happened that afternoon was the last thing I intended,' she told him as they faced each other on the drive. 'Nothing was further from my mind, and now I'm carrying the result of what we did.'

'And you aren't happy about it?'

'Yes, of course I am. I'm happy that I'm going to have another child. It is a privilege I never anticipated, but after losing Jamie and the dreadful aftermath, I'm not intending to change my lifestyle as it is now, except for doing fewer hours at the practice maybe.'

'Fair enough,' he said evenly, stepping to one side as she slid behind the wheel. 'And is this baby that you've been keeping to yourself going to get to know its father as it grows up?'

'If our lives had been as they were before we lost Jamie, it would have been ecstasy to tell you that I was pregnant,' she said sadly. 'Because our child would have been conceived in love, like he was. But it wasn't like that, was it? Too much water has flowed under the bridge since the days when we lived for each other and him.'

'But you *were* prepared to tell me that you're pregnant, Georgina, though in your own time. I suppose it could have been worse. I could have arrived to find you pushing a pram. And so is my part in this going to be sitting on the fence?'

'No, of course not,' she said, choking on the words. 'It's just that I couldn't go through what I suffered before if anything should happen to this child. I understood your despair but you never tried to understand mine. You shut me out, Ben, and it broke my spirit. Since I've come to Willowmere I've found a degree of comfort in the place and its people, but no one knows my past and that is how I would prefer it to stay.'

'So you don't want anyone to know that we were once husband and wife?'

'I'm not bothered about that, and in any case it's a problem that won't arise as you won't be around.'

'Don't be too sure about that,' he said dryly. 'I'm my own boss these days, and am due for a break anyway.'

Ignoring his comment and its implications, she expained, 'It's the reason for the divorce that I don't want to be common knowledge. I don't want anything to spoil Jamie's memory.'

'You can rest assured that I, of all people, won't be telling anyone why we broke up,' he said grimly. 'But, Georgina, I feel you need to know that if I had any intention of my stay here being brief, it won't be now. I'm going to be around until the birth *and after*, so please take note of that.'

He was stepping away from the car and, as she began to drive slowly out onto the road, he called through the open window, 'When I've settled my account at the pub I'm going home to tie up all the loose ends and then I'll be back. I'm not sure when, but I *will* be coming back.'

She had no reply to that. Still numb with the shock of seeing him strolling towards her along the lane, she left him standing at her gate.

As she pulled up outside the surgery, Georgina's thoughts were in chaos. There was relief that Ben now knew about the baby, tied up with panic at the thought of him coming to Willowmere and invading the solitary, safe life she had made for herself. Beneath it all there was a glimmer of happiness, because in spite of the circumstances, she'd given him something to be joyful about.

She did wish he'd let her know he was coming, though, so she could have greeted him with calmness in her sitting room, dressed in something that would have concealed her pregnancy during the first few moments of meeting, instead of hovering behind the car door in a state of shock.

Yet her surprise had been nothing compared to his when he'd realised she was pregnant, and straight away jumped to the conclusion that she was in a relationship with someone else.

James was at the surgery before her but, then, he always was, for the good reason that he lived next door. After they'd greeted each other, she asked how the interviews of the evening before had gone, hoping to bring normality into a very strange morning.

'I've found an excellent replacement for Anna,' he told her, observing her keenly, 'but there was no one that I could visualise as a new partner. I feel it might be wise to leave that until Glenn comes back to Willowmere. So it looks as if we might be turning to a locum again for the time being.

'And what about you?' he asked with a smile. 'How are you today, Georgina? You're very pale. Is the baby behaving itself?'

She managed a grimace of a smile. Apart from Beth, the remaining practice nurse, James was the only one who ever mentioned her pregnancy. Everyone observed a lot, but no one actually said anything outright and she wondered just how curious the locals were about her pregnancy.

With regard to herself, she'd been coping just as long as she didn't let her mind travel back to that afternoon in the sitting room of the house where she'd once known such happiness. But that frail cocoon had been torn apart just an hour ago when Ben had appeared and discovered why she'd wanted to talk to him.

James, in his caring way, had noted that she wasn't her usual self and suddenly she knew that she had to tell someone what had happened before she'd arrived at the surgery. She couldn't keep her life under wraps any longer if Ben was going to be around.

'My ex-husband turned up this morning,' she said in a low voice. 'I didn't know which of us was the most dumbfounded, though for different reasons. I had no idea he was coming, and on his part he had no idea I was pregnant.'

'Poor you!' James exclaimed. 'How long is it since you saw him?'

'It had been three years, until we met unexpectedly eight months ago.'

'And you are about eight months pregnant,' he said slowly.

'Yes,' she agreed flatly, 'the baby is his.'

'And what does he think about that?'

'He is delighted.'

'So is that good?'

'It might have been once.'

'I see. Well, Georgina, I don't want to pry into your affairs, but I'm here if you need me. Obviously you have a lot on your mind. Do you want to take the day off?'

She shook her head. 'No, thanks, James. I need to

keep myself occupied. I will remember what you've just said. You are a true friend.' And before she burst into humiliating tears, she went to start another day at the village practice.

'By the way,' he called after her as she went towards her room, 'St Gabriel's have phoned with appointments for Christine Quarmby. The neurologist will see her on Thursday and the rheumatologist the following day.'

She paused. 'That's brilliant. I pulled a few strings and it seems that it worked. I'm very concerned about Christine. I just hope my fears for her aren't realised. On a happier note, have you heard from Anna and Glenn yet?'

'Yes. They've arrived safely and are already working hard.' James filled her in on Anna and Glenn's assignment before she went to her room and called in her first patient of the day, grateful to have her mind taken off the shock of seeing Ben again.

The day progressed along its usual lines, with Beth still managing but relieved to know that a replacement for Anna had been found. The two nurses had been great friends and Anna had been delighted when James had taken on Beth's daughter, Jess, as nanny for his two young children.

The children were fond of Jess. Aware that she was going to be missing from their lives for the first time since they'd been born, Anna had been happy to know before she'd left Willowmere that the arrangement was working satisfactorily.

Georgina's second patient was Edwina Crabtree.

She was one of the bellringers in Willowmere who helped send the bells high in the church tower pealing out across the village on Sunday mornings and at weddings and funerals, but it wasn't her favourite pastime that she'd come to discuss with her doctor

'So what can I do for you, Miss Crabtree?' Georgina asked the smartly dressed campanologist, who always observed her more critically than most when their paths crossed. She had a feeling that Edwina had her catalogued as a loose woman as she was pregnant with no man around, and thought wryly that *loose* was the last word to describe her.

She was tied to the past, to a small fair-haired boy who hadn't seen danger when it had been there, and 'tied' to the man who had been hurting so much at the time that he'd become a stranger instead of a rock to hold on to.

Edwina was in full spate and, putting her own thoughts to one side, Georgina tuned into what she was saying, otherwise the other woman was going to have her labelled incompetent, as well as feckless.

'The side of my neck is bothering me,' she was explaining, 'just below my ear. I didn't take much notice at first but the feeling has been there for quite some time and I decided I ought to have it looked at.'

'Yes, of course,' Georgina told her. After examining her neck carefully and checking eyes, ears and throat, she asked, 'Do you ever get indigestion?'

'All the time,' she replied stiffly, 'but surely it can't be connected with that. I thought you would just give me some antibiotics.'

'Before anything else I want you to have the tests and

we'll take it from there, Miss Crabtree. If you are clear of the stomach infection, it will be a matter of looking elsewhere for the neck problem, but we'll deal with that when we get to it.'

When she'd gone, looking somewhat chastened, Georgina sighed. Oh, for a simple case of lumbago or athlete's foot, she thought. Edwina Crabtree had the symptoms of Helicobacter pylori, bacteria in the stomach that created excess acid and could cause peptic ulcers and swellings like the one in the bellringer's neck.

Christine Quarmby, on the other hand, had all the signs of Sjögren's syndrome, an illness with just as strange a name but far more serious, and she was beginning to wonder what strange ailment she was going to be consulted on next.

Willow Lake, a local beauty spot, was basking in the shafts of a spring sun behind the hedgerows as Georgina drove to her first housecall later in the morning, and she thought how the village, with its peace and tranquillity, had done much to help her find sanity in the mess that her life had become.

As the months had become years she'd expected that one day Nicholas would inform her that Ben had found someone else and it would bring closure once and for all, but she'd been spared that last hurt, and now incredibly he seemed determined to come back into her life. She couldn't help wondering if he would feel the same if she wasn't pregnant.

Robert Ingram owned the biggest of Willowmere's two estate agencies and he had asked for a home visit to his small daughter, Sophie. The request had been received shortly after morning surgery had finished and Georgina was making it her first call.

Apparently Sophie had developed a temperature during the night and a rash was appearing in small red clusters behind her ears, under her armpits and in her mouth.

From her father's description the rash was nothing like the dreaded red blotches of meningitis, but she wasn't wasting any time in getting to the young patient. She never took chances with anyone she was called on to treat, and children least of all.

When Alison, Robert's wife, took her up to the spacious flat above the business Georgina found the little girl to be hot and fretful and the rash that her father had described was beginning to appear in other places besides the ones he'd mentioned.

'It's chickenpox,' she announced when she'd had a close look at the spots. 'Have you had any experience of it before, Mrs Ingram?'

'Yes. I had it when I was young,' Alison replied. 'My mother had me wearing gloves to stop me from scratching when the spots turned to blisters.'

'Good idea,' Georgina agreed, 'or alternatively keep Sophie's nails very short, and dab the rash with cala-mine lotion. She should be feeling better once they've all come to the surface, and in the meantime give her paracetamol if the raised temperature persists. Has Sophie started school yet?'

'She goes to nursery school twice each week and

is due to start in the main stream in September,' her mother replied.

'We've had a few cases of chickenpox over the last couple of weeks,' Georgina informed her, 'so the infection is with us, it would seem. Sophie should be fine in a few days, but if there is anything at all that you are concerned about, send for me straight away.' She gave a reassuring smile to the anxious mother. 'I'll see myself out.'

When she went downstairs into the shop area she told Robert Ingram, 'I'm afraid that Sophie has got chickenpox, Mr Ingram. The rash is appearing quite quickly and she will feel much better when it is all out. But I've told your wife if either of you have any worries about her, don't hesitate to send for me.'

He nodded. 'Thanks, Doctor. I'm relieved that it is nothing more serious.' And they both knew what had been in his mind.

As she was about to leave, Robert didn't mention that he'd had someone in earlier, arranging to rent the cottage next door to hers for a minimum period of six months. He thought that Georgina would surely feel happier if the other property was occupied, as they were the only two buildings on Partridge Lane.

As he'd watched her drive off that morning Ben had felt shock waves washing over him. How could Georgina have waited so long to tell him that they were going to be parents again? he'd thought dismally. Yet knew the answer even as he asked himself the question.

Georgina had been the butt of his grief and despair when they'd lost Jamie and it would seem she hadn't been prepared to risk a repeat performance by letting him into her life again when they were going to have another child.

He'd felt as if his heart had been cut out when it had happened all that time ago, and if anyone had dared tell him that time was a great healer, he'd turned on them angrily. Now he knew that it was so. The pain was still there, but instead of being raw it was a dull ache and there were actually days when he managed not to think about it.

He didn't know how Georgina had coped over the last three years. When the divorce had come through and she'd disappeared out of his life, the shock of it had brought him to his senses, but not to the extent that he'd done anything about it because he'd been gutted at the way he'd treated her.

Then, unbelievably, they'd met in the cemetery. So what had he done? Without a word of remorse he'd made love to her, and ever since had wanted to tell her all the things he'd never said then.

He'd known that Nicholas knew where she was, that he always stayed with Georgina for part of the time when he was over from the States. Yet until then he'd never tried to persuade him to disclose her whereabouts.

But after that everything had changed, and he'd badgered his young brother for the information with no success.

Now here he was, in the place where she lived, because Georgina had written to him. But if the reception he'd just got was anything to go by, a happy reunion wasn't on the cards.

It was a sombre thought, but it didn't stop him from calling in at the estate agent and making arrangements to rent the cottage next to hers. After he'd collected his things from the Pheasant, he set off on the long drive back to London.

The afternoon seemed endless to Georgina as patients attending the second surgery of the day came and went, and when at last it was time to go, James said, 'I never finished telling you about the new practice nurse. Her name is Gillian Jarvis and she is free to start immediately. I'm expecting her tomorrow morning.

'Her husband has just taken on the position of Lord Derringham's estate manager and like the Quarmbys they'll be living in a grace-and-favour house on the estate. She has a teenage girl at sixth-form college and a younger boy who will attend the village school. The family have moved up north from the Midlands where Gillian was also a practice nurse.

'I'm relieved that is sorted, but we still need someone to replace Glenn either full or part time. However, I suppose we can hang on for a while until the right person comes along,' he said, as he made everywhere secure before they left.

James was aware that she was only half listening and asked, 'Are you going to introduce me to your ex-husband, or will you both still be separate items?'

'Yes and no,' she told him. 'Ben has gone back to London, but he intends to return. I don't know where he's going to stay, and neither do I know how he's going to fill his time. But he told me that with regard to work, he's a free agent, and he needs a break. He also said that he's going to be there for the birth and afterwards.'

And how could she object? It was his child as much as hers. But it wouldn't be like it had been with Jamie. They'd been a family, a happy threesome, wrapped around with love. This time it would be two separate families. Mother and child as one of them, and father with his child the other.

James was observing her sympathetically and she smiled sadly. 'I'm sure you'll meet him soon.'

What she'd said to James was still uppermost in her mind as Georgina took her evening stroll later that day. Her baby *was* going to know its father, as she didn't doubt for a moment that Ben would be back. He'd made that crystal clear. It would be as an older, more sombre version of the husband she'd adored, but a loving father nevertheless.

As she'd told James, she didn't know where he was going to stay. But it couldn't be with her. They might be about to start a new family, but it didn't mean she was going to accept that as a reason for pretending anything that wasn't there.

When she turned to wend her homeward way in the quiet evening the silence was broken by a train en route for the city, travelling across the aqueduct high above the river. Once it had gone there was peace once more down below, and a fisherman engaged in one of the quietest of sporting activities cast his rod over the dancing water.

* * *

It was two days later. Georgina had done some shopping in the village on her way home—meat from the butcher's, fresh bread and vegetables from the baker's and greengrocer's—and as was her custom, she went straight through to the kitchen to start preparing the food.

When she glanced through the window, her eyes widened. Ben was mending a gap in the fence between the two cottages, and as if conscious that he was being watched, he looked up and with hammer in hand gave a casual wave then carried on with what he was doing.

She drew back out of sight and hurried to the front of the house. Surely enough, the 'To Let' sign had been replaced on the cottage next door to one that said 'Let by Robert Ingram'.

Ben had never been in the habit of doing things by halves, she thought as she leaned limply against the doorpost. It was one of the reasons why he was so successful in his career. But this time he'd excelled himself.

Not only had he come to live in her village, but he'd taken up residence almost on her doorstep. Obviously he wasn't intending to miss anything that concerned his pregnant wife and the child she was carrying.

Maybe repairing the gap in the fence was an indication that though he'd sought her out he was going to stay on his own side of the fence, or perhaps on discovering that she was pregnant his interest had moved from mother to child, and until it was born he would be keeping his distance. If either of those things *were* in his mind, shouldn't she be relieved?

Contrary to all the thoughts that had been going through her mind since they'd met at her gate, she went out into the garden and, leaning over the fence, said stiffly, 'I've bought steaks and fresh vegetables and it's just as easy to cook for two as for one. It will be ready in about half an hour if you want to join me.'

He paused in the act of hammering a nail in and looking up, said, 'Er…thanks for the offer, but I've been shopping myself and have a lasagne in the oven.' He hesitated. 'It's big enough for two. It would save you cooking after a busy day at the practice.'

Taken aback by the suggestion, she gazed at him blankly and he groaned inwardly. After the other day's chilly welcome, he had promised himself that now he was established in the village he would take it slowly with Georgina. Keep in the background but be there if he was needed. So what was he doing?

'I only made the suggestion because I've had cause to discover that it's no joke coming home to an empty house and having to start cooking after working all day,' he said into the silence. 'At one time I was keeping the fast-food counters in the stores going, but that didn't last.'

His kitchen door was open. She could smell the food cooking and told herself that Ben asking her to dine with him was no different than her asking him over. They were both doing it out of politeness. It didn't mean anything.

'Yes, all right,' she agreed. 'How long before we eat?'

'Twenty minutes, if that's OK?'

'Yes. It will give me time to shower away the day and change into some comfortable clothes.' Turning, she went back inside with the feeling that she was making a big mistake.

CHAPTER THREE

WHEN Ben opened the door to her twenty minutes later, Georgina stepped into a bare, newly decorated hall that could only be described as stark. When he showed her into the sitting room, it was the same, and a vision of their London house came to mind, spacious, expensively furnished, in the leafy square not far from the park where she'd taken Jamie that day.

Yet Ben was prepared to live in this soulless place and she wondered what was in his mind. He was going to be involved, come what may, but their marriage had foundered long ago. It had hit rock bottom and wasn't going to rise out of the ashes because they'd made a child.

But that occasion had been the forerunner of an unexpected chain of events that had brought him back into her life. Not because he'd known about the baby. That had really rocked him on his feet. He'd come in reply to her letter. Curious, no doubt, to find his ex-wife surfacing from her hidey-hole.

'What?' he asked, observing her expression.

'This place must seem rather basic after our house in London.'

'It's adequate,' he said dryly. 'I long since ceased to notice the delights of that place.' He pointed to a small dining area of the same standard as the rest of the house. 'If you'd like to take a seat, I'll dish out the food.'

This is unreal, Georgina thought as Ben brought in a perfectly cooked lasagne and a bowl of salad, yet she had to admit it was nice to sit down to a meal that was ready to eat after a busy day at the practice.

'So what is there to do in the evenings in this place?' he asked as he served the food.

'Well, you already know the Pheasant in the village, which is the centre of the night life. Everyone congregates there to drink and chat in the evenings. Willowmere is a very friendly place, a small community where everyone cares about everyone else.'

'So you go to the pub every night, then?'

'I didn't say that was what *I* do. My evenings are spent clearing up after my meal and then taking a short walk. This is a beautiful place. I either stroll along the river bank or to Willow Lake, which isn't far away, and contrary to life in the big city, I'm meeting people I know all the time I'm out there, not just because I'm their doctor but because that's what village life is all about.'

She didn't tell him that it had been her lifesaver in the lonely months when she'd first come to live there, when the feeling of no longer being part of the life that she'd once thought would be hers for ever had been unbearable.

'After that I come home, have a hot drink and go to bed,' she concluded.

'So maybe you'll show me around some of these places that you're so fond of,' he said equably, as if not appalled at the similarity of their lives where there was work, lots of it, then coming home to an empty house and a scratch meal, and in his case, watching television for as long as he could stand it before going up to the bed they'd once shared.

'Maybe,' she said noncommittally. 'I suppose you think my life here sounds dull, but it is what I want. I don't ever want another relationship with *anyone*, Ben. Any love I have to spare will be for my baby.'

'Our baby!' he corrected, as his spirits plummeted.

'Yes, indeed. I'm sorry, Ben. It will be *ours*, yours and mine,' she agreed, 'but don't have expectations about anything else.'

'I won't,' he told her steadily, and steered the conversation into other channels. 'You haven't asked me what I'm going to do jobwise while I'm here.'

'No, I haven't, though I have wondered.'

'Don't concern yourself. I'll find something. Do you need any help at the practice or are you fully staffed?'

She gazed at him, open-mouthed. 'We do have a vacancy, but that would be coming down a peg, wouldn't it? I've seen your name mentioned a few times regarding paediatric surgery. You're a high-flyer these days, aren't you?'

'Some people might think so,' he replied dryly, and thought that though he might be good at his job, when it came to coping with grief he'd fallen flat on his face.

'It was just a thought. But if you don't want me around during your working day, just say so. What sort of a position are we talking about?'

'We need another doctor.'

'I see. Interesting. But don't be alarmed, Georgina. I'm not going to crowd you.'

'Not much!'

'You mean my moving in next door?'

'Well, yes.'

'I've rented the place so I will be close at hand if you need me when the baby comes.'

'Right.'

'What? Don't you believe me?'

'Yes, of course I do,' she said. 'I'm sure on some wakeful night on our child's part I will be grateful to have you near, but don't take me too much for granted, Ben.'

He didn't reply. Instead he said, 'Shall we take our coffee into the deluxe sitting room of my new accommodation?'

They spent the rest of the time together talking about the village and when he mentioned the practice again, and the part she played in it, she answered his questions warily.

'This James Bartlett sounds a decent guy,' he remarked. 'I'd like to meet him. Is he married?'

'James lost his wife in a motor accident five years ago, just a few weeks after she'd given birth to twins. Pollyanna and Jolyon are in their first year at the village school.'

'And he's never remarried?'

'No. James and the children live next door to the surgery with an excellent nanny and housekeeper to help out. His sister, Anna, was a nurse in the practice until she married a locum who was with us, and now they've left and gone to work in Africa, leaving James with two replacements to find.

'He's found someone to fill the gap of practice nurse but is hanging fire with the doctor vacancy, saying that he might wait until Glenn Hamilton, his sister's new husband, comes back from Africa to offer him a permanent placing, and in the meantime employ someone on a temporary basis as he did with him originally.'

'It puts more strain on you both, doesn't it, leaving the gap unfilled?' She was getting up to go, feeling they'd talked about the practice enough, and he said, 'You've missed your walk tonight, haven't you? I'm surprised that it takes you by the river. I would have thought it the last place to appeal to you.'

She turned away, thinking that she might have known that Ben would still be out to give her memory a nudge given the chance, and was tempted to tell him that she needed no reminders of what had happened to Jamie and never would.

'A river only becomes a dangerous place because of the elements above and the actions of those of us at its level,' she said in a voice so low he could only just hear it.

If he'd wanted to reply, he didn't get the chance as she was opening the door and telling him, 'Thanks for the meal, Ben.' Then she was gone, out into the spring dusk and back to the place where she'd felt content until now.

Ben watched her go from the window and felt like kicking himself for his apparent insensitivity. He hadn't meant it to be a hurtful comment. It had been said more out of consideration for her feelings, but in the past that hadn't always been the case and he couldn't blame Georgina for freezing up on him.

He'd been congratulating himself that he'd been making progress in getting to know his wife all over again but he'd blown it. Resisting the urge to go after her he turned away from the window, deciding that he'd already been guilty of one moment of bad timing—no point in risking another.

An owl hooted eerily and when Ben turned to look at the clock on the bedside table, it read 2:00 a.m. For most of his life he'd slept with the never-ending sound of London traffic in his ears, but not tonight. Except for the owl, there wasn't a sound out there.

When he raised himself off the pillows and padded across to the window, the moon was shining down on Partridge Lane and he saw the burnished brown of a fox's coat as it slunk along beside the trees on the opposite side.

To a city dweller like himself the rural scene outside his window was strange enough, but stranger still was the thought that next door Georgina was sleeping with their child inside her. Ever since he'd discovered that he was to be a father again he'd been throwing off the mantle of grief that had been heavy on him for so long.

Georgina saying that she wanted no commitments of any kind was something he would have to take in his stride. It was only what he deserved, but he was not going to give in easily. What they'd had before had been very special and he'd cast it and her aside and lived to bitterly regret it.

But now the fates were being kind. He'd found her, and not only was there joy in that, they'd made a child on that August afternoon, and his heart rejoiced every time he thought about it.

Georgina wasn't too happy about the way it had been conceived, but surely she realised that those moments had been more about hunger than lust, a coming together out of the lonely places that they'd found themselves in.

The fox had gone, the owl was silent, and for the first time in years, he was looking forward to what the next day would bring as he went back to bed.

In the cottage next door Georgina was also finding sleep hard to come by. The baby was moving inside her and it was nothing like it had been before when she'd been pregnant.

In those days Ben would have been beside her, sharing in the wonder of the moment by placing his hand gently on the place where the movements were coming from.

Tonight he was nearer than he'd been in years, but still far away in every other respect, and she told the little unborn one, 'Your father is next door and I don't know what to think about that. He didn't know about you until he came, and now he's going to stay. What are we going to do?'

* * *

There was no sign of Ben when she was ready to leave for the surgery the next morning, and Georgina was thankful. She needed a clear head for what she was going to be faced with during the day, and it was more than she'd had the night before.

The shock of his arrival in the new life that she'd made for herself wasn't as acute today and she intended to keep any thoughts of him at the back of her mind until such time as she could view everything more sensibly.

It was another bright spring morning, the kind of day that didn't lend itself to sombre thoughts, and a quick glance at the number of patients waiting to be seen as she passed by to get to her consulting room indicated that the village folk must be feeling the same, as for once, there weren't many.

On being introduced, she found Gillian, the new practice nurse, to be a pleasant, robust-looking woman who seemed to have hit it off with Beth straight away. As James had mentioned, she lived not far from the Quarmbys on the Derringham estate, though in a more prestigious house, her husband being the estate manager, and Georgina was reminded that tomorrow Christine would be keeping the first appointment that she'd made for her at St Gabriel's with her anxious husband by her side.

As she settled behind her desk she could hear the church bells ringing out across the village and thought that Edwina Crabtree's results on the possible stomach infection should be back soon.

The sound of the bells was also a reminder that

though there were the sights and sounds of new life all around, for one family in the village it was going to be remembering a life that was past as they buried an elderly relative that morning in the churchyard not far away.

That same family had just celebrated a birth and old Henry Butterworth's dying wish had been granted when he'd held his new great-granddaughter in his arms the night before he'd passed away peacefully in his sleep.

When she'd gone up to the Butterworths' remote farm on the fringe of the moors to sign the death certificate, Georgina had been met with a mixture of emotions from those there. There'd been delight at the safe arrival of the baby, grief at the passing of the old man, and relief that Henry had been spared further suffering from advanced Parkinson's disease.

As she'd driven back to the surgery on that day a week ago she'd been aware once again of the close family ties of the people in Willowmere. James and Anna had been a prime example of that in the way they'd cared for his motherless children, and Anna would never have left Pollyanna and Jolyon if she hadn't been sure they would be properly cared for by those that James had appointed to take her place.

It made the split between Ben and herself appear a poor example by comparison, but none of those she'd been thinking of had lost a child. *Her* family had ended up as two grieving strangers and how she wished with all her heart that it hadn't been like that.

There'd been no bitterness in her towards Ben. She'd understood his suffering and had felt just great sadness that it had driven her away from him into lonely exile when it should have brought them closer.

Of one thing she was sure, she could not go through that again, no matter how much they loved this new child when it came. But today the sun was shining in a clear blue sky, there was birdsong up in the trees, and as Timothy Lewis seated himself across from her in the middle of the morning, Georgina asked the man who owned Willowmere's secondhand bookshop, 'What can I do for you today, Timothy?'

He was a quiet, unassuming fellow who loved his books. As well as the literary treasures on the shelves of his quaint shop, he prided himself on stocking something for everyone, and whenever she had a moment to spare, Georgina would call in to find a book for bedtime, as sleep wasn't always easy to come by even when she'd had a busy and tiring day.

'I keep having the most awful headaches,' Timothy said in reply to the question. 'A couple of times a month I've been having them and when they come, I can't bear to lift my head off the pillow.'

When she checked his blood pressure, it was only slightly above normal and she asked, 'You haven't had a blow to the head at all?'

'No, nothing like that.'

'Do you feel sick when the headaches come, or have trouble with your vision?'

'Er, yes, both,' he replied. 'I sometimes feel better when I've been sick, and with regard to my eyes I always get flashing lights in front of them as the headache is coming on.'

'It sounds as if you have the symptoms of migraine,' she told him. 'They are easy enough to recognise. What isn't easy in a lot of cases of migraine is to discover what brings it on. Anger, excitement, stress are all factors, and so is diet.' She took some leaflets from a desk drawer and handed them to him. 'These have information on identifying possible triggers and managing the condition. For example, there are some foods that should be avoided, in particular chocolate and dairy foods such as cheese. Also red wine and citrus fruits can trigger it. How long do the headaches last when you get them?'

'It was a few hours at first, but the last time it was a couple of days and I had no choice but to shut the shop, which is my living going down the drain.'

'If they get any worse, come back and see me,' she told him sympathetically. 'In the meantime I can prescribe something to alleviate the pain, and make sure you get plenty of rest. And, Timothy, how about getting someone to help in the shop so that you don't have to close when they occur?'

'I suppose I might have to,' he agreed sombrely, 'but I'm used to my own space. When customers come in, I just leave them to browse. If they want to buy, fair enough, and if not so be it.'

'Come back if the headaches persist or get any worse,' she said as she showed him out. 'And in the meantime try to avoid stress.'

When he'd gone, Elaine, the practice manager, appeared with a message that James wanted a short meeting of staff and would she be free for half an hour first thing next morning before the start of surgery?

Elaine was facing the window and before Georgina could reply, she said, 'Wow! Where has *he* come from? Do you think he's just visiting or has come to live here?'

Georgina swivelled round in her chair and saw Ben strolling along Willowmere's main street in the direction of the shops.

'I know where he's from,' she said flatly as she waved her privacy goodbye. 'And I know why he's here in Willowmere.' Elaine looked at her questioningly. 'His name is Ben Allardyce. He's my ex-husband and he's moved into the cottage next to mine.'

'Really!' Elaine exclaimed, adding in quick contrition, 'I'm sorry, Georgina. I wouldn't have commented if I'd known.'

'It's all right,' Georgina replied. 'You couldn't be expected to know he was connected with me, and if you're wondering about the baby, Elaine, it's his. Ben is the father.'

Elaine was devastated to have been the cause of the reticent dark-haired doctor having to bring her private life into the open, knowing how *she* would feel in similar circumstances, and she said hurriedly, 'What you've just told me won't go any further, Georgina, I promise.'

'I know it won't,' she said wryly, 'but someone will put two and two together sooner or later, knowing village gossip, so there isn't much point in me pretending that Ben has nothing to do with me. Strictly speaking, he hasn't, not now. It's three years since we divorced, but there's nothing to say that *he* won't tell people what the connection is if they see us together. And about the practice meeting, yes, that is fine by me.'

When Elaine had gone back down to her office in the basement with her usual composure missing, Georgina thought that she couldn't imagine the petite blonde ex-accountant, in her late forties and who was the epitome of efficiency, ever having to admit to a failed marriage and an unexplained pregnancy. That, until Ben had come back on the scene, had been her affair and only hers.

She didn't see him come back from where he'd gone. There was too much going on with the patients for there to be time to stand at the window, hoping to catch a glimpse of him to confirm it hadn't been a dream the night before when they'd eaten at the same table in his cheerless rented house.

She wasn't surprised that Elaine had noticed him on the street. He'd always been a man that women took note of, though it had never made any impact on him. He'd only ever wanted her until they'd lost Jamie and then he'd withdrawn into his own grief-filled world and wanted no one.

As she drove home at the end of the day, Georgina was keen to see Ben again. If he'd been in her line of vision at any time during the day, she might have felt differently, but it was almost as if now that he'd entered her world, she had to keep registering his presence to make sure she wasn't imagining it.

She wasn't aware that he'd watched her drive off that morning from the front window of his cottage and had wished that they were going to spend the day together instead of him being left to his own devices, even though he'd known it was a vain hope.

Apart from the fact that Georgina had her commitment to the practice to consider, there was the way she'd reacted on first seeing him. There had been dismay in the dark hazel eyes meeting his, rather than delight, and it had been there again when he'd suggested he might help out at the surgery. But when last had he given her any cause to feel different?

The boot had turned out to be on the other foot. It was *she* who had given *him* joy with the promise of another child to love. After those first few agonised moments when he'd thought it might belong to some other man, he'd never stopped smiling, even though it had cut deep, knowing how long she'd waited to tell him. But that was a bed he'd made for himself and he had no choice but to lie on it.

In the middle of the morning he went into her garden and brought in the line of washing that she'd hung out first thing. On discovering that a fresh breeze had dried it, he fished out an iron and ironing board from one of the cupboards in his kitchen and applied himself to the task.

When the ironing was finished, he decided to go and find some lunch and then do some exploring of the rural paradise where she'd chosen to start a new life. He had passed the surgery with eyes averted and, unaware that he was being observed from one of the windows, had gone to the Pheasant for a ploughman's lunch, before familiarising himself with the delights of Willowmere.

He'd had a change of mind about that while he'd been eating, hoping that Georgina might want to show him around the village herself, which could be an indication that she wasn't as dismayed by his arrival as she was making out. Now he was listening for her car to pull up on the lane that was almost as quiet during the day as it had been during the night.

She was tired, he thought, noting her pallor and the droop of her shoulders as she got out of the car, but when he came out of his door and joined her on the driveway, she straightened up and with a steady smile asked, 'So what has *your* day been like?'

'Different,' he replied, 'and last night even more so.'

'In what way?'

'I saw a fox slinking along by the hedge over there and an owl was hooting somewhere nearby in the kind of silence I'm not used to. It was weird.'

'You weren't impressed, then?'

'Er, yes, I was. Both things were an improvement on the drone of the city traffic, be it night or day. I nearly went to explore the village when I'd had some lunch but thought that you might want to show me around the place yourself.'

'Possibly, but not on a week night. A short stroll by the river or around the lake is my limit, and tonight I have some ironing to do.'

He shook his head and she observed him enquiringly.

'What?'

'It's done. I brought the washing in and ironed it.'

She felt like weeping. It was so long since anyone had done anything for *her*. Instead, she said flatly, 'There was no need for you to do that, Ben. Please don't interfere in my life. I have it sorted. Don't try to change anything.'

'Surely you see that it's already changing with the child that you're carrying,' he said levelly. 'How were you going to manage when the baby came?'

'As I have managed for quite some time. On my own.'

She was tired and wishing she'd never got involved in the conversation that was taking place. It was turning out the way she'd hoped it wouldn't. Ben had been around for only a few hours and he was trying to take charge.

'What about antenatal care? What are you doing about that?'

He was making matters worse and she said stiffly, 'It is sorted. I'm registered privately with a gynaecologist at St Gabriel's. I wasn't going to take any chances with my being on my own. The sense of responsibility is far greater when one is about to become a single parent.'

'It doesn't have to be like that, Georgina,' he said steadily. 'I was the one who made you pregnant, which makes me even more responsible for our baby than you are.'

'Can't we just leave it for now, Ben?' she said dejectedly. 'I'm hungry and tired.' With a vestige of a smile she added, 'Which is not a cue for you to ask if I'm taking any vitamins.'

'Point taken,' he said with a smile of his own, and followed it by suggesting, 'How about I go to fetch some fish and chips? I saw a shop in the village that looked appetising. It would save us both cooking.'

'Yes, all right,' she agreed weakly, aware that it would be the second time they'd eaten together in a situation that was awkward to say the least, but until she'd got to grips with it, that was how it was going to be.

While Ben was gone she showered quickly and changed into a loose pink top and maternity jeans, and had plates warming in the oven and the kettle on the boil by the time he arrived with the food.

When he came inside, he looked around him curiously. This was the place that Georgina had made her home, he thought, when the one they'd made together had been too alien for her to want to stay there.

It was attractive, elegant in a toned-down sort of way, like the woman herself, who was making it clear that she was not going to change anything since he'd appeared on the scene.

With regard to himself he'd drifted into an existence of much work and very little play, but since coming to Willowmere, he was finding a new reason for living in being near his wife again. To him the term *'ex'* didn't apply. Georgina would be his wife until the day he died. He was a one-woman man and since he'd been without her, there had been no others.

'I feel better already,' she told him when they'd finished eating. Regretting the way she'd dealt with his earlier concern, she went on, 'Maybe we could go for the stroll I told you about. Willow Lake isn't far from here and for me that place *is* Willowmere. Needless to say, there are lots of willows there and they really are the most graceful of trees. It is where Glenn asked Anna to be his wife and they were married a month later before going out to Africa on a new and exciting venture.'

'You sound envious.'

The smile was back and this time it wasn't so hard to come by. 'No, not at all. I have lots of things happening in my life at the moment, and, Ben, if you think me cruel for not telling you I was pregnant, there were countless times during the months that have passed when I've started a letter or picked up the phone to tell you about the baby.

'In the end I sat down, wrote to you, and almost ran to the post office. Once the letter was on its way I felt so much better. It never occured to me that you might not be there to receive it. When you didn't get in touch I didn't know what to do.'

'But I found the letter at last, didn't I?' he said gravely. 'And you've given me a new reason for living. What more could I ask?'

It was there again, she thought. The implication that she was going to be the outsider in the forthcoming threesome.

'So shall we go for our stroll, if you really feel up to it, before the light fades?' he suggested, and she nodded. It could have been a special moment, but it hadn't turned out that way.

It was the oddest feeling, walking through the village with Ben by her side, Georgina thought. People going to the Pheasant hailed her as they would normally do, while at the same time casting curious glances at her companion.

Ben said, 'How are you going to explain me if anyone asks?'

'I'll tell them the truth, of course,' she replied. 'No
point in doing otherwise if you intend staying.'

'Oh, I intend staying,' he told her. 'Wild horses
wouldn't drag me away.'

'And would you be so definite about that if I wasn't
going to give you another child? You never made any
attempt to come looking for me before.'

'Maybe that's because I didn't know where you
were. Nicholas is very good at clamming up when he
has to. If you hadn't written to me everything would
have been as it's been since...'

His voice trailed away, and she said gently, 'Saying
his name isn't going to drag us back into the nightmare.
I had to smile the other night. *Oliver Twist* was on television, and it reminded me of when Jamie was Oliver
in the primary school Christmas play.'

He was laughing now. 'Yes, and how we thought he
was miscast as he looked too well fed. I always thought
he would have preferred to be the Artful Dodger.'

'And do you remember how they asked you to be the
Father Christmas, and we were on pins in case he recog-
nised you behind the whiskers?'

'Yes, I do,' he replied. 'I can still smell the glue that
one of the teachers used to stick them on me.'

At that moment they saw the glint of water ahead,
and as they stood beside the silent lake in the gloaming of a spring day, he said, 'You're right, Georgina.
Willow Lake *is* beautiful.' He turned to observe her
standing beside him with the so obvious signs of what

was to come in her changing shape and thought, *And so are you*.

They walked back to Partridge Lane in silence, each wrapped in with their own thoughts, and when their cottages came into view, Georgina said, 'Thanks for doing the ironing. I could have been more grateful when you told me it was done.'

He was laughing and she observed him in surprise. 'What a mundane comment to end the evening after visiting that idyllic lake,' he said. 'If you leave me a key under the mat tomorrow and the vacuum cleaner handy, I'll carry on with the chores. Just make a list.'

'If it got around that you were my new home help, it wouldn't fit in with your image in the medical world,' she told him jokingly, and marvelled at the moment of rapport that had suddenly surfaced.

They were standing at her gate, ready to separate, and she wondered if Ben was waiting to be invited in for the rest of the evening, and if that was the case, what should she do? But it seemed there was no cause to concern herself about that. He was turning to go into his rented cottage and said over his shoulder, 'Goodnight, Georgina. Sleep well.'

'And you, too,' she said weakly.

He was smiling. 'I most certainly will...now.'

CHAPTER FOUR

WHEN Georgina was ready to leave the cottage the next morning, Bryan Timmins, the farmer who delivered her milk, was coming up the drive. Looking at the now-occupied place next door, he said, 'Do you think your new neighbour will want his milk delivered, Dr Adams?'

'I would think so,' she told him. 'The person in question is accustomed to getting it from the supermarket and won't have realised that he can get milk delivered.'

'So can I risk leaving him a couple of pints, then?' the farmer asked.

'Yes, I'm sure you can. I'll tell him it was my doing.'

'Who is he? Do you know?'

'Er, yes, I do. His name is Ben Allardyce. He's a paediatric surgeon.'

'Another doctor, eh?' With a change of subject, he asked awkwardly, 'And how are *you* keeping.'

'I'm fine, Bryan,' she told him. 'And what about *your* pregnant lady? I didn't see Maggie at the antenatal clinic last week.'

'No, you wouldn't. The wife has gone to her mother's for a visit before the baby comes. We can't wait. If it's a boy, young Josh wants us to call him after some pop star that he's keen on. I shudder to think!'

'And if it's a girl?'

'He hasn't come up with anything for that so far. Have *you* chosen any names yet?'

At that moment Ben's door opened and as he eyed them questioningly Georgina said, 'Ben, may I introduce Bryan Timmins, who supplies me with fresh milk every day?' As the two men shook hands, she explained, 'Bryan owns the farm that we passed when I took you to see the lake. I've taken it on myself to arrange for your milk to be delivered. Is that all right?'

He was smiling. 'Yes, of course, that would be fine. It would seem to be another of the delights of living here.'

The burly farmer laughed, 'Aye, it is, though it's not all moonlight and roses, you know. There's the worry of foot and mouth, for one thing which is every farmer's nightmare, though I've never had that to contend with so far. Then there are trespassers who don't keep to the designated paths and trample the crops of some of us, but all in all it's a good life and a happy one, living in the countryside. You think so, don't you, Dr Adams?'

'Yes, I do,' she agreed, knowing that Bryan had yet to discover the connection between herself and her new neighbour.

When he'd gone, Ben said, 'You're off early, aren't you, Georgina? It's only eight o'clock.'

'James wants a short practice meeting before the day starts.'

'I see. Would it be all right if I popped into the surgery later in the day to have a look around and maybe meet the senior partner?'

'Er, yes, I suppose so,' she said, taken aback at the fact he hadn't lost interest at the practice. It would be another part of her life here that Ben was invading if he got involved in the work there. 'How do you want me to introduce you?'

'However it suits you best,' he said calmly. 'Your next-door neighbour, a colleague from the past...or you could tell them the truth, that I'm your husband. You said it wouldn't bother you if people found out, as long as they don't get to know the reason why we split up.'

'But you're not my husband any more, are you?'

'Legally, no, but there are more important things than paperwork and documents.'

'Such as?'

'Do I have to explain?'

'No,' she told him hurriedly.

It was neither the hour nor the occasion to start delving into the past. She didn't think there ever would be a right time for *that*. If they had to live side by side for however long it took, she would abide by it, and if Ben was intending taking a major role in their baby's life, there wasn't much she could do about that, other than apply for sole custody, and she could not do that to him.

He had suffered enough, they both had, and after the hurt she'd caused by not telling him she was pregnant for so long, to do that would be rubbing salt into the wound.

'What time are you thinking of visiting the surgery?' she asked. 'Early afternoon is always quietest, when we're back from the house calls and have a lull before the second onslaught of the day.'

'Twoish, then?'

She nodded. 'I'll tell James that you're coming to look us over.' And without further comment, she went to start her day.

The staff meeting that James had called didn't last long. In essence it was to welcome Gillian and to tell them that he was going to delay appointing another permanent partner until his new brother-in-law came back.

They all dispersed to their various duties after that except for Georgina, who stayed behind for a moment and said, 'Is it all right if Ben comes to have a look around when we're quiet this afternoon? He's interested in everything that's going on here and has even suggested that he would be willing to help out until Glenn gets back from Africa.'

She'd said it as a kind of warning, in case Ben did say something to that effect, and James stared at her in surprise.

'Really?' he exclaimed. 'And is he qualified?'

'Er…yes. His name is Ben Allardyce. He specialises in one particular branch of medicine, but in the past he has been a general consultant as well.'

'Are we talking about *the* Ben Allardyce? The paediatric surgeon?'

'Yes. He is my ex-husband. I think he's decided that he's going to need something to fill the days while he's in Willowmere, and that's where the suggestion came from.'

'I would welcome him into the practice on a temporary basis with open arms,' James said. 'But how would *you* feel about it, Georgina?'

'I'm not sure. I wasn't happy when he first suggested it, as he's already renting the cottage next to mine, but we do need someone, James, and it will be even more urgent when I'm off after having the baby. So feel free to ask him, if you so wish.'

He was smiling. 'I do wish, Georgina. I'll have a word with him when he comes this afternoon—just as long you're sure that you'd be happy with the arrangement?'

'I think one of the reasons he's offering is because he wants to make it easier for me during the coming weeks, so how can I object?' she said, with the feeling that she might be losing her strength of will.

Leaving James to take in what could be good news for the practice, Georgina went to start her day.

Edwina Crabtree's test results were back and they were positive for the presence of Helicobacter pylori. Georgina requested one of the receptionists to ask her to come in to discuss the findings.

It was today that Christine Quarmby was seeing the first of the two consultants that she'd referred her to, she thought as patients came and went, and wondered how long the sick woman would have to wait for a result.

* * *

Ben arrived at exactly two o'clock and as she saw him come through the main doors of the practice with a positive stride, Georgina felt a sudden rush of warmth. He had been so dear to her once, she thought. How could she not want him back in her life again?

But remembering the hurts from the past, she was still unsure. His decision to stay in the village was because of the baby rather than her, and could she blame him for that?

He'd been a loving father to Jamie, and gentle with his small patients in the London hospital where he'd worked. He was a natural with children. So the thought of another one of his own to love was obviously bringing him out of the depression that he'd fallen into three years ago.

'Hi,' he said when he saw her coming towards him. 'As you didn't leave a key or the vacuum handy, I've cleaned all the outside windows, yours *and* mine.'

'Great, so I'll be able to see who's coming up the drive,' she said, smiling as if her mind wasn't filled with the whys and wherefores of him actually standing beside her in the village practice. 'You seem determined to make yourself useful.'

'It makes a change, don't you think?' he replied sombrely, and she had no reply to that.

James came out of his room at that moment and when she'd introduced them, he said, 'Shall I show Ben around the surgery, Georgina, or would you like to do the honours?'

'I'll leave it to you,' she told him. 'The nurses are taking the diabetic clinic this afternoon and it will be the first time for the new practice nurse so I thought I'd be around to assist.'

She was chickening out and knew it, but Ben had been the one who'd said he wanted to meet James and it hadn't been her idea that he help out in the surgery, so she left them to it with a murmured 'I'll see you this evening, maybe' in Ben's direction.

'Sure,' he replied easily, but there was a look in his eyes that said he got her drift.

She came out of the nurses' room when he was on the point of leaving and he said, 'Nice place you and James have got here, Georgina. The practice manager seems extremely capable.' Remembering Elaine's comments when she'd seen him walking past the window, she almost laughed.

Bringing her back to the present, he said, 'James said you mentioned my working here to him, and we've come to an arrangement. I was surprised when he told me, as I thought you weren't keen on the idea.'

'Shall we just say that I could see the advantages of it after I'd given it some thought? It will take some of the strain off me.'

'Why do you think I suggested it?' he said evenly. 'I'm going to drive into town for the rest of the afternoon and will probably eat out, so I'll see you tomorrow, Georgina.'

'Yes, whatever,' she replied, and went back to her patients.

James was on top form as they were leaving at the end of the day. 'Ben is coming into the practice full-time,' he said jubilantly. 'He's starting on Monday.

Aren't we the lucky ones to have someone of his calibre on the staff for a short period?'

'Yes, I suppose we are,' she said, and wondered if Ben really was coming to work there for her sake.

As she went for her usual short walk that evening, the fact that it would be Easter at the end of the following week came to mind. She had thought of going away for the weekend while the surgery was closed, but it was a lovely time in the village and an ideal opportunity to drive to London to put fresh flowers on the grave where so much of her heart lay.

The main thought in her mind was that she'd hurt Ben a lot by being so slow in telling him about the baby. Did she want to hurt him further by going to London without his knowledge? It would be as if she was putting him in his place again, the place where he had been for three long years.

The situation he'd created by coming to live in the village had a strong feeling of getting to know each other all over again, and it gave her a mixture of pain and pleasure. There was comfort in knowing he was near, knowing that she could see him, touch him, and that she wasn't going to give birth to their baby without him.

But his presence was threatening the life she'd built for herself in Willowmere. Her hard-won contentment was disappearing in her awareness of all the things she'd tried to forget about him. His smile, the mouth that had kissed her, the surgeon's hands, long-fingered and supple, that had caressed her, and the trim, hard strength of him that she'd always thought would be there to protect, as well as arouse her—these were all things that could weaken her resolve to stay alone if she wasn't careful.

In her most upbeat moments she felt as if what had happened between them on the afternoon when he'd finally caught up with her at the cemetery had been meant. That the fates had decided to give them a push in the right direction, but those kind of thoughts were always followed by memories of the months before she'd said goodbye to a wonderful marriage.

As she walked homeward through woods carpeted with bluebells, she decided that she would tell Ben that she was driving to London on Good Friday. If he wanted to do the same, he could make his own arrangements.

The thought of being closeted together in the car for hours on end would be too much for their frail reunion to cope with, as would being together as she arranged the white roses of innocence on the grave.

But there was the coming weekend to get through first. Saturday and Sunday would be days when both she and Ben would have time on their hands, which could prove awkward.

She went up to bed at her usual time and steeled herself not to listen for him returning. It paid off and she went to sleep not knowing whether he was back or not.

When she opened the curtains the next morning, his car was in his drive. She wondered how she would have felt if it hadn't been. If he'd given up on her and gone back to London, discouraged by her lack of warmth. But as she looked down at the part of her anatomy where their child was curled up safely she knew that the die was cast. Ben would never let this one out of his sight.

When he'd first appeared, she'd made it clear that he had no part in her life any more. She'd said it because she'd been afraid that he might try to take over when he found out about the baby. But now that he was settled in the cottage next door it seemed as if, having made his presence felt, he was easing off and she wasn't sure what to make of it….

She was planning to go into the town herself over the weekend to get some ideas on the requirements of a new baby as it had been nine years since she'd last been pregnant.

But first there was Friday ahead of her and when she arrived at the surgery, she saw Edwina Crabtree in the waiting room, looking more dour than usual.

'I'm afraid that we've had a positive result on the stomach infection, Miss Crabtree,' she told her when it was her turn to be seen. 'How is the neck pain?'

'Just the same.'

'And the indigestion?'

'No different.'

'Now that I know what I'm treating, I'm going to prescribe medication to treat the stomach problem which should soon give you some relief from the indigestion and the neck discomfort.'

'I hope so,' was the flat reply. 'Spring is one of the busiest times for we bellringers. Lots of brides want the bells to be pealing as they come out of our church, and because it is in such a charming setting it is one wedding after another from Easter onwards.'

Was that a nudge for her? Georgina thought wryly when she'd gone, that the baby she was carrying would benefit from the blessing of the church. It would seem that so far Edwina, like most of the inhabitants of Willowmere, was not aware that the child's father was now there.

When she arrived home that evening, Ben appeared the moment she got out of the car and said, 'I've seen a café sort of place near the post office. Do you fancy eating there tonight?'

'I suppose it's not a bad idea,' she agreed. 'It will be the Hollyhocks Tea Rooms that you've seen. We get lots of walkers stopping off in the village on the lookout for some good food as Easter approaches, and the Hollyhocks is the answer. The people who own it are friends of mine.'

'Does that make any difference? Are you sure that you'll be happy for us to be dining there if that's the case? Only I feel that we have things to discuss and in a place like that we're on neutral ground.'

'You make us sound like enemies.'

'I didn't mean to, but we're not exactly on the same wavelength, are we?' he commented dryly.

She didn't reply to that. What did he expect? They'd been living separate lives for the last three years. A week back in each other's company wasn't going to cancel that out.

'Give me a few moments to get changed and while I'm gone perhaps you could phone and make sure they have a table free.'

* * *

'So what is it that you want to discuss?' she asked when they were seated at a table by the window in the village's most popular place for dining without frills.

'I was looking at baby things when I was in the town yesterday—prams, cots and lots of other items our new arrival will need and…'

He'd seen her expression and didn't finish the sentence.

'You took it on yourself to do that without consulting me,' she said. 'I've thought a few times that since you found me pregnant, you see me as just a means to an end.'

The colour drained from his face but his voice was level enough as he said, 'If you'd let me finish, I was intending to suggest that we go shopping this weekend. No point being on the last minute with everything. But as you seem to think I've stepped out of line, maybe it isn't a good idea.'

Georgina felt the wetness of tears. He hadn't taken her up on her last comment but had taken it on board. She could tell by the set of his jaw and she wished she hadn't been so hasty. But it was all part of her uncertainty, the feeling of not being in control. Since coming to Willowmere she'd managed to achieve it to a degree, until the moment she'd seen him walking towards her in the lane.

Ben was reading the menu as if the subject was closed, but she couldn't leave it at that and told him, 'I was thinking of going shopping, too.'

'And were not intending consulting me from the sound of it.'

'I hadn't got any further than considering it. You've

not been here long, don't forget, and I'm used to doing things on my own, making my own decisions. I'm not going to get out of the habit in five minutes. I'm sorry if I upset you, but please don't rush me, Ben. By all means, let's go shopping together. We can order what we need on the arrangement that it is to be delivered once the baby has arrived safely.'

There was a question in the dark hazel eyes looking into hers. 'Why? Is there any reason why it might not, a problem that you've not told me about?'

'Not at present, but as we are both aware, sometimes things can go wrong.'

'What is it that you're not telling me, Georgina?' he persisted in a low voice.

'It's just that the gynaecologist is keeping a close watch on my blood pressure. It's all right at the moment. I check it all the time, but as we both know in pregnancies it can soon go sky high.'

'Who is this fellow?' he questioned. 'Does he know you had a difficult time with Jamie? I'll have a word with him to make sure he's knows what he's doing.'

She had to smile. 'You won't do any such thing. What about professional ethics?'

'Nothing is going to happen to this child if I can help it,' he said with a grim sort of calm that tore at her heart, 'and if it means checking up on the gynaecologist, I'll do it.'

'You're taking over again,' she reminded him. 'Ian Sefton is the best. I've made sure about that, Ben. Now, shall we decide what we want to eat? I'm starving.'

She'd introduced him to Emma and Simon, the

husband-and-wife team who owned the place, and now Emma was poised ready to take their order. Once that was done, they chatted about less personal things until the food arrived.

It was as they were strolling back home that Ben said, 'When is your next appointment to see this guy?'

'The week after Easter. You're not going to suggest that you go with me, are you? I'm quite capable of dealing with that part of the pregnancy myself.'

He sighed. 'Yes, I do know that. You don't really need me back on the scene, do you? You're extremely capable, but I'm afraid you are going to be lumbered with me. I feel we've been blessed with this little one that you are carrying and I'm sure you must feel the same.'

Tears were threatening again and she told him, 'Of course I do. How could I feel otherwise? But just give me time, Ben. It's been so long since anyone cared if I lived or died.'

'Silence doesn't have to mean not caring,' he replied. 'It's just that sometimes shame gets in the way.'

'We both did the best we could,' she said flatly.

'Yes, but mine wasn't good enough, was it?'

'We've done enough heart searching for tonight, Ben,' she protested.

'Yes, we have,' he agreed. 'Let's get you home and tucked up in bed with Baby Allardyce.'

Georgina had come to a standstill and he said, 'What's wrong? Are you all right?'

She was unbuttoning her jacket. Reaching out to take his hand, she placed it on to her expanding front and said in a low voice, 'Can you feel your child moving, Ben?'

'Oh, yes!' He looked at her, his dark eyes full of wonder. 'I can indeed. It's fantastic, Georgina.'

'Yes, it is,' she said softly. 'It keeps me awake sometimes, and when it does, I always wish I could share the moment with someone else.'

So he was just 'someone else', Ben thought sombrely. Not the beloved husband or the expectant father, but he wasn't going to be dismayed. In just a week they'd come a long way and every day was going to bring them closer together if it had anything to do with him.

Like tomorrow, which would be a big step forward when they went shopping together. It was all going to come right, he told himself. He just needed to be patient and maybe one day they might be a happy family once again. Nothing would ever replace Jamie, but there would be acceptance of it at last if he and Georgina could start fresh.

With regard to her antenatal appointment, Georgina would have to accept his anxieties. She'd had a difficult pregnancy when she'd been carrying Jamie. There had been problems with her blood pressure for most of the time, and she would not have forgotten *that*. He certainly hadn't. So far all seemed to be well, or she would have said, but he would be keeping a close watch.

They were happy and relaxed as they chose a pram, baby bath and a pretty white crib, along with a host of other things, and when they were paid for on the understanding that delivery would be made once the baby

was born, there was only one moment of seriousness
when Ben asked, 'How's the blood pressure?'

'Fine,' she said. 'You will be the first to know if ever
it isn't.'

Once they'd finished shopping for the baby they
strolled around the stores and dawdled until it was time
for lunch. As they went to find somewhere to eat, Ben
said, 'The other day I heard the farmer who brings the
milk ask if you'd decided on any names for the baby.
Have you?'

She shook her head. 'Nothing definite. Have you any
ideas?'

'I might have. If it's a girl, how about Aimee? The
French spelling of it?'

'We thought of that last time, didn't we?' she reminded him, and saw that he was smiling.

'Yes. We wanted Jamie for a boy, and chose Aimee
for a girl because it sounded like Jamie without the *J*.
What name would you choose for another boy?'

'Arran, maybe?'

'I like that. Arran Allardyce sounds good.'

They were waiting for a table to be free in a bistro
in one of the stores, and after the brief discussion about
names, silence fell on them.

Georgina was thinking that twice in the last few days
Ben had been able to talk about Jamie as if he'd found
some acceptance at last, and it warmed her heart.

Shopping together for the baby had been delightful.
Having Ben beside her had felt so right. It had been like
taking a step back in time to when all had been perfect

between them, and now they were discussing names like any excited parents.

But they weren't like other parents, and they were going too fast. She needed some calm in her life while she adjusted to how it was going to be, instead of how it had been.

He was pushing it, Ben was thinking as he observed her closed expression. Why couldn't he have been satisfied with what they'd done together so far, without pinning Georgina down about names for the baby?

When they arrived back in Willowmere in the quiet Saturday afternoon, Ben noticed that cricket was being played on a field behind the vicarage. Observing the flashes of white against the fresh green of the pitch, he said, 'I might have guessed there would be cricket here. Does the village have a team of its own?'

'Yes, but today it will be just a friendly match as the season doesn't actually start until Easter, does it?' she replied.

'I might go to watch when I've dropped you off,' he said, 'or do you want to come?'

'No, thanks,' she told him with the feeling that she needed some time alone.

As if he'd picked up on something in her tone, Ben looked at her sharply. 'You've had enough of me for one day? Is that it?'

She shook her head. 'No. If you want to know, it's me that I've had enough of.'

He was stopping the car in front of their two cottages

and he turned to where she was sitting unmoving in the passenger seat and said, 'I'm not sure what you mean by that and am not going to ask. I'll see you later, Georgina. Why not have a rest while you have the chance?'

'I'll think about it,' she promised, knowing that she needed ease of mind as much as she needed ease of body.

The first person Ben saw when he arrived at the cricket match was James Bartlett with his two children, and the other man flashed him a welcoming smile. He was dressed in whites so was either a player or a stand-in, Ben decided, but as it was the interval at that moment and tea and cakes were being passed around, he couldn't tell which.

James had taken to this estranged husband of Georgina's, much to his surprise, as he'd been prepared to dislike the man who had obviously caused Georgina anguish in the past, but on meeting Ben he'd found him to be pleasant, intelligent, and a man he could communicate with.

What had gone wrong between them he didn't know, but he sensed an awareness of each other that told him feelings of some kind still ran strongly in them both.

'Do you play?' he asked the newcomer as he and the children took Ben to the pavilion for some refreshments.

He smiled. 'No. Not really. I used to play on the fathers' team when it was sports day at my son's school, and he and I used to play cricket in the back garden sometimes, but that's about it.'

James frowned in surprise. 'I didn't know that you and Georgina have a child. She's never said. Does he live with you?'

'No,' he said levelly. 'We lost Jamie in an accident when he was six years old. He was drowned.'

'Oh! I'm so sorry!' James exclaimed as Georgina's reserve and reticence were explained. He knew from bitter experience that some things just couldn't be talked about because they hurt too much, and it seemed that where he had lost a wife, Ben and Georgina had lost a child.

'It was losing him that broke up our marriage. Grief can be a cruel thing,' Ben said as one of the ladies behind the counter passed him a mug of tea. 'I take it that Georgina had never mentioned either him or me to you.'

'No, she hadn't,' James confirmed. 'So why have you come to Willowmere after all this time?'

'We met up by chance last August. I realised how much I still cared. She wrote to me some time ago, asking that we talk, but I was away and didn't get the letter until recently. I came here hoping for a reconciliation and discovered that she was pregnant, which means that I'm not budging. Whether she wants me here or not, I'm staying. I want to be there for her at the birth and afterwards. I let her down once when she needed me desperately and am not going to do it again.

'And do you know what, James? I've never talked to another living soul as I've talked to you today, but there is just one thing. Georgina is wary of me and I don't blame her, so could I ask you not to mention our conversation to her?'

'Yes, of course,' was the reply, 'and if ever there is anything I can do for either of you, Ben, you have only to ask.'

At that moment his children came up, asking for ice cream, and as Ben observed Pollyanna and Jolyon he thought that in spite of losing his wife the man standing beside him was truly blessed.

CHAPTER FIVE

WHEN Ben had gone to watch the cricket, Georgina lay on the sofa in her sitting room and thought about the time they'd just spent together.

They'd been happy as they'd chosen the baby's layette, perfectly in tune like any expectant parents shopping for an addition to their family. But now she was wondering if it was wishful thinking on her part. Theirs was a strange relationship, and where Ben seemed supremely confident that it was all going to work out, she was alternating between doubt and hope all the time.

The more she saw of him the more she craved to have him near, yet when they were together she was wary, and knew he sensed it. He'd asked her to watch the cricket with him and she'd refused because she felt that he was always one step ahead of her, taking her breath away and undermining her confidence in her own abilities at the same time.

He'd described her as capable, and most of the time she was, but not where he was concerned. What was

Ben expecting them to do once the baby had arrived? Set up house together as if the past didn't exist?

The sexual chemistry was still strong between them. It always would be. But she had to keep telling herself that there was more to a relationship than that. Understanding came high on the list.

She'd been taken aback when he'd wanted to discuss names for the baby. Obviously she'd given it some thought, yet had felt the time for that would be once it was born. Maybe he'd brought up the subject because today he was happy and relaxed like he used to be in the old days and now she was wondering if she was going to be able to live up to his expectations.

The phone trilled into her thoughts and when she picked it up it was Nicholas ringing from Texas, as he sometimes did.

After they'd exchanged greetings he said uncomfortably, 'I keep phoning Ben but there's no answer. He's been to Scandinavia, but I would have expected him to be back by now. I don't suppose he's appeared on your horizon, by any chance? He was desperate for your address before I left the country, but I kept my promise.'

She was fond of Ben's likable young brother and told him, 'As a matter of fact, Ben *is* here, and is intending to stay. He's over the moon because I wrote to him with my address, and when he turned up here he found that I was pregnant after we'd met unexpectedly in the summer.'

'That's fantastic!' he cried jubilantly, and then sounded less exuberant. 'But how do *you* feel about all this, Georgina?'

She sighed. 'I'm delighted about the baby, of course, but he and I haven't had a very good track record since we lost Jamie, have we?'

'Yes, but haven't I always said that the two of you belong together?' he said gravely. 'You can both be forgiven for losing the plot after something like that. Give it time, Georgina. On a more cheerful note, I *will* be over for the christening of my new nephew or niece. That is really great news.'

When he'd rung off, she thought that Nicholas was another optimist who thought it was going to be easy, but she was the one carrying the baby, the one who had fled from the aftermath of grief and vowed that she wasn't ever going to be hurt like that again.

With a sudden need for reassurance she reached for the jacket she'd taken off when she'd arrived home and, picking up her door keys, set off for the cricket ground.

James was batting at the wicket when she got there, but there was no sign of Ben amongst the spectators as she looked around her. She could hear children's laughter coming from behind the pavillion, and when she went to look, she smiled.

James wasn't the only one at the crease. There was another match taking place. Ben was the batsman, with a minuscule cricket cap on his head and a children's bat in his hands, pretending to brace himself against the tennis ball that Jolyon was about to bowl at him. Pollyanna was the wicket keeper behind a small set of stumps.

This is how he used to be, Georgina thought wistfully. It was turning out to be a day of turning back the clock.

When the ball hit the bat he flicked it high enough for Pollyanna to catch, and as the children gleefully shouted 'Out!' he turned and saw her behind him.

'This is a nice surprise,' he said. 'What made you change your mind?'

'I came to tell you that Nicholas has been on the phone and I've put him in the picture about what's happening here,' she explained. 'He's coming over for the christening.'

He laughed. 'That's great!' The children tugged at his arms, pleading with him to carry on with the game, and he gave her an apologetic smile. 'I won't be long. Are you going to sit and watch us?'

'I am, indeed,' she told him, with the appropriate amount of enthusiasm, and settled herself on one of the wooden seats that were scattered around the pitch.

They stayed until the match was over and the sun was sinking in the sky. As they were leaving, James said, 'The children want to know when you are going to play with them again, Ben. You've made a hit there.'

'Not with the bat,' he said laughingly. 'They're great kids, James.'

'They're a grubby pair at the moment,' their father said. 'It's going to be into the bath with them before supper.'

'He's a great guy too,' Ben said as James trooped off with a tired but happy child on either side. 'It's a pity he hasn't found them a loving stepmum.'

'I agree,' she told him. 'But James has yet to find

someone he can love as much as he loved his wife, and that's the problem. He would never marry for convenience. I firmly believe that one day the right woman will appear and everyone will be delighted.'

'If you feel up to it, why don't we offer to take the children out for the day some time soon, to give him a break?' he suggested. Partridge Lane came in sight and he glanced over at her. 'I've really enjoyed today. Shopping for the baby this morning and playing with James's kids this afternoon.'

'Yes, I can tell you have,' she said softly. 'Dare I remind you of something that used to make you really angry?'

'What?'

'Time really does heal. Doesn't it, Ben?'

'Yes, it does,' he agreed sombrely. 'But the scars remain.'

'They do, but we can live with them, can't we?'

'We have to,' he replied, and there was no bitterness in his voice.

In that moment she felt closer to him than she'd been in years. If they could have talked like this all that time ago they might have salvaged something from their marriage, she thought wistfully.

They arrived at their separate properties, and as they halted he said, 'As you arrived at the match shortly after I did, I take it you didn't have a rest?'

'Er, no, but I'm not an invalid, you know. It's like I tell my mothers-to-be at the antenatal clinic at the surgery—having children is a natural thing, to be taken in one's stride with common sense and pleasure.'

And what about high blood pressure and it's effects? he thought, but didn't voice it, even thought the memory was crystal-clear of the scares they'd had when she was expecting Jamie.

'Yes, of course it is,' he agreed. 'And I was not intending to fuss. I was merely going to suggest that I'll rustle up some food while you have a rest, if you are agreeable?'

'I'm agreeable,' she told him thankfully.

'I'll give you a knock when it's ready,' he promised as they separated.

Once Georgina was inside the first thing she did was check her blood pressure. The gynaecologist had warned her to keep a close watch on it, because it had been up slightly the last time she'd seen him.

However, today the readings were as they should be, and she breathed a sigh of relief.

On Monday morning of the week leading up to Good Friday, Georgina awoke to the knowledge that it was Ben's first day at the practice, and she was immediately wide-awake.

It was going to be very strange, she thought. They'd both been doctors all their working lives, but in different situations. She had always been in general practice and Ben hospital-based, so this was going to be the first time they'd worked together. She couldn't imagine what it was going to be like.

He was bringing in his milk as she was setting off, and he called across, 'I'll be right behind you.'

As she was pulling up outside the surgery she could see his car following, and felt her heartbeat quicken.

Georgina began to calm down as the day progressed. He was efficient, yet pleasant with both patients and staff. To the uninformed he was just another doctor at the surgery. James and Ben had arranged that all young patients should be passed to him, thereby receiving the benefit of his experience, and in any spare time that Ben might have he would share the general workload.

It was late morning before they had a chance to talk. He came out onto the forecourt of the practice as Georgina was about to set off on her home visits and said, 'James suggests that I tag along so that I can get to know the area better. Is that all right with you?'

'Yes, of course,' she told him. 'How's it going?'

'Fine,' he said easily, as if walking into a strange practice where his ex-wife worked was a doddle.

As she drove up the steep road that led to the moors and the peaks beyond, Ben wasn't missing a thing. 'It's rather remote and bleak up here, and very sparsely populated,' he commented as they drove the last mile to the tops. 'I could do your calls in these parts if you want.'

'No way!' she protested. 'The people who live in the cottages and farms up here are my friends.' She could have told him they were amongst those who'd made her welcome when she'd first come to Willowmere, lonely and lost.

At that moment a stray sheep came from nowhere. It ran across the road in front of the car and she had to swerve to miss it.

'Wow!' he exclaimed. 'Never a dull moment. The next time we have lamb for dinner I'll be asking where it's come from.' Suddenly his tone changed. 'Stop the car! There's someone lying beneath that outcrop of rock over there.'

'I see him,' she said, braking sharply.

By the time she'd eased herself out of the car Ben was bending over the motionless body of a man in walking clothes. He called, 'Fetch your bag, Georgina.'

Grabbing her bag out of the boot, she hurried over, fishing her mobile phone out of her pocket.

'Looks as if he's fallen over and hit his head,' he said, nodding towards the high face of rock beneath which he was lying. 'See the gash there on the side? I've got a pulse, but his breathing is shallow. We're going to have to get an ambulance up here, Georgina. Have you got a signal?'

'Thankfully. Right, I'm through.' She gave the information required and hung up. 'The ambulance is on it's way.'

Ten minutes passed. Ben and Georgina were monitoring the man's vital signs and Ben said grimly, 'They'd better hurry or we're going to lose him. Get ready to help me resuscitate, Georgina. OK, he's stopped breathing.'

They immediately began the resuscitation procedure. As the ambulance pulled up, the accident victim was breathing shallowly once more.

When the paramedics had gone, sirens wailing, Ben said, 'Phew! That was touch and go.' He turned to her as they walked slowly back to the car. 'Are you all right? It couldn't have been easy for you, crouching down beside him.'

'I'm fine,' she told him. 'Just relieved that we came upon the poor man. Do you think he stepped over the edge not realising there was a steep drop at the other side?'

'I don't know,' he replied. 'It's beautiful up here, but there can be dangers in this sort of rugged terrain. What would you have done if I hadn't been with you?'

'The best I could, I suppose. At least it's not snowing.' He was observing her sharply and, tuning in to the direction of his thoughts, she said, 'Don't worry, Ben. I've lived here long enough to know how to manage. Now, we'd better get moving or our next patient will think we've got lost. It's Ted Dawson at Summit Farm. His wife rang in to ask for a visit as he's got a lot of back pain and is barely mobile. Otherwise, knowing Ted, he would have come to the surgery as he's not one to make a fuss about nothing.

'The Dawson's are the most hospitable people. If I know Ellie, she'll be offering us homemade cakes and coffee.'

Ben's expression brightened.

'It's just a shame we won't be able to accept, as we're behind already with the home visits after what's just happened at Hellemans Crag.'

He groaned and said laughingly, 'So, do you think the farmer's wife could make us up a lunchbox?'

A barred gate leading to a farmyard had appeared in front of them, and they drove up to the farmhouse. After Georgina had introduced Ben to Ellie and Ted, they each examined the stricken farmer in turn.

After they had exchanged comments, Georgina told

the patient, 'We both think that you might have a slipped disc in your spine, Ted, but only an X-ray can decide that. We need to get you to hospital.'

Ted sighed. Looking around the pleasant farmhouse, he said, 'I can't afford to be off my feet in this kind of job, Georgina. Farming's not for stretcher cases.'

'I know,' she said sympathetically. 'So the sooner we get you sorted, the better, don't you agree? And in the meantime, can't those three sons of yours give you a hand?'

'They would if they were here,' Ellie chipped in. 'They're all at university now, but we'll sort something out until Ted is on his feet again.'

'Shall I pass the message around that Summit Farm can do with some help?' Georgina asked.

'Aye, if you would,' Ted said reluctantly. 'By the way, don't forget to have a cuppa and a piece of Ellie's cake before you go.'

'We'd love to, but I'm afraid we haven't time,' she said, and as they packed up, told them about the injured man they'd come across.

Almost on cue, Ellie said, 'So take a piece with you to eat in the car.' As Ben's amused glance met hers, Georgina knew she hadn't better refuse *that* offer.

'I can't believe that we dealt with a case of that kind on your first day at the practice,' Georgina said as they went to get their cars at the end of the second surgery. 'It would have been difficult if you hadn't been there.'

'So I *am* useful for something?' he said quizically.

'You're in a league way above the rest of us at the

practice, but don't make a big thing of it. It was great working with you, Ben.'

It was true, she thought as she drove home. Why couldn't she accept that living with him again could be just as good?

With the anxiety of working with Ben now having disappeared, Georgina still had to face telling him she was going to the cemetery on Good Friday, and it was approaching too quickly for her liking. Thursday was upon her almost before she knew it. She had to tell him that evening.

It was late in the afternoon, and on her way home she stopped off at the florist's on the main street of the village to pick up the white roses that she'd ordered earlier in the week.

As she came out of the shop, holding the flowers and smiling at something the girl behind the counter had said, she froze. Ben's car was parked behind hers and he was watching her through the window on the driver's side.

When she drew level, he wound it down and said levelly, 'I saw your car parked and wondered where you were. Could it be that you were intending to go to the cemetery and weren't going to tell me? What is it, Georgina? Don't you want me with you when you go there? Do you think I'm going to entice you back to the house again? I would never have expected you to be so unforgiving.'

'I'm doing what I've done at special times of the year,' she told him steadily. 'The only difference is that since I've been pregnant I've travelled by train instead of using the car. I'll be getting a local train from the station here in Willowmere early in the morning to connect with a mainline train from Manchester to London, if you want to come.'

'I do want to come, but I won't be going on this occasion,' he said, in the same sort of level tone. 'I've arranged to meet a colleague from Scandinavia. He's interested in the work I did out there, so we're spending the day together.'

His glance was on the perfection of the flowers she was holding. 'So, as I can't accept your lukewarm invitation, I'll make my own arrangements for visiting Jamie.' And, leaving her deflated, he pulled out from behind her car and drove off.

So much for her making a situation out of something that should have been handled tactfully, Georgina thought bleakly, and knew what she had to do.

Ben was home before her and when he answered her knock on the door, she said contritely, 'I'm sorry, Ben. I didn't mean you to find out like that. It was unkind of me.'

'So how did you want me to find out?' he asked dryly.

'I don't know!' she told him exasperatedly. 'I keep telling you that I'm used to doing things on my own.'

'And you want it to stay that way?

'No. Not exactly, but the cemetery was the place where we met that day and since then nothing has been the same. Going together would bring back memories not just of our meeting there but what happened afterwards.'

'You don't want to remember that, then?'

She looked down at her unaccustomed width and wondered how he could ask such a question.

'I will never forget it as long as I live,' she choked. 'I have far more reason to recall it than you have.'

He stepped forward and touched her cheek gently. 'Yes, I know you have. Don't let me interfere in your routine regarding Jamie. Tell him I love him, and I'll come see him soon.'

'Yes, I'll do that,' she promised, 'but don't you think he knows? I won't linger in London. I expect to be back late afternoon...and maybe next time we'll be able to go together.'

It was five o'clock when the local train from Manchester stopped in Willowmere's small station and Georgina smiled as she stepped onto the platform, bright with its tubs and baskets of flowers. She could hear the jangling kind of music that told her the Easter fair had arrived. If Ben wasn't too late home, maybe they could have a wander around the sideshows and other attractions after they'd eaten.

So far he hadn't seen much of village activities and in a perverse sort of way she was keen to introduce him to country life, even though she was still adjusting to his presence.

The fair was a yearly event. Everyone turned out for it, and as she heard the noise of it she thought of tomorrow's wedding in the village. Edwina and her friends wouldn't be too thrilled at having the music from the fair drowning their efforts on behalf of the happy couple.

On the short distance to Partridge Lane it occurred to her that Ben in his present confident state of mind might suggest that they marry again, and if he did, what would she say?

There was no way she would agree for the sake of convenience or propriety. If she ever took his name again it would be because it was something she wanted with all her heart, and at the present time she didn't know what she wanted.

She wasn't to know that since yesterday his confidence had been at a low ebb. The fact that she'd intended going to London without him had been a sharp reminder that he'd blundered into the life that she'd made for herself, and she wasn't prepared to give it up so easily.

He arrived home at seven o'clock and the first thing he did was knock on her door to check if she was back. When she opened it to him, he observed her keenly.

'How did it go?' he wanted to know.

'Fine,' she told him. 'The trains were on time, no trouble getting a taxi. I spent an hour in the cemetery and then returned to Euston to get the train home.'

'And do you feel better for going?'

She smiled across at him. 'Of course. Need you ask? And now I've got a question for *you*. Can you hear the fair?'

'Yes. Where is it?'

'On spare ground beside the river. Shall we go once you've eaten?'

'I've already had something in Manchester,' he said. 'What about you?'

'I made a meal when I got in.'

'And you feel up to it.'

'Yes, but I don't think I'll be risking any of the rides. They do throw one about rather.'

'As your resident physician I agree that is good thinking,' he said lightly. 'I'll go and change into something comfortable and be back shortly,'

When they set off in the early April evening to where the fair had been set up, Ben thought that Georgina hadn't had much to say about her day except for the bare details. Remembering their discussion of the previous day, he decided she must be thinking that the least said would be soonest mended.

As they wandered around the various stalls and sideshows he won a soft toy for hitting the target on a shooting range, and when presented with a coconut for a good score at skittles, asked wryly, 'What are we going to do with this?'

Cries of alarm suddenly came from behind and someone shouted, 'Look out!'

They could hear the pounding of hooves coming towards them and as Georgina and Ben swung round the crowd behind them scattered as a white-faced teenage girl on a pony bore down on them with the animal out of control.

It took a split second for Ben to realise that someone was going to get hurt and that someone might be Georgina, and as the animal came charging towards them he grabbed the bridle. The impact almost wrenched his arm out of its socket and slammed him up against the supports of a nearby sideshow, but at least it had halted the frightened animal and no one in the crowd had been hurt.

The girl was shaking from head to foot. 'It was the music that made her bolt,' she said. 'I should never have brought Dinky near the fair but I couldn't resist, and nearly killed somebody.'

She turned to Ben. 'Thank you for saving me and my horse and some innocent person.'

He nodded. 'Fortunately no one was hurt, but another time do take care, young lady.' He smiled at her crestfallen expression. 'The next time you come to the fair, I suggest you leave Dinky at home.'

'I will,' she promised fervently, and with an apologetic smile for the onlookers rode off slowly towards a quieter part of the village.

Georgina was by his side, aware that every time he moved his arm and shoulder he was wincing, and she said, 'I'll take you to A and E to have your arm looked at.'

He shook his head. 'No, Georgina. I'm all right. Let's go home and I'll bathe it.'

'I'll bathe it,' she told him, and he smiled.

'All right, whatever you say. If it's still painful in the morning, I *will* go to A and E.'

When they got home she removed his shirt with gentle hands and saw a livid red weal across a shoulder that was already swollen and discoloured.

'Can you move it?' she asked anxiously.

'Yes,' he said calmly. 'It will be all right when the swelling goes down. I've just wrenched my shoulder joint.'

She was observing him doubtfully. 'I do think we should go to A and E to have it X-rayed.'

'I'll see how it feels when I've been in the bath,' he conceded.

'Let me put witch hazel on it first,' she insisted. 'It's so good for inward bruising and strains.'

As she rubbed the age-old remedy gently all over his back and shoulders Georgina was thinking that this was the first real physical contact they'd had since the day they'd made love. The opportunity to go back in time to when his wellbeing had been as important to her as breathing was a moment to treasure.

He was observing her whimsically over his shoulder and commented, 'I could really get to like this, though not the reason for it. That girl shouldn't have been any-where near the fair with her pony. The kind of music they were playing was enough to frighten any animal. Someone could have been killed.'

He was reaching for his shirt and she said, 'Let me help you,' and held it out for him while he eased his arms into it. As she was pressed up against him, fasten-ing the buttons, the baby moved inside her and she reached for his hand as she'd done on that other oc-casion.

It was a timeless sort of moment, yet in reality it only lasted seconds, and when it was over he reached out and took her face between his hands and kissed her gently on the mouth. Starved of the passion that had once been one of the mainstays of their life together, she kissed him back with a fervour that brought him rigid with surprise and pleasure.

When at last he put her away from him gently Ben said, 'I can't think of a better way of making me forget that my back hurts, Georgina. Does it mean that I'm forgiven?'

'I could say that I forgave you a long time ago,' she said breathlessly, 'but there was never anything to forgive. We just found ourselves travelling along different roads and there was nothing left to hold on to. But it doesn't mean that I've forgotten how it used to be.'

He was reaching out for her again but she shook her head and told him, 'As your doctor, I recommend rest and quiet. A repeat of what just happened is not in keeping with that. I suggest that you go home, have a warm bath and a hot drink, and we'll see how the patient is in the morning.'

'All right,' he agreed, and paused on the doorstep to comment dryly, 'I note that you managed to hang on to the cuddly toy. I wonder what happened to the coconut?'

When he'd gone, Georgina sank down onto the sofa and thought what a strange day it had been. It had started with her self-imposed solitary pilgrimage to London, followed by their visit to the fair that had changed from pleasure to panic in just a few seconds.

Then last, but by no means the least, in the emotionally charged moment that they'd shared after feeling the baby move, she had let her heart rule her head, given way to longing, and now she was feeling guilty because she'd given Ben cause to hope when she still wasn't clear in her mind about the future.

But exhaustion was kicking in and she went slowly upstairs to her lonely bed and tried not to think about how right it had felt when she'd been in Ben's arms.

As sleep began to slide over her she thought drowsily that it was almost as if the little unborn one, be it Aimee or Arran, was playing a little game of its own by making its presence felt at meaningful moments.

Next door Ben was having a leisurely soak to ease an aching shoulder and planning to sleep on the side not affected, wishing at the same time that he could awake the next morning to find Georgina beside him.

Outside in the lane in the dark spring night the fox slunk by once more on the lookout for an unsuspecting meal.

CHAPTER SIX

WHEN Georgina went to check on Ben's injured shoulder the following morning, he assured her that it was much better but, noting painkillers on the worktop in the kitchen, she insisted on being shown the affected area. When she saw the swelling and amount of bruising that had come out during the night, she said that they should have it looked at in A and E.

'I can move it all right,' he told her, 'so there is no fracture, but if you insist, I'll go.'

'*We'll* go,' she said. 'I'll drive.'

'*I'm* supposed to be looking after *you*,' he protested.

'I don't need looking after,' she told him firmly.

'So I've gathered, but don't forget when you go to see the gynaecologist next week, I *would* like to be there. What time is the appointment?'

'Three in the afternoon, between surgeries.'

She understood his concern. It had not been an easy pregnancy when she was expecting Jamie, but so far all was well, and she was not going to take any risks regarding the baby's safety. It was a precious gift, conceived in a moment of madness, and where at first she hadn't liked the thought of that, now she saw it differently because of the joy it was bringing with it.

Ben had been X-rayed in A and E at St Gabriel's, the main hospital for the area, and he'd been right. There were no broken bones, just a lot of soreness that could take a few days to ease off.

As they were about to leave, he said, 'I'm told they have a new paediatric centre here that is quite something.'

'Yes, they have,' she said.

'I know the manager of the unit. I'm sure he'll let us have a look round when he knows who you are.'

She was right. Ben's name brought immediate recognition, and they were shown round the centre by one of the doctors. Not only was it state-of-the-art, with every kind of up-to-date equipment, it was bright and sunny, with lots of things to take young patients' minds off their problems.

As they were leaving, Ben shook the doctor's hand and said, 'Many thanks for showing us round. My wife and I are most impressed.'

Georgina didn't comment on it when they left but he did. 'I know what you're thinking,' he said wryly. 'You're not my wife any more. I felt it more appropriate to introduce you like that as you are so obviously pregnant.'

'And so avoid any gossip?'

He glanced at her sharply. 'Yes, but on your account, not mine. I know what hospital grapevines are like. I don't give a damn what people think of *me*, but you are known in these parts.'

'Yes, I am,' she agreed levelly. 'I'm known as a woman who hasn't been open to any advances from members of the opposite sex since she came here, and who gets on with her life without burdening others with her problems and heartaches. Until you came back into my life James was the only one who knew anything about me and he has never heard the full story.'

'He has now. *I* told him,' he said coolly, stung by her words. 'I also told him that he was the only person I'd ever opened up to.'

She stared at him with surprised hazel eyes. 'When was this? You've barely met the man.'

'It was at the cricket match last weekend…and I like the guy.'

'Well! The new you is certainly full of surprises.'

They were back in the car ready to drive home and he said, 'Here's one more. I want to buy you an Easter egg like I used to when Jamie was with us, so can we stop off somewhere? Then we have to decide what we're going to do with the rest of the day. After all, it is Easter Saturday.'

Picking up on his mood, she said, 'I suggest we give the fair a miss after yesterday's near catastrophe. How about a picnic by Willow Lake?'

'Agreed as long as I help to prepare the food.'

She shook her head. 'No, rest your shoulder. I'll do the catering. I'll shop for it when we get back to the village and you can go on home and do your own thing for a couple of hours.'

And now she was making a salad to go with smoked salmon, and buttering crusty bread to be eaten with it before they went on to meringues and the apple tart that she'd bought at the village baker's.

As she bent to get fruit juice from the fridge, the Easter egg, resplendent in a fancy box with her name piped across in icing was there at her elbow, and she paused. Was she falling into a trap of her own making, allowing Ben to charm her with his concern and happy memories from the past when the future still wasn't clear?

'Do you remember how we used to call Jamie "Chocolate Chops" at Easter time,' he'd said, while they were waiting for her name to be piped on to the egg.

'Yes,' she replied softly. 'I remember everything the three of us did together, and I know that you do, too, Ben.'

It had been a tender moment that the girl behind the counter had broken into by saying laughingly, 'Your husband's name is Ben? That's a nice short name to go on an Easter egg. I've only just managed to get Georgina on yours!'

When Ben had bought Easter eggs for Jamie, he'd always bought one for her, and it would seem that he hadn't forgotten. In the pleasure of the moment she'd suggested the picnic and could hardly change her mind now, but for the rest of the holiday weekend she was going to retreat behind what few defences she had left.

When Ben had first arrived in Willowmere, she'd told him she didn't want a relationship with *anyone*, and had meant it. But she was realising that the bond between them remained unbroken. It might be battered and bent, but it was still there and always would be.

* * *

Next door Ben was also in a more sombre mood, remembering how Georgina had described herself at the hospital. He'd taken it on board at the time but pushed her words to the back of his mind. Now they'd come back to plague him and he wondered if they'd been a reminder that nothing had changed. That there might be precarious harmony between them but he wasn't to take it for granted. Her not wanting him with her when she went to see the gynaecologist fitted in with that.

Yet when she appeared carrying a picnic basket covered with a white napkin, she seemed happy enough, and he resolutely put his uncertainties to one side.

If the fair hadn't been in full swing at the other side of the village, Willow Lake would have been the star attraction on a sunny Easter Saturday, but as it was, there were just a few people there. Some out for a walk, others just sitting beside the water's edge, enjoying the peace of the place or having a picnic like themselves.

As Ben was opening up a couple of folding chairs and a small table that he'd taken from the boot of the car Georgina looked away and, seeing her expression, he asked, 'What's making you look like that?'

She managed a smile. 'Just a memory, that's all.' Before he could question her further, her attention was caught by the approach of Christine Quarmby, for once without her gamekeeper husband.

'Do I take the absence of your husband to mean there's a shoot taking place on Lord Derringham's estate?' she asked Christine after introducing Ben as her next-door neighbour and pretending not to notice the glint in his eye.

'Yes,' was the answer. 'His lordship has people staying with him over Easter, and Dennis is on call all the time. He wishes he wasn't as he's concerned about me, but I tell him that his job is our bread and butter, and I have to learn to be less reliant on him. It might sound ridiculous, Georgina, but I feel better now I know what is wrong with me.

'I'm not jumping for joy, far from it, but for anyone who is waiting for the results of tests and a diagnosis, it's like wandering in the wilderness. I've read all I can find about Sjögren's syndrome and searched on the Internet so I know the score. But it isn't going to stop me from leading as normal a life as possible.' She smiled at Ben, who had been listening intently. 'And now I'll go on my way having had my exercise for today.'

When she'd gone, he said, 'Is it secondary Sjögren's?'

'Yes. It stems from rheumatoid arthritis in Christine's case.'

'That's tough.'

'Yes, indeed. There is no known cure at the moment, but hopefully there will be one day.'

They'd left the picnic basket on the backseat of the car and now she went to get it and asked, 'Are you ready to eat?'

'Yes,' he said absently. 'It seems a long time since breakfast.'

His voice was flat. She sensed a change of mood in him and knew she wasn't wrong when he said, 'It isn't working, is it, Georgina? If I asked you to marry me a second time, what would you say?'

She was speechless with surprise. What had happened to his brisk confidence? Into the silence he said, 'You would say no, wouldn't you? You don't miss an opportunity to hammer it home that you were happier before I came on the scene. But I'm afraid I'm not going anywhere. You're going to have to endure having me here in Willowmere because the baby you're carrying is just as much mine as yours.'

She found her voice. 'What has brought this on?' she croaked. 'We've been getting on fine these last few days.'

'*I have,*' he replied. 'I can't vouch for you. I'm going to start looking around for a property to buy, so that our situation won't be so claustrophobic, and also so that when it's my turn to have the baby, it won't be in a bare rented house.'

'You've certainly been making your plans!' she exclaimed, unaware that he'd just said the first thing that had come into his head. 'So are you going to put the London house on the market?'

'No. We need somewhere close to where Jamie is, don't we?'

'You've certainly changed your attitude in the last couple of hours,' she said in a low voice. 'I'm sorry I haven't come up to scratch.' She got to her feet. 'I'll leave you to it as I've suddenly lost my appetite. I'll walk back. I need the fresh air.'

He was about to protest, but she didn't give him the chance, and as he watched her walk away beside the lake's clear waters he thought sombrely that if James's sister had fond memories of Willow Lake, *he'd* just spoilt it for Georgina.

He didn't stay long, ate some of the food without tasting it, then packed up and drove back to the cottage, taking note on his arrival that her car wasn't there.

She hadn't gone far. Georgina had driven up the hill road that led to the moors and was seated, gazing blankly in front of her, the car a solitary vehicle parked against the skyline, with the rugged grandeur of the peaks on either side.

Back there by the lake Ben had told her out of the blue that he'd given up on them being reconciled and it had taken hearing it put into words for her to acknowledge that her protestations that she wanted to stay as she was had been just a way of protecting herself from any more hurt.

She *did* want them to be a proper family again when the baby came. But Ben had taken on board what she'd said earlier, and as she'd been so definite, he'd had a change of mind. Now he was talking about buying a property in Willowmere that was not so close as they were now, *and* was in favour of them bringing up their child separately.

It was what she'd wanted at the start, because she'd been confused by his arrival in Willowmere, but the more they were together the more she wanted them to be like they'd been before. Instead she'd blocked every move he'd made towards that end. 'If I asked you to marry me a second time, you would say no, wouldn't you?' he'd said, without giving her the chance to reply, and now she was having to accept that she'd played the 'I am my own woman' card once too often.

If she were to tell him now that the answer would be yes if he asked her to marry him again, he wouldn't believe her. She could hear herself saying what sort of a woman she had become as they were leaving the hospital that morning. Warning him once again that she wasn't going to fall into his arms and take up where they'd left off three years ago.

So, what now? she thought miserably. The sensible thing would be to carry on as normal. It was just a matter of weeks before she gave birth and that was the most important thing in both their lives. If afterwards Ben kept to his word and moved out of their close proximity, she would have to console herself with the knowledge that at least he was in Willowmere, and accept that once they were parents again, she might be the one who had to do the begging.

When she arrived back at the cottage, Georgina saw that Ben had returned and she hurried inside, only to have to open the door to him seconds later and find him on the step, holding the picnic hamper.

'You haven't eaten since this morning, have you?' he said, bringing the moment down to basics. 'So why not make use of this?' Placing it in her hands, he turned and went without commenting that she should be eating for two, but she was pretty sure that was what he was thinking.

She stayed in for the rest of the weekend, saw Ben drive off and return a few times but he didn't call again, and when Easter was over, she set off for the practice on Tuesday morning, grateful for the chance to be near him.

As she waited for her first patients to present themselves, she thought that it was typical of life's twists and turns that when Ben had joined the practice she'd thought it wasn't a good idea from her point of view. Now his presence there was assuming the proportions of a lifeline, if only he would come out of his consulting room and say something.

As if he'd read her thoughts, the door across the passage from hers opened and he was there, smiling a tight smile and asking dryly, 'How was the Easter egg?'

It was hardly what she'd expected to be the first topic of conversation when they came face to face again, but she held on to her composure and said, 'I've eaten the George part and saved you the Gina bit. Perhaps you'd like to call round for it?'

'Yes, perhaps I would,' he said, unconvincingly, and she thought that the gap between them was widening. Then he asked, 'What arrangements have you made with James for tomorrow, when you see the gynaecologist?'

'I'm taking the afternoon off. Are you coming?'

'Yes, I'm coming. I thought we'd sorted that? I'll have to meet you there, though, and come straight back, as it will be two doctors missing from the surgery all afternoon if I don't.'

'Yes, whatever is best for the surgery,' she agreed.

It was a moment to tell him that she really *did* want him there beside her when she saw their baby on the scan, but if she told Ben that he might find it hard to believe after what had happened between them at that travesty of a picnic.

As Michael Meredith seated himself opposite her minutes later, Georgina wondered what had brought the local celebrity to the surgery. The man was a well-known botanist turned writer who wrote about the flora and fauna of the countryside and was something of a recluse.

Unmarried and in his sixties, he was rarely seen at the surgery, but today he had made an appointment for some reason that she was about to discover.

He was a pleasant man with a well-modulated voice and open expression, and as they exchanged smiles she asked, 'What can I do for you today, Mr Meredith?'

'I'm in severe pain at the bottom of my back and down my right leg, Dr Adams,' he informed her. 'I was clambering over some rocks to get a rare specimen a couple of days ago and slipped and jarred my hip. Within a short time the pain came and it is the kind of agony one can't ignore.'

'If you would like to lift your shirt and loosen the belt of your trousers, I'll take a look,' she told him. After examining his lower spine, right hip and knee, she said, 'I think you might have damaged the sciatic nerve which is the biggest nerve in the body. It passes behind the pelvis, then backwards to the buttock, from where it runs behind the hip joint and down the back of the thigh. When it reaches the knee, it separates into two separate nerves, known as the tibial nerve and the common peroneal nerve, and the pain that you've described are in those areas. In the meantime I'll give you some strong painkillers and a letter to take to the radiology department at St Gabriel's and they'll X-ray you while you're there.'

'What, straight away?' he exclaimed.

'Yes. You might have to wait a little while but it will be done on the spot. I should get the result within the week and in the meantime don't go rock climbing.'

He was smiling as he got up to go. 'There's no like-lihood of that in my present state.'

Or in mine, Georgina thought as the botanist bade her goodbye.

When Beth came round with a tray of coffee in the middle of the morning, she said, 'You don't look very chirpy this morning, Georgina. Pregnancy gets weary-ing towards the end, doesn't it? And the hormones start playing tricks. One moment the mother-to-be is happy, and the next she's all droopy.'

'That decribes me exactly,' she told Beth, but knew her depression wasn't anything to do with hormones.

As she came up the lane that evening, drenched by a sud-den downpour that had caught her unawares on her solitary stroll, Ben's door opened and they came face to face for the second time in the day.

'You're wet through!' he exclaimed, taking in the vision of her hair lying damply against her head and the loose dress that she'd changed into when she'd arrived home from the surgery clinging to her ample waistline.

'Yes, I do know that,' she said wryly, 'and I didn't do it on purpose, so if you'll excuse me, I'll go and change into some dry clothes.'

'And then will you come back for a moment?'

'Er, yes, if you want me to,' she agreed doubtfully, 'but I don't want a lecture.'

'You won't get one,' he promised quickly. 'And now will you go and get out of those wet clothes? I can't run the surgery on my own if you get pneumonia.'

'Yes, all right,' she agreed flatly. 'I'd hate to be a nuisance.'

She was unzipping the dress even as she opened her front door and as soon as she was in the hall stepped out of it and then went to towel her hair dry.

Exhaustion always seemed to creep over her at this time of day and, instead of changing into fresh clothes, Georgina wrapped herself in a warm robe and padded across to the house next door.

When she'd left him by the lakeside, Ben had forced himself to stay where he was. He'd wanted to chase after her and give Georgina the chance to reply to his outburst, but hadn't done so because he'd believed he was right and her abrupt departure had only added to that feeling.

They'd been in harmony for days until she'd outlined what she wanted from life as they'd been leaving the hospital, and it had made him see that they were not going anywhere as a couple.

It had been a pleasant enough moment when he'd taken her to buy an Easter egg, and when she'd followed it up with the suggestion that they have a picnic, he'd been all for it, but it hadn't stopped him remembering what she'd said before that. It had kept going round and round in his mind and his optimism had suddenly been in short supply.

Now he was regretting letting it show, as instead of bringing everything out into the open it had made the future more uncertain, with the only thing to hold on to being the arrival of the baby.

'You're tired,' he said when he opened the door to her.

'Yes,' she agreed, and thought she wasn't just that, she was miserable and lost and lonely. Her time was drawing near and she had no stable plans for the future. She'd known where she'd been heading before Ben had come to Willowmere. Had been ready to step into the role of single mother, but his coming had changed all that.

Just as she'd been beginning to accept that there could be a second chance of the family life that had been so important to them in the past, she'd driven Ben away by harping on how she was content with her lot as a woman alone.

Unaware of her heartsearching, he was trying to think of a reason for asking her to call back after she'd dried out. The truth of it was, he just wanted to be with her for a while, without the trappings of the surgery around them.

'I've made a hot drink to warm you up after the soaking you got,' he said. 'It can get chilly once the sun goes down.'

'Thanks for that,' she told him, feeling some of the chill of her body and mind disappear at the first sign that Ben might be relenting.

'How's the blood pressure?' he was asking, and she flashed him a pale smile.

'All right so far. It's the first question Ian will ask tomorrow afternoon.'

'Talking about blood pressure going up, ours in particular, do you remember that poor guy who'd fallen down the rock face?'

'Yes, of course I do.'

'When they got him to A and E they discovered he'd suffered a subdural haematoma from the fall and had to operate on him smartly.'

'And how is he now?'

'Doing all right, from what I can gather. I had to do a bit of pulling rank when I rang the other day to ask how he was, with my not being a relative, but the sister in charge mellowed when she knew I was one of the doctors who'd treated him up on the tops.'

'Why didn't you tell me before?' she asked, her eyes questioning above the rim of a mug of hot chocolate.

'Why do you think?' he asked dryly. 'I've been giving you the space that you are so keen to have.'

She put the mug down and got to her feet, too tired to get involved in emotional matters. 'Thanks for telling me about the walker.' She didn't comment on his last remark because it had been partly true. She did want her own space and she always would. But she wanted him more.

'What was it that you asked me to come back for?' she asked from the doorway.

'I just wanted to confirm the arrangements for tomorrow. I'll try to be there for quarter to three,' he said, improvising quickly, and with a brief nod, she went.

* * *

Once again sleep was long in coming, and as she lay wide-eyed beneath the covers, Georgina was thinking about how Ben's patience and understanding had been easing her into a new beginning after his arrival in the village, and now it had all fallen apart. They desperately needed a better understanding. Perhaps seeing the baby on the scan tomorrow would be a step towards it, but Ben wasn't one for going back on his word.

When she arrived at the consultant's rooms at a quarter to three there was no sign of him. Her heart sank, but maybe she was being a bit previous. There was still time for him to arrive.

She was beginning to feel weepy and vulnerable as the minutes ticked by and he still didn't appear, but consoled herself with the thought that it was because her hormones *were* all over the place as Beth had suggested, and there were other body changes to contend with, too. So by the time she was shown into the presence of the gynaecologist, she was resigned to the fact that Ben wasn't coming. All the fussing and insisting that he was going to be there had been for nothing.

Ben had arrived on time but, having parked his car, had just crossed the busy main road to get to the large Victorian building that housed the private rooms of various consultants when a young boy walking in front of him with his mother had gone into a fit.

It had appeared to be the first time ever, as the woman had been transfixed with shock. Ben had been beside them in an instant, loosening the child's clothing and checking that his tongue hadn't gone back and blocked the airway.

'We mustn't move your boy,' he'd told her. 'He will come out of it gradually. Has he had a convulsion before?'

'No, never,' she sobbed.

'I'm going to phone for an ambulance,' he announced. 'I'm a children's doctor and I will stay with you until they get here. Try not to be too alarmed. He won't remember a thing when he comes round. But he needs to be taken to hospital to be examined.'

He was glancing at his watch. It was ten minutes past three. Georgina would think he wasn't coming. The woman had seen him checking the time and begged, 'Don't leave us. I'm terrified. I've never seen anyone in a fit before.'

'I won't leave you,' he promised, and prayed that the ambulance wouldn't be long. It came in ten minutes, but it took another five for him to feel he could safely leave the woman and the boy, who was now coming out of what was very likely to be an epileptic seizure.

He ran the rest of the way and told Ian Sefton's receptionist, 'I should have met Georgina Adams here at three o'clock, but have been delayed. Is she in with Dr Sefton now?'

'Yes,' the receptionist said. 'I'll buzz him and let him know that you've arrived.' After doing so, she looked up and smiled. 'You can go in, Dr Allardyce.'

'I'm so sorry,' Ben said as he faced Georgina and the consultant. 'A child in front of me on the street had a seizure as I was approaching this place. His mother was almost hysterical and I just had to stay with them until an ambulance came. Have I missed the scan?'

Georgina was smiling. Ben had come after all. He'd always been a man of his word. How could she have doubted him?

'All is well with the baby and mother,' Ian Sefton told him. 'I will show you both the scan in a moment, and you will see that the head hasn't yet moved down into the pelvis. That is normal enough in a woman who already has had a child. So now the picture show, which I'm sure you must be eager to see. There is your baby,' he said, and they gazed enraptured a the image.

Georgina reached out and took Ben's hand in hers, saying in a low voice, 'I thought you weren't coming and I'm ashamed.'

'Don't be,' he told her huskily, with the wonder of the moment sweet upon him. 'We've made a child, Georgina, and we're going to give it all the love that we never got the chance to give Jamie.'

'I want to see you again in a fortnight now that you're into your third trimester of the pregnancy,' the consultant was saying. He turned to Ben. 'I've checked the blood pressure myself, even though as a doctor Georgina is quite capable of monitoring it, and at this stage I'm satisfied there are no problems coming from that direction. I know that she had a difficult pregnancy with your first child, so I'll be keeping a keen eye open for any signs of hypertension.'

When they'd left the building, and were going to their separate cars, Ben said, 'I'm relieved that so far your blood pressure is behaving itself. I've been dreading…'

He hadn't put it into words, so she said it for him. 'That we might lose this child as well?'

'It just seems too good to be true. Everything does.'

'Not quite everything,' she said gravely, and as she wasn't going to beg, got into her car and set off for Partridge Lane, leaving Ben to make his way back to the practice for the rest of the afternoon.

She didn't see him that evening, which was something of an anti-climax after those incredible moments at the gynaecologist's. Having the afternoon off meant that she ate earlier than usual and had her walk earlier. She'd expected that he would be home by the time she got back, but there was no sign of Ben's car on his driveway. Feeling tired and disappointed, she decided to go to bed.

When she'd undressed and put on the roomy night-dress that he'd once ironed for her, Georgina stood motionless by the wall that separated the two cottages. The longing to have Ben beside her through the night was so strong she felt that he must surely sense it on the other side of the wall.

But nothing moved. There was no knock on her door or urgent ringing of the phone and, turning away, she climbed slowly into bed. It was as she placed her head on the pillow that she heard it and it was not the kind of sound she was longing for.

There was hammering coming from the other side

of the wall and the whirring of a hand drill, and she thought wryly that Ben's thoughts must be a million miles away from hers if he was putting shelves up or hanging pictures.

Since he felt that they still had separate agendas for the future, Ben found the evenings never-ending with Georgina next door, so near physically yet so out of reach in every other way. He needed something to occupy himself with and had decided he was going to fill the empty hours by making a cot for the baby.

They'd bought a crib but he knew that infants soon outgrew their first sleeping place and the thought of their child lying in a cot that he'd made for it was appealing. He'd bought all that was needed for the venture on his way home and was now hard at work in the spare bedroom, unaware that the noise of his labours could be heard through the thick stone walls of the cottage.

'What were you doing last night, putting shelves up?' Georgina asked the next morning as they were about to leave for the surgery in their separate cars.

'Why? Could you hear me?' he exclaimed. 'I'm sorry if I disturbed you.' Intending that the cot was going to be a surprise, he replied, 'No. I was repairing a loose floorboard.'

'Oh, I see,' she replied, and let the matter drop.

CHAPTER SEVEN

As they drove to the practice they passed Jess, the nanny, taking James's children to school. When they arrived at the surgery, Georgina said, 'Are we going to do as you suggested and take Pollyanna and Jolyon out for the day?'

He didn't reply immediately and she wondered if he was remembering Jamie and thinking that he was always involved with other people's children, never his own. Yet surely the baby she was carrying was going to take some of that kind of ache away? And it had been Ben's idea in the first place.

He was observing her thoughtfully, and she wasn't to know that his hesitation was on her behalf. She was nearing the end of her pregnancy, had a demanding job at the practice, and should be resting whenever possible. But he knew what Georgina would say to that. It would be the same thimg she said to the women at the antenatal clinic at the surgery. Pregnancy was a natural thing, not an illness. But with regard to the woman he adored there was the spectre of possible blood pressure problems in the background.

He longed to hold another child of theirs in his arms,

but she came first. Three long and lonely years had shown how much she meant to him, and he'd resigned himself to accepting it if she didn't want him back in the fullest sense. As long as he could be near her and the baby when it came, so that he could watch over them, he would stay on the fringe of their lives for ever if he had to. It would be better than nothing.

She was waiting for an answer. 'Yes, if you like,' he said with assumed easiness. 'But only if you feel up to it and whatever we do isn't too strenuous.'

'I'll mention it to James, then. How about this coming Saturday?'

'Fine by me,' he said, unable to stop his spirits from lifting at the thought of spending some prime time with her. 'Where should we take them?'

'There's a stately home not far from here that gets lots of visitors. The inside is full of beautiful pictures and antique furniture, which wouldn't be of much interest to Pollyanna and Jolyon, but in the grounds there are brilliant amusements for children and lots of animals for them to see. Once we've done the rounds, there are grassy slopes where visitors can picnic if they don't want to use the restaurants.'

'That sort of place would be ideal for keeping a couple of youngsters happy for a few hours,' he agreed. 'Hopefully the picnic will be an improvement on our last one.'

'Thanks for reminding me of the day you gave up on me,' she said quietly, and preceded him into the roomy stone building that was the centre of healthcare in the village.

* * *

'That would be great,' James said, when Georgina aproached him about having the children for the day. 'It will give me the chance to do a few things I haven't been able to get to for ages. What time shall I have them ready?'

'Ten o'clock, shall we say? It will take us an hour to get there.'

'They'll love it,' he enthused. 'Especially if Ben is there. Don't be surprised if Jolyon turns up with his cricket gear.'

'I never did find out where Ben got that cap from,' she said laughingly.

'It probably belonged to one of the junior team and had been left hanging around the pavillion.' He smiled.

Georgina was smiling too as she drove to the local children's boutique, a small but classy place called Ribbons and Rompers. The owner, Tessa Graham, had asked for a visit. After leaving James to his own activities, she was making the shop her first stop.

When Georgina arrived there, she saw that the shop blinds were still down and there were no signs of life around the place. She rang the bell outside a door at the bottom of stairs that led to an upstairs apartment, and it was a few moments before it was opened. Tessa was revealed hunched in a towelling robe and looking pale and listless.

As she led the way upstairs the shopowner said weakly, 'I've got the most awful stomach cramps, Dr Adams, and have been vomiting and had diarrhoea for most of the night. I think I passed out once. I found myself on the bathroom floor and don't recall how I got there.'

'It sounds as if you might have food poisoning,' Georgina told her, 'or a severe gastric upset of some sort.' She was looking around her, could see into the kitchen and it was spotless, as was the rest of the apartment.

'Have you eaten anything in the last twenty-four hours that could be suspect?' she asked.

'I went to a barbeque last night and had some sausage that could have done with being cooked a bit longer, but apart from that I can't think of anything else that could have caused it. I'm usually very fussy about what I eat.'

'Maybe not fussy enough this time,' Georgina suggested. 'It could be the sausage that has caused this, so don't eat any food until you haven't been sick or had diarrhoea for several hours, and then only small amounts of very plain food. In the meantime, try small sips of water and gradually build up your fluid intake. Make sure you drink regularly. The only comfort to be had from this sort of thing is that once the stomach has emptied itself and the colon likewise it can only go on for so long and then it must be allowed to settle. Send for me again, Tessa, if the symptoms persist or get worse, but I think it will have been the sausages that have upset you.'

When she arrived back at the practice, Ben was closeted with a patient. As soon as he was free he asked, 'Have you spoken to James?'

'Yes, he's happy for us to have the children for the day.'

And are we sticking to plan A?'

'Yes, and I think we should pray for good weather as these dry, sunny days aren't going to last for ever.'

He nodded, and in a more serious tone said, 'Have you decided what you are going to do about the practice when you have the baby? Are you going to take the full maternity leave? I can't believe we haven't discussed it.'

'That's because of the confusion in our lives,' she told him. 'But you're right. It needs to be sorted.'

'So why don't I take you out for a meal tonight and we'll talk about it while we're relaxing? It will save us having to cook.'

If he thought she was going to be relaxed while they were discussing the future, Ben was very much mistaken. But the idea of dining together, as they'd done a few times when he first came to the village, was appealing, and she said, 'Yes, that would be nice.'

James had overheard the conversation and said, 'There is something that has just cropped up that might influence your plans, or otherwise. You know that I wouldn't want to lose you, Georgina, as the practice wouldn't be the same without you, but if you decided you wanted a break from work until your little one is older, I've had a registrar from St Gabriel's on the phone. He wants to move into general practice and as his contract with the hospital is up at the end of May, he asked if there was any likelihood of a vacancy in Willowmere.

'His name is David Tremayne and he met Anna and Glenn in A and E last winter on the day when there was a near tragedy on Willow Lake. It was frozen over and when the ice began to melt someone fell through and nearly drowned.

'It must have stuck in his mind and he's coming in for a chat. He sounded a very capable guy but, Georgina, I want us to do what is best for you. So let me know once you've decided. And enjoy your meal.'

She smiled. It would be great just getting dressed up and going to a nice restaurant, but the real pleasure would be in the opportunity to spend some time alone with Ben. If only he felt the same as she did, she would stand over a hot stove if she had to.

When he'd first come to Willowmere, he had been desperate for her company. Now it was just the opposite. It was she who longed for his, but ever since he'd said that it wasn't working out between them, it had been in short supply socially.

She was seeing plenty of him at the surgery but that was a different ball game. They were there to work.

When she opened the door to him dressed in a long black skirt and a low-necked top, relieved by a silver choker, he said, 'Very nice! It reminds me of how it used to be before we were married. You opening the door of your parents' house to me all dressed up for the evening ahead. You're a beautiful woman, Georgina.'

She patted her midriff laughingly and questioned, 'Like this?'

'Yes, like that. Pregnancy suits you.'

'Next thing you'll be saying I should try it more often,' she teased, still in a light-hearted mood, but his reply was serious.

'I suggest that we focus on getting *this* little one safely into the world.'

'Yes, of course,' she told him. 'I've started putting my feet up for half an hour each evening when I get home.'

'They're not swelling, are they?'

'Just a little, but they'll be down by morning.' She pushed him gently to one side as she locked the door, and then they were off.

'So where are we heading?' she asked half an hour later as Ben turned the car onto the hill road in the dusk of a spring night.

'A new place that was recommended to me by a patient,' he explained. 'It's described as a farm restaurant and she said the food was delicious.'

'Ah! I know it!' she exclaimed. 'I noticed it when I was up there visiting a patient a few weeks ago. I remember thinking that someone had invested a lot of money in it, considering that it's rather out in the wilds.'

'Yes, that may be, but don't you think that people are prepared to travel miles for some good food?'

As they were shown to a table in a tastefully presented dining room that was already half-full, it seemed as if Ben's comment that the population would travel far for some good food had been correct. When it was put in front of them, they had their answer in succulent steaks and crispy home-grown vegetables.

They ate silently and with relish after a long and busy day, and it wasn't until they were relaxing over a coffee for Ben and a herbal tea for Georgina that she said, 'Until you came I intended to take full maternity leave from the practice, for obvious reasons. I was on my own, and I didn't think I could bear to leave the baby in someone else's care any sooner than I had to. If that someone was you it would be a different matter. But now you're involved in the practice as much as I am.'

'I don't have to be if James takes on another doctor. He might decide to do that if this registrar from St Gabriel's is the right man for the job.'

'You said you were going to look for a property,' she reminded him. 'That could affect any arrangements we made—especially if it was out of the area.'

As if! Everything he cared about was here in Willowmere.

'Have you seen anything suitable?' she continued.

'No, not yet. I haven't had a lot of time for house-hunting so far.'

She nodded. 'The weeks are speeding past. Some-times I can hardly believe that I'm carrying our child and will soon be giving birth.'

He didn't have that problem, Ben was thinking. The baby was always in his thoughts. *As was his beautiful wife.*

Ever since he'd found out that Georgina was preg-nant it had been like stepping out of darkness, but it wasn't stopping him from feeling that he didn't deserve it after the way he'd acted in the past. Calm, clinical doctor that he was, neither did it prevent him from waking up in the night with the dread in him that some-thing could go wrong.

After they'd seen the scan at the gynaecologist's rooms, Ian Sefton had phoned him that same night, and he'd been tense as a violin string when he'd heard his voice at the other end of the line. But it had been merely a social call to say that until he'd seen them together he'd had no idea that he was the father of Georgina Adams's baby.

'She *was* my wife once,' Ben had explained in clipped tones, 'but we lost our little boy in a tragic accident and our marriage broke down.'

'Sadly, that can happen,' the other man had said gravely. 'But you're back together again and starting a new family, which has to be good. Before I take up any more of your evening, the reason I called is because I'd very much like to chat with you some time. I'm a great admirer of your work, and often paediatrics and gynaecology walk hand in hand.'

'Yes, why not?' he'd agreed. 'Some time after the baby is born, perhaps.'

'You're not listening,' Georgina was protesting.

'Sorry. I was thinking about a phone call I had from Ian Sefton the other night.'

'Not about me, I would hope!'

'No. That would hardly be ethical, would it? He wants me to meet up with him when it's convenient, to discuss our respective professions.'

'That's nice.'

'Yes, I suppose so. Let's talk about babycare. There are a few options open to us. My staying at home while you go back to work is one of them. It would give me lots of time with the baby.'

'I wouldn't want you to do that,' she told him.

He stilled. 'Why?' *Because I'm not really your husband?* he thought.

'Ben, your skills are too important to be hidden away. I know there are times when you feel that your life is full of other people's children instead of your own, but those same children need you. You can't disappear out of their lives.'

'So what, then?' he questioned.

'I don't know. James isn't rushing me into a decision now that he's got you, and if you want to go back to what you do best he will still have David Tremayne in the practice, which gives me ample time to decide what my future role in it will be. It will depend largely on what sort of arrangements we make for the future.'

Georgina was giving him an opening, but he remained silent, and her hopes faded. It seemed that Ben hadn't changed his mind. They were going to be together, yet apart, with just one precious bond to bind them.

With the departure of the sun that had beamed down on Willowmere during daylight hours there was a chill in the air when they left the restaurant and Georgina shivered in the flimsy clothes she was wearing.

Ben had seen the shudder and was already taking off his jacket and draping it around her shoulders protectively. The simple, caring gesture brought tears to her eyes.

He saw them and wanted to know, 'What's wrong?'

'Nothing,' she told him, managing a watery smile, and thought that their lives were full of contradictions.

When he turned the car into Partridge Lane, she said hesitantly, 'Would you like to come in for a nightcap?'

Of course he would like to! He would *like* to go inside with her and stay there for evermore he thought, but he knew that Georgina was still holding back. He'd lost her trust once and she wasn't going to risk any further heartbreak even though the bond was still there.

In his most despondent moments he told himself that if it hadn't been for the baby, she would have sent him away long ago, but almost as if by divine providence they'd been given something to unite them in joyful anticipation.

'No, thanks just the same,' he said easily, trying not to choke on the words.

She nodded as if that was the answer she'd been expecting, and went inside.

When they went to call for Pollyanna and Jolyon on Saturday morning, the children were watching for them from the window of Bracken House. When James opened the door, he said, 'These two young ones have been looking for you ever since breakfast-time and are bursting to know where you're taking them.'

'We're going to a place where there are lots of animals and exciting things to do,' Ben told them. 'We're going to have a picnic while we're there, as well.'

Georgina smiled as the children, with eyes like saucers, listened to what he had to say.

'You'll have hit the jackpot with that,' James said.

Pollyanna was hopping with excitement, but Jolyon,

always the deeper thinker of the two, wanted to know, 'Are we going to play cricket?'

'Yes, if you want to.' Ben smiled. 'Go and get your bat and ball and the stumps.'

The little boy didn't waste any time. He was back within minutes and they were off, waving their good-byes to James as the car pulled away from Bracken House.

The weather was holding out for them and there wasn't a cloud in the sky. Georgina was determined that there weren't going to be any in *her* sky on this bright Saturday morning.

When they arrived at their destination, Ben looked around him at green lawns, silent statues and fountains in profusion in front of a beautiful old house.

'This is great!' he exclaimed, and turned to the children. 'What do you want to do first?'

'See the animals,' they chorused.

'Right! So that's what we'll do,' he said. 'Afterwards, how about some ice cream before we go on all those exciting things in the play areas?'

'Yes, please!' they said.

'And then can we play cricket?' Jolyon asked quietly.

'Then we will play cricket,' Ben assured him, gently ruffling the solemn little boy's hair.

This was what he'd been denied, Georgina thought, as her heart ached with tenderness. They both had.

As if he'd read her thoughts, Ben said, 'Are you all right, Georgina? Tell me if you're feeling tired, won't you?'

She smiled up at him, and he wanted to take her in arms and tell her how much he loved her, but it was the children's day. He didn't want his emotions running riot to spoil it for them.

They did everything they'd come to do, and when it was time for the picnic that Georgina had set out on a grassy slope behind the gracious house Ben told Jolyon, 'When we've had our lunch we'll play cricket.'

'I'll be the wicket keeper, if you like,' Georgina volunteered.

'Great stuff,' Ben said approvingly. 'Jolyon, you can be one of the opening bats and I'll be the other. Pollyanna can be the bowler.'

'She can't do over-arm throws,' Jolyon whispered in his ear. 'I'll be the bowler and Pollyanna can bat.'

James was waiting at the gate when they arrived home. Grubby, tired and happy, the children couldn't wait to tell their father about their day. He said, 'I can tell they've had a really good time. Are you going to come in for a drink?'

'No, but thank you for the offer,' Georgina told him. 'My feet are aching, but we've had a lovely time too.'

'It's been great,' Ben said. 'Your children are terrific, James. You are very fortunate to have them.'

'Yes, I know,' he said in a low voice as he watched them scamper towards the house after saying their thanks and goodbyes. 'Yet I ache all the time because Julie isn't here with us.'

'Georgina and I can sympathise with you. We know all about the agony of loss, but we are at last coming through it, and the world seems a different place.'

* * *

They were home, and Ben was making tea in her kitchen while Georgina sat with her feet up. When he came in, carrying two steaming mugs, she said, 'That was lovely what you said to James. We *are* coming through it, aren't we?'

'Yes,' he said soberly. 'Since I came here I've been remembering only the good times we had with Jamie.'

'That is how it should be,' she told him. Remembering what James had said about his wife, she said, 'Rightly or wrongly, James has kept the faith.'

'And we didn't because our love wasn't strong enough,' he commented.

She turned away to hide the hurt that his words had caused and then, facing him again, said steadily, 'Maybe so, but we've been given a second chance, haven't we?'

She was giving him another opportunity to say what was really in his mind, but again he didn't take it. Instead, he said, 'If you say so. But it doesn't alter the fact that I drove you away. And *you* let me.'

'I'm sorry we got involved in this sort of a discussion,' she told him as she rose to her feet. 'It has spoilt the last few moments of a lovely day. I'll see you on Monday, Ben.'

'So that's it, is it?' he said dryly. 'It's only half past four and I am dismissed.'

'I'm sure you can find something to do. Why not watch the cricket again? You enjoyed it last time, if I remember rightly.'

'I might just do that,' he replied, 'and when it's over make a day of it by dining at the Hollyhocks.'

And what was that meant to be? Georgina wondered

when he'd gone. A hint about where he could be found later?

She wasn't sure she wanted to take him up on it. He'd put the dampener on her hopes with his disparagement of their past relationship, yet after a rest and a shower she was changing into one of her flowing dresses and preparing to walk the short distance to the Hollyhocks as if Ben was willing her to appear.

He was seated at a table by the window and when he heard Emma greeting her as she came in, he rose to his feet and smiled his welcome as if they'd parted on the best of terms.

As he pulled out a chair for her he said in a low voice, 'I'm sorry about earlier. I don't deserve you.'

'No, you don't,' she agreed, and now it was her turn to smile, 'but I'm here, aren't I?'

'Yes, you are, and I hope it isn't only because you're feeding two,' he teased.

'That *could* be the reason, or it might be because there's nothing on television worth watching. Then again it could be because this child of ours is kicking away inside me in protest at the behaviour of its parents and I thought you ought to know.'

He sighed. 'Not parents…parent. I was the one casting the gloom.'

'So let's change the subject, shall we?' she said lightly. 'Are you going to accompany me the next time I go to see Ian?'

He raised a questioning eyebrow in her direction. 'I thought we'd already agreed on that. Yes, of course I am,' he said decisively.

* * *

Unlike the occasion when they'd dined at the smart new restaurant up on the tops, the night was mild as they walked slowly back to their respective cottages.

As they turned on to the lane a badger ambled in front of them, then disappeared into the darkness. Georgina said, 'The people at the post office feed them every night, and they never fail to turn up.'

He'd only been in the place a matter of weeks yet everything that had happened since he'd arrived was engraved upon his mind. Even the smallest happenings, and the big ones, all about being with Georgina again, would stay with him always, like stars in a dark sky, with the moment when he'd discovered she was pregnant the brightest star of all.

He ached to sleep with her again, to be able to reach out in the darkness and hold the pliant warmth of her in his arms again. And then when daylight came to have breakfast together. Just simple things but for those starved of them precious beyond belief.

Did *she* ever feel like that? he wondered. If she did, she hid it well. She'd made a point of telling him that day at the hospital. How she was her own woman and not interested in any of the advances of the opposite sex, and he'd known that it included himself.

It had been a blow to the heart, but even worse had been the knowledge that *he* was to blame for it, and it could be that any warmth she was showing towards him was either out of pity or put on just to get the waiting time over until the baby was born.

Georgina was observing his expression and commented, 'I thought we had banished the gloom.'

'We have,' he said firmly, and told himself to be satisfied with what they'd got, instead of wishing for the moon.

He wasn't invited in for a nightcap this time. If he had been he would have accepted, yet it didn't matter. He'd just told himself to think positive and that was what he was going to do. He did that in every other aspect of his life, but what there was, or was not, between Georgina and himself was as delicate as gossamer.

As Georgina lay looking up at the night sky through her bedroom window, the day that was past was occupying her thoughts and they were a jumble of pleasure and pain. There'd been the happy hours with the children that had made the longing for a family of her own so bad she could almost taste it.

Then the fall to earth over what Ben had said about the quality of their love in time of need, and last but not least she'd been back up in the clouds as they'd walked home together in the gloaming.

Her spirits had been up and down more times than a yo-yo and in the middle of it all was the longing to be not just the mother of Ben's baby but the cherished wife that she'd once been.

The resident owl hooted to announce its nocturnal presence and taking comfort from that small moment of normality, she slept.

CHAPTER EIGHT

WITH no problems apart from the usual discomforts of pregnancy, Georgina was counting the days to the birth. The baby's head was down in the right position now and when she was called out to the Quarmbys' cottage on Lord Derringham's estate one morning, Christine said on opening the door to her, 'Dr Adams! I wasn't expecting it to be you that came. Shouldn't you be resting?'

'I'm fine, Christine,' she told her laughingly. 'Just a little out of breath and my feet are rather puffy at the end of the day, but that is all. *You* are the one I am concerned about, so tell me what's wrong today, my dear.'

'It isn't me this time,' she explained. 'It's Dennis. He would have come to the surgery as he doesn't like a fuss, but I didn't think he should drive.'

'So what's wrong and where is he?' she asked.

'He's falling about all over the place, can't keep his balance. The moment he got up this morning it was there. The room was spinning and he couldn't stand up straight. He's gone back to bed.'

'And this is the first time it has happened?'

'Yes, to this extent. He's had a few minor dizzy spells before but they've only lasted a matter of minutes. Today it's much worse.'

'This kind of thing can be due to low blood pressure,' Georgina said when she'd tested it and examined the gamekeeper's eyes and ears, 'but I think not in your case, Mr Quarmby. Have you had any headaches?'

'No, but my ears have been tender and painful,' he mumbled irritably, and she thought that for once Dennis Quarmby wasn't in control and he wasn't liking it.

She nodded. 'Vertigo, which it most likely is, comes from a disturbance of the nerves in the canals in the ears. I'm going to prescribe some antihistamine tablets that will help to restore your balance, and in the meantime you need rest and quiet.'

He groaned. 'And while I'm having that the poachers will be out on the estate in full force if they know that I'm laid low.'

'You should soon be much better once you start taking the medication,' she told him, 'and don't get stressed. If the attacks persist we'll look into it further, but for now just take the tablets and keep calm.'

Dennis Quarmby's glance was on his wife hovering anxiously beside the bed and he said, 'I can't be ill, Doctor. Christine needs me. This vile thing that she's got isn't getting any better and I can't bear to see her suffer so.'

'Hush,' Christine said gently. 'We both know that it isn't going to go away, but we love each other, Dennis, and as long as that never changes, we'll be all right.'

He reached out, took her hand in his, and said gruffly, 'Aye, Chrissie, nothing can take that away from us.'

Driving back down to the village Georgina's thoughts were back there with the Quarmbys. Sjögren's syndrome was an incurable autoimmune disorder related to the rheumatoid arthritis that Christine had been diagnosed with and, as she'd said, it wasn't going to go away. In fact, it could get worse, so the outlook was bleak.

But those two had something more precious than gold in the way they loved each other. She and Ben had been blessed with that kind of love once. Would it blossom again in the last days of spring when their child came into the world?

When she arrived back at the surgery, Ben said, 'You look very solemn. Is everything all right?'

With the Quarmbys still at the forefront of her mind she told him, 'Yes. I suppose so. I've just been with two people who love each other very much.'

'And?'

'It reminded me of how we used to be.'

She saw him flinch and regretted the words as soon as she'd said them.

'Maybe they've never lost a child,' he commented flatly.

Contrite, she reached out to take his hand in hers, but as if he hadn't seen the gesture Ben walked through the main doors of the surgery towards his car. Deflated and upset, Georgina watched him drive off on his own calls.

* * *

David Tremayne had been for an interview with a view to joining the practice at the end of May when his contract at St Gabriel's was up. When he'd gone the three doctors had all expressed their approval of the possible newcomer, having been impressed by his brisk yet friendly manner and his unmistakable enthusiasm for his calling.

In his early thirties and unmarried, he was tall and very attractive, and Georgina thought that a mother somewhere must be proud of her handsome son.

James had asked Ben to sit in on the interview even though he was just a temporary member of the practice, and the more she saw them together the more Georgina was aware that the two men had taken an instant liking to each other.

When the interview was over, she had carried on for the rest of the day with an easier mind regarding her own arrangements and that evening when Ben arrived home from the surgery, he came to have a chat about the day's events.

'So what do you think about David Tremayne?' he asked.

'He seemed a really nice guy,' she replied, 'but it's how good a doctor he is that matters most. I do hope that he can join us when he's free, but first James and Elaine will have to sort out the admin side of it.'

The next subject was her appointment with the gynaecologist the following day. 'I'll meet you at his rooms, as I did the last time,' he said. 'Just in case I'm on the last minute getting away from surgery. I presume you're taking the afternoon off as you did before? Have you any concerns to discuss with him?'

'No. Not really. I keep getting a touch of indigestion, which I suppose is because the baby is pressing on my digestive tract, but apart from that I'm all right.'

'Blood pressure still behaving itself?'

'Yes. I seem to have escaped that problem this time.'

'Good.'

She made tea for them, and he perched himself on a kitchen stool while he drank it. He'd been cooler since she'd mentioned the Quarmbys to him, still caring but withdrawn, while she was aching for love and tenderness.

Ben's thoughts on the matter were that what she'd said had been a veiled reproach and he'd thought grimly that no one regretted what had happened to their marriage more than him, but at least he was trying to make up for it.

Georgina was early for the appointment with Ian Sefton and as she sat in the empty waiting room, leafing through a magazine while she waited for Ben, the man she was waiting to see came through on his way back from one of his clinics at the hospital. When he saw her, he stopped for a quick chat.

'Hi, Georgina,' he said. 'Did Ben tell you I phoned the other night to suggest we might meet up to discuss our work? I didn't realise that you and Ben Allardyce were a couple until he joined you at your last appointment.'

'There didn't seem any need to mention it,' she

replied, playing it down. 'We've only just renewed our acquaintance.'

'Yes, he told me. Ben said that you'd been apart, but were together again now and starting this new family.' Moving towards his consulting room, he said good-naturedly, 'I'll be ready for you as soon as he arrives. While I'm waiting I'm going to have a quick cuppa. Those clinics can be gruelling places.'

So Ben had told him that they were together again, she thought. But that wasn't strictly true. So why had he said it? To impress? She didn't think so. That wasn't his style.

As soon as Ben arrived, the receptionist smiled across at them, and said, 'Mr Sefton is ready for you, if you'd like to go in.'

'So, any changes or problems?' Ian asked as he examined her.

'I'm experiencing Braxton Hicks contractions more often,' she told him, 'which I know is normal, so I'm not going to mistake them for labour pains. They're too far apart, for one thing.'

'Yes, they're spaced-out contractions of the uterus and become more noticeable as pregnancy progresses,' he replied.

'And my blood pressure was up this morning. Not all that much but when I checked, it was up.'

She was aware of Ben tensing beside her but avoided his concerned expression as the gynaecologist said, 'Ah, now, that is a different matter. Where the Braxton Hicks are no cause for concern, hypertension most certainly is. So let's see what is going on with that.'

When he tested it for himself he said, 'Yes, it's up, though as you said not a lot. Nevertheless, it's going to mean resting to get it down. At this stage we can't take any chances, Georgina, as I'm sure I don't need to tell you.' He turned to Ben. 'Take the lady home and put her to bed for a couple of days and we'll see how the hypertension is then.'

She groaned. 'I'm needed at the practice.'

'We'll manage without you,' Ben told her levelly. 'You and the baby come first.'

'I do know that,' she told him in chilly tones. The idea of him giving Ian Sefton the impression that all was well with their relationship was still niggling at her.

When they left the building, Ben said, 'Why the drop in temperature?'

'There isn't one. I was just a bit taken aback when Ian Sefton said that you'd told him we were together again.'

'What did you expect me to say? That the baby is a mistake, that we're playing cat and mouse with each other all the time? It was easier to pretend that all was well between us. So, why didn't you mention your blood pressure while we were at the surgery this morning?'

'Because I had the appointment this afternoon. I would have told you about it if I hadn't, but there didn't seem any reason to alarm you at that stage.'

'And at what stage would you have thought it necessary if we hadn't been coming here?'

'Look, Ben,' she said wearily. 'I'm doing what I've

been told and am going home to bed, so calm down. Nothing is going to happen to this baby.'

'And what about something happening to *you*?' he called after her retreating figure, but there was no reply. Georgina was already in her car and pulling away from the forecourt of the building, leaving him with no alternative but to return to his patients.

As she drove back to Willowmere Georgina's annoyance was draining away. How could she have belittled Ben's consideration for her by not telling Ian Sefton the full story? She should be grateful that he cared. He'd lost a child and he would have been living with the thought that there would never be another. Why should he feel that he had to spell out what was happening in their lives to a stranger? She was getting to be a bit prickly. Dared she blame it on hormones?

Their heated exchange of words had put their relationship on an even more shaky footing, and as she pulled up in front of her cottage she was wondering where they went from here.

She rang James on the bedside phone once she was settled against the pillows and, as she'd known he would be, he was totally supportive. 'We will cope all right here,' he assured her. 'Ben is a tower of strength, and if it isn't possible for you to come back before the baby comes, we have David Tremayne joining us towards the end of May. So you will be free to return whenever you feel ready once you have the baby.'

When she'd put the phone down Georgina turned her head into the pillow and wept. She wanted this baby just as much as Ben did, but its coming would be marred if she and he had separate lives.

She'd put a key through his letterbox before going into her own place so that he could let himself in if he wanted to. Sure enough, seconds after he'd arrived home early that evening he was bounding up the stairs and knocking on her bedroom door. That nearly brought the tears back. The only man she'd ever slept with having to wait to be invited into her bedroom.

'Have you eaten?' were his first words when she called for him to come in, and that made her smile the tears away. He'd obviously put their earlier crossing of swords to one side and was about to take on the role of head nurse.

She shook her head. 'I wasn't hungry when I got home but I'm peckish now.'

'So shall I go and raid the larder?'

'Yes, if you like, though anything will do, Ben, just a slice of toast or whatever. But make something substantial for yourself while you're there.'

Twenty minutes later he appeared with a tray on which was an omelette and a soft roll, tea in a china cup, and a small vase with just one early rose in it. As she raised herself up off the pillows she said softly, 'Not so long ago you said you did not deserve me. It is the other way round, I think. I'm sorry for what I said earlier. Can you forgive me?'

He placed the tray on the bedside table and replied with a quizzical smile that gave no hint of anything other than light-heartedness, 'Yes, if you promise to eat every crumb. Before I go back downstairs, what about dessert? I've brought some fresh fruit in with me and some ice cream, and I caught the Hollyhocks on the point of closing and coaxed a couple of cream cakes from Emma.'

'I'd like a cream cake. Let's save the fruit and ice cream for tomorrow. Now, will you please go and have *your* meal? You must be starving.'

He was, Ben thought as he went downstairs, but it was the love they'd once had that he was hungry for. Tarnished and neglected, it hadn't disappeared during the lonely years. It was still there if only they could forget past hurts and walk into the light together with a new brother or sister to Jamie.

His nerves had knotted when Georgina had announced that her blood pressure was up, and once they'd eaten, another check would be a good idea.

He was going to suggest he stay the night and was expecting her to protest that it wasn't necessary, but he wasn't going to take no for an answer. The baby was due very soon and it was vital that he should be there for her now…and afterwards.

When he went back upstairs Georgina was asleep, her dark mane splayed across the pillow and her breathing regular enough, considering the weight she was carrying. He'd brought the cream cake with him and placed it on the bedside table when he'd removed the empty tray.

As he kissed her gently on the brow she stirred in her sleep and murmured his name, and in that moment he thought tenderly that she had been keen to make it clear that she was her own woman, but as she'd said his name it had been as if once more she was *his* woman, and for that to be so was all he would ever ask.

While she was sleeping he went next door to collect his things for the night ahead, and when he got back she was awake, face flushed with sleep, eyelids drooping and about to check her blood pressure.

'I'll do that,' he said gently, and when it was done, he was smiling. 'It's normal,' he announced. 'It must have just been a blip, but we do need to keep a close watch on it.'

'So can I get up, Doctor?' she teased, as relief washed over her.

'No. I'm afraid not,' he replied in a similar manner. 'Maybe tomorrow, but for now stop where you are. I intend to stay the night and no protests, please.'

'All right,' she agreed meekly.

'How would you feel if I moved in after the baby is born?' he said, but she shook her head.

'I don't know, Ben,' she said awkwardly, 'let's wait and see.'

'I would be in the spare room—as I will be tonight,' he commented dryly.

'Yes, I know,' she said lamely. 'But if you hadn't come to Willowmere I would have had to cope alone, and I've got used to doing that.'

'All right,' he said levelly. 'Just be sure you don't put the baby at risk with your independence.' On that word of warning, he turned and went downstairs.

He came back up again some time later, to make up

the spare bed and to bring her some supper, but that was the last she saw of him as the night closed in upon them.

The next morning she went downstairs and found Ben making the breakfast. Before he asked, she told him that her blood pressure was normal.

'Good,' he said with a tight smile, and placed bacon and eggs in front of her.

'Your're angry with me, aren't you?' she said in a low voice. 'I know I deserve it. It must seem as if I'm throwing all your kindness back in your face, but it isn't like that, Ben. I'm confused and apprehensive about the future, and I suppose you are the same.'

'Not at all,' he replied. 'The future will take care of itself. I have to be off, Georgina. The surgery opens in ten minutes.'

She'd spoken to the gynaecologist in the middle of the morning and told him that her blood pressure was back to normal and he'd warned her to take care as it could happen again and he wanted to see her again the following week. In the meantime, if she wanted to go back to work there was no reason why not, but to do fewer hours and not overtire herself.

So after another day of rest Georgina had presented herself at the practice once more, free of the anxiety that the minor scare had caused, and had suggested to James that she work afternoons only until the baby was born.

He had agreed immediately and Ben, who had now moved back into his own cottage, watched over her from the sidelines.

Maggie Timmins had given birth to a baby girl earlier in the week, and she was doing well. Every morning when he delivered the milk Bryan had an update on mother and baby to relate.

'What does Josh have to say about his new baby sister?' Georgina had asked when he'd first come with the news.

'He was disappointed at first,' his father said, 'but now that he's adjusted to it he'll sit with her for hours.'

'Have you chosen a name?' she'd enquired.

'Yes,' he replied promptly. 'Rhianna.'

'That's lovely. And Maggie, how is she?'

'Rather nervous after all this time, and we can't wait to bring her home, but doing fine otherwise.'

As Bryan had driven off, Ben's door had opened, and he'd asked, 'Was that the happy father?'

'Yes,' she'd told him. 'It will be your turn soon.'

He'd nodded, for once having no reply, because he was aware that in everything else in his life he was a positive thinker, but when it came to Georgina and the baby he was like a nervous jellyfish.

He knew the reason, of course. Ever since they'd lost Jamie he'd found it impossible to take anything for granted, which had its advantages in his work, but not in his private life.

Georgina had managed without him for three years. She was one of Willowmere's full-time, permanent GPs and extremely capable into the bargain. He knew that she wanted him to be near for their child when it came, but he wasn't getting the impression that it was going to be by her side and in her bed with his wedding ring on her finger.

In the days that followed April showers and spring sunshine were constant reminders of the time of year, and as the calendar moved slowly towards an event that was always celebrated in Willowmere on the first of May, Georgina found herself facing Clare, the owner of the picture gallery, at the other side of her desk.

The two were good friends, and Georgina had been very supportive when Clare had been diagnosed with ovarian cancer some months ago. The smart, middle-aged woman had been operated on to remove the affected organs and was now at the end of a course of chemotherapy and back into organising village affairs once more, something she excelled in.

When she saw her friend seated opposite, Georgina hoped that Clare's presence at the surgery didn't mean any further complications with regard to her health.

It seemed as if that was not the case as her first words were, 'I've come to ask a favour of you, Georgina.'

'Really?' she questioned. 'What is it?'

'The May Day committee has asked me to approach you.'

'Whatever for?'

'They want to know if you will crown the May Queen.'

'Clare, I would love to,' she said regretfully, 'but the baby will be due any day then and I wouldn't want to let them down.'

'We appreciate that, but if you couldn't be there, I would act as stand-in for you. You've only been resident in the village a short time compared to some of us, but you are liked and respected, so please say you will.'

'Yes, of course I will,' she said immediately. 'Pollyanna, James's daughter, has been telling me that she's one of the attendants, and I believe that the Quarmbys' teenage daughter is to be the May Queen, which is good. Christine needs some brightness in her life, but she isn't well enough to be involved actively with her daughter's dress and such.'

'That's under control,' Clare assured her. 'You'll never guess who's offered to make the dress and train…my mother. She's been a gem since I've been ill. I was dreading what she would be like, as Mum can be a tartar over little things, but she's supported me all the time and it's made the cancer problem a lot easier to cope with.'

'That's wonderful,' Georgina said softly. 'When Ben and I lost our son almost four years ago, we had no parents to turn to. Mine died within a short time of each other just before he and I were married, and his were killed in a pile-up on the motorway. So, "tartar" or not, you must cherish her.'

The crowning of the May Queen was an ancient tradition still practised in many English country villages and rural areas to celebrate the coming of summer, a teenage girl being selected to be the Queen and younger ones chosen to be her attendants.

A maypole decked with flowers and with ribbons hanging from it would be erected in the centre of the village green where the crowning ceremony would take place, and once it was over children would dance around the maypole each holding a ribbon.

It was always a special occasion in Willowmere and Georgina thought that Ben would want to watch the proceedings. He was becoming more attracted to village life with each passing day, and whatever they ended up doing in the future he would want their baby to be brought up in the fresh air and friendliness of the countryside.

What he would say when he discovered she'd accepted the honour that the folks of Willowmere were anxious to bestow upon her she didn't know, but if she was mobile and not in the labour ward at St Gabriel's, she would perform it with the greatest of pleasure.

When she told him he smiled and said, 'It is a nice thought but—'

'I know,' she interrupted. 'You were going to say I might be occupied elsewhere. I've cleared that with Clare. She will perform the crowning ceremony if I can't be there.' She paused and smiled. 'I'm glad this child of ours will be a spring baby.'

'Why especially?'

'It was spring when you came back into my life, when daffodils were nodding in cottage gardens and there were newborn lambs in the fields.'

Surely he would understand the message in what she'd just said, Georgina thought, and take her up on it, but he just smiled a wry smile and carried on trimming the hedge around his garden.

So much for that, she thought. Was Ben still of the opinion that in spite of the closeness of their lives in recent weeks, it still wasn't working? Had he actually been into the estate agent's to see what properties were for sale in the village? She hoped not.

There was one house that had been for sale in recent weeks that she'd always longed to live in. It was a large, detached property, built out of local limestone, and it stood among the green fields of Cheshire.

She'd always thought what an attractive house it was, though not the kind of residence for a single mother, and she wouldn't have been able to afford it in any case if it had ever come up for sale, but it was on the market now and no doubt would soon be snatched up by someone with an eye for solid elegance.

When she'd seen the photograph of it in the estate agent's window, she'd gazed at it enviously and hoped that it wouldn't be bought by someone who would start pulling it apart. Obviously it wasn't going to appeal to Ben. He'd lived alone in the house in London for three years and that was a delightful place, but from what he'd said it may as well have been a stable for all the pleasure he'd derived from living there without his wife and son.

So she couldn't see him getting an urge to buy The Meadows, as the house was called, while he had the up-keep of a large property in London to contend with. And it was like he'd said, they needed somewhere close by when they went to visit the grave so that Jamie would never feel they had deserted him, and the London house would always be somewhere for his brother, Nicholas, to stay if he had business in the capital when he came to the U.K.

It was early morning. As he handed the solicitor next door to the estate agent's a cheque for the deposit on the purchase of the only house that had caught his imagination in Willowmere, Ben was telling himself that he was crazy to be thinking of buying a house as big as The Meadows.

If Georgina didn't want to stand beside him in front of the altar in the village church and repeat the vows they'd once made in the uncomplicated life that had been wrenched out of their grasp, he was going to find himself rattling around the place like a lost soul.

But the moment the estate agent had shown him a photograph of The Meadows he'd asked to view it, and after that he hadn't been able to get it out of his mind. Incredibly it was standing empty and there was no chain involved in the sale so it would soon be his, or theirs if he should be so lucky.

Sometimes he thought Georgina still loved him, but on other occasions, he wasn't at all sure. Maybe when he told her he'd bought The Meadows, he would have a clearer picture of her feelings. If she expressed concern about them still having the London house, he would tell her the good news regarding that.

The last time he'd spoken to Nicholas he'd said that he was considering buying a property in the capital as in the future he would be spending six months in every year there. When he'd suggested that he buy theirs,

Nicholas had jumped at the chance, delighted to become the new owner of the house in the tree-lined square.

It would mean that the loving bonds they still had with their son would remain unbroken because his favourite uncle, who was someone else that Jamie had loved and who had loved him, would be close by for him and for them when either together or apart they brought the white roses of remembrance.

CHAPTER NINE

To Ben's relief Georgina was still asleep when he arrived back at the cottage. He didn't want her to know anything about the house until the baby was born. That way she wouldn't feel that he was forcing the issue of their future relationship in any way.

He didn't know if she was aware that The Meadows was for sale, or even if she knew there was such a place. But she would one day soon and he would be able to tell from her reaction whether he'd made a big mistake in buying one of the most attractive houses in the neighbourhood.

He'd asked the estate agent not to reveal any details of his purchase to anyone, especially his ex-wife, and so far it was all going to plan. Surveys had been satisfactory and he'd got a completion date for the first of May.

He wasn't to know that she hadn't been asleep all the time he'd been absent. She'd heard his door close down below when he was setting off, and had gone to the window and watched him walk down the lane with his familiar purposeful stride, thinking how much she loved him still.

She'd presumed he'd gone to buy a morning paper, so had gone back to bed and dozed off again, but when eventually she surfaced he was puttering around the garden. When she'd showered and dressed, she went down and asked Ben where he'd been. For a moment he looked taken aback. Then he rallied and said he'd been for a walk, which was easy enough to believe on a bright April morning.

Once a month there was a farmers' market in the village hall that was always well attended by local people and others from outlying areas, eager to buy fresh free-range eggs, farmhouse cheeses, and bacon and hams from the pig farms, to name just a few of the wholesome foods on display.

There was also a café at the back of the hall where the husband-and-wife team from the Hollyhocks served snack meals. Altogether it was an occasion not to be missed.

As she was finishing a leisurely breakfast, Ben appeared and suggested that they walk to Willow Lake for exercise, which Georgina thought was odd as he'd already been out doing that same thing. But the suggestion was appealing and when they arrived, they found that the trees from which it had got its name were now bedecked with the new growth that spring brought as they hung over its still waters.

As she looked around her Georgina was remembering Anna and Glenn, now far away in Africa, and how he had proposed to her at this very spot. Would there be a second time round for her and Ben? she wondered. And if there was, would it be for the right reasons?

He was observing her questioningly and, putting to one side wistful thoughts, she said, 'How about we go to do a big shop? There is a farmers' market in the village hall today, the first one since you arrived in Willowmere. When you see what is on sale you'll understand what I mean by a "big shop".'

He was smiling, 'Lead on, then, and surprise me still further with your country customs.'

With a sudden drop in spirits Georgina thought that they were on each other's wavelength in all but one thing…they didn't sleep in the same bed.

There were so many times in the night when the child inside her moved and she longed for Ben to be there to share the special moment of tenderness and joy, but she thought sombrely it would be breaking the rules that they seemed to be living by. He seemed contented enough in his role of onlooker, which made her think all the more that he'd given up on them making their wedding vows for a second time.

As they moved from stall to stall, with Ben carrying their purchases in a large hessian bag that Georgina had brought with her, they were stopped frequently by patients and friends that she'd made during her years in Willowmere. All of them were ready to welcome Ben into their midst, in spite of the curiosity of some who would have liked to know where Dr Adams had been hiding the man by her side.

As they were turning into Partridge Lane on the way home, a luxurious car passed them with a chauffeur at the wheel, and the man on the backseat smiled and waved.

'Who was *that*? Ben exclaimed.

'Lord Derringham,' she told him laughingly. 'He owns an estate up on the tops. Dennis Quarmby is his gamekeeper.'

'I wouldn't expect that you see *him* at the surgery very often,' he commented dryly.

'No. He has private medical care, but I was called out to his wife a few times last year when she was pregnant and was having some problems. He's a decent sort and well liked amongst those who live in the area. Needless to say, he has a very impressive residence that puts every other house for miles around in the shade.'

The comment brought The Meadows to mind and he wondered what she would think when she saw it. There had been a tricky moment earlier when one of the stall-holders had asked Georgina if she was aware that it had been sold and she'd enquired without much show of interest if the farmer's wife knew who'd bought it.

'No, I don't,' had been the reply, 'but there's a rumour going around that it isn't anyone local, and everyone thinks it's a shame.'

On Monday evening Ben came knocking on her door. 'I answered the phone to David Tremayne this morning. He wanted to speak to James, and he and I had a brief conversation. He's still keen to join the practice and is hoping that there will be some definite news on his appointment soon.'

'James and Elaine were discussing it this morning,' she told him. 'It would seem that it's all going ahead satisfactorily, but I can understand that he's anxious to get things sorted.'

'Which makes two of us,' he commented with an edge to his voice.

'What do you mean?' she asked, startled by his tone.

'I would have thought it was obvious. His coming means you can take as long as you want away from the surgery after the birth, but so far your plans, if you have any, seem to be a closely guarded secret.'

'You make it sound so simple,' she said heatedly. 'But it isn't and well you know it!' Before she could say anything she might regret, she grabbed a jacket off the hall stand and marched off down the drive.

He groaned as he watched her go. It was unfor-givable to take out his irritations on Georgina, but he was keen to know what direction their relationship was going in. So far a blissful reconciliation seemed as remote as the silver moon that had appeared on the heels of a glorious sunset.

Until tonight he'd been determined that there would be no persuasion from him. Georgina had to be sure that she really wanted him if they ever got back together, that it wasn't because of the baby but because she still loved him. And so what had he done? Tackled her about it in a manner that had sounded more like bullying than concern.

The only thing to do was to go and find her, bring her home and apologise, even though what she'd said before she'd rushed off had made him feel that he was still not forgiven.

When he went out into the lane, there was no sign of her, and he hesitated. The lake wasn't far away, had she gone there to calm down? He hoped not. It could be unsafe out there in the dark, and suppose she started labour while she was alone?

He was moving in that direction with a fast stride even as he thought it, but there was no one there when he arrived, just the lake and the trees bowing over it.

The village centre was just the opposite when he got there, with the Pheasant as the focal point. It was a mild night and the tables outside were fully occupied. From the buzz of noise issuing from inside it seemed as if it was the same in both parts, but Georgina wasn't amongst the throng.

Gillian Jarvis, the new nurse at the practice, was there with her husband, and when she saw him in the doorway, she came across and asked if he was looking for Georgina. 'We saw her going into the surgery as we drove past,' she said.

With a brief word of thanks, Ben turned on his heel and set off in the direction of the limestone building beside the village green and, sure enough, the lights were on inside when he got there.

He called out as he went in so as not to alarm her and found her sitting in the swivel chair behind her desk, staring into space. She turned at his approach and observed him unsmilingly. Reaching out, he took her hand and lifted her carefully to her feet. When they were facing each other he said gently, 'I'm sorry I took my bad temper out on you, of all people, Georgina.'

The dark hazel eyes looking into his were mirroring

the pain inside her as she told him, 'I behaved no better, Ben. I'm sorry, too. Let's go home.'

'Yes, let's,' he agreed, wanting to hold her close and tell her how much he loved her, yet wary of doing so in case it pushed their relationship further back than it was already.

As they walked the short distance home Georgina said regretfully, 'Have you eaten since you came home from the surgery?'

He shrugged. 'You know me—first things first. I had something on the stove but left it to tell you about David Tremayne. I was keen to see your reaction.'

'You turned the hotplate off, I hope?' she said, as she thought that he'd certainly got her reaction, and it hadn't gone down too well. Her face softened. It hadn't stopped him from coming to look for her, though.

They separated at her door. Ben returned to his cooking and Georgina sat gazing into space as the future that was so hazy didn't become any cleaner.

It was there again, the feeling deep down inside her that, though Ben was thoughtful and caring, it was the baby who held his heartstrings, and could she blame him if that was the case after what they'd lost that day in the park?

She went upstairs to bed as the light was fading and willed herself to blot out everything except the child that was moving inside her. Soon her doubts and dilemmas were submerged in sleep.

Next door, Ben was also deep in thought and he wished they were happier issues that crowded his mind. These should be joyful days for them both, he told himself. Full of excitement and anticipation. If they had a normal relationship, they would be, but neither of them were prepared to make the first move because they didn't want to be hurt again.

It was Friday evening at the end of a week that had passed slowly and uneventfully for the two doctors. They'd each had their evening meal and were seated in the small gardens at the back of the cottages, watching the sun set. When Ben looked across at her, Georgina was staring straight ahead as if she was seeing something that he couldn't see, and out of the blue she said, 'It could be some time before we're able to visit the grave once the baby arrives. Let's go tomorrow.'

Ben was frowning. 'I don't think so. It's a long drive for you in your present state. Why don't I go on my own?'

She was shaking her head emphatically. 'No, I have to go. Something is telling me that I must.'

'What do you mean?' he said slowly. 'Do you feel that the baby might be early so you don't want to leave it any later? If that's the case, it could be risky. I'm quite capable of delivering my own child, but I'm not too keen on having to do it on the motorway or in some other most unsuitable surroundings.'

'I *have* to go,' she insisted.

He sighed. 'What has brought this on? If it means so much, yes, we'll go. We can pick up the flowers on the way. But I don't understand the sudden urgency.'

She was calming down now that he'd agreed and said in a placatory manner, 'The next time we go Jamie will have a new sister or brother. On this occasion I want it to be just the two of us…and him.'

'Fair enough, but I insist we go to the house while we're there so that you can have a rest before we set off back.'

She didn't reply and he knew she was remembering the last time they'd both been there. How it had set off an incredible chain of events that would soon be bearing fruit in the gift of another child, and he still didn't know if that would be the limit of it.

A far as he was concerned, her suggestion had come out of nowhere. He'd been taking it for granted that they would be staying close to base during the last days before the birth and suddenly they were embarking upon a long and tiring journey. It was a fact that pregnant women sometimes behaved out of character due to hormone changes and he supposed that today's sudden urgency fell into that category.

He wasn't to know that for Georgina there were no such misgivings. There had just been an overwhelming urge in her to do what she'd been doing for all the years she'd been apart from Ben. Yet she didn't blame him if he was upset at the way she was making light of his anxieties on behalf of the baby and herself.

They were up early the next morning and while Ben was at the local garage, filling up the tank with petrol, Georgina checked her blood pressure. It was steady, with no increase to concern herself about, and she breathed a sigh of relief, knowing that if it had been up, Ben would have dug his heels in and refused to go, and it would have been common sense to agree.

As if he'd read her mind his first words when he came back were concerning it, and when she'd reassured him, he looked happier about what they were doing, though still unsure of the wisdom of it.

The miles were speeding past and all the time Georgina sat quietly in the passenger seat, speaking only rarely, but each time he looked at her she had a smile for him, and Ben thought that it was going to be the first time they'd visited the grave together, except for the day when he'd found her there and both their lives had changed for ever. Maybe her tranquillity was a way of telling him that it was going to all come right for them?

They'd stopped off in the town to buy the white roses before going onto the motorway and had recently stopped again for an early lunch before they hit the London traffic. As the capital city drew nearer Georgina could feel a strange kind of peace stealing over her. As if all the anxieties and frustrations of past weeks and years were leaving her. She'd seen it in the sunset, the promise of happiness, yet didn't understand how the sad thing they had come all this way for could bring that about.

They'd held hands as they'd placed the flowers on the white marble, united for the first time in a bond of love for their son from which grief had been wiped away, and when they'd said their goodbyes to him and walked back to the car they'd still been holding hands as if neither of them wanted to let go.

When Ben had suggested that they go to the house

so that she might rest for a while, Georgina had agreed without hesitation, and this time she hadn't slumped into his arms, caught up in the in the trauma of a painful return to the place that had once been her home.

Instead, she'd walked around the familiar rooms before letting Ben tuck her up on the sofa for an hour, and as he'd watched over her his thoughts had gone to Nicholas who would soon be living there with maybe children of his own one day.

Whether he and Georgina would ever live together in The Meadows was another matter, but for the moment he was going to put those thoughts to one side.

When it was time to leave, he asked, 'Are you content now that you've been to the cemetery?'

'Yes,' she told him gravely. 'Today it was how it should be for him, the two of us together. The longing to be here came over me suddenly and everything else seemed far away. The birth being so near, the thought of visiting the house again, the long drive, all seemed blurred. All I wanted was come to where we were once so happy.'

'And do you think we will ever be that happy again?' he asked as he helped her into the car.

'Maybe not,' she said softly, still with peace upon her. 'How it was before could be a hard act to follow, but today we've made a move in the right direction, haven't we?' And as the car pulled out of the square she closed her eyes and slept.

She woke up when Ben pulled in at a service stop on the motorway not far from home, and as she observed him questioningly he said, 'I think I might have a flat tyre. Do you want to stretch your legs and have a wander around inside? I'll come and join you as soon as I've changed it.'

Georgina nodded. 'Yes, I'm stiff all over. I'll wait for you outside the restaurant. We may as well eat here to save cooking when we get back.' And left him to sort out the tyre.

It was a big place. There were shops of various kinds along the passage that led to the restaurant on the first floor and, considering the time of day, there weren't many people about.

After pottering around for a while she lowered herself onto the seating outside a toy shop next to the restaurant and positioned herself where she could see Ben when he came in at the main entrance below.

As she glanced around her she saw a young family approaching. Mother, father, with a small boy of a similar age and colouring to how Jamie had been and just as fast in his movements. He was running on in front, watched dotingly by his parents, and as she smiled at him he stopped abruptly beside her.

When Georgina glanced to see what had caught his attention, she saw that it was the wooden display case next to where she was sitting. Inside it were some of the toys sold in the shop.

It was glass fronted and locked and after hesitating for a moment, the boy reached out and pulled at the handle to get to the toys. As he did so, the whole thing began to topple towards him.

She heard his mother scream and his father's footsteps pounding on the tiled floor as she heaved herself towards him and dragged him out of the way. And then there was nothing but pain and darkness.

Ben was smiling as he came through the main door. They would be home safe and sound in minutes. There had been no need for him to fuss like he had. It had been a wonderful day with those special tranquil moments with their son followed by that quiet time in the home they'd once shared, and all the time he'd been able to feel Georgina's contentment around him in unspoken promises.

When they were back home, he was going to ask her to marry him again. He should have done it before, instead of being so set on waiting until he saw how things were when the baby came. That was how it ought to be, making their vows to each other once more as a separate thing that wasn't tied in with anything else except their love for each other. And if he was taking too much for granted after this wonderful day together, at least Georgina would know how much he still adored her.

As he stepped onto the escalator he heard a crash and someone screamed above, then a voice bellowed, 'Phone for an ambulance and tell them the lady's pregnant, due any time by the looks of it!' As his happy bubble burst around him Ben was leaping up the moving staircase in sick dismay, praying that it wasn't Georgina who was being described, yet knowing it would be too big a coincidence if it wasn't.

At the worst he was expecting to find that she'd gone into premature labour, but it was worse than that, much worse. She was lying very still on her side, curled up in a foetal position with her arms folded protectively across her stomach. Two security men were frantically removing the large wooden display case that she was lying under.

He was by her side in a flash, telling them in a voice as cold as steel, 'I'm her husband and I'm a doctor. Tell me what happened.'

There was a woman weeping silently just a foot away and she said chokingly, 'Your wife saved our little boy. He'd seen the toys inside and was pulling at the handle. She saw what was about to happen and dragged him away as it started to fall, but didn't have time to protect herself. We are so sorry.'

Not as much as I am, he thought grimly as he registered a faint pulse and shallow breathing. He was shuddering to think what might have happened to the baby. But for the moment she was his main concern. He could see a deep gash on the side of her head and her legs were bleeding from cuts that the glass in the doors of the display unit had made when they had shattered. Any other injuries would not be immediately visible until she was examined in Accident and Emergency at St Gabriel's, which was the nearest hospital as they were so close to home.

The ambulance had been mercifully quick and after they'd taken Georgina down in the lift on a stretcher they were soon away with sirens blaring.

Ben had caught a glimpse of the child who'd innocently been the cause of the accident clinging to his mother's hand, and with a pang thought how much like

Jamie he was. Had this been another reason why Georgina had felt impelled to leave the safety of Willowmere? he'd thought incredulously. And now that they'd made peace at their son's grave was he going to lose her?

Ian Sefton was waiting for them when the stretcher was wheeled into A and E with Ben granite-faced beside it, and he said, 'We've got a team standing by for Georgina but first I'm going to check the baby's heartbeat on the foetal monitor to make sure it's OK.' It was with great relief he announced, 'We have a heartbeat. That's the good news. But it's not quite as strong as I would like it to be.'

Ben nodded with hope hard to come by as he gazed at Georgina still and bloodstained on the bed.

'I'll be standing by in case I have to do a Caesarean section,' the gynaecologist said, and Ben thought that was how he would be if it was someone else's wife and child, but on this occasion he was on the receiving end and was numb with the horror of what was happening to their hopes and dreams.

He'd had high blood pressure on his mind while Georgina had been carrying the baby because it had happened once before, or had thought that some other medical problem might put her and the baby at risk, but from out of nowhere had come a different kind of danger, horrifying and unexpected.

A child in danger had been something that she hadn't been able to ignore and she was paying the price. Why, oh, why, hadn't he told her how much he loved her before this?

* * *

Severe concussion, broken ribs and deep cuts, especially to the head and legs, were the total of Georgina's injuries, and one of the doctors commented to another that if she hadn't been carrying so much extra weight, it might have been a lot worse.

She still hadn't regained consciousness when she started to haemorrhage, and then it was panic stations with the theatre on standby for the Caesarean section that Ian Sefton had anticipated.

At just past midnight Arran Allardyce came into the world, and Ben wept at the nature of his coming, even though from all appearances he was a lusty infant. His mother, on the other hand, still hadn't surfaced from the accident and the anaesthetic she'd been given during the operation, and was not aware of his arrival. As Ben kept a vigil by her bedside, with the baby sleeping peacefully beside them, he was willing Georgina to come back to them so that he could tell her how much he loved her.

As dawn brightened the night sky Georgina opened her eyes, removed the hand that he'd been holding out of his clasp and passed it slowly over her stomach. Ben saw that her eyes were awash with tears,

'I'm so sorry, Ben,' she said weakly, 'but I had to save the boy. Did you see how much he looked like Jamie?' Tears were rolling down her cheeks now as she begged, 'Can you forgive me for losing another of our children?'

'I can forgive you anything,' he said softly, 'because I love you more than life itself. And what's this about losing the baby? If you turn your head sideways, you will see young Arran Allardyce, strong and healthy despite a slightly early entrance into the world, sleeping peacefully beside you, Georgina, unharmed and totally beautiful, just like his mother.'

Her smile was brighter than the sun that would soon be in the sky as she cried joyfully, 'So Jamie has a brother! How absolutely perfect, and how wonderful that you still love me as much as I love you.

'That day when we were having the picnic and you said that the second chance we'd been given wasn't working, it made me realise just how much I wanted it to, and ever since then I've been afraid to plan a future in which we were together in every sense of the word in case you were right.'

'Will you marry me when you've recovered from all the dreadful things that have happened to you during the last twenty-four hours?' he asked softly.

'Those will be forgotten when I hold our baby in my arms,' she told him, 'and, yes, of course I'll marry you, Ben. I've always felt as if I was still your wife in any case, but now we can start living again, waking up each morning in the same bed, you and I together like it used to be, with Arran close by in the nursery.'

Ian Sefton was approaching and when he reached the bedside, he said whimsically, 'You had us all worried for a while, Georgina. I'd almost decided I would have to emigrate if I let anything happen to you and the baby. This husband of yours was all scrubbed up ready to take over if I put a foot wrong.'

'Were you really?' she asked Ben.

'Yes, I'm afraid so,' he replied. 'There was too much at stake.'

'So, do I get an invitation to the wedding for a job well done?' the gynaecologist asked.

Ben was smiling. 'You do indeed,' he told him, and then added in a more serious manner, 'You were the best, Ian. We can't thank you enough.'

When he'd gone, Ben lifted little Arran carefully out of his crib and placed him in his mother's arms, and as he gazed at them in that special moment it seemed as if it had been a good idea after all to buy The Meadows. There would be no more confusion in their minds regarding the future. They were a family again.

That same evening they were visited by another family, one that might not have been so complete if it hadn't been for Georgina's instinctive reaction at the motorway services.

When the parents and their small son stood beside her bed the young one's father said, 'So what do you say to the lady for saving you from being hurt by the display case, Dominic?'

'Thank you for saving me,' he told her in a voice that indicated he'd been rehearsing the little speech.

'And?' his mother prompted, placing a gift-wrapped parcel in his hands.

'This is for your baby,' he said shyly. 'What are you going to call him?'

'We're going to call him Arran,' she told him gently, 'and I'm sure he will love what is inside this present when he is a bit older.' Then she turned to his parents.

'You didn't have to do this. I'm just so pleased that Dominic wasn't hurt. We lost our first child in an accident and I wouldn't wish that sort of grief on anyone.'

When they'd gone, she asked Ben, 'Were you angry when you knew what I'd done?'

'Horrified, yes, but not angry.' he told her softly. 'It would have been amazing if you hadn't stepped in, being the nearest to him. In those kind of moments there is no time for thinking, do I, or don't I? One just goes ahead and does it.'

brought Georgina and baby Arran home to the cottage

CHAPTER TEN

IT WAS an occasion they would long remember when Ben
brought Georgina and baby Arran home to the cottage
in Partridge Lane and in the hours that followed it was
as if the whole village was sharing their happiness.

And there was more to come. Ben still had a couple
of pleasant surprises for her but felt they could wait for
a day or two. The injuries she'd received from the
broken glass were healing satisfactorily and the hospital, as was usually the case, was leaving the fractured
ribs to heal of their own accord. But she was still a little
weak from the trauma that had followed when Ian
Sefton had been forced to do a Caesarean baby to save
its life and hers.

Arran was fine. Every time they observed him they
rejoiced. Ben was taking time off from work to be there
during the first important days of his son's life and so
that Georgina could rest as she recovered from the
accident and her delivery.

It was an irksome situation when she was raring to be
back to her usual fitness but, acknowledging that it was

a necessary procedure, she had to be content with welcoming a constant stream of wellwishers from the comfort of the sofa while Ben took charge of everything else.

On the second afternoon of her return Clare was one of the callers and after she'd held the baby reverently and then handed him back to his watchful father she said, 'I know it's pushing it, Georgina, you've only been home a couple of days, but it's the May Queen crowning on Saturday. Would you feel up to doing the ceremony?'

'I'd love to,' she told her. 'I'm feeling stronger all the time and as long as Ben and Arran are there beside me I'll be fine. How are the preparations going?'

'All right so far,' was the reply, 'and now that you're prepared to do the crowning, my last worry is sorted. My mum has finished the dresses, the music is organised and refreshments are in the capable hands of our Hollyhocks friends.'

'And how are you amongst all this activity?' Georgina asked, not overlooking that the woman sitting opposite was coping with a very worrying health problem, as well as the May Queen arrangements.

'Not so bad,' she replied. 'The chemo took it out of me but, as I've said before, my mother gives me lots of support. It has taken something like this to bring us together. I've always been very self-sufficient and capable, and now that I'm sick and apprehensive of what lies ahead, it's bringing out the best in her.'

'*We* have something to ask of *you*, Clare, haven't we, Ben?' Georgina said, and he nodded.

'Will you be Arran's godmother?'

She watched Clare's eyes fill with tears and knew what was coming next.

'I can't think of anything I would love more,' she choked, 'but a godmother needs to be someone there for him long term and I can't promise that, can I, in my present state?'

'I know how much Georgina values you as a friend,' Ben told her, 'and with your courage and spirit, you'll be an inspiration to our son. So do please say yes.'

She was smiling now. 'How can I say anything else after that? Thanks for being so kind. You can count me in.'

The godfather slot had always belonged to Nicholas, and when Ben had rung him from the hospital to say that the baby had arrived and that Georgina was doing as well as could be expected, he'd said, 'Don't give me that hospital jargon, Ben. What do you mean?'

He'd been appalled when Ben had told him the full story, but had perked up when he'd discovered that there was a second role they wanted him to play in their lives, that of best man, and the knowledge that the two people he cared for most were going to remarry had left him on cloud nine.

It was drizzling out of a grey sky when the villagers awoke on Saturday morning and as Georgina gave Arran his first feed of the day, with Ben propped up against the pillows beside her, she wailed, 'I don't believe it. We've had nothing but sunshine for days and just look out there!'

But by the middle of the morning the rain had gone

and blue skies had appeared, with the sun shining extra brightly as if to compensate for its earlier absence, and all was hustle and bustle around the village green.

A wooden platform had been erected at one end, with steps leading up to it for the crowning ceremony, and in the middle of the green was the maypole with its bright ribbons wrapped tightly around it until such time as they were needed.

On the dot of twelve Willowmere's own brass band began to lead the May Day procession around the village with the vicar at the front and the Queen and her attendants walking sedately behind in their pretty long dresses.

They arrived at the village green at exactly twelve o'clock and the first people Georgina saw when she and Ben took their positions on the platform, with Arran cradled safely in his father's arms, were the Quarmbys, with Dennis puffed out with pride as he saw his daughter approach the rostrum and Christine, pale but very happy by his side.

When Georgina looked away from them, Pollyanna was waving from her place in the Queen's retinue, and James, another proud father, wasn't far away from her with Jolyon by his side. But she thought contentedly that the proudest father of all was standing beside her with his son in his arms and all was well with her world.

The crowning of the May Queen and the festivities that had followed it were over and in the early evening Georgina and Ben were pushing the pram homewards when he said, 'That was a great day, but I've got something that could top that or, on the other hand, maybe it won't.'

'What is it?' she asked, eyes bright with curiosity as they walked the last hundred yards to the cottage.

'You'll find out tomorrow, not before,' he said teasingly, with his dark eyes adoring her, and she pulled a face but didn't pursue it.

The sale of The Meadows had been completed a couple of days ago.

He was in possession of the keys to the lovely old house and was eager to see Georgina's reaction, all the time wondering if he should have let her have a say in where they were going to bring up Arran. But at that time he hadn't known what direction they were going in and had faced the fact that he might have to resell it or live there alone.

It was Nicholas offering to buy the London house that had made up his mind for him and he had yet to find out what Georgina would think of *that*.

'So do you want us to walk or drive to where we're going?' he questioned the next morning when they'd finished breakfast and Arran had been fed.

'It depends how far,' she replied.

'It's a mile or so.'

'Then we'll walk. May I ask in what direction?'

'Towards the Timmins farm. Baby Rhianna is home now and thriving.'

She was smiling. 'We're not going on a comparing-babies outing, are we?'

'We can call on them if you like but, no, that isn't where we're going. You'll just have to wait and see.'

The house was aptly named, Ben thought as they walked past fields where sheep and cattle grazed on the greenest grass he'd ever seen, and as they turned a bend on the lane on which it stood it was there, silent and empty, waiting for *them*.

'I wonder who's bought The Meadows,' Georgina said regretfully. 'Maggie Timmins has heard that it's a townie.'

'She's heard right.'

'What do you mean?'

'Well, you can hardly call me a country boy, can you?'

'You!' she cried. 'You, Ben! You've bought The Meadows for us.'

He held out his hand and on the flat of his palm were the keys.

'I hope you're going to like it.'

'Like it!' she whooped, throwing her arms around him. 'I've always loved this house. When, though? How? What made you…?' she gasped excitedly.

'It was when I knew that I couldn't live without you any more.'

Her excitement was lessening. 'But can we afford two houses? What about our house in the square?'

'It's sold.'

'And you never consulted me!'

'I didn't need to. Someone you love is going to live there and we'll be able to visit whenever we want.'

She was bewildered. 'Who?'

'Who is your favourite man…next to me?'

Light was dawning. 'Nicholas?'

'Yes. My young brother wants a house in London and is only too pleased to buy ours, so Jamie won't be all alone there while we're up here. He'll have his uncle Nick close by.'

Her radiance was back as she held him close and told him. 'I can live with that, Ben.'

He jangled the keys in front of her again. 'So now can we go inside?'

'Just try and stop me,' she told him as she picked Arran up out of the pram and cradled him in her arms.

As they walked around the spacious rooms and took in the views from every window Ben was jubilant. They were going to be so happy in this place, he thought. Their son was going to grow up in the beautiful Cheshire countryside in one of the nicest family homes around.

Just a few weeks ago it would have been a dream, now it was a reality, a reality where Georgina still loved him, they had a son, and they were going to live in this gorgeous house.

James had been round to the cottage to see Arran and to discuss Georgina's future role at the surgery and they had come to a decision that she was going to take the full maternity leave and then would return part time if a suitable arrangement could be made regarding Arran's care during those hours.

In the meantime, it would leave James and David Tremayne as full-time doctors, and Ben would be able to go back to paediatrics.

* * *

When Edwina Crabtree, bellringer in chief, heard that there was to be a wedding in the village very soon and that the two participants were Dr Adams and the ex-husband she'd produced from nowhere, she nodded approvingly. They now had a child and if there was one thing that Edwina liked to see it was all loose ends tied up neatly.

In her own staid way she liked Georgina Adams—soon to be Allardyce once more. Dr Adams was always kind and tactful when she was forced to consult her and in honour of the occasion, she was going to see that the bells pealed out across Willowmere on her wedding day more joyously than they'd ever done before.

An invitation to the wedding reception at The Meadows had mellowed Edwina even more until she discovered that she wasn't the only one to receive such a thing, that half the village had been invited.

Unaware of the prim campanologist's good feelings towards them, Georgina and Ben were making their preparations for a second taking of their marriage vows.

Pollyanna was to be the only bridesmaid and was being quite blasé about the occasion, saying that she didn't want pink again as it was what she'd worn as a bridesmaid not so long ago to her aunt Anna, now far away in Africa. So a pretty dress of pale green had been produced and she was delighted.

Nicholas was due any time from Texas to do the double act of best man and godfather at Arran's christening, which was to take place shortly before the wedding, and when she heard about that arrangement, Edwina was positively beaming.

For Georgina and Ben the days were filled with tenderness and contentment and it was all going to come together in the village church, the two ceremonies that would set the seal on the future that they'd thought they would never have.

The christening was in the morning and the wedding was in the afternoon. Those present were just Clare and Nicholas, as godparents, and Georgina and Ben in the church that was decked out with flowers for the wedding later.

As they each made their vows with regard to the tiny child in his godmother's arms there was a feeling of timelessness around them in the old stone church, of baptisms, weddings and funerals, some recent, others long gone.

When the vicar took the baby from Clare, dipped his fingers into the baptismal font and christened him Arran Benjamin, there were tears on his mother's lashes.

On seeing them, his father took her hand in his and held it tightly because he knew from where they came. They had another son, absent but cherished beyond belief, and one day they would tell Arran about his brother.

The moment had passed. The baptism was over and Arran was back in his mother's arms as they made their way outside and proceeded to Georgina's cottage where the four of them would remain until it was time to get dressed for the wedding.

As they ate a snack lunch the church bells were pealing triumphantly across Willowmere and Ben said, 'Surely that can't be for us!'

'I believe it is,' Clare told him. 'Edwina and her friends are in fine fettle today.'

They were going to use the same ring as before, which had never been off Georgina's finger since the occasion when Ben had placed it there. Today it was safely in Nicholas's pocket but would soon be back where it belonged.

When Georgina came slowly down the stairs some time later, beautiful in a calf-length dress of oyster silk that emphasised her dark eyes and hair, she was carrying beautiful flowers from the garden of the house that would soon be their home.

Ben was waiting for her at the bottom step in his own wedding finery and when he opened his arms, she went into them like a ship into harbour... And the wedding bells continued to swing high in the bell tower as they pealed out for two people who had once lost their way and were about to be united in the love that had been mislaid rather than lost.

MILLS & BOON
MEDICAL
Pulse-Racing Passion

Set your pulse racing with dedicated, delectable doctors in the high-pressure world of medicine, where emotions run high and passion, comfort and love are the best medicine.

MILLS & BOON
True Love

Romance from the Heart

Celebrate true love with tender stories of heartfelt romance, from the rush of falling in love to the joy a new baby can bring, and a focus on the emotional heart of a relationship.

JOIN US ON SOCIAL MEDIA!

Stay up to date with our latest releases, author news and gossip, special offers and discounts, and all the behind-the-scenes action from Mills & Boon...

 millsandboon

 millsandboonuk

 millsandboon

might just be true love...

MILLS & BOON

THE HEART OF ROMANCE

A ROMANCE FOR EVERY KIND OF READER

MODERN

Prepare to be swept off your feet by sophisticated, sexy and seductive heroes, in some of the world's most glamourous and romantic locations, where power and passion collide.
8 stories per month.

HISTORICAL

Escape with historical heroes from time gone by. Whether your passion is for wicked Regency Rakes, muscled Vikings or rugged Highlanders, awaken the romance of the past.
6 stories per month.

MEDICAL

Set your pulse racing with dedicated, delectable doctors in the high-pressure world of medicine, where emotions run high and passion, comfort and love are the best medicine.
6 stories per month.

True Love

Celebrate true love with tender stories of heartfelt romance, from the rush of falling in love to the joy a new baby can bring, and a focus on the emotional heart of a relationship.
8 stories per month.

Desire

Indulge in secrets and scandal, intense drama and plenty of sizzling hot action with powerful and passionate heroes who have it all: wealth, status, good looks…everything but the right woman.
6 stories per month.

HEROES

Experience all the excitement of a gripping thriller, with an intense romance at its heart. Resourceful, true-to-life women and strong, fearless men face danger and desire - a killer combination!
8 stories per month.

DARE

Sensual love stories featuring smart, sassy heroines you'd want as a best friend, and compelling intense heroes who are worthy of them.
4 stories per month.

To see which titles are coming soon, please visit

millsandboon.co.uk/nextmonth

LET'S TALK
Romance

For exclusive extracts, competitions
and special offers, find us online: